The Camera Never Lies

TESS DALY

The Camera Never Lies

CORONET

First published in Great Britain in 2011 by Coronet
An imprint of Hodder & Stoughton
An Hachette UK company

1

A CIP catalogue record for this title is available from the British Library

Hardback ISBN 9781444734188
Trade Paperback ISBN 9781444731538
Ebook ISBN 9781444734201

Typeset in Sabon MT by Hewer Text UK Ltd, Edinburgh

Printed and bound by CPI Group (UK) Ltd, Croydon, CR0 4YY

Hodder & Stoughton policy is to use papers that are natural, renewable
and recyclable products and made from wood grown in sustainable forests.
The logging and manufacturing processes are expected to conform
to the environmental regulations of the country of origin.

Hodder & Stoughton Ltd
338 Euston Road
London NW1 3BH

www.hodder.co.uk

For my mum – who always encouraged me
to write – feel free to skip the sexy bits.

Acknowledgements

My most grateful thanks go to my editor, Charlotte Hardman – whose belief and support helped get this novel off the ground – for listening with endless patience as I regaled (or rather bombarded) her with stories of the good (and the not so good) times spent in the wonderfully wacky worlds of television and fashion, for tolerating my endless script changes, for bringing cupcakes, and for general handholding throughout this debut novel writing process. Here's to the sequel . . .

Huge thanks also to Mark Booth and to everyone at Hodder for all their support and kindness. I'd like to thank my agent, Polly Hill, for all her hard work and constant feedback – without her, none of this would have been possible. Special thanks to my family for putting up with me sneaking off after bath times to work on this book. Finally, thanks to you for reading it. I hope Britt Baxter gets under your skin like she got under mine. Happy reading!

1

This particular Thursday started out looking like it was going to be one of the best days of Britt Baxter's twenty-six years.

It was one of those blissfully mild, blue-skied April mornings, when even the air in central London smells fresh. Britt stepped out of the taxi onto New Burlington Street, a few short steps away from the bustle of shoppers and tourists on Regent Street. She usually took the tube – unless it was a special occasion and she happened to be wearing over three inches heels. But today she was late for an extremely important – possibly life-changing – appointment, so she had splurged on a cab and would make up for it elsewhere. That Essie nail polish in Midnight Blue could always wait another week.

She checked her watch: she had exactly eight minutes to get to her 9 a.m. meeting, just round the corner amongst the bespoke tailors and fashion houses on Mayfair's Savile Row.

As she hurried along, Britt caught her reflection in a sandwich shop window. *Not too bad*, she thought – although considering the amount of time and money she'd spent getting ready she should look bloomin' sensational. Rather than risk one of her all-too-frequent bad hair days,

Britt had splashed out on a professional blow-dry to tame her mane of curls into submission. Over the years she had spent a small fortune on products to try and find something that would control her thick, unruly tresses. Her bathroom was crammed with so many mousses, foams and gels that her best friend Jessie had nicknamed her Boots Baxter. 'Got any special offers today?' Jessie would joke. 'Buy-one-get-one-free on curl serum, perhaps?' *Well, it was alright for Jess with her sleek, neat bob*, thought Britt fondly. For her part, she only had to glimpse rain on TV for her hair to puff up into a halo of frizz.

Britt had spent several hours the night before agonising over what to wear for her big moment, before finally deciding on her treasured black Diane von Furstenberg wrap dress (a bargain in the Net-A-Porter sale). It screamed class yet clung to every curve and gave her an eye-popping cleavage. She had teamed the dress with a pair of snakeskin Alaïa heels, a Mulberry tote and her swishy Reiss cape.

She wouldn't usually get this dressed up for a casting – in fact bookers usually preferred you to look as natural as possible – but this job was different. And judging by the number of heads that swivelled in her direction as she sashayed along, her wrap dress parting to reveal a flash of long, tanned leg with every stride, she certainly looked the part.

Although she was from a little village called Larkbridge Britt looked like she hailed from California rather than from Carlisle. Her mate Jessie joked all Britt needed was a red swimming cossie and she could be an extra on *Baywatch*. She was a petite size eight with slender, golden-skinned limbs and a cracking 32D chest. With her large, wide-apart green eyes, perfect pout and a profile that would give Yasmin Le Bon a run for her money, hers was the beauty type of your classic fifties pin-up. Yet even though she'd had a successful career as a model, inside Britt still felt like that gawky teenager who on holidays would walk to the sea hiding behind a lilo in the hope that nobody would see her long, skinny legs and hipbones jutting from her swimsuit.

Britt had been spotted by a model agent at the age of seventeen and had worked steadily ever since, mainly in catalogue shoots, magazine editorials and commercials, but although she'd been to countless castings with top designers, she'd never landed a big-name catwalk show or lucrative worldwide advertising campaign. At five foot seven and a half she was just too short to be a top fashion model – and besides, she loved Green & Black's vanilla caramel nut ice-cream, full-fat Coke and the odd packet of Frazzles way too much to starve herself down to a catwalk size four.

But then, last month, in the middle of what had been a rainy and worryingly work-free March, something incredible had happened. Out of the blue, Britt had been summoned to Berlin for a casting with Zauber, the top German fashion label, who were on the hunt for a new girl to front their advertising campaign. She had headed off to the meeting at the brand's head office on the city's hip Rosenthaler Strasse with little hope. After all, Zauber was known for its edgy designs – they were bound to go for one of those scarily skinny, bug-eyed models who were the current big thing. Britt's heart had dropped even further into her grey suede Topshop ankle boots when she had been summoned to a meeting room in which a

3

panel of seven people waited behind a long table, like a fashionista firing squad. Her eyes had nervously skimmed the panel, taking in a man dressed all in black with a shock of Warhol-white hair, a woman in sunglasses who looked a dead ringer for US *Vogue* editor Anna Wintour (*surely it couldnt be, couldn't it?*), and a bored-looking bloke slouching at the end in a leather jacket, who she recognised as the latest hot young photographer. But then Britt had noticed that at the very centre of the panel, in the seat of power, was a small, chubby woman in her mid-fifties who was about as far from the frosty fashion-bitch stereotype as you could possibly get. With her corkscrew-curly brown hair laced with grey and half-moon glasses, she looked like she'd taken a wrong turn out of a school governors' meeting and ended up sitting there by mistake. And the biggest shock of all was that the woman was smiling at her warmly. As far as Britt was aware, nobody in fashion had smiled since 1998.

'My name is Frieda Koch, and I am Zauber's creative director,' the woman had said in lightly accented English. 'I was very excited when I saw your portfolio, Britt, so I'm thrilled you could come to meet us today.'

After gesturing for Britt to take a seat, Frieda had explained that for its next season's campaign, Zauber was taking a radically different direction. Rather than their usual type of model, they were looking for someone glossy and curvy (well, curvy in modelling terms). A girl who was bursting with health; who looked like she loved life, food and sex.

'In short, we want a girl who looks exactly like you,' smiled Frieda, as Britt had struggled to take in the fact that it looked very much like she had just landed the job

4

of a lifetime. 'Congratulations my dear, I will arrange a date in London with your agent to sign the contracts and take care of the formalities.'

And today was to be that day.

In modelling terms, it was like winning the EuroMillions jackpot. In an instant, her status would be elevated from catalogue girl to campaign queen. She could wave goodbye to those cruel cattle-call castings that usually took a two-hour slog through driving rain to get to, finally arriving only to be shown to a room with a hundred or so other girls eyeing each other competitively from behind their portfolios, all after the same job. No, after nearly ten long years pounding the pavements, she would be the Zauber girl, with all the respect and recognition that entailed within the fickle fashion world. Heck, she'd even be able to take a taxi without worrying about the expense.

Number 183 Savile Row was an imposing four-storey redbrick building with a glossy, black front door. Britt checked the list of names next to the buzzers and found Zauber's British HQ on the fourth floor. She suddenly felt sick with nerves.

She was just checking her make-up in her compact and plucking up the courage to press the buzzer when her BlackBerry started vibrating. It was Scott, her agent at Gawk Models.

'Why on earth are you answering your phone when you're supposed to be sitting in a meeting with Zauber right this freaking minute?'

Scott was American, flamboyantly gay and had a mouth on him like Joan Rivers.

'If you get off the bloody phone,' said Britt, 'I'll go in.'

'Now remember, Britt, your whole career depends on you not screwing this up. If you get this advertising campaign you will be splashed across every billboard in every city in the world and beyond. Oh, and PS – I was out for drinks with the editor of German *Vogue* last night and word on the street is that Matthew McConaughey will be starring in the shoot alongside you.' His voice dropped to a reverent whisper. 'Matthew freaking Mc-Hot-aughey!'

'Wow, really?' Britt's nerves seemed to suddenly double in intensity.

'The job is basically in the bag,' Scott went on, 'you just need to sign the contracts with Frieda Koch, so—'

'So, don't Koch it up,' laughed Britt.

'Right. If she says jump, you find a freaking trampoline – got it?'

'You worry too much, Scottie.'

'Go get 'em, tiger,' grunted Scott in mock manly tones.

As Britt put her phone back in her bag it vibrated again. It was a text from her boyfriend, Alex: 'Dolce booked for 8 p.m. Don't forget! A xxx'

As if, Britt smiled to herself. She had been looking forward to tonight for ages. Not only was Dolce her favourite restaurant but tonight was to be a double celebration: her landing the Zauber campaign and Alex's well-deserved promotion. He had been working for the local council since moving down from Carlisle to live with her a year ago, and was meeting with his boss today to 'discuss his future'. It looked like Alex was a dead cert for a step up both in pay and prestige. He certainly deserved it, and with the extra cash coming in, they would finally be able to afford the deposit on a place of their own. For the last few days they had talked late into the night, planning their future together, and had even gone to look round a flat they had spotted for sale nearby. As the estate agent had shown them round, Alex had looked at the airy second bedroom and whispered to Britt: 'This would be perfect for a nursery, wouldn't it?'

'Oh my God, he's going to propose!' Jessie had squealed when Britt had told her friend about it the following day. And although Britt had laughed it off at the time, she was beginning to think dinner tonight would be the ideal occasion . . .

2

Britt pushed the buzzer next to the glossy black door and a few moments later a crackly German voice said, '*Ja?*'

'Oh, hi, this is Britt Baxter for Frieda Koch,' said Britt nervously.

'*Sehr gut*. Come straight up, please.'

Britt took the lift to the fourth floor to be greeted by a startlingly tall, skinny man with a neatly clipped blond goatee. He was wearing a black polo neck, and trousers that looked two inches too short for him. Britt presumed they were the height of fashion in Berlin.

'*Guten morgen*, Miz Baxter,' he said in a sing-song voice. 'My name is Herman, I am Frau Koch's executive assistant. Please, come zis way.'

He showed her into an office, the walls, floor and furniture of which were all bright white. There was a single black orchid in a square crystal vase and the walls were covered with moody black-and-white photos of pouting models – the stars of previous Zauber campaigns. In the far corner was a huge black marble sculpture, all smooth lines and shiny curves, with two enormous protrusions sticking out of the side that made it look like an ancient fertility statue of a naked tribeswoman, or Katie Price in her Jordan days. And, at a large desk, in stark contrast to the frosty minimalism of her office, sat Frieda Koch.

'Ah, the beautiful Britt, it is so very lovely to see you again.' Frieda stood up and held out her arms to her, reaching up to kiss Britt on both cheeks. 'Let me take your coat. Can I get you anything to drink? Herman makes a quite marvellous goji berry and ginseng tea.'

'Mmm, that sounds delicious, Frau Koch.' Britt realised she could have murdered a cappuccino, but doubted that dairy or caffeine would be allowed near the building.

'Please, you must call me Frieda,' Frieda Koch smiled.

Once again, Britt marvelled at how unlike your typical fashionista Frieda was. She was swathed in layers of voluminous, jewel-coloured material, which only served to emphasise her plumpness, and her plain face seemed untouched by Botox, fillers or even make-up. The only clue to her profession was the strikingly chunky chrome and wooden necklace resting on her motherly bosom.

'We're all so excited about you being our new Zauber girl,' Frieda said as Britt took a seat opposite her. 'Matthew McConaughey and you will make a fabulous couple.'

'It all sounds wonderful,' Britt enthused, trying to hide her excitement. *Scott was right – Matthew McConaughey!*

'The shoot will be on Copacabana Beach in Rio and will involve you spending several weeks in Brazil in May. Will that be convenient?'

Britt gulped, not believing her luck. 'Oh, yes, I'm sure that will be fine,' she grinned. *Really, could this job get any better?*

'I'm glad to hear that.' Frieda smiled at her again as Herman returned with the tea.

'I'll be *Mutti*,' twinkled Frieda. 'You know, Britt, the moment I saw your portfolio I knew that you would be perfect for us. Not only are you very beautiful, your body is quite exceptional.'

'Um, thanks,' said Britt. She had never been very good at taking compliments.

'There is something about you I like. You have a very fresh, very English quality.'

'Oh. Ah! Thank you!'

'There are just a few small matters to deal with before we can draw up the contracts,' said Frieda. 'Herman, could you please also fetch some of those delicious flax and quinoa crackers for us? Thank you very much.'

She watched her assistant leave and then turned back to Britt. 'Please, let us make ourselves a bit more comfortable over here,' she said, gesturing to a white leather sofa near the sculpture. 'I find sitting at a desk so frightfully formal, don't you? I know we are going to be bosom buddies.'

She said this with a half-laugh and Britt thought she looked surprisingly nervous, even a bit unsure of herself – what could she have to be nervous about? Seeing this human side of Frieda Koch made her feel more at home. Perhaps she really could be friends with this powerful woman?

As Britt sank into the cushions, she felt like pinching herself. This was it: she was about to hit the big time! *Just show me the dotted line and I'll sign*, she thought with a shiver of excitement.

'Now, as the Zauber girl, you will obviously be working very closely alongside me,' Frieda said once they had sat down. 'I like to take a . . . personal interest in our models, and in return I hope you will be happy to

10

cooperate with me in all matters. Do you think that will be okay?'

'Oh, yes, of course,' said Britt. 'It's a huge honour to be asked to represent such a prestigious brand, and I'm very excited about working with you, Frieda.'

For years, she'd imagined a day she might be saying words like these, hardly daring to dream she'd one day be the face of a major campaign.

'I'm very glad to hear that, Britt.' Frieda nodded and smiled. 'Very glad indeed.'

And then something rather strange happened. Without warning, Frieda leant over and put a hand on Britt's thigh. Britt stared at it in surprise, unsure what to do. Seconds ticked by. The hand stayed put.

'I have another meeting shortly, Britt, so I thought it might be nice if we signed the contract in a more relaxed setting,' said Frieda. 'Perhaps over dinner tonight in my hotel room? After all, we have a lot to celebrate. The start of your relationship with Zauber – and, of course, with me.'

Britt was so thrown by the turn of events that it occurred to her that perhaps Frieda was just unusually touchy-feely, but then her hand started to slowly slide up Britt's leg and snaked under the flap of her dress, leaving Britt in little doubt as to what that night's meeting would involve.

'Bloomin' 'eck, gerroff, will you!' she cried out, stunned. Over the years, Britt had been hit on countless times by male bookers or photographers. It pretty much went with the territory, and she had never had any problems giving them the brush off. But this was the first time a woman had ever invited her onto the casting couch

– and Britt had absolutely no idea how to handle it.

Immediately regretting her outburst, she tried to recover her composure. 'I'm so sorry, Frieda, I would have loved to meet you tonight but I'm afraid I already have plans. With my *boyfriend*. But I'd be happy to come back here to see you again tomorrow, or any other day this week.'

Frieda's eyes had narrowed to tiny slits. 'Well, Britt, that is a very great shame. I would hate for you to miss out on this fantastic opportunity. If you really are serious about wanting to be the new Zauber girl, then I suggest you try and reschedule your plans. I'm staying at the Mandarin Oriental.' Frieda stood up to signify that the meeting was over. 'I shall expect you at 8 p.m. tonight. I would strongly advise you to be there if you want this job.'

Oh, but Britt so desperately wanted this job – and she needed it. She might still be stunning, but at twenty-six the work was starting to dry up and if she didn't hit the big time soon it was never going to happen for her. A model's career was like a footballer's: you made your fortune when you were young, because once you hit a certain age you were all washed up. The problem was, Britt had spent most of her career playing for Northend Thistle FC rather than Manchester United. Zauber was probably her last hope. But sleep her way onto the billboards? It just felt so . . . *sordid*.

'I'm not really sure if I understand . . .' she trailed off, still desperately hoping that she might have misread the signs.

'Well, let me try and help clarify the situation,' smiled Frau Koch, although Britt only now noticed how the warmth of her smile didn't quite reach her eyes. 'There are a great many girls who would be prepared to do whatever it takes to land such a prestigious campaign, and if you are unwilling to ... cooperate with me, then I'm afraid Zauber will just have to find someone else.'

3

Oh God, would Alex understand if she went through with it? The job was a once-in-a-lifetime opportunity. It was her ticket to fame, fortune and designer freebies. She tried to imagine what it would be like to kiss Frieda Koch. It wouldn't be too bad, surely? No doubt it would be like kissing a man, only a bit less prickly. And then after the kissing, things would probably just progress naturally. It would be fine – perhaps she'd even enjoy it. They would have some champagne, Britt would slip out of her dress, Frieda would take off her kaftan and then . . . and then . . . *Oh Christ, no.* No, no, *no.* She couldn't do it. No way.

With her dreams of supermodel stardom collapsing around her, Britt realised with horror that she was about to cry.

'I'm very sorry, Frau Koch,' she said, desperate to get out with her dignity intact. 'But you'll have to find another girl to, um, cooperate with. I'll see myself out.'

And with that Britt grabbed her things and dashed towards the door – slamming straight into Herman. As he half fell away from her, holding a tray aloft and frantically trying to regain his balance, his legs were a blur. He gave Britt a long, level look that seemed to say *This is the end of my life as a dignified human being, as a real person – and it is all your fault.* Then suddenly he was on his backside, his legs with their too-short trousers waving in the air.

'*Meine Kräcker!*' he wailed. Crumbs of flax and quinoa were scattered over the spotless white floor. He looked close to tears.

'I'm so sorry!' cried Britt. Her immediate reaction was to stop to help, but she had to get out of that place. Moments later, she clattered down the front steps, blinking back tears.

Since she'd been inside, the sky had clouded over and a chill breeze now whipped round her bare legs. She was standing on the pavement wondering what on earth she should do when a builder working on scaffolding across the street wolf-whistled and shouted, 'Alright, darlin'?' Usually she just ignored this sort of thing – or occasionally smiled if she was in a particularly good mood – but not today. 'I'm not a piece of meat!' Britt screeched furiously, storming off in the direction of Piccadilly Circus tube. There was definitely no way she could justify a taxi now.

She had just skulked into Pret to grab a medicinal double espresso and an almond croissant when her phone rang. It was Scott.

'Sooo,' he trilled. 'I've got a bottle of Cristal here on my desk with your name on it!'

'I didn't get it,' said Britt, flatly.

'What?'

Britt sobbed. 'Oh, Scott, it was awful. Frau Koch told me that if I wanted the job I had to meet her tonight in her hotel room and . . .'

There was such a long pause at the other end of the line that Britt thought she must have been cut off, but eventually Scott spoke, his voice low and simmering. 'And what?'

'And I'd have to . . . well, you know,' muttered Britt. 'Go to bed with her. Do, um, lesbian stuff.'

Another long pause, then: 'So you said, 'Frau Koch, I can't wait, and by the way I'll bring the vibrator and crotchless knickers'?'

'Are you kidding me?' Britt asked in disbelief. 'I'm not prepared to sleep my way to the top – it's not my style. I thought you'd understand that!'

'Oh, you did, did you? Well, let me spell it out for you, babe.' Scott was suddenly almost squeaking with rage. 'In model years you're practically pensionable, and if you need to frig a freaking fräulein to get a job like this then you do it! How do you think some of those supermodels got to be so goddamn *super* in the first place?'

'I . . . I'm sorry . . .' Britt was so stunned by his reaction that she barely registered the jibe about her age.

'This was going to be your big chance, Britt! Jesus! Do you think there's any chance we might be able to salvage something from this?'

Britt thought back to Frau Koch's look of icy contempt as she'd dashed out of her office. 'I very much doubt it.'

Scott sighed. 'Okay, babe. Come and see me at the agency tomorrow. In the meantime, I'll make a few calls, see if I can dredge something else up.'

The first drops of an April shower were starting to fall when Britt finally arrived at the tube, but when she walked up to the entrance she noticed a large handwritten sign: 'Piccadilly Line suspended due to staff shortages'. Darn, it was raining steadily by now. By the time Britt eventually found a bus that was heading in the direction of her flat in Clapham, her precious snakeskin shoes were ruined and the £50 blow-dry was a total write-off.

As she stood in the crowded bus, shivering in her sodden dress, she thought about phoning Alex. He had a knack of knowing exactly the right thing to say to make her feel better and put everything in perspective. But it was a big day for him too, and she didn't want to worry him, so instead she sent a text: 'Hey gorgeous. Best of luck at work, can't wait to see you tonight. Love you xxx'.

Britt knew Alex would understand about Zauber. In fact, he was sure to help her see the funny side and they'd probably be laughing about Frau Koch's wandering hands by this time tomorrow. As someone with a 'proper' job, he was always amused by the tales Britt told him about working in fashion, about how hysterical fashion folk could get over a statement heel or a flared trouser (because of course it was always 'trouser' or 'jean' on Planet Fashion, never the plural).

Alex had always laughed off Britt's suggestions that he try modelling himself – although there was no doubt that he had the looks for it. Until a couple of years ago, Alex had looked set for a career as a professional rugby player. Although a serious back injury had put paid to his sporting ambitions, he still trained regularly and at six foot three, with broad shoulders, rock-hard thighs and the most gorgeously firm bum, he still had a rugby player's physique, only miraculously without the smashed nose and cauliflower ears. With his lush lips, shaggy chocolate-brown hair that was always flopping into his blue eyes, and classically chiselled bone structure, Alex looked like he'd be more at home in a photo shoot than a scrum. The only souvenir of his time on the pitch was a scar just below his eye that gave his boy-band features a dangerously sexy edge. Britt still looked at him occasionally and melted, marvelling at how she had managed to bag such a drop-dead gorgeous bloke.

Britt had known Alex since he was the scrawny, annoying kid who flicked rubber bands at her during GCSE geography, but they hadn't started dating until a couple of years ago when they had bumped into each other at a pub near home while Britt had been visiting her mum. Britt was stunned that the obnoxious fourteen-year-old had grown into such a total babe – and a real gentleman, too. After a few months of long-distance dating they had fallen head over heels in love. At the time, Alex was working in bars and labouring to make ends meet until he figured out what to do, now that a career as a professional sportsman was out of the question. After moving down to London to live with Britt last year, he had found a job at the local council, working on their Fitness for Kids programme. It wasn't brilliantly paid, but he was glad to be using his sporting talent and he proved a natural with children. And it was wonderful finally to be living together.

The bus stopped at the end of her road and Britt picked her way around the puddles to her front door. She had started renting the tiny one-bedroom flat, which was on the top floor of a pretty, mint-green terraced Victorian villa in Clapham, shortly after moving to London at the age of nineteen. Being close to central London meant that the rent was extortionate, but Britt adored the area. It had a real villagey feel that reminded Britt of home – except with a Starbucks, Bikram yoga studio and Waitrose. She suddenly had a pang of worry about how she would afford the rent with no prospect of work, but at least Alex would be able to cover it until something else came along.

As soon as Britt unlocked the front door her enormously plump tabby cat, Kate Moss, padded over and started rubbing around her legs, purring like a hairdryer, and by the time she had made herself a cup of tea and watched a couple of episodes of *Friends* Britt was beginning to feel a bit brighter. Hadn't Scott hinted that he might have another job for her? He had never let her down in the past. She began to look forward again to dinner that evening.

Having a long soak in a bath filled with her favourite Laura Mercier Crème Brûlée bubbles seemed far more restorative than spending hours blow-drying her hair, so Britt just tied it into a low bun and drowned it in Frizz-Ease. Years of working with some of the industry's best make-up artists had taught her how to pull off a naturally glowing complexion in five minutes flat. With the help of her pinky-gold Nars cream blush in Orgasm, Laura Mercier tinted foundation, lashings of Max Factor mascara and a slick of Elizabeth Arden Eight Hour cream on her lips and lids, she was ready to go.

The rain was hammering down by the time Britt was ready to set out for dinner that evening, so with a pang of guilt she called up the local minicab firm, her earlier pact with herself to steer clear of taxis fading fast. When a car horn outside announced that her cab had arrived, she slipped a leather biker jacket over the top of her Topshop Baxter skinny grey jeans, See by Chloé chiffon blouse and Kurt Geiger spike-heeled boots, and dashed out into the rain.

Dolce was an Italian restaurant in Kensington. Despite the chichi location and brick and leather-panelled minimalism of the interior, it was a warm, friendly place – and the food was incredible. Britt gratefully ordered a Bellini and some nibbles and sat to wait for Alex.

Twenty minutes and two Bellinis later, Britt was starting to worry. It really wasn't like Alex to be late. But as she tried his mobile again, the door swung open and there he was. As he shrugged off his drenched coat and handed it to the waiter at the door, Britt once again thrilled at how good-looking her boyfriend was. Even with his hair plastered over his face in wet ribbons and sodden jeans, she fancied him rotten and contemplated paying for the drinks, skipping dinner and whisking him home.

Alex wore a look of fierce concentration as he picked his way through the tables towards where she was sitting. As she leaned in for a kiss, she caught a whiff of beer fumes. So that was why he was late: he'd been out drinking with workmates. Well, she certainly couldn't begrudge him a pint.

'So,' grinned Britt, 'I've managed to polish off two plates of crostini, a bowl of olives and some of those cheese-filled risotto balls while I've been waiting, so if I get thrown out of the models' union I'm blaming you!'

But Alex didn't laugh; he didn't even return her smile as he sat down.

'Sorry, love.' He stared at the table, his shoulders slumped.

'Hey, is everything alright?'

Alex eventually lifted his head to meet her gaze. He looked like a broken man. He finally opened his mouth to speak: 'I've got some bad news . . .'

4

'I didn't get a promotion, Britt,' Alex said flatly. 'I got made redundant.'

Britt's first thought was *Oh God, poor Alex*. She knew just how hard this would hit him. But very quickly a second thought wormed its way into her head. *The rent!* With both of them out of work, there was no way they could afford to stay in the flat, never mind afford the deposit for the flat they'd seen. And as for an engagement ring . . .

As the waiter poured them both a glass of the very expensive Chianti Britt had ordered before the bombshell, Alex explained what had happened. The council was being forced to make drastic cuts across all departments and his boss had had no choice but to let him go.

'He told me how pleased he was with my work, how much they liked me, blah blah blah, but as I was the last in I was going to have to be the first out,' he said. 'So that's it. As of tomorrow I'm unemployed.' He drained his wine and immediately reached for the bottle and poured himself another brimming glass. 'Oh God, love, I don't know what I'm going to do. It took me so long to find this job, and now . . .'

Britt reached for his hands and gave them a reassuring

squeeze. 'You are talented and brilliant and we will get through this, okay?'

But Alex just shook his head, looking utterly miserable. 'I can't believe I thought I was getting a promotion. What a prat . . .' He took another long swig of wine and waved to the waiter for another bottle, then suddenly realised something. 'God, I'm so sorry, sweetheart, how did it go at the Zauber meeting? At least one of us isn't a total lost cause.'

Britt looked at Alex's expectant smile. Her stomach lurched but suddenly a little white lie seemed like by far the kindest choice.

'Oh, well, it's not completely in the bag . . . yet.' She blushed furiously. 'You know what these flaky fashion people are like! Ha ha! It should all be sorted by early next week. If not before. So that's all really great!'

Yeah, great job, Baxter, thought Britt. *Really bloody convincing.* But at least it would give her time to sort something else out.

The rest of the evening was miserable. While Britt did her cheerleader bit, trying to rally Alex and cheer him up, he just pushed his food moodily round his plate while polishing off two bottles of wine and several shots of sambuca. By the time the taxi arrived, he was quite frankly legless, and Britt had to help him into the car.

'Birchwood Road, Clapham, thank you,' Britt requested as the driver glared at Alex, now slumped against her shoulder.

'He better not throw up in my taxi.'

'No, he's fine, he's just, um, tired.' But Britt wound down the window just in case.

As they drove home, Britt wondered how her life had

23

gone so badly wrong. In a matter of hours she'd gone from being a supermodel-in-waiting with the prospects of a flashy engagement ring and three weeks in Rio with Matthew McConaughey, to a failed model with a drunk and redundant boyfriend and the prospect of imminent homelessness. She was usually a half-cup-full kind of girl, but as the rain hammered away at the window and Alex snored drunkenly beside her, Britt wondered: *How on earth are we going to cope?*

5

Gawk Models was located at the end of a quiet, cobbled mews street in Notting Hill.

It was just after 9 a.m., but Britt was already on her second coffee of the day. The first had been to get her up and out of bed after last night's disastrous dinner. This one – a triple-shot latte – was to help her deal with Scott.

From the outside, Gawk HQ looked like a country cottage, all flower-filled window boxes and pastel paint-work. Inside, it was utter chaos, with bookers shouting across the room to one another, Radio 1 blaring and phones that never seemed to stop ringing. The walls of the open-plan office were lined with floor-to-ceiling racks of model cards, and there were huge boards covered with Polaroid snaps of the wannabes who every day made the pilgrimage to Gawk's famous offices, dreaming of a glamorous catwalk career. It was never that simple though, and hordes of pretty young things were turned away, their teenage dreams broken by the sharp tongue of the agency team. Very few were lucky.

As she walked in, Britt glanced at the photos of all the hopeful young faces and remembered the magical moment when she had first been asked: 'Have you ever thought about being a model?' At the time, she had felt like Cinderella being offered an invitation to the ball. Well, her only hope now was that Scott would be able to make like the fairy godmother, wave his magic wand and miraculously conjure up another job. Britt felt sure that Alex wouldn't be hit quite so hard by the news that this month's rent was overdue – oh, and by the way, she didn't actually get the Zauber job after all – if she had something else up her designer sleeve.

'Hi, Ella.' She greeted the receptionist at the front desk, above which hung a giant neon 'GAWK' sign. 'Is Scott around?'

'Hey, babe, yeah, he's at his desk. Be warned though – he's in the mother of all fashion-monster moods today.'

'I'm afraid that might well have something to do with me.'

'Ouch. Good luck, hon.' Ella gave her an encouraging smile and went back to her flashing phones. 'Gawk Models, thank you for holding . . .'

Britt picked her way between the bookers' desks to where Scott was tucked away in a corner taking a call. A black cap covered his bleached-blond hair and he was wearing a khaki T-shirt and skinny jeans that seemed to hang off his scrawny frame. In the almost ten years that she had known him, Britt couldn't remember once seeing Scott eat. He seemed to exist on a diet of Marlboro Lights and fickle fashion gossip.

'Do you understand English?' Scott was yelling down the phone. 'Five foot five is way too short to be a fashion model! The only place you'll get work is in the lads mags, love.' He slammed the phone down.

Britt stood in front of his desk, smiling with more confidence than she was feeling.

'Well, well, well, if it isn't the blessed Sister Britt,' Scott snapped. 'How's life up at the convent this morning?'

'Ha ha, very funny,' she sighed. It looked like he hadn't forgiven her for refusing Frieda's advances.

'Just to keep you in the loop,' Scott went on, 'I got a phone call earlier from Herman at Frau Koch's office, who took great pleasure in telling me that the new Zauber girl is Diamond Lopez.' A hot young Latina model. 'Looks like sweet little Diamond wasn't quite so sniffy about a little Koch action.'

'Please, can we just drop it,' sighed Britt.

'Okay, okay. Sorry, babe. Come on, let's go outside, I'm gagging for a cig.'

They wandered out into the mews, squinting in the bright morning sunshine, while Scott chattered away about the latest dramas with Jesus, his fiery Spanish boyfriend. Britt was desperate to know if he had any other work up his sleeve for her, but he was well into his second cigarette by the time Britt finally managed to get a word in.

'So, did you ever hear back from that casting I went to for the Boden catalogue last month?' she asked casually.

'They went with Alenka Alekshashkin. Apparently you weren't quite tall enough.'

'Oh, right.' *This wasn't good.* 'How about the Lynx TV commercial?'

'They decided they wanted a red-head,' said Scott, rolling his eyes. 'Fucked-up, right?'

'How about Primark? They've given me lots of work in the past. Is it worth giving them a call?'

Scott shook his head. 'Sorry, babe, already done it and the answer's no. You're way too old.'

Britt struggled with a rising sense of panic. 'Look, I know I screwed up the Zauber deal, but you've got to help me. Alex has lost his job and if I'm not working we won't be able to afford to stay in the flat. Is there nothing you can put me up for? Come on, there aren't many models as professional or hard-working as me. You know that.'

Scott took a long, final drag on his cigarette. 'Well, there might be something . . .'

'I'll do it!'

'You're not going to like it . . .'

'Please, Scott, I'm desperate. I'll literally do anything. Even get my kit off,' she joked.

'Shame you didn't say that to Frau Koch: you'd still have a career,' he shot back, but with a smile. 'Okay, here's my plan. We send you out to Japan for six months. I'll hook you up with our sister agency in Tokyo, they'll get you a room in a model apartment and set you up with some go-sees. You'll have to work freaking hard, but you've got the right look for their market – even though you are a bit on the *senior* side. I can sort out the details and have you in Tokyo by next week.'

Britt's heart plummeted. Her initial reaction was *No bloody way*. She would rather move back to her mum's cottage and pull pints in the village pub than be stuck thousands of miles away from Alex for so long. And while she might have jumped at the chance when she was seventeen, right now the thought of building a career from scratch in a strange city felt utterly daunting. Besides, Alex would probably hate the idea. He worried about her when she was working abroad and although he denied it, Britt knew he got jealous about the attention she attracted from other men.

'Is there nothing a bit closer to home?' she asked Scott.

'There's no easy way to put this, hon, but you're just not in fashion,' Scott said apologetically. 'No-one is using the curvy babes these days – it's all about the skinny Eastern Europeans or the industry wants quirky girls who look like they're from another planet. You look like you're from Malibu. I don't mean to sound harsh, but career-wise Zauber was your last hope.'

So that was it: Tokyo or bust – quite literally.

'Okay, let me think about it,' she said. 'I'll call you.'

All the way home on the train Britt tried to work out how to break the news to Alex. She imagined sitting him down on the sofa: 'Now I've got some good news and some bad news,' she would tell him calmly. 'The bad news is that I didn't get the Zauber job, but the good news is – tah dah! – I've got a job in Tokyo!' The problem was, she very much doubted that Alex would think that qualified as good news. Maybe she should tell him that something really terrible had happened, like she was being sent to prison, then say: 'Just joking! I'm only going to Japan for a little while instead! Hahahaha!' No, that wasn't going to work either. *Oh God, this was going to be awful.* Perhaps she should have sex with him first to soften him up . . .

It was gone midday when she arrived home but Alex was still in bed, fast asleep, with Kate Moss draped over him like a fat, furry stole. The bedroom reeked of stale booze, so she threw open the window to let in some fresh air.

'Hey, sleepyhead,' said Britt, ruffling Alex's hair and dropping a kiss on his forehead.

'What time is it?' He raised his head an inch then dropped it back on the pillow. 'Jesus, I feel terrible.'

'Here, drink this.' She handed him a glass of water fizzing with a cocktail of Berocca and Alka-Seltzer. 'You'll feel better after a shower.'

By the time Alex had got showered and dressed, Britt was serving up fried eggs and bacon for them both. He sat down at the table looking sheepish.

'Did I behave like a total arsehole last night?'

'Not a *total* arsehole, no – although I think we might need to apologise to Dolce for overturning the table.' Alex looked horrified. 'Joke!' she added quickly.

'God, I'm so sorry. I'd just been so sure I was getting a promotion that when I found out I was actually being made redundant . . . It hit me really hard. I just don't know what I'm going to do.' He held his head in his hands. It was clear that a night's sleep hadn't helped him feel any more positive about the future. 'Anyway, love, what have you been up to this morning?'

Britt realised she would have to come clean. 'Alex, I need to tell you something important,' she said. 'Please don't say anything until I've finished, okay?'

He nodded warily, so Britt took a deep breath and launched into the speech that she'd been rehearsing all the way home from her meeting with Scott.

'I didn't get the Zauber campaign,' she said, not daring to look up to see how Alex had taken her bombshell. 'The creative director told me I'd have to sleep with her to get the job and I wasn't prepared to do it. I didn't tell you last night because I didn't want to make you feel any worse than you already did.' Britt didn't even pause to take a breath: she was on a roll and couldn't let Alex interrupt her for fear that she'd lose it. 'Besides, it doesn't actually matter because I've just been offered the most fantastic opportunity in – wait for it – Tokyo!' She stole a glance to see Alex's reaction, but immediately had to look away. The horror etched across his face was too much to bear. 'Scott has said that I've got the perfect look for the Japanese market and he reckons I'll be able to work non-stop and the money is amazing! The agency will get me a fantastic apartment and there're lots of other English girls out there who can show me the ropes. Isn't that brilliant?'

She finally looked up to see Alex staring at her intently. 'Can I speak now?'

Britt nodded.

'I don't want you to go,' he said passionately. 'I need you here. I want us to work through this together.'

'I know, hon, but it's a once-in-a-lifetime chance! If I take this we might still be able to afford the deposit on that flat. It'll only be for a couple of months or so. Maybe you could even come and visit me in Tokyo. We haven't had a holiday for ages, and I know how much you like sushi and, um, karaoke . . .' Britt tailed off, aware she was babbling.

Alex reached out for her and pulled her onto his lap. 'Come here, beautiful.' He wrapped his strong arms around her and held her tightly against his chest. 'You don't have to do this if you don't want to,' he said. 'There'll be other jobs, right? Something will come along.'

'But it's an amazing opportunity,' she said feebly.

Alex sighed. 'Look, it's your career and I won't stop you if you think it's the right move. But only if it's what you really, truly want.' He drew back from the embrace and looked searchingly into her eyes. 'So, is it, Britt?'

She couldn't meet his gaze. The thought of leaving him for weeks on end tore her apart. But how could she tell him that at the grand old age of twenty-six her career had hit the rocks and this was her last chance?

'Yes, it is,' she said eventually. 'I think Tokyo will be the making of my career. I really want to go.'

She only hoped that Alex couldn't tell that she was lying through her teeth.

6

'Auntie Briiiiitt!' The front door of Jessie's house flew open and Britt was caught up in a tangle of limbs and showered with sticky, chocolatey kisses by her six-year-old goddaughter Poppy, four-year-old Willow and toddler Rose. 'We're baking muffins for the school fête, come and see!'

With Poppy and Willow each taking a hand and Rose pushing from behind, Britt happily let herself be dragged along to the kitchen. After the stress of the last couple of days, she couldn't think of a nicer dose of TLC than spending time with Jessie and the girls.

After she'd told Alex about Tokyo yesterday morning he'd spent the morning moping around the house, and she was exhausted with the effort of trying to stay upbeat and positive for him while she felt like she was crumbling inside. If there was one person with whom Britt could be completely honest about the whole mess, it was Jessie.

She found her friend standing in the kitchen, looking flustered. She was poring over a recipe book. The whole room was dusted with flour, while smeary chocolate hand-prints (and, weirdly, footprints) covered all the surfaces. Every single pot, pan and utensil seemed to have been taken out of the cupboards and used.

'How's it going, Nigella?' said Britt, surveying the chaos. 'Looks like the domestic goddess has been at the tequila ice-cream again . . .'

'Thank God you're here, Baxter!' Despite having a family of five to cater for, cooking was not Jessie's strong point. 'I don't have any baking powder, so do you think I could just leave it out altogether? And would raspberry jam work instead of real raspberries? And what the hell is glycerine?'

'Leave it with me,' smiled Britt, putting on a spare apron. 'Um, Jess, what have you got tied in your hair?'

Her friend patted her head absent-mindedly. 'Oh that – it's a pair of knickers. The girls were running riot and I couldn't find a hair-band this morning so I used these instead. They work perfectly well,' she said, adding a little defensively, 'and they *are* clean.'

As much as Britt loved her own small-but-perfectly-formed flat, she felt truly at home in the chaos and clutter of Jessie's house with its huge, homely kitchen. Although Jessie had been a full-time mum since Poppy had come along six years ago, her husband Tom had a good job working in the City and they had been able to afford a five-bedroom semi in Streatham – a short hop from Clapham – where it was still possible to pick up a house for less than a million. Britt visited whenever she could. Not only did she love catching up with her friend, but the toy-strewn rooms and air of shambolic cosiness was exactly the sort of place Britt wanted for her and Alex.

Britt and Jessie had met in primary school and had been best mates ever since. They had made an odd couple as kids: Britt, tall and lanky with a wild mess of frizz; Jessie short and chubby, her poker-straight brown hair cut into a bob. And although Jessie grew her hair in her teens, nothing much else had changed. She was just an inch or so over five foot and for most of the last six years had either been pregnant or on a diet. Always ready with a self-deprecating quip, Jessie said she looked like Sonia from *EastEnders*, only without the trumpet.

While Jessie made them both cups of tea, Britt tried to rescue the muffin mixture, sending Poppy and Willow running about the kitchen to fetch ingredients from the cupboards while little Rose sat under the table sucking a chocolate-coated spoon.

'Right, try this.' Britt offered the bowl to Jessie, who dipped in a finger.

'Mmm, that is incredible!' She scooped up another fingerful. 'God, I'll have to do an extra set of squats with Davina tomorrow to work that off.' Jessie also owned every celebrity fitness DVD ever produced.

Britt started dolloping the mixture into muffin cases. 'How's Tom?'

'Oh, fine, but busy as ever. Things have gone a bit crazy at the bank and he's working late most nights, but' – she dropped her voice to a whisper – 'we're going to send the kids off to Tom's parents and have a dirty weekend in Brighton together next month!'

Jessie and Tom were the most brilliant advert for marriage. After three kids, they still acted like love-struck teenagers. They had met eight years ago when Jessie moved down to London with Britt and got a job working as a shop assistant at Gap. In her first week there, Tom had come in looking for a pair of chinos and had left with Jessie's phone number. A year later they were married – and almost nine months to the day after that,

Poppy had arrived. Both short of stature, brown-haired and generous to a fault, Jessie and Tom were different sides of the same coin. Britt sometimes thought that about her and Alex too, although right now it felt like they weren't even part of the same currency.

Once the muffins were out of the oven, Jessie split one of them into pieces for them all to try. One was never going to be enough though, and it soon led to two more being shared. And then another five. And then she insisted Britt take home a couple for Alex just to get them out of the house.

'I'll just have to get some Mr Kiplings for the fête,' said Jessie breezily. 'Okay, anyone who's under seven needs to get in the bath right now!'

There was a chorus of moans. 'Can Auntie Britt do the bath tonight, Mum? Pleeeease?'

Britt smiled. 'Last one upstairs is going to be caught by the Tickle Monster!'

For the next hour she chased the girls around the house, played tea parties in the bath, helped them all into their pyjamas and tucked them up in bed, then finished with a triple-helping of bedtime stories and goodnight kisses. By the time she made it back downstairs, Jessie had cleaned up the kitchen and was cracking open a bottle of red wine and a big bag of crisps.

'They're carrot and beetroot,' said Jessie, grabbing a handful. 'Much less fattening than potato. Probably.'

The pair of them slumped together on the sofa with their wine glasses. Jessie clinked her glass with Britt's.

'So, how are you, doll? And how did the big dinner at Dolce go? I need news!'

'Well, it was . . .' Britt trailed off. Suddenly the stress

of the last few days came flooding out and she broke into big, shoulder-shuddering sobs.

'Oh my God, what's happened?' Jessie desperately rummaged through her pockets and pulled out a crumpled tissue. 'Is everything okay with you and Alex?'

'Yes, it's fine – well, actually, it's not fine, but . . .' Britt noisily blew her nose. 'Oh, Jess, I don't know what I'm going to do. Everything's such a mess.'

'Shh, it'll be okay, love,' said Jessie. 'Just start from the beginning.'

So Britt told her everything that had happened – losing out on the Zauber job, Alex being made redundant, their money worries, Scott's offer to send her to Tokyo – while Jessie kept her supplied with wine and tissues.

'Okay, first things first,' she said, when Britt had finally ground to a tear-stained halt. 'Don't go to Tokyo. You will get another job. You are absolutely beautiful and hard-working and something else will come along.'

'No, I won't. I'm unemployable, apparently.'

'Bullshit.'

'It's true. Scott says I'm too old and don't look enough like an alien.'

'Yeah, because that ET was such a babe,' snorted Jessie. 'Well, what about Alex, then? Couldn't he get a similar sort of job elsewhere? Really, the two of you are so bloody gorgeous I'm surprised you don't have people stopping you in the street and begging you to work for them.'

'To be honest, Jess, I'm really worried about Al,' said Britt. 'He seems to have just gone to pieces since being made redundant. I've never seen him so depressed. It's like all the fight's gone out of him, like he's just . . . given up. It's so out of character.'

'Hmm, I guess it's a male pride thing,' said Jessie. 'Put yourself in his shoes – imagine how humiliated he must be feeling at losing his job and having to rely on you for support. I'm sure he'll snap out of it in a little while but in the meantime, if it's just a question of money, you know that the two of you are always welcome to stay in our spare room for as long as you want. Tom and the girls would love to have you here, not to mention how much I'd enjoy you being around.'

Britt nearly burst into tears all over again at Jessie's kindness. The thought of decamping to her house until they'd weathered the current financial storm was extremely attractive, but Britt knew that as much as Alex loved Jessie and her family, he would be too proud to even consider it.

'No, that's lovely of you but we couldn't possibly,' said Britt. 'I hate to say it, but I think my only option is to try my luck in Japan.'

Jessie took a long sip of wine. 'I really don't think you should go, hon. If Alex is taking this as badly as you say he is, what will happen to your relationship if you disappear off to Japan for months?'

'I'm not going over there for a bloody holiday!' Britt snapped, then, quickly regretting it, said, 'God, sorry, Jess.'

Jessie gave her a 'Don't worry about it' smile.

'Of course I'm worried about what will happen if I go,' Britt went on. 'I'm worried Alex will fall apart. I'm worried we'll fall apart. But I can't just sit at home waiting for a job that might never appear, can I?'

When Britt got back to the flat later that evening she found a note from Alex: '*Out for some beers. A* x ' She felt a twinge of annoyance. That was all he'd done since his last meeting at work. Was he planning on drinking his way through every last penny of his redundancy pay-off? And then another horrible thought wormed its way into her mind. With her disappearing off to Japan for weeks – perhaps months – what if Alex met someone else? She had seen how other women looked at him when they were out together: like lionesses sizing up a particularly juicy zebra. She didn't doubt how much he adored her, but what if he got drunk one night and some floozy came on to him? The thought made her feel queasy with fear.

Later, as Britt lay in bed, Jessie's words rang through her head again: '*What will happen to your relationship with Alex if you disappear off to Japan?*' Just a few days ago she was dreaming about a wedding and babies; now she was worrying if they even had a future together. She tried to imagine what life would be like without him. If they split up, she wouldn't just lose her lover, she would lose her best friend – well, apart from Jess. Right now, it didn't bear thinking about. With her mind whirling, it took Britt ages to get to sleep.

The last time she looked at the clock it was after 1 a.m., and Alex still wasn't back.

Britt wasn't sure what time Alex finally reappeared, but when she woke the next morning he was spread-eagled on the bed next to her, still fully dressed, softly snoring. Britt gently stroked his stubbly cheek and kissed his neck, but he didn't stir. She was struck by an overwhelming wave of love for him, but it was tinged with fear. It felt like he was slipping away from her and she could do nothing but watch him go.

Britt padded out of the bedroom in her dressing gown, made herself a coffee and then sat down at the kitchen table and picked up her phone. She had to put all this right.

'Well, good morning, Miz Baxter – or should I say *Konnichiwa?*'

'Hey, Scottie,' said Britt. 'Sorry for calling you at the weekend, but I've come to a decision.'

7

Britt stared at the bewildering array of buttons on the panel next to the airport toilet. One of them must flush the bloody thing, surely? There were instructions, but they were all in flipping Japanese. She tentatively pressed one of the buttons and little jets of water squirted out of the seat, while the next one along set off a dryer. When Britt pressed another and classical music started playing, she just gave up. After an eleven-hour flight crammed next to a man the size of a Sumo wrestler, she wasn't in the mood to negotiate with a smart-arse toilet.

Britt looked at herself in the bathroom mirror, taking in her lank hair, dull skin and the large red spot on her chin that must have sprung up somewhere over northern Russia. The only thing she'd be up to modelling right now was an ad for Clearasil. She scooted back into the cubicle and changed out of her tracksuit into a pair of jeans, cashmere hoody and biker boots. She scraped her hair into a messy bun and applied tinted moisturiser, bronzer, mascara. Hardly cover-girl material, but it would have to do.

After picking up her bags from the luggage carousel (she'd managed to squeeze everything she would need into two large holdalls) Britt wheeled her trolley out into the Arrivals hall across a beige marble floor so shiny that she could see her reflection in it. As she scanned the crowd of people lining the exit, checking for the one carrying a board with her name on it, she realised she was standing a good few inches taller than everyone else in there.

Scott had told her that someone from the Tokyo agency, Scout Models, would be there to meet her, but she couldn't see anything resembling either 'Britt' or 'Baxter' on any of the signs. After looking for a fruitless few minutes, Britt dialled the mobile number of Akiko, her contact at the agency.

The phone was answered instantly. 'Yes?'

'Oh, hi, is this Akiko?'

'Yes.'

'Hello Akiko, my name's Britt Baxter, I'm with Gawk Models in London and I'm at Tokyo Narita airport. I just wondered where you'll be meeting me?'

'I'm at a shoot,' the voice snapped. 'Get a taxi and I'll meet you at the agency in two hours. The address is 5-2-48 Minami-Azabu, Minato-Ku.'

'Sorry, I just need to grab a pen.' Britt rummaged in her hand luggage, trying not to drop the BlackBerry. 'Would you mind repeating that?'

The voice at the other end of the line huffed, reeled off the address again and then abruptly ended the call. Britt was surprised. The Japanese were famously polite.

There seemed to be worryingly few signs in English, so finding the taxi rank – and then trying to explain to the driver where she wanted to go – was a struggle. But once Britt was settled in the backseat (after experiencing a little thrill at the self-opening taxi doors) she finally allowed herself a shiver of excitement at what Tokyo would have in store for her. Maybe this wasn't going to be so bad after all? Okay, so she would far rather be here on holiday with friends, but it was certainly going to be an adventure. And the best thing was that in the days before she left, Alex seemed to be getting his old spark back. In the four days since Britt had phoned Scott to tell him she would try her luck in Japan, he had cut down on the boozing, shrugged off the self-pity and even started making enquiries about getting a new job. It was as if Britt's decision to come to Japan had given him just the kick up the bum he'd needed to sort himself out, too.

It had been so hard leaving Alex at the Departures gate in Heathrow. 'I love you more than life itself, Britt,' he had whispered, holding her so tightly that he'd lifted her off the ground. 'I promise I'll be the man you deserve by the time you get back.' And they had kissed for so long that the couple behind them eventually had to tap them on the shoulder to start the queue moving again.

Her last glimpse of Alex was turning round to wave as she went through Passport Control. Seeing him standing there, running his hand through that unruly mess of dark chocolate hair, he had looked heartbreakingly gorgeous in a navy sweatshirt that brought out the startling blue of his eyes.

'I love you,' he had mouthed with a smile. Fighting back the tears, Britt tucked the memory away like a treasured photo and tried to ignore the wrenching pain in her gut.

As the taxi drove through Tokyo's rush-hour traffic, Britt had to gasp at the sheer futuristic madness of the city. She felt like she was in a computer game. A crazy network of flyovers whizzed overhead, punctuated by the gazillion-floored, neon-lit skyscrapers. And the crowds! Whenever the green man flashed up at a pedestrian crossing, torrents of people would flow across from all angles. Then the crossing light would go red and *bam* – people instantly disappeared and the cars zoomed across. Highly organised chaos seemed the best way to describe it.

An hour and a half after leaving the airport, Britt's taxi finally pulled up outside a modern white and chrome office block. Situated on the sixteenth floor, Scout Models was pretty much identical to its London counterpart: the same décor, same photo-covered walls and constantly ringing phones. A nodding, smiley receptionist directed Britt to one of the frosted-glass-fronted offices to wait. She was just settling down onto the black leather sofa when the door opened.

'Britt Baxter? I'm Akiko, Scout Models' senior booker.'

The girl was wearing a tailored black shift dress with her hair tied back in a high, swingy ponytail. Her face was perfectly made up with flicks of sixties-style black eyeliner and a slash of bright red lipstick that matched the scarlet soles of her patent Christian Louboutin heels. She was so petite that she must have been even smaller than a size zero. A size minus one, perhaps? Britt felt like an elephant next to her.

'Your book, please.'

Britt handed her portfolio over and Akiko flicked through the photos in silence.

'Okay,' she said finally, putting the book to one side and crossing one glossy leg over the other. 'First of all, you too fat. You need to lose weight – start with ten pounds and then we see how you look.'

Britt was stunned. She opened her mouth to say something but then shut it again.

'You will have to do something about the sun damage on your face.'

'I'm sorry?'

'The freckles,' snapped Akiko. 'They will need to be covered up. Do you have any tattoos?'

Britt shook her head, still dazed.

'Well, I guess that's something.' She became aware that Akiko had an American accent; perhaps that would explain the total absence of Japanese manners.

'We have arranged for you to share an apartment with another model in the Roppongi district,' she said. 'Here are the keys, a map of the city, a subway map and a train map. Here is two hundred thousand yen to assist you in settling in. Do you have any questions?'

Britt had a million of them, starting with, 'How much is two hundred thousand yen worth?' swiftly followed by, 'Why are you such an evil cow?' but she figured it would be better if she spoke to her again when she wasn't giddy with jet lag and needing a shower. She mutely shook her head.

'Right then,' said Akiko, showing her to the door. 'Your first casting is tomorrow morning at 11 a.m. at the Chikako Corporation.'

'Tomorrow?' Britt had been expecting at least a day to settle in.

'Yes.' Akiko handed over a slip of paper. 'Here is the address. Don't be late, it is considered extremely rude.' And with that she turned on her shiny heel and click-clacked off down the corridor.

* * *

45

Britt knocked on the door of her new apartment. She'd found it amid a street of bars, restaurants and nightclubs. It was on the eighth floor of a block that looked like a giant, grey Rubik's Cube. It was getting dark when she arrived, and she was exhausted and dizzy with hunger.

No-one answered. Britt unlocked the door with the keys Akiko had given her. 'Hello?' she called tentatively. 'Is anybody home?'

She found herself in a tiny living room with cream walls, cream curtains and a laminated wood floor, the only furniture being a small table with two chairs. There were no pictures on the walls, no books, in fact nothing to suggest that anyone lived there apart from a massive hi-tech cross-trainer that took up most of the cramped space.

Britt was just about to go looking for her bedroom when she became aware of a muffled grunting sound coming from behind one of the three doors leading off the living room. She froze, listening to the increasingly frenzied gasps and moans. *Oh lord.* She had walked in on her new flatmate having sex.

Britt immediately turned to leave, but tripped over the cross-trainer and sent one of the chairs skittering across the floor with an almighty crash. The grunting abruptly stopped.

'Who's there?' asked a girlish voice from inside the room.

'Um, hello! It's me – Britt Baxter. I'm supposed to be moving in today.'

'Oh, cool, yeah, they mentioned something about that.' Broad Texan. 'I'm just in the middle of something, but come in and say hi.'

'Into your bedroom?'

'Sure! In fact, come and join in.'

Bloody hell. What happened to polite handshakes and getting to know each other with bland conversation about the weather? Perhaps she could just say a quick hello, then make her excuses?

Britt gingerly pushed open the door. Just keep looking at their faces, she kept telling herself. But all she found was a tiny blonde girl in a lycra vest and leggings lying on the floor by the side of the bed. She pushed herself up onto her elbows as Britt came in. With her honey-blonde hair, blue eyes and dimples, the girl had the all-American prettiness of a cheerleader, but her skin-tight workout gear revealed a painfully skinny body.

'Hey there, Britney, I'm Pebbles,' she chirped. 'Real nice to meet y'all. I've just got a few more reps with the Thighmaster then you're like *totally* welcome to have a go.'

And with that she lay back down again, positioned a bendy blue contraption between her legs and squeezed it together with a grunt. Britt almost burst out laughing.

'That's sweet of you to offer, Pebbles, but I'm a bit tired after the flight. Oh, and it's Britt, not Britney.'

'You're welcome to use the cross-trainer, too.' *Grunt.* 'And I have free weights and an Abdominator under the bed.' *Grunt.* 'Lazy bones make fat butts, as my momma likes to say!'

Britt wondered what Pebbles and her momma would make of her own exercise regime, which consisted of occasionally walking up the escalators at tube stations and going for a gentle jog every month or so.

'So, where y'all from, Britney?' panted Pebbles.

'Um, it's Britt. I'm from the north of England, but I live in London.'

'Oh my goodness!' Pebbles suddenly sat bolt upright, sending the Thighmaster boomeranging across the room. 'D'y'all know Prince William? I just lurve him.'

'Um, not really, no . . .'

But Pebbles wasn't listening. 'Hey, why don't we go out to celebrate our first night as roomies?' She jumped up and grabbed a towel. 'We can grab something to eat!'

After showering and changing, Pebbles and Britt locked up the apartment and plunged into the crowd of tourists, salary men and office girls streaming along the pavements outside. As they wandered along, Britt stared around her in a daze. The noise, the sky-high buildings festooned with neon, the wafts of sweet and spicy smells, the restaurant windows filled with plastic recreations of the food they served inside: it was total sensory overload. And unlike most other places she had been to in the world where they at least used the same alphabet, she couldn't even begin to guess at what all the signs meant. 'This is so exciting!' Britt said as she peered behind the curtained door of a little restaurant that from the look of the plastic models in the window seemed to specialise in tempura. 'I've really been looking forward to trying some authentic Japanese food.'

Pebbles wrinkled her cute little pixie nose in disgust. 'Ew! I can't even be in the same room as raw fish. It's so totally gross. And they serve rice with, like, everything! It's like, duh, *hello?* Carbs after 9 p.m.? – I don't think so!' It looked like Britt's plans for a slap-up Japanese feast would have to wait. 'But don't worry, honey,' Pebbles smiled. 'I know the perfect place.'

'So that's a box of Chicken McNuggets, a Big Mac, small fries and two Diet Cokes,' said Britt.

While Pebbles nibbled at a single McNugget (after carefully picking off the batter coating), Britt wolfed down her burger and fries. Then she remembered she was supposed to be losing ten pounds. Shite. Her first night in Tokyo, culinary capital of the world, and she was stuck in McDonald's with a sushi-phobic borderline anorexic.

Over dinner, Britt learnt that Pebbles was nineteen and from a little town called Sulphur Springs in Texas (where she actually *had* been a cheerleader). Although she told Britt she had only planned on staying in Tokyo for six weeks to earn a bit of money before college, a year later she was still there – and Britt got the impression it wasn't out of choice. But when Britt asked her why, Pebbles abruptly changed the subject.

'So how old are you, Britney?'

'It's *Britt*. I'm twenty-six.'

'Oh my gosh, I always imagined I'd be married and a momma by twenty-six!'

Yeah, so did I, thought Britt sadly, her thoughts instantly turning to Alex. 'I live with my boyfriend and we . . . well, we might be getting married.'

'And you left him to come out here? What are you, like, totally nutso?'

'I needed the work.' Britt shrugged.

'Well, I've been here for nearly a year and for the past six months I've had, like, three jobs.'

Britt was stunned. If sweet little size-zero Pebbles

couldn't get work, what hope was there for her? 'My agent told me that there's lots of work around,' she said.

Pebbles shook her head sadly. 'This is the place where modelling careers go to die.' She sucked up the last of her Diet Coke and then leant over the table towards Britt. 'Seriously, honey,' she whispered, her blue eyes wide. 'I'm sorry for you. You don't know what you've let yourself in for.'

8

Britt looked up at the emerald-green glass skyscraper soaring high over her head. She checked the slip of paper with the address Akiko had given her yesterday. Chikako Corporation. Yes, this was definitely where the casting was taking place.

She checked her BlackBerry: 10.30. Great, half an hour early. She had left the apartment at 8 a.m. and walked to the casting as she hadn't had a chance to get her head round the subway system yet. It was as warm and sunny as a British summer day, and – despite the jet lag and Pebbles – Britt was bursting with caffeine-fuelled positivity.

Another model was already sitting in the waiting room when Britt arrived at the office on the twenty-first floor. Tall and waifish with near-translucent skin and huge, dark eyes, the girl looked like she'd walked out of *The Lord of the Rings*. Britt half expected her to have pointy ears beneath the curtain of white blonde hair.

'Hi,' Britt smiled. She was keen to make some friends in Tokyo beyond Pebbles.

The girl stared back, her face a mask of icy inscrutability.

'I'm Britt.'

Not a word.

'What's your name?'

Nothing. Perhaps she didn't speak English, or maybe she was shy. She did look very young.

Britt had given up on the small talk and had started flicking through a magazine when a voice like a Soviet submarine commander boomed out, 'Vladlena Popolovich.'

'Have you been in Tokyo long, Vladlena?' smiled Britt, encouragingly. But her name was the only information that the girl seemed willing to offer. A few moments later, a secretary poked her head round the door and Vladlena was summoned to the casting. She clomped out of the room like the Terminator in leggings and ballet pumps.

On the dot of 11 a.m. the secretary reappeared. 'Mr Takahashi will see you now, Miss Baxter. This way, please.'

Britt was shown into a vast meeting room with windows stretching floor to ceiling along its entire length. It was empty of furniture except for a row of a dozen or so chairs, which were all occupied by identically dark-suited Japanese businessmen. In Britt's experience, there were usually only two or three people at go-sees: a casting director, booking agent and perhaps the photographer or artistic director. This must be a pretty important job to require a whole roomful of decision-makers.

'*Hajimemashite,*' said Britt, smiling and bowing in every direction as she had learnt from her guidebook: *Hello, I am honoured to make your acquaintance.*

The men stood and smiled and bowed then all sat down again. She noticed one of the men in the middle of the row whispering something to the man on his right, who then addressed Britt.

'I am Mr Murai, Mr Takahashi's interpreter,' he said. 'Mr Takahashi has asked if you will walk, please.' He gestured back and forwards in front of the row of chairs.

Britt smoothed down her floral Topshop dress (which perfectly suited the 'pretty not tarty' dress code Akiko had recommended for go-sees during her briefing), pushed her shoulders back, her hips forwards and sashayed along the line of expressionless men wearing what she called her 'fashion face': a fierce pout and blazing eyes.

After she had walked up and down the room a couple of times she stopped in front of Mr Takahashi, struck a pose, then smiled expectantly at the panel.

Mr Takahashi and the interpreter conferred. 'Again, please,' Mr Murai translated.

And so Britt repeated her walk, this time adding a couple more laps for good measure. As she strutted back and forth a dozen pairs of eyes followed her, silently and intently, like she was a tennis ball in a tense Wimbledon final.

More whispering.

'Take off your dress now please,' said the interpreter.

Britt gawped. 'I'm sorry?'

'Please remove your dress.'

'What – here?'

The interpreter nodded, as if getting undressed in front of an office full of men was the most natural thing in the world. Britt realised that the job must be a lingerie or swimwear ad, but why on earth hadn't Akiko warned her? Her bikini line needed serious attention. Nevertheless, she reluctantly stripped down to her mismatched M&S undies. Thank God she'd decided against the skimpy Agent

Provocateur thong she had planned to wear that morning to avoid a VPL.

'Please walk again.'

As Britt set off once more, it dawned on her that apart from Mr Takahashi and the interpreter, none of the other men had actually said a word the whole time she had been in there. Was it likely that they had anything to do with the casting decision? Had they just come along for a free show?

'Now, please turn all the way around very slowly,' said the interpreter.

What next? Britt wondered crossly. *Bend over and touch my flipping toes so you can get a proper eyeful?*

It looked like Mr Takahashi had seen enough.

'Congratulations, Miss Baxter, you have been chosen for the job,' said the interpreter. 'You will need to be at the location at 7 a.m. tomorrow morning. We will send a car to pick you up.'

Mr Takahashi smiled. The interpreter smiled. The men from Accounts or IT or wherever the hell they worked all smiled. Britt smiled.

'Uh, can I get dressed now?' she said eventually.

'Ew, that is, like, totally perverted!' Pebbles' tiny hands flew to her mouth. 'I can't believe you had to take your clothes off in front of all those men!'

The pair of them were in Britt's bedroom, where she had spent the entire evening in a frenzy of plucking, exfoliating, polishing and waxing, determined to look her best for the next day's shoot.

'Yeah, well, I got the job so I guess it was worth it,' said Britt, rubbing fake tan into her shoulders. 'Can you be a love and help me do my back?'

54

'Sure.' Pebbles bounced off the bed. 'So, what is this gig, anyhow?'

'Apparently it's a TV car commercial.' Britt had finally managed to get a few more details out of Akiko about the job, and it sounded pretty high profile.

'Omigod, you'll probably be, like, sprawled across the bonnet in a bikini!'

'Not a problem,' smiled Britt, checking herself in the mirror from every angle. 'This time I'm going to be ready for anything.'

Early the next morning, Britt arrived at the location where the advert was being filmed and was hustled straight to Make-up before being pushed towards Wardrobe. The room was buzzing with activity, people muttering urgently into walkie-talkies and rifling through the rails of clothing and rows of shoes. Britt felt like she was on a movie set. It all seemed very glamorous and exciting. Last night's three-hour grooming marathon had definitely been worthwhile.

'Name?' said a smiling Japanese girl clutching a clipboard.

'Britt Baxter.'

The girl – who evidently didn't speak much English – looked blank, so Britt leant over and pointed out her name on the list.

'Ah, okay!' The girl rummaged through a rail of costumes. 'You wear this, please.'

She held out a grey flannel suit with a knee-length A-line skirt, a cream frill-collared blouse and a pair of mid-heeled shoes. It was the sort of get-up a Mormon might have rejected as a little on the frumpy side.

Britt stared at the outfit. 'There must be some mistake.'

But the girl didn't seem to understand and just smiled and nodded, pressing the outfit into Britt's hands along with a leather briefcase and a pair of near-opaque American tan tights. 'You hurry, please,' she said, pointing to a curtained-off changing room. By the time Britt had smoothed the tights over her perfectly stubble-free legs and buttoned up the blouse, there was barely an inch of her meticulously tanned body on show.

She followed the clipboard-girl outside to where another three girls dressed in similar suits to her own were waiting, hoping someone else might be able to sort out the costume mix-up.

'Okay, extras, listen up!' A man, who Britt assumed was the director, clapped his hands for attention. Thankfully he spoke perfect English. 'So what's going to happen is that you four are going to be standing on the pavement and then the car is going to drive past and I want you all to turn your heads to follow it. You got that? Stand, drive, turn heads. Okay, let's go!' The director started striding off, but Britt hurried after him.

'Um, excuse me! Hi. Sorry about this, but I think I might be wearing the wrong outfit. My name is Britt Baxter.'

The man looked down a cast list. 'Britt Baxter . . . Right, I have you down as Second Businesswoman.' He glanced at her suit. 'You look like Second Businesswoman to me.'

'The thing is . . .' Britt shifted uncomfortably. 'I think I was meant to be in a bikini.'

The man looked at her with barely disguised disgust. 'This is a commercial for a new five-door family hatchback. Not *Beverly Hills 90210.*' He stalked off, shaking his head as if to say, 'These sex-obsessed English girls are all the same . . .'

And then the penny finally dropped. Britt stood there, feeling like a total idiot as she realised that of course there was no mistake.

Mr Takahashi just had a very thorough auditioning technique.

It took a dozen or so takes and a lot of hanging around before the director was happy, but Britt enjoyed the buzz of being on set and got chatting to a few of the extras. She was pleased to discover they'd had more positive experiences of working in Tokyo than Pebbles had. All in all, it was a pretty easy way to earn $500.

She had arranged to meet Pebbles at a bar that evening, so after the car dropped her back at the apartment Britt jumped in the shower – having to bend almost double to fit in the tiny cubicle – and tied her hair in a fashionably messy knot. Then she rummaged through her suitcases to find something suitable for Friday night cocktails.

Maybe it was because she spent her life getting dolled up for shoots, but she usually steered clear of full-on glamour in her spare time, and she eventually decided on a pair of her favourite American Apparel leather-look leggings teamed with an oversized boyfriend T-shirt and killer Zanotti heels. Slinging a parka over the top, she dashed out of the door, looking forward to telling Pebbles about her day over a few Mojitos.

She finally found The Happy Drinker, the bar where Pebbles wanted to meet, down a narrow alley piled with bin bags. It was off a street that looked like Soho with sex shops and seedy-looking clubs. A red neon sign with a large flashing arrow pointed the way down a narrow flight of steps to an entrance, from which came the low thump of 'Single Ladies' by Beyoncé.

In the dim light, Britt could see that the room was lined with booths, most of which were occupied by groups of businessmen with their ties loosened, downing shots, while heavily made-up Western girls in tight dresses wandered around with trays of drinks. Some of the men turned and stared at Britt as she stood in the doorway. The place felt . . . sleazy.

She spotted Pebbles sitting on a stool at the mirrored bar with a much older Japanese man. She was wearing a vest top and denim hot-pants with a pair of pink cowboy boots. As she got closer, she saw the man had his hand on her leg.

'Hi, Pebbles,' said Britt cautiously.

'Hey, roomie! This is Mr Nakamura. Mr Nakamura, this is my flatmate, Britney.' She dropped her voice to a reverent whisper. 'She's friends with Prince William, you know.'

The man nodded and smiled.

'You want a drink, honey? Mr Nakamura here is buying.' Pebbles gave the man a flirtatious wink. It was only just after 7 p.m., but from the way her roommate was giggling and swaying on her stool, Britt was pretty sure that she was wasted.

All sorts of things were running through Britt's mind, none of them pretty. She had heard tales of hostess bars in Japan where Western girls earned money for 'entertaining' businessmen, but surely Pebbles couldn't be mixed up in that? She seemed like such an innocent.

59

'Would you excuse us for a moment?' she asked Mr Nakamura, dragging Pebbles off to a quiet corner.

'Pebbles, who is that man?'

'He's a friend,' she pouted, swaying slightly.

'What kind of friend?'

'A friend who buys me drinks sometimes! Jeez, *Mom*, chill out.' With a swish of her hair, Pebbles turned to go back to the bar and promptly stumbled over her feet. She was definitely drunk.

'Right, we're out of here,' said Britt, grabbing her arm.

'Hey, let me go, I wanna stay!' wailed Pebbles, trying to wriggle free.

But Britt was stronger – and sober – and easily dragged her up the stairs. Then, ignoring her howls of protest about carbs, she pulled Pebbles into the nearest noodle bar and ordered them each a big bowl of chicken ramen soup, the only thing she could fathom on the menu.

'Right – eat,' she ordered when their food arrived. Pebbles started reluctantly spooning up the soup. 'The noodles as well,' warned Britt.

They ate in silence. After a while, Pebbles put down her spoon and stared at the table. She looked like she was going to cry.

'I wanna go back to Sulphur Springs,' she said in a small voice. 'I hate it here.'

'Well, why don't you then?'

'Because I can't afford the flight.' Pebbles' bottom lip started wobbling. 'I've got no money. Not a cent. I owe the agency thousands. Why do you think I have to get Mr Nakamura to buy my drinks?' A fat tear trickled down her cheek.

'Hey, it's okay, I can lend you the money,' said Britt

gently. 'I earned five hundred dollars today.'

Pebbles gave a snort of laughter. 'Yeah, and after the agency have taken commission and deducted the rent and everything else they charge you for, you'll be left with a couple of bucks, tops. Did they tell y'all what the apartment is gonna cost you a month? Three hundred thousand yen.'

Britt did a rough calculation in her head. Over £2,000 a month each for that tiny box room? And then there were bills, food, travel and living expenses on top of that. She'd have to do several jobs a week just to break even! That couldn't be right. Pebbles must have made a mistake.

'The agency kept telling me how much money I was gonna make, but then I got here and found I owed them money before I'd even started,' wailed Pebbles. 'And then they charge you interest on the debt! We're gonna be trapped here, like . . .' – she sobbed – '. . . like, for ever!'

'Shh, don't worry, love, it's all going to be okay.' Britt hugged the now furiously sobbing Pebbles. 'I'll go and see Akiko at the agency tomorrow. I'm sure I can sort everything out.'

But as she spoke, Britt felt an icy shiver of panic travel down her spine. What if Pebbles was right?

10

This time, Britt intended to be ready for Akiko and her bloody Louboutins. She got up at 6 a.m. and spent an hour blow-drying her hair, sectioning it off with clips like she'd learned from a professional stylist. Then she carefully straightened each section with a barrel brush until it swished about her shoulders in a glossy curtain. Next up, make-up. Britt went for the works: primer, foundation (to cover the despised freckles), bronzer, rosy blush, a subtly defined eye, loads of mascara and a gloss of lipstick. The outfit was equally important: she had to look like she meant business. So – J Brand jeans, stack-heeled Chloé loafers, a silk T-shirt and a chic navy Joseph blazer. She looked at her effect in the mirror: Cindy Crawford kicks corporate butt.

When Britt came into the living room Pebbles was working up a storm on the cross-trainer in a Hello Kitty vest and knickers, doing penance for the carbs she'd been force-fed last night.

'Wow, y'all look hot!' she drawled. Britt eyed Pebbles' emaciated frame and felt a surge of pity.

'How are you feeling today, love?'

'I'm doing just fine,' panted Pebbles. 'Much better for a workout, that's for sure! Size zeroes are heroes – am I right, honey?' At least she seemed to have recovered after her meltdown.

'Um, sure,' said Britt. 'Whatever you say. See you later.' She grabbed her keys, Mulberry bag and the sheaf of maps then headed for the door.

'Give 'em hell, roomie!' she heard Pebbles shout after her.

Britt felt like the frosted-glass walls of the pristine white office were closing in on her.

'So you're saying that the rent for the apartment is automatically deducted from whatever I earn,' she said, struggling to contain her panic.

'Correct.' Akiko's face was emotionless. 'The rent is three hundred thousand yen per month.' That was nearly £2,500 according to Britt's calculation! 'We also deduct agency commission at thirty-five per cent and various living costs, including your weekly Shiatsu massage.'

'My weekly *what*?'

'All models must come to the agency once a week for a Shiatsu massage,' said Akiko. 'It is essential.'

'I'll do without the massages.'

'Not an option. After twelve-hour photo shoots and four hours of castings a day, your body will need it.'

Britt was beginning to wonder if Akiko was actually a robot, albeit one with a knockout wardrobe. Today she was wearing a tailored pinstripe trouser suit and another pair of Louboutin heels – although her feet were so tiny they looked like they should be in Start-rite.

'What about that cash you gave me when I arrived?' asked Britt in last-ditch desperation. 'I thought that was to cover the rent?'

63

'That was a loan. Which will need to be repaid. And there will, of course, be interest charged.'

Britt's head was spinning. How the hell was she going to save up enough to start sending money back to Alex to cover the rent on their flat, let alone afford a flight back home? Pebbles *was* right.

Akiko looked pointedly at her watch – black diamond-encrusted Chanel, natch.

'Now if there's nothing else, I have a meeting with the fashion director of *Elle* Japan,' she said, thrusting a sheet of paper at Britt. 'I've printed off a list of your castings for the next few days.'

Britt stared at the long list of appointments, the first of which was in just a couple of hours' time. It looked like she was in demand. Well, that was something at least. She gathered up her things and started for the lift.

'Oh, and I trust you are doing something about your weight problem,' Akiko called after her as she left. But when Britt turned round to respond she had disappeared. *In a puff of smoke*, thought Britt, punching furiously at the lift button, while sucking in her midriff.

Emerging onto the busy street, Britt vowed to put her money worries to the back of her mind and focus on the job at hand: getting more work. *If the flow of work continues*, she thought, trying to be positive, *I've made a good start on getting together some cash to take back home.*

With taxis definitely out of the question, she realised she would have to brave the Tokyo Metro to get to the next appointment, across town in Ginza. She checked her map and then walked the short distance to Hiroo station. It wasn't just the language barrier that was making Britt nervous about using Tokyo's public transport: she remembered seeing a photo of Japanese commuters being pushed onto already filled-to-capacity subway carriages by a couple of guards until they were packed like grains of rice in a sushi roll. The image made London's tube trains seem positively light and airy in comparison.

To Britt's relief, the signs and ticket-machine instructions at the station were translated into English and – despite the bewildering number of lines – after poring over the subway map she found the route heading to her next appointment.

On the platform, there were neat queues of people waiting to board the train, rather than the sprawling free-for-all of London. There were signs indicating where the pink female-only carriages stopped, but as the other women on the platform seemed to be ignoring them, so too did Britt. She joined one of the queues and managed to get on without being shoved on by one of the white-gloved guards. So far, so painless.

The train was busy, though, and at each stop more and more people ploughed single-mindedly onto the already packed train. Britt found herself gradually being jostled and pushed into the middle of the carriage where she clung onto an overhead strap, squeezed up against the surrounding passengers.

In her heels, Britt was a good few inches taller than most of the other people in the carriage. She was just staring over the heads at the on-board map, trying to work out how many stops she had left (and exactly how she was going to fight her way out of the carriage) when she became aware of a strange shuffling noise coming from just behind her. She looked round to see a group of suited businessman with blank faces standing directly behind her; the noise abruptly stopped. None of them seemed to have noticed it or else they were feigning ignorance, so she looked forward again. But the noise started up, this time with a rubbing sensation against the back of her legs. Britt swung round again, and once again it stopped. It reminded her of the childhood game of Grandmother's Footsteps.

By now it was so crammed in the carriage that it was difficult to turn round to see what was going on behind her without elbowing the little old lady crushed up to her side. All Britt could do was stand there with a growing feeling of unease, wondering what on earth the strange sensation could be.

11

Britt left the station feeling pleased with her small triumph. Britt Baxter: 1, Tokyo Subway: 0. With an hour to kill before her next casting, she popped into a café and had a cappuccino and a hot vanilla cream puff – two fingers up at diet-Nazi Akiko. Then she braved a vast, futuristic shopping plaza for her first taste of window-shopping, Tokyo style. She stood on the escalator gazing around her, dazed by the sheer scale of the place. It made the average British shopping centre look like Larkbridge village store.

Amongst the kitsch boutiques and electronics emporiums, Britt zeroed in on a shop selling designer denim. Some women have a thing for shoes, others handbags – for Britt it was jeans. Promising herself she would only have a quick look (and *definitely* wouldn't risk the temptation of trying anything on), she rifled through the rails until she came to a pair of Paige jeans with an irresistible little kick-flare. They were just her size – and they were reduced! Her good intentions instantly forgotten, Britt headed happily off to the fitting rooms, enjoying the buzz that came with finding what might turn out to be Perfect Jeans.

She was shown to a cubicle that had lights so bright

you could perform a surgical operation under them, and mirrors positioned to show the shopper's cellulite from every angle. She was just shrugging off her blazer when she caught sight of her back view. *What the hell was that on her jeans?* Britt twisted around so she could get a better look. It seemed to be a large damp stain. She didn't remember sitting in anything. In fact, she'd been standing the whole way on the subway. And then, in a horrific split-second, everything fell into place. The shuffling sound on the subway . . . the stroking feeling on the back of her legs . . . the man pressed up behind her . . .

Oh. My. God.

Squealing with revulsion, Britt ripped off her J Brand jeans and then used up an entire pack of wet wipes she had in her handbag in a frenzy of hand sanitising. This was even worse than the time an ageing French playboy with halitosis and too-tight jeans had grabbed her from behind while she was dancing in a Paris nightclub with some of her model mates and had started grinding his erection against her to 'I'm Too Sexy' by Right Said Fred. They had all been laughing about that after a few drinks, but she couldn't ever imagine seeing the funny side of *this*. Still shuddering with disgust, Britt wriggled into the Paige flares – not even caring that the labels were still on and that they didn't quite fit round the bum – and then marched straight to the cash desk to pay. From then on, she vowed she would only travel on the subway in one of the women-only carriages.

Dumping her poor, violated J Brands into a bin outside the shop (two hundred quid down the drain, but she couldn't face taking them back to the apartment and washing them), Britt was just looking for a public toilet to give her hands a more thorough disinfecting when her BlackBerry rang. She looked at the screen and her heart leapt. *Alex!*

'Britt! How are you, beautiful?'

'Oh, Al, it's so lovely to hear from you!' And with that, she promptly burst into tears.

'Hey, love, why are you crying? What's happened? Are you okay?'

Britt felt like begging him to come and rescue her. But if she told him the truth, that she was chronically homesick and didn't know how she was ever going to get back to Britain – oh, and that someone had just wanked over her favourite jeans – then Alex would be so furious he would insist she got on the first flight home. And really, when it came down to it, what was the point of worrying him? It wasn't like he could just conjure up a plane ticket out of thin air – he couldn't afford it.

'Oh, I just miss you, that's all,' she sniffed. 'I'm fine, honest.' She gushed about how many castings she had lined up. That bit at least was true.

'And how about your job hunt?' she asked. 'Any luck finding something?'

'Oh, you know, still looking,' said Alex breezily. 'There doesn't seem to be much around at the moment. But with you making so much money out in Tokyo, perhaps I can be a house-husband!'

Britt felt a twinge of anger. If he knew what she was going through! But immediately she knew that wasn't fair. Alex was doing his best to find a job, she was sure about that.

'It's just not the same without you here,' he said after

they'd chatted for a few minutes. 'How long do you think you'll be out there for?'

'I'm not sure. A few more weeks I should think.'

'Okay. Well, hurry home. I miss you – as does Kate Moss. She's gone on hunger strike. She's down to one tin of KiteKat a day.'

'I love you, gorgeous.'

'You too. Be good, baby.'

The weeks flew by in a frenzy of work. Every single day Britt was either schlepping her portfolio around the city on castings, or working fourteen-hour days on photo shoots. They certainly knew how to get their money's worth in this town. At home, a typical shoot would average six to eight different outfits a day; here it was as many as sixty. No wonder so many models turned to binge-eating, booze or drugs, cracking under the weight of the workload. And the working day started early, often at 6 a.m., so if a job was out in the suburbs she would find herself leaving the apartment at the same time as the pissed-up businessmen were spilling out of the bars neighbouring their apartment. On several occasions she'd had to step over businessmen passed out cold in the gutter.

Yet apart from Akiko – who Britt christened the Wicked Witch of the Far East – all the Japanese people she met and worked with were unfailingly polite and professional. And she soon learned to love Tokyo. The city was a mass of contradictions. On the one hand it was a vision of caffeine-fuelled futuristic craziness, but at the same time she could be walking down the busiest shopping street, turn a corner and suddenly find herself in a tranquil Japanese garden overlooked by a temple, where the only sound was koi carp fish blowing bubbles on the surface of a pond. She just wished Alex could be there to enjoy it with her. She missed him like crazy – but she was worried about him, too. They spoke every few days, but whenever she raised the subject of him finding a job he changed the subject.

Britt asked Jessie if she'd seen anything of Alex when she called for a gossip.

'No, I haven't, but Tom went out for a drink with him the other night.' Jessie sounded a bit shifty.

'How does he seem? Be honest, Jess.'

She sighed. 'Not great I'm afraid, love. Tom said he was really putting away the beers – and for him to even mention that must mean that Alex was drinking a hell of a lot. He misses you, Britt.'

Well, there was nothing Britt could do about him right now. She just had to focus on earning enough money to get home.

Britt had been in Tokyo for a month when she came back to the apartment one evening after a late-running shoot to find a note written in a childlike scrawl on a pink heart-shaped Post-it pinned to the cross-trainer: *'Hey Britney, guess wot? Im goin home to Texas!!!! Mr Nakamura gave me the money 4 the ticket. At airport now, no point hangin around!! Come visit me in Sulphur Springs soon. Thanx for bein a gr8 roomie xxxxxxxxxx ps. I left u the Thi-master. Lol!!!'*

So that was it – Pebbles had left the building. Britt would miss her. Okay, so her habit of dropping to the floor and doing 100 press-ups whenever Britt cooked a full English breakfast because she thought she had '. . . like, *totally* inhaled the fat molecules' was a little annoying, but Pebbles had been her only pal. Britt's attempts at befriending the other Western models had been met with indifference.

To bat away the feeling of loneliness, Britt went in search of a slap-up raw fish dinner. She ended up sitting in a sushi restaurant at the counter next to an older Japanese guy, who spent the evening pouring her endless glasses of sake and trying to explain exactly what she was eating using a hilarious mixture of mime and sign language.

The last thing she remembered was fleeing a karaoke bar after her new friend coerced her to join him in a drunken rendition of 'Islands in the Stream', then tried to grope her boobs. She woke up late the following morning with a thumping hangover to find herself lying on the bed, fully dressed, with the Thighmaster wedged between her knees.

The make-up artist cocked her head to one side to admire her handiwork. 'Okay, all done. Cool, right?'

Britt looked in the mirror. She was wearing a huge pink wig that had been teased and curled into a candy-floss bouffant. A pattern of hearts and stars had been painted on one cheek and a rainbow on the other. Her eyes peered out warily from under a veil of glitter and a sweeping pair of silver false lashes. Britt wasn't sure what the idea behind the magazine shoot was supposed to be, but the overall effect was My Little Pony on acid.

'*Kawaii!* Cwazy hot!!!' gushed the stylist in a heavy Japanese accent.

'Yeah,' agreed the photographer, whose jeans were hanging down below his boxers. 'Cwazy cool.'

The stylist led Britt to the dressing room where she showed her the outfits for the shoot. First up was a silver catsuit, so tight that she instantly regretted the muffin she'd had for breakfast. It looked like she would have to be sewn into it.

'Um, can you excuse me just for a moment?' smiled Britt apologetically. 'Comfort break.'

Humming along to the Kings of Leon album that was blaring out over the studio speakers, Britt wandered off to find the toilet. On the way she pulled out her BlackBerry to check if she'd had any calls – and froze in shock at what she saw. *What the hell?* Sixteen calls from Alex in the last hour! There was a text, too. The three-word message left Britt sick with dread: 'Please call. Urgent.'

12

Rushing into the toilets, Britt locked herself into a cubicle and pressed Alex's number, her hands shaking.

'What's happened?'

'It's your mum. She's fine but she's in hospital. She collapsed in the post office this morning. They think it's a stroke.'

Oh, no. Oh God, no. Not Mum.

Britt felt like someone had punched her in the stomach. 'Is . . . is she okay?'

'She's conscious, but it's too early to tell exactly what's happened. They're doing tests now.'

There was a rushing sound in Britt's ears and the room started to spin. She shakily pulled down the toilet lid, rocked back down onto it and put her head between her legs to stop herself fainting. She was closer to her mum than anyone in the world. She was her only family.

'I've got to get home.' The tears were starting to tumble down her cheeks. 'I have to get a flight. Oh Al, I don't know how I'm going to afford a ticket home. What am I going to do?'

'What do you mean, love? I thought work was going well out there?'

'I didn't want to worry you, but the agency is taking such a large portion of my earnings that I haven't managed to save up much money, and . . . Look, I can't really explain now. I just need to get home!'

There was a long pause at the other end of the line. 'I haven't really got enough money for a ticket. I'm so sorry, Britt . . .'

Despite her fears for her mum, Britt was suddenly furious. *Why was Alex so bloody useless?*

'Look, I'll call Jessie and see if she can help,' said Alex. 'Leave it with me.'

'Don't bother,' sobbed Britt, and jabbed at the button to end the call.

It was only when she was standing on the subway on the way back to the apartment, willing the train to go faster, that Britt caught sight of her reflection and realised she'd dashed out of the studio without removing the pink wig. She looked like The Joker from *Batman*. Thankfully it was the sort of thing that wouldn't get you a second glance in Tokyo.

By the time she had made it back to the apartment, Britt had formulated a plan. She would borrow the money from Scout Models as an advance on her earnings. After all, she had been working pretty much non-stop. Akiko would understand. She had to.

But Akiko didn't understand.

'You have a catalogue shoot tomorrow and a location job for *Elle* Japan the following day,' she said when Britt called her. 'Impossible for you to leave now. Next Monday is earliest you can go.'

'But my mother's in hospital and I have to get back to

see her! I'll send you a cheque for any money I owe you, plus the interest. Please, Akiko, I'm desperate!'

'I cannot authorise that.'

Britt saw red. 'Well, authorise *this* then. I quit!'

She slammed down the phone. The fleeting feeling of satisfaction was all too quickly replaced by panic. No job. No way home. Now what?

She went online to trawl through the cheap flight websites, but there was nothing under a thousand quid. Fighting panic and struggling to blank out the image of her mum lying in a hospital bed hooked up to drips and covered in tubes, she went to the bathroom to take off her make-up. As she peeled off the false lashes and brushed away the glitter, she wondered whether she could possibly ask Pebbles' friend Mr Nakamura for help?

The door buzzer sounded. Britt answered the intercom, but whoever it was didn't speak English so she trekked down to the front door. It was a motorbike courier with a package for her.

On the way up in the lift, she tore open the envelope and gasped – a British Airways ticket to London Heathrow, leaving in four hours' time. Jessie had come to the rescue! Britt raced back to the apartment muttering a silent prayer of thanks to her wonderful friend. Unlike her boyfriend, who hadn't come close to being there for her. She felt a pang as she realised she was beginning to lose all respect for Alex.

Leaving behind anything that she couldn't jam into her bags, Britt rushed out of the apartment and headed for the subway to Tokyo station, where she boarded a Narita express train to the airport.

* * *

76

Eleven hours later, after landing at Heathrow, Britt took the train to London, then the tube to Euston and then the train up north. And less than twenty-four hours after leaving Tokyo, she ran through the doors of Cumberland Infirmary, her bags bumping about her bruised and exhausted legs. She caught sight of her reflection in a mirror door and realised she still had traces of glittery make-up smeared over her face.

'I'm Molly Baxter's daughter,' she panted to one of the nurses sitting on a desk at the Neurology unit, who directed her to a ward down the corridor. Fearing the worst, Britt pushed open the swing doors and scanned the beds for her mum.

She found her at the far end of the room by the window. Molly was sitting up in bed wearing a white towelling robe, reading *Vogue*. Her long hair, still lustrously auburn, was swept back with a hair-band. Her skin was make-up free, but glowing and radiant. There were no tubes, no drips and no machines bleeping. She certainly didn't look like a stroke victim. In fact, she looked more like she was waiting to have a facial at a swanky spa.

'Mum!' Britt dropped her bags and threw her arms around Molly, sobbing with relief and exhaustion. 'God, I was so worried! How are you?'

The two of them clung together, laughing and crying.

'Mum, why are you laughing?'

'Oh, Britt, it's so wonderful to see you, you've got some glitter on your cheek,' smiled her mum. 'I'm fine, really. I'm so sorry for giving you all a scare and dragging you back from Japan. I told Alex not to bother you, but he insisted.'

'Don't be silly, Mum, there was no way I wouldn't be

here!' Britt sat on the bed, clutching Molly's hand. 'So what happened?'

'Well, I'm not really sure, pet. One moment I was standing in the post office, the next I woke up in here with a handsome doctor standing over me. No-one really seems sure what happened. They want to do a few more tests, but they've said that I can go home.'

Molly had celebrated her sixtieth birthday the year before but was still a beautiful woman. Britt had inherited her striking looks – the strong nose, wide mouth and high cheekbones – from her mum, while her height and frizzy brown hair came from her dad. Well, that was what she had gathered from photos. Britt had never actually met her father, Ben Baxter. He had been killed in a car accident at the age of thirty-four when Molly was four months pregnant, leaving the young widow to raise their only child with the help of her parents, Britt's beloved Nanna Eileen and Grandpa Roy, who had passed away within a few months of each other four years ago. Molly, a teacher at the local primary school, had had a few relationships since her husband's tragic death, but nothing long term. Ben had been the love of her life, she would tell Britt wistfully as they flipped through old photo albums.

Like her mum, Britt had grown up into a strong, independent woman who would always cope with a problem rather than burdening someone else with it. She was fiercely loyal and would do anything to help a friend in need. And she was also a hopeless – or rather, hopeful – romantic and a firm believer in The One. Until recently, it had seemed that was Alex, but now Britt wasn't sure he was The Two or even The Three.

After a final visit from the doctor (a dead spit for George Clooney in *ER*, only with a bald patch), Molly was discharged and they got a taxi back home to Larkbridge.

As they pulled up outside the little redbrick cottage with its green front door, square windows festooned with climbing roses and squat chimney – a child's drawing of a house – Britt felt herself relax for the first time in months.

Inside, little had changed since Britt was growing up. The hallway walls were crowded with photos, paintings and keepsakes, including a pair of Britt's baby shoes in a box frame. The house always had a homely smell thanks to the wood-burning stove in the living room, and the coffee that her mum ground fresh every morning. It had caused quite a stir in Larkbridge village store when Molly Baxter had switched her usual order from tea bags to coffee beans, but now visitors popping round to the redbrick cottage for elevenses would always ask for one of Molly's cappuccinos, rather than a brew, with their shortbread fingers.

Upstairs, Britt's bedroom still had her teenage posters on the walls, a pile of teddies on the single bed and her old clothes hanging in the wardrobe. After a long bath, she rifled through the rails and chose a baggy navy jumper, a cast off from her grandpa, and pulled it on with a pair of leggings. After making sure Molly was comfortable in an armchair with a rug over her legs, ignoring her grumbling ('I'm not an old woman,' she had huffed), Britt had put on her wellies, walked over to the village store and bought milk and the ingredients to make pea and ham soup for dinner. Then she picked up Salty and Biscuit, Molly's border collies, from a neighbour where they had been staying and set out for a walk across the fields.

As she clambered over a stile, Britt paused at the top and stared out over the valley. There was a late afternoon mist above the trees by the river and the only sound was a couple of ponies cropping the grass in the next field. Britt pulled out her BlackBerry: no reception. She smiled and turned it off. Then she took a deep breath of the damp, earthy air, and all her problems – the Alex crisis, her non-existent career, the growing debts – just seemed to vanish into the mist. It was good to be home.

For the next week, Britt holed up in Larkbridge cooking hearty, healthy meals for Molly, walking the dogs and watching TV (although her mum's telly only got BBC1, BBC2 and ITV, so the choice was fairly limited). Alex phoned the cottage every day, but whenever her mum mouthed, 'It's Alex,' Britt shook her head furiously.

Molly had to return to hospital for tests, but although the cause of her collapse was still unclear, the doctors seemed confident that there was no cause for concern. That evening, Britt took her to the local pub for scampi, chips and half a shandy to celebrate.

One afternoon, when Britt was in the middle of baking a batch of scones and Molly had gone shopping, there was a knock at the door. The dogs jumped around, barking furiously. 'Hold on a minute!' she shouted above the din, wiping her dough-covered hands on her grandpa's jumper, which she had barely taken off. Her hair was tied into two plaits that she'd clipped on top of her head to stop them getting dusted with flour and she hadn't worn any make-up since she arrived, let alone tackled basic maintenance such as shaving her armpits.

There was another, more angry knock.

'Okay, okay, I'm coming,' Britt grumbled, and opened the door. 'Alex! What the hell are you doing here?'

13

'I've come to see you, stupid.' He held out his arms to her. 'Don't I get a kiss after six weeks?' Britt had spent so long feeling furious with him that she had forgotten just how drop-dead gorgeous he was. Alex was wearing a white T-shirt that clung to his biceps and a pair of old jeans, with a sweatshirt slung around his waist and a rucksack over his shoulder. His shock of cocoa-coloured hair was even messier than usual, there were dark shadows beneath his eyes and a shadow of stubble on his jaw, but God, he was fit. Britt wasn't sure whether to rip his head or his clothes off.

They had an awkward embrace on the doorstep, bashing noses as they tentatively kissed, then they went through to the kitchen where Britt busied herself making coffee. She didn't quite know how to feel. On the one hand she fancied the pants off him and seeing him reminded her of just how crazy in love they had been mere weeks ago, and how desperate she had been to get married – even have his babies. But so much had changed since then. And she just couldn't reconcile the old, wonderful Alex with this new, slightly hopeless version.

They sat at the old oak table in the kitchen in silence, drinking their coffee.

'You've been avoiding me,' he said eventually.

'Oh.' Britt bent down to stroke the dogs and decided to change the subject. 'So how did you get up here today? I didn't hear the car on the drive.'

'By train, walked from the station.'

'Why didn't you drive?'

'I sold the Beetle, Britt.'

'What the hell did you do that for?' His ancient red Beetle was his pride and joy. At times it had seemed he loved the car more than her.

'To pay for your ticket back from Tokyo, of course,' he said quietly.

Britt was stunned. 'But I thought Jessie . . .'

'She offered to help, but I'm your man; it's my job to look after you.' Alex reached out for her hand. 'Look, I know things are tough between us right now, but you can't hide away up here baking scones for ever. I need you to come back to London so we can figure out what we're going to do.' He gently stroked her hair. 'I need you to come back because I miss you.'

Then he leant over the table and slowly moved towards her for a kiss. This time, everything fell into place. His lips pressed against hers, first softly, and then more insistently. Then his tongue lightly brushed her lips before gently probing inside her mouth. Britt reached across the table and put her hand behind his head, crushing him to her. The kissing became harder and more passionate. Britt felt something deep inside her melt and saw stars pop behind her closed eyes . . .

'Oh, hello, you two!'

They sprang apart to see Molly standing at the door, laden down with shopping bags. 'Alex, what a lovely surprise. Are you staying?'

'Just for a night, Mrs B, if you don't mind. Then I'm going to take Britt home with me.'

'Don't I get any say in this?' Britt snapped. 'Mum needs me here.'

'Shh, I'm fine,' said Molly. 'In fact, I told Alex he should come up and get you. Your life is in London, love, and I'm not far away. I promise I'll call if I need you.'

That night, Britt slept fitfully in the little single bed, while Alex lay on the floor next to her. She knew that Alex wanted to have sex with her – and not so long ago she'd have been desperate for him, too. That evening, after dinner, he had climbed into bed with her and started to kiss her, as he had in the kitchen, but she hadn't been able to recapture that spark. She just gave him a quick peck and then turned over. *We haven't had sex for nearly two months*, she thought, lying in bed listening to Alex breathing nearby. *Shouldn't I be just a little bit bothered about that . . . ?*

Next day, they waited together in silence for the bus to take them to Carlisle station. Britt was worried about leaving Molly on her own, but also about going back to London. She would have to deal with her landlord's messages about the overdue rent. She had to meet up with Scott to try and find another job. And she and Alex would need to sit down and discuss their future – if they even had one together. Was their relationship even worth fighting for?

It had been Scott's idea to meet at Butch Bakes, a trendy new cupcake café in the heart of Soho. Not because he was fond of cakes – he would go straight before letting buttercream pass his lips – but because it was currently the hottest meeting spot in London. Located just off Old Compton Street, it sold kinky S&M-themed cakes and cookies. The café's plates, cups and teapots were decorated with what looked like a pretty pattern of pink roses, but on closer inspection were revealed to be little willies. It brought a whole new meaning to the phrase 'cream tea'.

Britt had only been back in London for a couple of days, but both of them had been miserable. She had spoken to her landlord, who was sympathetic as she had always been a good tenant, but told her she would need to cough up the rent they owed by next month or move out. And then this morning she'd had a huge row with Alex. It had started after she'd confessed to him what a disaster Tokyo had been and he'd made some off-hand comment about how she should have listened to him and never gone out there in the first place. Britt had flown into a fury and all the weeks of simmering resentment over his inability to find a job had come flooding out.

'How . . . how *dare* you!' she had screeched. 'At least I was trying to earn some money! As far as I can tell, all you're doing is sitting on your backside all day, drinking!'

Alex had stormed out and Britt had called Jessie in floods of tears, but rather than cheering her up, Jess had made her feel more wretched than ever by gently reminding her that Alex had sold his beloved car to get Britt home, and perhaps she had been a little bit hard on him?

So she wasn't exactly looking forward to meeting up with Scott, who she was sure would have a few choice words to say about her Tokyo disaster – not to mention the weight she'd piled on eating scones and dumpling-filled stews in Larkbridge.

She found him sitting at the café window table, checking out the passers-by.

'Britt!' He leapt out of his seat and passionately air-kissed her. 'Let me look at you, babe.' He held her at arm's length and looked her up and down. 'Oh my, what happened to the sashimi and seaweed diet in Japan? No cupcakes for you, sweet cheeks.'

But Britt needed sugar, and when the waiter came round she ignored Scott's raised eyebrow and ordered a plate of Fondant Fannies with a pot of English Bonkfest tea.

As expected, he was not sympathetic. 'That's the way it works, babe,' he shrugged. 'I told you it would be a hard slog out there. Sounds like you got lots of work, though.'

'Yeah, my portfolio's looking really good,' enthused Britt. 'Any chance I'll be able to find something over here now?'

Scott sighed. 'You know I love you, Britt, but I can't help. After screwing up the Zauber deal and running out on Tokyo, Jo Brand is looking a more likely candidate for the catwalk than you.' He took a sip of his green tea. 'I hate to say this, but I think it's time for you to look for something different to do. Let's wait until the dust has settled and review in, say, six months?'

'But I'll be homeless by then!'

'I'm so sorry, babe, but blame the game, not the player.'

So that was it. She was unemployable. So was Alex. It was time for Plan B.

Now Britt just had to work out exactly what Plan B was.

14

After leaving Scott, Britt wandered up to Oxford Street and spent a few hours mooching around the stores. Like most girls, Britt liked to comfort shop – or comfort window-shop. Even if she was at home, she would get deep satisfaction from clicking online at Net-A-Porter and filling up a virtual shopping bag with thousands of pounds' worth of Lanvin and Balenciaga, although she would never press the button to checkout. A girl could dream, after all. But today, wandering around Selfridges and trying on armfuls of clothes she couldn't afford just made her feel even worse, especially because her usual size eight was now feeling worryingly snug. She couldn't even fit a pair of Topshop boyfriend jeans over her thighs – and they were supposed to be baggy!

By the time Britt got back to Clapham, the afternoon rush hour was just beginning. Tired and depressed, she arrived home to find Alex sitting on the sofa, watching sport on TV. *Just for a change*, thought Britt bitterly, chucking her bag on the table and heading for the kitchen. But although the last she'd seen of him that morning had been the front door slamming so violently it had sent Kate Moss skittering under the table in terror, Alex was now smiling broadly at her. He looked strangely pleased with himself – cocky.

'And just *what* exactly are you so happy about?' snapped Britt.

'I've got a job,' he grinned. 'And so have you, if you want one?'

Britt stood staring at him, wondering if she'd heard correctly.

'You were absolutely right, Britt, I've been useless,' he went on. 'I had been so excited about the thought of buying a flat and building a life with you, that when I got made redundant I just . . . well, stopped trying. And then when you went to Tokyo I felt I was losing you as well, which made me even more depressed.' He shrugged apologetically. 'I love you so bloody much, Britt, and I know I've let you down these last few weeks, but let me show you I can make it up to you. I made some calls this morning and found an opening at an agency that provides waiters and bar staff for events and parties. I went to see the boss today and she offered me a job on the spot – and there's one for you, too, if you want it. The pay's not brilliant, but it's something at least, and we'd be in it together. What do you reckon, beautiful?'

Britt tried to take it all in. A waitress? What a comedown. It would be fine if she was a teenager and just starting out, but she was twenty-six and had already had a successful career. Well, it had been successful, until recently . . . But Alex was right – it was something. Which was a hell of a lot better than the big fat nothing they would have otherwise.

Britt looked at Alex, his face more hopeful and positive than she had seen it look in a long time, and smiled. 'Let's do it,' she said.

* * *

Sylvia Service was an event-staffing agency that prided itself on its high standards and professionalism – or, as the brochure put it, 'Why settle for silver service, when you can have Sylvia Service?' It was run by the eponymous Sylvia, who – from what Alex had told Britt after his initial meeting with the woman – had devoted her life to her business, and was as fiercely proud and protective of the agency as if it were her child.

Along with a dozen or so other new recruits, Britt and Alex had been summoned to attend an induction day at the company's headquarters at a grey office block in Enfield. A secretary had shown them into a meeting room containing a large table, chairs, a white board, tea urn with polystyrene cups and plates of cheap biscuits. Britt was just nibbling on a broken Pink Wafer when the door burst open and in marched their new boss.

In her late forties, Sylvia dressed like it was still 1985. She was wearing a pair of acid-wash jeans trimmed with tassels and rhinestones with a white mohair jumper cut low to show off a substantial cleavage so luminously fake-tanned, it could probably have been seen from space. Her long hair was bleached blonde but had a sickly yellowish tinge, like it was stained with nicotine, while her fringe was extravagantly backcombed and crisp with hairspray. It looked like it would shatter like a meringue.

'Right everyone, take a seat. Let's get started.' Her accent was broadest Essex.

As the rest of the group refilled their polystyrene cups with tea and settled down, Sylvia spotted Alex and came bustling over. 'Ooh, here he is, my rugby hunk!'

'Hi, Sylvia,' smiled Alex. 'Thanks again for giving us a go.'

'Happy to give you a go *anytime*, sweetheart!' Sylvia tittered with a wink. She had a thin, pinched face that was lavishly coated in foundation and her pink frosted lipstick had bled into the deeply etched lines around her mouth.

'This is my girlfriend, Britt,' said Alex.

Sylvia's nostrils flared.

'Hello, Sylvia, thanks so much for the opportunity. I've worked as a waitress before so I won't—'

'You'll need to tie your hair back,' Sylvia snapped. 'Can't have that great bloody bush hanging in your face when you're handing round foie gras tempura.' And with that, she marched to the front of the room, leaving a lingering scent of cigarettes and a perfume so sickly sweet it might have been Eau de Haribo.

The training session started. Whenever Sylvia needed a volunteer it was always Alex who was called to the front. Snappy with the rest of the new recruits, she turned into a giggling schoolgirl around him. Did she think Britt was all that stood between her and Alex's pants?

'I think our Sylvia has taken a bit of a shine to you,' Britt said to Alex as they sat together on the train home. It had been a long day, but they now knew everything there was to know about fish knives and cheese boards.

'Well, you can't blame her.' Alex threw an arm round her shoulders. 'She's not a robot.'

Britt gave him a playful punch and snuggled against his chest. He dropped a kiss on her forehead and she smiled up at him. Seeing Alex in action today – even if it was only learning to pour champagne – had reminded her of the confident, charming man she had fallen in love with.

Britt and Alex were soon working at events and parties several nights a week. Alex was given all the plum jobs such as manning the cocktail bar. Britt was a natural waitress, smiley and efficient, but as far as Sylvia was concerned, Britt couldn't do anything right.

The hours were long and Britt's feet were a mess of blisters, but they finally had money coming in. And with some of the financial pressure taken off, their relationship started to improve. One night, while working at a record industry party, they sneaked a few of the cocktails and ended up snogging like horny teenagers on the night bus home. They had barely made it through their front door before ripping each other's clothes off and having urgent, dirty sex on the kitchen table. Lying in bed together afterwards, wrapped in Alex's strong arms with her face nuzzled into the warm skin of his chest, Britt basked in the blissful glow of intimacy that had been missing for so long.

'We should do this more often,' she murmured happily.

'No time like the present,' smiled Alex, tracing his fingers exquisitely slowly around her nipple, over her flat stomach and then much, much lower . . .

Sylvia told them it was going to be the party of the year. The Russian oligarch Igor Lesbiak, owner of the world's second largest aluminium company, was throwing a birthday party for his only daughter, and no expense had been spared for darling Dasha's sweet sixteen.

The night was starting with a private concert from JLS and Pixie Lott at the Royal Albert Hall for Dasha and 300 of her closest friends, and then it was on to a lavish after-party in the dinosaur room of the Natural History Museum. A top Michelin-starred chef had been flown over from Paris to prepare the canapés, and two elephants had been borrowed from Moscow State Circus and painted bright pink (the birthday girl's favourite colour) and decorated with Swarovski crystals. There was a casino and cabaret, but the highlight of the night promised to be surprise guest Justin Bieber jumping out of her birthday cake and serenading Dasha with his hit song 'Baby'.

Wandering around with a tray of mini-hamburgers and chips, Britt gawped at the sparkly pink elephants dwarfed by the dinosaur skeleton in the museum's cavernous hall. Almost as impressive a sight was the array of diamonds and designer labels worn by the guests, most of whom were still doing their GCSEs. She caught sight of Alex in action with a cocktail shaker at the bar and gave him a little wave. He looked gorgeous in a uniform of tight black T-shirt and black jeans. Unfortunately for Britt, Sylvia spotted the exchange and collared her when she went back to the kitchen for another tray of canapés.

'If you don't pull your finger out, I'm putting you on elephant-shit-shovelling duty,' she hissed. Tonight Sylvia was looking like Krystle Carrington from *Dynasty* in a blue taffeta cocktail dress with enormous flounced sleeves. 'Now go and pour champagne.'

Britt went over to the bar to get a bottle. 'Sylvia's on the warpath, I'd better get going,' she whispered to Alex.

Working round the room refilling glasses, Britt found herself next to the birthday girl. Dasha was a plain-looking girl who had inherited her father's close-together eyes and wide nose. (Quite what she'd got from her mother it was hard to tell, thanks to the extensive handiwork of a plastic surgeon in Beverly Hills.) Dasha was groomed to within an inch of her life, with a mane of blonde hair extensions, glossy golden skin, a perfect manicure and diamonds the size of Smarties at her ears, throat, wrists and even ankles.

'Champagne?' smiled Britt, offering the bottle. She enviously recognised Dasha's silver Versace cocktail dress from the cover of that month's *Vogue*.

Without acknowledging Britt, Dasha stuck out her glass and continued chatting to her friends, who were hanging adoringly on her every word. Britt had filled her glass and was just moving on to the next group when she heard a splutter and a shriek right behind her. She turned to see Dasha dabbing at her heavily lip-glossed mouth in disgust.

'What the fark is this?' she barked furiously. Years of an exclusive boarding school education had obviously left their mark on her accent.

'Champagne.' Britt double-checked the bottle. 'Moët.'

'Are you trying to farking poison me? I HATE Moët! I ONLY drink Cristal!'

'Oh, I'm sorry, I didn't know that. Shall I get you a glass of Cristal instead?'

Just then Igor Lesbiak loomed out of the crowd, his bald head reflecting the flashing disco lights. 'Is everything okay, my little *lapochka*?'

Dasha had worked herself into a frenzy of outrage. 'This . . . this imbecile filled my glass with Moët. You know Moët makes me blotchy, Daddy.' She started to wail. 'How can this happen on my farking birthday?'

Igor Lesbiak rounded on Britt. He was a short man, almost as broad as he was tall, and she towered over him. 'You stupid bitch,' he hissed.

Frozen to the spot, Britt was just wondering what to do

when suddenly she heard a familiar voice from just behind her.

'Don't talk to her like that.' It was Alex. He sounded calm, but Britt knew that tone. The last time she had heard it was shortly before he had decked some drunken bloke who had tried to grope her in a bar.

'I will talk to her like I please,' spluttered the Russian.

Sylvia rushed over just in time to hear Alex say, 'Money can buy crystal-studded elephants, but it can't buy class.'

There was a moment's horrified silence. 'I'm so sorry, Mr Lesbiak,' gasped Sylvia. 'I will deal with this!' And she dragged both Britt and Alex out of the room.

'You're fired!' shrieked Sylvia, jabbing a pointy red talon in Britt's face.

'What the hell are you firing Britt for?' said Alex. 'She didn't do anything.'

'She's a troublemaker.'

'No, she's not, she's a bloody good waitress.'

'Well, then you're fired instead,' she said to Alex. 'Shame, you were set for big things.' She turned back to Britt. 'But you're skating on thin ice, my girl,' she hissed. 'Very thin ice indeed.'

15

By the following morning, the pair of them were laughing at the memory of Sylvia's look of slack-mouthed horror. Although Britt would never have admitted it, she had been worried Alex might fall to pieces after Sylvia sacked him, but he seemed to be taking the whole thing in his stride – in fact, if anything, it appeared to have given him a new lease of life. After breakfast he sat down at the computer and spent the rest of the day fine-tuning his CV and searching websites for a job that would make use of his fitness skills. It seemed the old Alex was back.

It was a few days later and Britt had been booked to work at a party at an art gallery in the hip Hoxton neighbourhood of east London. As usual, the team met in the venue's kitchens an hour before the party was due to begin to be briefed by Sylvia. Britt sneaked in a few minutes late and stood at the back of the group, trying her best to keep a low profile. After the Dasha disaster she imagined she probably wouldn't be Sylvia's favourite.

While Sylvia ran through the list of the canapés they would be serving that evening, Britt turned to the girl standing next to her, a sweet university student called Sally.

'Do you know what this party's for, Sal?' she whispered.

'Some fashion thing. Sounds dead glam.'

'Oh, good.' *Not good.* Britt hoped she wouldn't know any of the guests. 'Any idea who's throwing it?'

'Apparently Matthew McConaughey is going to be here! It's for that German brand, Zauber or something?'

Shit. Okay, this was bad. Very, very bad. Perhaps she could sneak out, pretend she was ill at home in bed and never even got there? Britt looked round, trying to plan an escape route. Yes, she could just grab her coat and made a dash for the back door . . .

Too late – Sylvia had already spotted her. 'You – you're on canapés,' she said, thrusting a pile of napkins at her.

Canapés? She'd be sure to bump into Frieda Koch if she had to walk around with a tray! Urgent evasive action was required.

'Er, Sylvia? Sorry about this, but would it be okay if I'm on cloakroom duty tonight? I've . . . got a sore foot.' Britt mimed a limp.

Sylvia's lip curled with contempt. 'Canapés, now,' she spat.

Hovering by the door to the kitchen, Britt stared warily out at the party. She was dreading venturing out into the crowd. The walls of the gallery had been covered with life-sized black-and-white posters of the new Zauber girl, the impossibly sexy Diamond Lopez, posing on Copacabana Beach swathed in a variety of stunning gowns – and, of course, draped around a shirt-less Matthew McConaughey. And there in the middle of the room, her arm wrapped around the honey-skinned Diamond, holding court to a group of the fashion industry's great and good, was the dumpy figure of Frieda Koch. Britt couldn't believe she'd once thought of her as motherly; right now, she looked as menacing as Jabba the Hutt.

Britt worked her way slowly round the room until she was near to where Frau Koch was standing. She gulped. There was nowhere to hide. She would have to go over there.

'. . . and so I said to Karl Lagerfeld, darlink, of course you can't have Diamond for the next Chanel show,' Frieda was telling the group. 'She only works for Zauber!'

As everyone laughed, Britt tentatively waved the tray in their direction, keeping her head down and trying her best to stay invisible.

'Ah, these look delicious!' said Frieda. 'Miuccia Prada recommended a raw food chef to me and I had him flown over from Milano.' Then to her horror, Frieda turned to Britt. 'Tell me, vot exactly are these?'

Britt kept her eyes firmly on the tray, blushing furiously. 'Turnip carpaccio topped with beetroot gelée and toasted spelt grains.'

Britt looked up to see Frieda Koch's cold eyes staring straight at her. There was absolutely no doubt she had recognised her. For a horrible moment Britt thought she was going to say something, but then she just turned her icy smile on the rest of the group.

'That sounds wonderful. Who would like to try one? Diamond, my dear?'

Everywhere Britt looked in the crowd there was a photographer, stylist, model or editor who she had met or worked with before. But thankfully, the drab black uniform proved a pretty decent disguise, and after making a couple of circuits of the room without being recognised Britt started to relax.

And then – disaster. She was just scurrying past a

97

group of people to dispose of an empty champagne bottle when she heard someone call her name.

'Britt?'

She spun round to see a fashion editor from *Cosmopolitan* magazine with whom she had worked a few times in the past.

'I thought it was you!' The woman leaned in for an air-kiss. 'How are you, darling?'

'Oh, hi.' Britt thrust the empty champagne bottle behind her back. 'I'm, yeah, really good, thanks. You know. Busy!'

'You must come and meet some people.' To Britt's horror, the woman steered her over to join the group she'd been chatting to. 'Everyone, this is Britt Baxter, she's with Gawk Models.'

As if things couldn't get any worse, Britt then saw that Matthew McConaughey was standing with them. Smiling, he raised his glass to her in greeting. Automatically, Britt did the same – only to realise she had just waved an empty bottle at him. *Nice one, Baxter. Proper smooth.*

'So, Britt, what are you up to these days?' asked the fashion editor.

'Oh, this and that,' she said breezily, trying to brazen it out. 'I've got some really interesting projects on the go.'

'May I just say, I *love* your tunic,' interrupted a woman in a red turban. 'Such a strikingly utilitarian vibe. Is it Yohji Yamamoto?'

'Oh, this old thing?' Britt looked down at her uniform. 'No, it's by, um . . . Mr Nakamura. Don't you just adore his cutting?'

The woman in the turban looked momentarily

confused. 'Oh, right, of course . . . Yes, he's an absolute genius.'

Britt was just wondering how to excuse herself from the group when there was a furious tap on her shoulder.

'And what the hell do you think you're doing?' It was Sylvia. 'Someone's spilt their drink near the toilets. Go and clear it up before someone goes arse over tit.' And with that she thrust a mop into Britt's hand and bustled off.

Everyone was staring at Britt, not quite sure what to say. She stood with the mop in her hand wishing the ground would swallow her up.

'Well, I'd better go,' she finally managed. 'Lovely to see you again – and great to meet you, Matthew. Loved your work in that film about, erm, surfing. Let's do lunch sometime!'

Oh God, oh God, oh God.

By 11 p.m. most of the guests had left and Britt was tidying up the empty glasses, relieved that her ordeal was finally coming to an end. And then suddenly out of nowhere, there she was. Frieda Koch. Smiling up at her like a Great White shark at a goldfish.

'Vot a pleasant surprise to see you again, Britt. Such a shame things didn't work out with us, but I am very pleased to see that you have found another job.' Frieda looked pointedly at her mop. 'You would be a little too . . . *curvy* for Zauber these days.'

With that she turned and left Britt standing there, feeling like she'd just been slapped round the face.

It was past midnight by the time Britt got home. She was exhausted, miserable and desperate for a consolatory cuddle from Alex. The thought of climbing into bed and spooning his duvet-warmed body was all that was keeping her going. But he wasn't in bed; he was on the sofa, surrounded by about a dozen empty beer cans, snoring heavily. Kate Moss was licking at a half-eaten takeaway pizza still sitting in its box on the floor.

Not bothering to even get undressed, Britt crawled into bed and cried herself to sleep.

16

'But I thought you said that Alex was finally getting his act together?' Jessie reached over and spooned some more pilau rice and rogan josh onto her plate. They were having dinner at The Spice Boys, Britt's local curry house.

'He is – well, he was. I thought I'd got the old Alex back for a while. But then last night I came home and found him passed out cold on the sofa, stinking of booze.' Britt thought back to the furious row they'd had that morning, which had ended in her accusing Alex of having a drink problem and him slamming the door – again. Kate Moss was turning into a nervous wreck. 'Oh, I just don't know what to do, Jess. One moment he's my gorgeous Alex, the love of my life, the next it feels like I don't even know the guy.' Britt drained her glass. 'Sorry, it feels like I've been moaning about my relationship problems for ages.'

'Don't be silly, it's important to talk about it.' Jessie went to tear off a piece of naan bread and then stopped herself. 'Oh God, I need to stop eating this. I don't think the Zone diet allows garlic naan.'

'How about beer?' Britt topped up their glasses from a large bottle of Cobra.

'Oh, I think that's okay,' Jessie grinned. 'So what's going on with the waitressing gig?'

'Still doing it. Right now it seems like my only option. Actually, I've got quite a fun job tomorrow night. I'm working at a party for that TV breakfast show, *Rise & Shine*. Should be loads of celebs.'

'Ooh, do you think Josh Bailey will be there?' squealed Jessie. 'I cause a riot every morning when I switch off *CBeebies* on the dot of 7.45 so I can watch him do the daily Hollywood gossip report.'

'I hadn't even thought of that!' said Britt. 'Do you know, Jess, I think there's still a poster of him on my bedroom wall in Larkbridge! God, that man is *so* sexy . . .'

Britt tugged self-consciously at the hem of her skirt, which barely covered her knickers. Instead of their usual black uniform, the Sylvia Service team was dressed to suit the event's Pyjama Party theme, which meant boxer shorts with *Rise & Shine* T-shirts for the boys and silky baby-doll nighties and fluffy Marabou mules for the girls. Sylvia had warned them all to make an effort, so Britt had blow-dried her hair into big bouncy curls, which she gathered into a low side ponytail, and spent a good half-hour working on her make-up. After dusting on Guerlain bronzer (Britt's secret weapon on lingerie shoots) she used a palette of grey Nars shadows to create smoky, sultry eyes, layered on the black mascara and finished with a coat of pale pink Clinique lip-gloss. She might be skint, but she was buggered if she was going to start buying cheap make-up.

It was fun to get herself all dolled up; Britt couldn't

remember the last time she'd had a glam night out, even if tonight she would be serving the cocktails rather than drinking them. Shame Alex hadn't been there to see the results of her labours. He had left their flat at lunchtime to watch football with some mates in the pub and had yet to return.

The party, which was to celebrate five years of *Rise & Shine* being Britain's favourite breakfast show, was at a private members' club in Soho. When Britt arrived there were already crowds of paparazzi and fans waiting at the door, anxious for a glimpse of JLS or one of the X Factor finalists.

Inside the club, the breakfast theme had been taken to extremes, with cushion-strewn beds replacing the sofas, and canapés of baked-bean brioches and mini frying pans of fried quails eggs with pancetta rashers. The specially created cocktails on offer included the Rise Fizz, a blend of prosecco, espresso and prune essence, and the Shine-tini, which was pink grapefruit vodka with an egg-white foam. As well as the show's presenters and crew, the guests included the usual rent-a-celeb mix of reality TV contestants, glamour girls and wannabe WAGs.

Britt picked up a tray of canapés and headed out into the crowd, weaving amongst all the familiar faces. She spotted Cherry Smith, star of the *Rise & Shine* sofa, and instantly made a beeline for her. Britt had seen an interview with her in *Heat* magazine the other day, and remembered reading that she had started her career as a model before landing a job as a TV weather girl. Cherry had worked her way up through the ranks to become the highest-paid female presenter on television, fronting big Saturday night entertainment shows. In her late thirties, however, there had been a scandal involving a teenage footballer and a bag of Class As and Cherry had disappeared off to rehab, presumably never to be heard of again. But then a few years later she was back, looking better than ever and giving weepy interviews about how her therapist had helped to battle her demons and change her life – although she was not quite so forthcoming about the plastic surgeon who had changed her face. Widely lauded as a 'survivor' and with channel bosses under pressure to employ more middle-aged women, Cherry had landed the plum job co-hosting *Rise & Shine*.

Tonight, Cherry's blonde hair was swept into an elaborate up-do and she was wearing a full-length black satin negligée split to the thigh, which also showed off her gym-toned arms and a shiny, plumped-up cleavage. *It was what Sylvia would want to look like if she had the money*, Britt thought.

There were two men standing with Cherry, a weasly-looking bloke with a thin black moustache in a cheap-looking shiny suit, and another guy, probably in his forties, who – despite being a good few inches shorter than the rest of the group – had an air of calm confidence that suggested he was someone pretty important. He had closely cropped fair hair and was wearing jeans, a blazer and a pair of trendy geek-chic glasses, his one concession to the night's dress code being a pair of well-worn tartan slippers.

Britt offered her tray to the trio. 'Smoked kipper vol-au-vent?'

'Bless you, darling, so kind, but I'm gluten intolerant,' smiled Cherry. 'Do pop back if you have anything without pastry. Toby, Gaz, will you have one?'

The man with the moustache – evidently Gaz – grabbed one without even acknowledging Britt, then turned to Cherry with an oily grin. 'Now what about that exclusive you promised me, Cherry?' He had a rough London accent. 'You know how much *The Daily Splash* would love an interview . . .'

As Cherry giggled flirtatiously, the other member of the group – Toby, she assumed – reached for a canapé from her tray. 'Thanks,' he said to Britt with an appraising smile. She turned to go, but realised that he was staring at her intently, almost like he wanted to say something to her. *What was that all about?* she wondered, moving on.

There was a huge screen at the end of the room showing a compilation of 'special moments' from the last five years of *Rise & Shine*. Britt glanced over to see a clip of Cherry interviewing the prime minister together with her co-anchor, the silver-haired – and -tongued – Ken Chudleigh. Smiling Cherry and Brummie family-man Ken were hugely popular with the public, although, Britt realised, Ken didn't look all that clean-cut now, lounging on one of the beds with a pair of giggly blondes wearing transparent nighties and over-the-knee socks.

The next clip was of the show's Hollywood correspondent, Josh Bailey, interviewing Julia Roberts. Now *this* was more interesting. Britt manoeuvred herself behind a pillar, out of the way of Sylvia's beady eyes, so that she could watch. Born and raised in Chicago, Joshua J. Bailey had started his career in Broadway musicals, but at the age of twenty-two a Hollywood producer had plucked him out of the chorus line and cast him in the lead role of his new project. The movie, *Dance Delirium*, was your typical tale of boy-wants-girl, boy-learns-to-dance, boy-gets-girl, but was really just a vehicle for its hot young star's dazzling moves and buff body. The film, in which he played high-school rebel Mitch Rider, had been a smash hit and Josh – or JJ Bailey as he was then known – became a pin-up for a generation. A sequel was then rushed out, but *Dance Delirium 2*, in which Mitch Rider went to Spain to learn flamenco, was a spectacular flop, and by his mid-twenties Josh's movie career was floundering. Struggling to find work, he had come to the UK, appeared in a few washing detergent ads and then got a break as the Hollywood correspondent for *Rise & Shine*. Charismatic, flirtatious and ludicrously good-looking, Josh was an instant hit with the show's housewife-heavy audience – and, as she watched him charming the pants off Julia Roberts on screen, Britt could certainly understand why.

'Pretty good, this guy, isn't he?' asked a familiar American voice behind her. 'A knockout in the sack as well, apparently.'

And Britt swung round and looked straight into the smiling eyes of Joshua J. Bailey.

17

He was even better looking in the flesh than he was on screen. Like Tom Cruise, only taller. His strikingly green eyes were delicately almond-shaped, almost feline, but framed by heavy, masculine brows and a straight, strong nose. With his wavy dark hair, wide Persil-white smile and cleft chin, Josh was perfect leading-man material. Britt noticed he was wearing a navy T-shirt, jeans and brown boots. Obviously he didn't given a toss about the party's dress code.

He was still smiling, those cat-like eyes locked on hers. *God, he was gorgeous.* Seconds ticked by before Britt realised he was waiting for her to say something.

'Kipper vol-au-vent?'

Josh laughed. 'Delicious.' He leaned in towards her and dropped his voice to a husky whisper. 'The vol-au-vents don't look so bad, either.'

And with that he took one of the canapés, flashed that dazzling smile again, and sauntered off into the crowd.

As a teenager, Britt had spent many nights lying in her bed, staring at her poster of the divine JJ Bailey, wondering what she would say to him if they were ever face to face. Well, now it had happened and all she'd said was: 'Kipper vol-au-vent?' But then Josh Bailey had actually told her (well, okay, sort of *hinted* to her) that he thought she was delicious. *Blimey!* She wouldn't wait to tell Jessie.

Britt scuttled off to the kitchen to fetch some more canapés. She loaded up a tray with mini cornets of Crunchy Nut Cornflake ice-cream and headed back into the throng, running over the encounter with Josh in her head as she handed out the cones. Had he *really* been flirting with her, or was he just being friendly? She definitely needed to get Jessie's opinion – though obviously she'd gloss over her own less than impressive performance . . . God, what if she bumped into Josh again tonight? Perhaps she should plan something witty to say?

Britt was lost in thought when suddenly she felt someone grab her bum and give it a long, hard squeeze. Yelping, Britt let her tray clatter to the floor, sending cornflake ice-cream flying everywhere and splattering the people in front of her.

'Oh God, I'm so sorry!' wailed Britt, gathering up the spilt napkins from the floor and trying to clear up the mess. As she knelt there mopping at the puddles of melting ice-cream, she tried to look round to see who was responsible for her humiliation – and was stunned by what she saw. There, standing just behind her and still openly leering at her bum was one of the most respected men in broadcasting: Ken Chudleigh. He looked like a podgy uncle in a maroon silk dressing gown and monogrammed slippers, and when he saw Britt looking at him, he arched a silver eyebrow suggestively. The bloody nerve . . .

Just then Sylvia appeared out of the crowd. There was a gleam of triumph in her eyes as she bore down on Britt.

'Right, that's it! You're fired. Clear up this mess, then get the hell out.'

'But I . . .' Britt looked round for Ken, but he had disappeared. And besides, what was the point in trying to tell Sylvia what had really happened? It wouldn't make any difference: she had been looking for an excuse to get rid of her for weeks.

Britt had piled up the tray with the sodden, sticky napkins and started back to the kitchen, feeling utterly humiliated and depressed at losing her job, when she felt an arm snake around her waist. It was Ken again.

'I've just called my chauffeur to pick us up,' he whispered in his famous Brummie burr, his moustache tickling her ear. 'I've got a room at the Metropolitan Hotel where we can . . . get to know each other better. How does that sound, sexy lady?'

Britt turned to look at Ken's jowly, drink-flushed face. She had just lost her job. She had been humiliated in front of a crowd of celebrities that included sex god Josh Bailey. She had ice-cream in her carefully blow-dried hair. Her boyfriend was probably passed out in a gutter somewhere. (Okay, so that wasn't really Ken's fault but . . . but they were both men, weren't they?) In that moment, the months of stress, worry, disappointment and exhaustion distilled into single, furious focus.

Britt grabbed a Shine-tini from a passing waitress and chucked the drink in the face of *Rise & Shine*'s most important star.

'Oh, and by the way, Ken,' she shouted, her voice trembling with emotion, 'Paul Daniels called – he wants his toupee back!'

There was a shocked silence. The drink was dripping down Ken's gobsmacked face, turning his white shirt pink. Britt heard someone gasp in horror, and realised it had been her. *Shit.*

But then something remarkable happened. Ken started to smile, and then to laugh, and soon the whole room was in hysterics. By some amazing stroke of luck, everyone seemed to find the whole thing hilariously funny. Apart from Sylvia, that was. She grabbed Britt and dragged her to the door, her eyes popping in fury. 'How . . . how *dare* you embarrass me like this?' she spluttered. 'You've been nothing but trouble from the start!'

As she passed the bar, Britt saw Josh Bailey, an amused look on his face. They reached the door and Sylvia shoved her outside, throwing her handbag out after her.

'And if you think you're getting paid for tonight after that little performance, missy, then you've got another think coming!'

Britt stood outside the club, shivering in her skimpy outfit. It had started to drizzle. There were three or four paparazzi standing by the door, obviously hoping for a drunken celebrity exit shot. They ignored her. *So this is what people mean when they talk about hitting rock bottom*, thought Britt, as she stood on the pavement, wondering what to do next. She didn't have any cash and didn't fancy walking the streets trying to find a cashpoint while looking like a working girl from one of Soho's seedier establishments in a nightie and high heels.

She was just thinking about asking one of the paps for a loan when she heard someone behind her. 'Hey! Excuse me!'

Britt spun round to see the short, fair-haired man who she had seen chatting with Cherry earlier that evening walking purposefully towards her. He could only have been about five foot five, but his aura of powerful self-belief seemed to add at least a foot to that.

Oh God, I'm in trouble, thought Britt.

'That was quite a performance in there,' the man said. He had the soft, cultured voice of a university professor, but he looked at her with the directness of a mover and shaker.

'I'm so sorry. Obviously I'll pay for any dry cleaning bill . . .' Britt trailed off, mortified at the tears that were springing hotly to her eyes. 'I'm just having a really shitty day.'

'Don't worry, no harm done. It was about time someone put Ken in his place,' he smiled. 'I'm Toby Livingstone, executive producer of *Rise & Shine*.'

Britt shook his hand, grateful for a friendly face. 'Britt Baxter, unemployed waitress.'

'Well, waitressing's loss might just be TV's gain. I hope this doesn't sound like a line, but you've got a great look, Britt, and you can obviously think on your feet – plus, you certainly know how to turn heads.'

She grimaced, thinking back to her theatrics a moment ago. But then something truly remarkable happened: 'Have you ever thought about working in TV?' Toby said. 'We're always looking for new on-screen talent and I think you'd be perfect.'

Britt couldn't believe what she was hearing. 'Is this some kind of wind up?'

Toby smiled. 'No, not at all. I'm totally serious. In fact, would you like to come to the studio for a screen test next week?'

18

Britt sat nervously in the *Rise & Shine* green room, waiting for Toby to arrive. The breakfast show had come off air an hour ago and the studio was pretty much deserted. She picked at the remains of a pain au raisin sitting on a half-eaten platter of pastries on the coffee table in front of her. *Just breathe*, Britt told herself. Petrified wasn't the word.

After the *Rise & Shine* party, Britt had floated home on cloud nine courtesy of a chauffeur-driven car summoned by Toby. When she arrived back at the flat, Alex – who was surprisingly sober – had been instantly suspicious when she excitedly told him what had happened.

'I'm betting that bloke is after one thing, and it's sure as hell not your interviewing skills,' he said.

'It's not like that, honestly!' Britt was indignant. 'Toby really thought I had promise.'

'Well, I just don't want you to get your hopes up, that's all.'

She knew he was talking sense, but Britt wanted to get her hopes up. She *needed* to. It was only after Toby had called the next morning and scheduled her screen test for the following Monday that Alex started to believe that perhaps this guy wasn't trying to get Britt into bed after all. Still, every time he warned her not to get too excited over the next few days she felt a pang of annoyance. This could be her big break – why couldn't he be more pleased for her?

But if Alex wasn't overjoyed, her mum and Jessie certainly were. Molly immediately asked if she could get her Ken Chudleigh's autograph (Britt thought it best not to mention the groping incident) and Jessie's squeal of excitement would have probably been heard in Larkbridge.

'Oh my God, you're going to be famous!' she shrieked. 'And – ooh! You're going to be working with Josh Bailey!'

Britt laughed. 'Woah, slow down there, lady. Let's see how the screen test goes first.' But inside she felt a thrill of excitement. *Just imagine – getting to work with Josh Bailey!*

Britt glanced at the green-room clock: 10.06. The flock of butterflies in her stomach was working itself up into frenzy. She pulled out a compact from her handbag and reapplied her lip-gloss. Britt had spent ages planning her outfit, in the end deciding on a hip but approachable vibe: silver-grey draped jumper from Whistles, skinny black J Brand jeans, vintage denim jacket and black suede Office wedges. She'd blow-dried her hair straight and tied it into a high swingy ponytail. With tiny diamond studs in her ears and a chunky rose-gold Michael Kors watch, Britt felt she was ready (well, as ready as she'd ever be) for her close-up.

Just then the green-room door swung open.

'Hi, Britt, good to see you again.' Toby was standing in the doorway. He was wearing jeans, brogues and a perfectly ironed white shirt. They shook hands and Britt hoped he wouldn't notice how clammy her palms were.

'Right, if you're ready?' He held the door open for her and they set off through a maze of corridors.

As they walked, people they passed smiled and greeted Toby and he'd nod curtly in return. One girl wearing a headset tried to ask something as they bustled past, but he cut her off in mid-flow.

'Not now, Sarah. Come and see me in my office later,' he barked.

Britt obviously hadn't been wrong in assuming he was a pretty important person.

He now turned to Britt. 'There's no need to be nervous, this is going to be very simple,' he told her. 'We're going to try you out for the position of style correspondent, so I'll just get you to talk about fashion and that sort of thing.' *Bingo*, thought Britt happily. *My specialist subject*. 'There'll only be a few people around,' he added, 'so hopefully you won't feel too much like a performing monkey.' Toby pushed through a pair of heavy swing doors and Britt found herself standing in a cavernous studio. 'Okay, so this is where 'the magic' happens.'

Most of the space was in semi-darkness and crowded with light stands, cameras and props. Wires snaked across the floor and dozens of black lights hung from the ceiling, like bats clinging to the roof of a cave. Toby led her across the floor to the actual part of the studio seen by viewers. It was a surprisingly small, brightly lit space at the back of the room decorated with a fake stripped-wood floor and a fake window looking out over a fake London skyline, in front of which sat the famous *Rise & Shine* red sofa. Under the bright studio lights the set looked rather tired and shabby, with chipped paint and scuff-marks on the floor. Britt was a little disappointed: she had been expecting something a bit more glamorous.

She stood with Toby in front of the sofa. 'First things first, we need to get you miked up,' he said. 'Stewie, can you please do the honours?'

A guy wandered over from out of the shadows. He was dressed like he'd just come off the beach, in knee-length cargo shorts, a T-shirt and flip-flops, and was wearing a tangle of leather thongs round his wrist. He had messy dark blond hair that was sun-bleached at the ends and blond stubble on his chin. Although he was slightly shorter than Britt he was a well-built bloke, with wide shoulders and muscular calves, and despite working in a TV studio he had the healthy weather-beaten look of someone who'd spent a lot of time outdoors. When he smiled, his eyes crinkled as if he was squinting into bright sunlight.

'This is Britt,' Toby told him. 'Be gentle with her, it's her first time.'

'Hi,' smiled Britt. The guy had a kind face, which made her instantly relax.

'Right,' said Toby. 'Stewie will get you wired for sound then I'll run through what we're doing. I'm going to be sitting up in the gallery, so I'll speak to you over talk-back. And relax, you'll be great.'

After Toby had left, Stewie got to work, fiddling with the wires on a small battery pack. 'So you're a telly virgin then, are you, Britt?' He had an Australian accent.

'I am,' she said. 'I'm a bit nervous, to be honest.'

'Nothing to worry about. Toby's a top bloke. You'll be right. Okay, just spin round for me, mate.'

She turned around and he clipped the battery pack onto the back of her trousers.

'Now, can you just put this up under your top?' She might have been mistaken, but as he handed her the wire this hunky Aussie bloke looked almost bashful. She slid it under her jumper so the mic was poking out at the top and watched him clip it in place.

'There you go, live to the nation,' Stewie said with a smile. 'Good luck.'

The first thing Toby wanted her to do was describe a model's outfit for a feature on high street shopping. *So far, so easy*, thought Britt. Except the 'model' turned out to be a runner called Charlie with a nasty dose of acne and a *World of Warcraft* T-shirt.

'I'm afraid you'll have to improvise a bit,' said Toby apologetically over her mic. 'Okay, are you ready?'

Britt nodded mutely, worried that her voice would come out as a terrified croak.

'Right, and – cue Britt!'

So this was it. Her chance at a new career – a new life. She couldn't screw this up. In an attempt to hide her total panic, Britt plastered on a smile and took a deep breath.

19

'So here we have . . . um, *Charlotte* wearing this season's must-have high-waisted jean teamed with a gorgeous floral blouse,' Britt gushed, trying her best to ignore Charlie, who was now gawping at her while scratching his bum. 'The blouse is from Zara, but is a dead-ringer for one that Phillip Lim showed on the catwalk in his spring/summer collection. Charlotte, if you could just turn round for me?' The runner shuffled in a circle. 'As you can see, these fabulous Topshop jeans really tick all the boxes for this season's key seventies trend, hugging the bum and thighs and then flaring out from the knee. I would really recommend a stack heel with this style of jean, like the gorgeous See by Chloé sandals Charlotte is wearing here—'

'That's great, Britt, thanks,' interrupted Toby in her ear. It was impossible to tell from his voice if it genuinely was great or whether he was just being polite.

Toby then ran through the next part of the audition, which was to test her interview skills. Britt had to sit on the famous sofa (which she did with a little thrill of excitement) and chat to a top fashion designer about their new collection. In the absence of Vivienne Westwood or Stella McCartney, however, Charlie was standing in again. He slumped opposite her and started tapping moodily at his iPhone.

Britt beamed brightly. 'So, tell me, Charles, what was your inspiration for this fabulous new collection?'

Charlie looked up briefly. 'Dunno,' he grunted. 'Flowers?'

Suddenly Toby muttered something over talkback. Britt's focus was instantly thrown and she looked round, flustered.

'Um, sorry, I didn't quite catch that?'

'I said to ask him what he thinks about the controversy over skinny models,' said Toby. 'I know it's hard but you'll really have to concentrate, Britt, and get used to this. If this was live you'd have the director talking in your ear the whole time.'

'Of course, right, I'm sorry.' She turned back to Charlie. *Damn, she hadn't handled that at all well.* 'So what do you think about the controversy over skinny catwalk models?'

'Don't really mind,' snickered Charlie. 'As long as they're fit.'

'Yes, of course, you are well known for your love of beauty – both female and male,' said Britt, recovering her composure. 'It's been widely reported that you're marrying your long-term partner, David. So are congratulations in order?'

'Leave it out, I ain't no batty boy!' said Charlie indignantly.

Britt heard Toby chuckling in her ear and felt a surge of hope. *She could do this.*

Finally, Britt had to read from the autocue. She had always enjoyed drama at school and this was just like reciting a poem in front of the class. As the words scrolled down the screen, she read steadily and confidently.

'. . . and I'll be bringing you all the hottest style news and fashion gossip at the same time tomorrow,' she smiled, coming to the end of the link.

'Thanks, Britt,' came Toby's voice. 'Come up to the fourth floor and we can have a chat in my office. Stewie will point you in the right direction.'

She looked round to see the Aussie sound technician walking towards her.

'You sure you haven't done this before?' he grinned.

'Was it okay?'

'Okay? You were epic.' Stewie helped her unclip the battery mic. 'I reckon I'll be seeing you again.' He glanced at her, one eyebrow raised. 'Well, I hope I will, at any rate.'

'Fingers crossed,' smiled Britt.

Toby's office was testament to five years of *Rise & Shine* success. As well as the teetering piles of tapes and paperwork on his desk, there was a shelf of awards and framed press cuttings hanging on the walls documenting the show's meteoric rise to the top of the ratings. Next to a large window (with the riverside views that had been faked in the studio downstairs) was a pair of yellow sofas facing each other with a glass coffee table between them. Toby was sitting on one of them, next to a petite, dark-haired girl Britt hadn't seen before. Both of them smiled broadly as Britt came in.

'Take a seat, Britt,' he smiled, gesturing to the sofa opposite. 'This is Rashida Jones, one of our assistant producers.'

With her pretty heart-shaped face, huge dark eyes and

glossy black hair cut in a bob, Rashida barely looked old enough to have left school – let alone be in charge of a major TV show. She had flawless skin the exact shade of milky coffee; Britt couldn't place her heritage – she looked Italian, but with a name like Rashida she assumed she was Indian.

'Well done, Britt,' she said. 'I was sitting in the gallery with Toby and I thought you did really well for your first time.'

Britt smiled, but inside her heart sank. That sounded to her a lot like: '. . . really well for your first time . . . but total crap compared to the professionals'.

Toby leant towards her, his elbows resting on his knees and fingers laced. 'So Britt, how did you think that went?'

'Okay, I guess,' said Britt carefully. 'I really enjoyed it, and I'm sure I would get better with practice.'

'Well, I thought you were fantastic,' he said.

Britt was stunned. 'You did?'

'I did. And both Rashida and I think you'd be a great addition to our team. We'd like to offer you a three-month contract with *Rise & Shine* as our style correspondent, presenting a daily fashion slot. Rashida here will be in charge of the content – coming up with ideas for features and supervising the researchers. Initially it will be a temporary position, but we'll review the situation after three months and if it's working out then we can discuss a more permanent position.' He smiled expectantly at her. 'How does that sound?'

It took a moment for it all to sink in. She had just been offered a job as a presenter on one of the top shows on TV. Her money worries would be over. She would be able to stay in her flat after all. Surely this was too good to be true?

'I think that sounds pretty incredible,' she said eventually. 'In fact, I'm trying my hardest not to jump off this sofa and give you a great big snog.'

Toby and Rashida both laughed. 'Well, I wouldn't mind, but I'm not so sure about my wife,' said Toby. 'Perhaps we should just shake on it instead?'

Britt reached over the coffee table and pumped their hands enthusiastically.

'Welcome to the team,' smiled Rashida, pulling her in for a kiss. She smelt of a gorgeous musky fragrance that added to her allure. 'I'm really excited about working with you. I think this style slot is going to work fantastically well.'

'Now I'd like to strike while the iron is hot,' said Toby. 'So how about we start you off on tomorrow's show?'

'Tomorrow?' *But that is . . . the day after today!* 'But I haven't had any . . . I don't know if I . . .'

'Don't worry,' said Toby. 'It'll just be a quick chat on the sofa with Cherry to introduce you to the viewers. I'll brief you on the questions before the show in the morning. Okay?'

Britt didn't really have any other option but to agree. In less than twenty-four hours, there would be several million people watching her over their breakfast cereal.

For the rest of the meeting, they took care of the technicalities such as how much Britt would be paid (a hell of a lot more than she'd been earning as a model for the last few years), her wardrobe allowance (more River Island than Roland Mouret, but still) and transport provision (a chauffeur-driven car to the studio every morning at – *oh*

Christ – 4.30 a.m.). Toby also arranged for her to have a meeting with the show's PR manager Jill after the next day's broadcast to get some promotional shots done for a press release.

'And then if everything works out we'll get some press interviews set up,' said Toby. 'But don't worry, I'm not going to throw you to the lions just yet!'

After the meeting, Rashida accompanied Britt back through the labyrinth of corridors to the lifts. As they walked, the assistant producer chatted away, asking all about Britt's modelling career, and she found herself really warming to the gorgeous Rashida, who had the sort of petite, perfectly proportioned body that Britt had always envied as a gangly teenager. She was like an Asian Kylie Minogue.

On the way they passed down a corridor that was lined with huge glossy photographs of all the *Rise & Shine* presenters. There was Ken smiling with avuncular benevolence and looking far chubbier than he did these days, then Cherry (with a good twenty years airbrushed off her), the sports reporter, weather girl and, at the end of the row, all chiselled cheekbones and perfect hair, was Josh Bailey. It seemed to Britt that his smouldering cat eyes were staring straight at her and following her down the corridor.

Suddenly Rashida's mobile trilled and she stopped to retrieve it from her pocket.

'Sorry, Britt, I'd better take this,' she said, glancing at the screen. Then she put the phone to her ear, a playful smile on her lips. 'Well, hello, Mr Bailey,' she purred.

Britt's ears pricked up – could that be Josh? Sure enough, it soon became clear that she was talking to the gorgeous American, and Britt couldn't help but listen in.

'Yup, I've sorted the location for your Jessica Alba interview in Cannes,' Rashida was saying, then broke into a flurry of girlish giggles. 'Of course I've booked you a decent hotel! How does the Hôtel du Cap-Eden-Roc sound?' She paused to listen. 'Yes, I thought you'd be happy with that.' She smiled, turning away from Britt, as if for privacy. 'I'm really looking forward to it, Josh,' she said quietly, her voice full of hope. 'I can't wait to spend some time alone with you.'

Britt gawped: it sounded very much like Rashida and Josh were – if not an item – then at least engaged in a very serious flirtation. She felt a twinge of jealousy. Lucky Rashida.

Rashida ended the call and turned to Britt with an apologetic smile. 'Sorry about that,' she said.

Britt was dying to find out more, but just then one of the doors in front of them flew open and Cherry emerged, carrying a Louis Vuitton suit carrier under one arm and a small yappy dog under the other.

'Shh, Anthea darling, Mummy's taking you home now.'

'Sorry, Cherry, have you got a moment?' called Rashida.

Cherry turned round and pushed her tortoiseshell sunglasses up onto her head. 'Can't this wait, Rashida? I'm running late for my Pilates trainer.'

'I just wanted to introduce you to Britt Baxter. I think Toby mentioned to you she was coming in for a screen test. She's going to be starting on the team tomorrow as our new style correspondent.'

Cherry quickly rearranged her features into a

professionally dazzling smile. 'Oh, yes, of course, you're the waitress! Such a funny night, you really were the talk of the party.' She air-kissed Britt on both cheeks. 'Welcome to our little family, darling.'

Rashida checked her watch. 'If you're heading off, would you mind pointing Britt in the right direction? I've got a pre-record starting any minute.'

'It would be a pleasure,' smiled Cherry.

'Great, thanks. Well then, I'll see you tomorrow, Britt. We'll send a car to pick you up at 4.30 a.m. Try and get a decent night's sleep.'

'I think that's not very likely!' said Britt. 'Thanks again, Rashida, I really appreciate you giving me this chance.'

Britt set off down the corridor with Cherry, Anthea yapping furiously all the while.

'Isn't this exciting?' Cherry gushed. 'So tell me, darling, what have you done in television before?'

'Well, nothing actually. This is my first job. I still can't quite believe it!'

Cherry spun round to look at her. 'Gosh, you're so brave!'

'Brave? What do you mean?'

'Taking a job on live television with absolutely no experience at all!' Cherry locked hold of her arm and looked deeply sympathetic and concerned. 'I mean, most people would want to cut their teeth on something pre-recorded so any mistakes can be edited out.' She gave a little tinkling laugh.

I don't have a clue what I'm doing, thought Britt with a sudden stab of terror.

'Well, best of luck, darling,' said Cherry. 'I'm sure it

will all go swimmingly.' As she disappeared off towards the car park, Britt stood frozen to the spot as the enormity of the challenge that was facing her began to sink in. Had she just made the next spectacular mistake of her life?

20

Britt had never suffered a panic attack before, but standing on the pavement outside the studio she felt pretty sure this was what one felt like. Shallow breathing? Yup. Sweaty palms? Definitely. Fear of total humiliation in front of millions of people? Oh lord. Britt was sure she might even throw up, the nerves were that bad.

Britt started to walk shakily in the direction of Waterloo station. Hopefully the fresh air would calm her nerves. *It'll be alright, Toby wouldn't have given you this job if he didn't think you were up to it*, she told herself. *Yeah, but Toby won't be the one on the sofa hyperventilating tomorrow morning . . .*

By the time she'd made it back to Clapham, Britt had managed to calm – or at least control – her nerves. What was the worst that could happen, after all? She would make a complete tit of herself and get sacked on her first day. People would quickly forget. Unless of course she did something so hilariously stupid it ended up going viral on YouTube . . . But even then, compared to the world's bigger problems, that didn't seem *so* terrible. Besides, she couldn't wait to see Alex's face when she told him that she'd actually got the job.

He was sitting on the sofa watching a cookery show when she walked in.

'So, how did it go, love?'

She came and sat next to him on the sofa. 'How do you fancy going to the pub for a pint with *Rise & Shine*'s brand-new style correspondent?'

'You're kidding. Really?'

Britt nodded, grinning broadly.

'Oh my God, that's fantastic!' Alex threw his arms around her. 'Congratulations, beautiful, I just know you're going to be a huge star.'

He kissed her all over her face over and over, yet there was a note of sadness about him, which unnerved her. She had felt him slipping away from her again since Sylvia sacked him, but neither of them seemed to have the will to tackle their problems. It was like there was one of Dasha's big pink sparkly elephants lurking in the room.

Alex never wanted to do anything these days apart from slob around the flat or go to the pub. He wasn't even doing much exercise, which was totally out of character. Because he got so upset when Britt nagged him about finding a job she had simply stopped mentioning it – and he had given up all pretence of looking for one. It wasn't like they were even arguing – far from it. In fact, Britt would have almost preferred a bit of shouting and door-slamming to the listless, sad-eyed lump that her boyfriend had become.

He didn't seem that interested in sex any more, either. One night last week she'd gone all out in an effort to put the sparkle back, digging out his favourite pink and black Agent Provocateur undies and stockings teemed with a pair of killer heels. She strutted into the living room and straddled him on the sofa with what she hoped was a seductive manner, but he just made an apologetic face and said he had a bit of a headache. *A headache?* What was he, a fifties housewife? He couldn't even be bothered to make up a decent excuse.

But now wasn't the time to tackle any of this. Her problems with Alex would have to wait. Right now her focus was on a live broadcasting debut in less than twenty-four hours' time.

As expected, Britt did not sleep well. After an 8 p.m. bedtime she woke up almost every hour during the night, checking the time on the clock radio before rolling over and falling back into a fitful doze. At 3.30 she stopped bothering trying to sleep and padded to the kitchen to brew coffee in her little stove-top espresso maker. She had a long, hot shower (with her hair in a shower cap to protect yesterday's blow-dry) and then wriggled on a pair of leggings and a sweatshirt. As there hadn't been time to sort out her on-screen wardrobe, Toby had told her to bring some of her own clothes with her, and she'd packed a large selection in a bag the night before.

On the dot of 4.30 a.m. Britt's phone beeped with a text to say that her car was waiting downstairs. The smartly suited driver jumped out as soon as she came outside, opening her door for her and putting her bag in the boot. As she sank into the luxuriously upholstered backseat and opened the complimentary bottle of Evian, Britt finally allowed herself a shiver of excitement. *I could get used to this.*

It was early July and the sky was already light as they flew through the deserted London streets. The driver was a cheery cockney named Reg who chatted happily for the whole journey, telling her about the time he had been booked to pick Dale Winton up from The Ivy. The presenter had emerged accompanied by Cilla Black, Christopher Biggins and Paul O'Grady and the four of them had ended up singing show tunes all the way back to Dale's pad. Reg's endless chatter suited Britt just fine: anything to take her mind off her impending ordeal.

They finally rolled up outside the studio. Reg waved her off with a cheery 'Best of luck, Miss Baxter!' and then a security guard checked Britt's name off a list and directed her up to the fourth floor, where she found Rashida waiting for her outside the lift. She was carrying a walkie-talkie and a clipboard and looked unfairly fresh-faced for the hour.

'Good to see you Britt. How are you feeling?'

'A bit nervous, I'm afraid.' Understatement of the century.

'Really, you'll be fine,' she said, her lovely smile giving Britt's confidence a little boost. No wonder Josh had a soft spot for her . . .

Compared to yesterday, the corridors were buzzing with people. Rashida led her past doors – each of which had a plaque with the name of one of the presenters – until they reached a door labelled 'Guest Dressing Room 3'.

'Right, here we are.' Rashida tried the handle.

It was a tiny box of a room containing a clothes rail and a dressing table with a fold-up chair. There was another, marginally more comfortable-looking chair squeezed into the corner, partially hiding a large dark stain on the blue carpet. There were light bulbs around the dressing table mirror, but when Rashida switched them on only a couple lit up.

'Sorry, it's not exactly luxurious – we'll get these fixed.'

'No, really, it's great.' Britt put her bag of clothes down on the chair. 'Thanks, Rashida.'

'Now there's coffee in the green room and if you want breakfast just grab one of the runners to get you something. When you're ready, Make-up is just down the corridor – I think some of the guests are in there at the moment, but our head make-up artist, Fran, is expecting you. The other presenters have already gone into their pre-show conference, but you'll be on at the end of the show so there's lots of time.' Rashida paused at the door. 'Hey, just relax,' she smiled. 'You never know, you might even enjoy it.' And with that she was gone.

The make-up room had a wall of brightly lit mirrors along one side, in front of which was a long counter and stools. The counter was covered with brushes, palettes, pots and bottles. All three of the stools were occupied, the one furthest from the door by a pretty young actress who Britt thought she remembered from one of the soaps. *Coronation Street*, perhaps? She was nursing a mug of something hot and looked knackered and sulky. Next to her was a government minister, trying to cling to his dignity while a make-up artist dusted powder on his bald patch, a sheet covering the front of his suit like an overgrown baby's bib. And sitting at the third stool was a woman who Britt didn't recognise, doing her own make-up in the mirror. When she caught sight of Britt's reflection she spun round and hopped off the stool.

'Oops, sorry about that, I never have time to do my own face before everyone else and I tend to scare people if I don't have at least a bit of blusher on!' She held out her hand. 'You must be Britt. I'm Fran.'

The head make-up artist was in her mid-thirties, with sandy brown hair tied in a messy ponytail. Her face had that effortlessly flawless glow that all professional make-up artists seemed to have and cute dimples when she smiled, which seemed to be often. She pulled out the stool for Britt.

'Right, make yourself comfortable.'

Fran set to work, smoothing moisturiser over Britt's face and then applying foundation. Under the firm strokes of her expert hands, Britt started to relax. She might be a total novice in a TV studio, but a make-up chair was familiar territory.

'You've got a really beautiful face, Britt.' Fran dotted concealer around her eyes. 'Toby mentioned that you're a model?'

'I am – or rather I used to be. I got old.'

Fran laughed. 'Well, try not to make the same mistake in television. They're not so keen on that here, either.'

Britt giggled; she knew that she and Fran were going to be friends.

They had been chatting for a while, during which time the politician and the actress had both left, when the door flew open and Toby rushed in. He looked stressed.

'Ah, Britt, there you are.' He pulled up a stool. 'Just wanted to brief you on what's happening later. The idea is that you're going to have a chat with Cherry about your new role presenting this fabulous new feature we're calling "Style Spot". We want to get across to the viewers that it's like a daily fashion magazine covering beauty, shopping, celebrity style, expert tips – that sort of thing.'

Britt nodded. 'So what will Cherry be asking me?'

Toby waved his hands dismissively. 'Oh, just stuff about you, really – being a model, working in fashion, that sort of thing. Nothing complicated.'

Suddenly a girl wearing a headset poked her head round the door. 'Toby, Ken's been at the croissants again. Some idiot forgot to hide them. There are none left for any of the guests.'

Toby grimaced. 'Sorry, Britt, I've got to go. You're on at 8.45. You'll be fabulous.' And with that he jumped up and headed for the door.

'Hang on Toby, I . . .' But he had already disappeared.

'Don't worry, it'll be easy,' said Fran. 'Cherry's a total professional, just let her take the lead.'

Once Fran had finished with her, Britt popped to the green room. Pouring herself a mug of coffee, she glanced at the TV in the corner to see what was happening in the studio. It was just after 8 a.m. and Ken and Cherry were in the middle of interviewing the minister. They appeared to be taking a good-cop-bad-cop approach, with Ken taking the lead with the hard-hitting political questions and then Cherry asking about his children or his favourite biscuit when things got too serious. It was a master-class in TV presenting: the minister got his message across, while the viewers weren't bombarded with political jargon over their Coco Pops. Ken and Cherry made it look so easy, especially as Britt knew they'd have someone shouting in their ear the whole time. As she imagined herself sitting there in less than an hour's time, her heart started hammering in her chest.

It was going to be a total disaster.

21

Britt was walking back to her dressing room with her coffee, wondering if it was too late to back out, when she bumped into Ken coming out of the studio humming to himself. His eyes went straight to her cleavage like a tit-seeking missile, but his leer quickly turned into a beaming smile.

'Britt, isn't it? Hello, ducky.' He went in for the standard showbiz cheek double-kiss, although somehow managed to get her mouth instead, his moustache tickling her lips. 'Now, you're not planning on chucking that coffee over me, are you?'

She blushed. 'I'm so sorry about my behaviour that night, Ken. It really was inexcusable.' She did regret what she had done, but at the same time couldn't help thinking . . . *but you're not half a letch.*

'Shhh, don't give it another thought,' he chuckled. 'You can make it up to me another time.' He slid his hand over her shoulder and pulled her close to him, giving her a squeeze. 'Now if you need any help with this presenting lark, just you come and ask your Uncle Kenneth. I'll be happy to give you a few tips. Over dinner one night, perhaps?'

'Um, great.' She wriggled out from under his arm. 'Thanks, Ken. Better dash.'

Back in her dressing room she found several messages on her BlackBerry, including one from Alex: 'Good luck, gorgeous. I'll be watching. Break a leg xxx '

At 8.35 a.m. the assistant floor manager, a chubby Geordie called Dave, came to fetch Britt from her dressing room with a cheery 'Alright, pet?' By now, proper stomach-churning, mouth-parching fear had kicked in. Had anyone had ever thrown up on live TV before?

There was a green light outside the studio doors; they were currently off air. 'We're just coming to the end of a travel VT about holidays in Turkey, then it's the ads,' Dave told Britt as he led her towards the sofa. 'And after that, you're on.'

He showed Britt where to sit and she immediately felt her face burning as she prickled with sweat under the bright studio lights. Oh God, what if she got damp patches under her arms? Her pale pink silk blouse would act like blotting paper at the first sign of moisture – her first TV appearance and she was going to end up in next week's *Heat* magazine with a big red ring of shame around her sweaty pits!

'Cherry will be along any minute, so make yourself comfy,' said Dave. 'And don't worry, you'll be fine!'

'So everyone keeps telling me,' muttered Britt.

She sat alone on the sofa, staring out on to the busy studio floor. There seemed to be dozens of people there to witness her humiliation – although that was obviously nothing compared to the millions and millions watching at home.

Four or five cameras were pointing in her direction, like snipers trained on a target. She looked around desperately for a familiar face but couldn't see anyone that she knew. Her TV debut was in a matter of seconds and right now she was struggling to remember her own name. But, just when she was seriously thinking about doing a runner, Britt felt someone sit on the sofa next to her and she looked round to see Stewie smiling at her. 'G'day, mate. How're you holding up?'

'Oh, Stewie, thank God!' She was so pleased to see him. 'I've got no idea what I'm supposed to be doing. Please, have you got any tips?'

He started to mic her up. 'Okay, well, as far as I can tell, the best way to handle an interview is just to imagine you're sitting in a pub having a chat over a beer – only without the swearing. Keep your answers short. Let Cherry keep the conversation moving.'

'But what if I don't know the answer?'

'Do what the politicians do – talk about what *you* want instead. Just waffle on about how excited you are to be joining *Rise & Shine*.' He clipped the mic to her collar. 'But this isn't *Question Time*, mate; I think you'll be fine.'

'Do you think it's too late to back out?'

'Nah, course not, but it would be a shame. I reckon you're going to surprise yourself.' He stood up and winked at her. 'But if you *are* pants, then I'll buy you a beer, so really it's win-win.'

Just then Cherry came bustling across the floor, looking calm and unruffled in an immaculate beige shift dress.

'Hello, darling, super to see you again.' She sat opposite Britt on the sofa, patting at her blonde bob – so heavily hairsprayed it looked like a helmet. 'All ready?'

Britt nodded mutely.

'Lovely, looks like we're ready to go.'

Britt looked out at the studio floor again, where the floor manager had raised his arm to indicate they were about to go live. Cherry plastered on a smile, turning to face a camera with a little illuminated red light. The floor manager pointed in her direction and they were away.

'And welcome back to *Rise & Shine* . . .'

It felt like it was over in seconds, although – as Stewie later told her – she had been on for three minutes. After an initial hiccup when Cherry asked the name of the new fashion feature and Britt's mind went blank (she was pleased then to have the director talking in her ear) she felt the whole thing had gone rather well. In fact, by the end of the interview, she was happily chatting away about anti-ageing serums with aplomb.

'So tune in next week when I'll be recommending the best products for giving your skin a youthful glow,' said Britt. 'Not that you'll be needing anything like that for years yet, Cherry!' she added with a cheeky wink.

As Cherry laughed, Britt felt a thrill of exhilaration. *She really could do this!*

Stewie met her as she walked off set. 'You were ace. Reckon you owe *me* a beer after that.'

Britt gave him a quick kiss on the cheek.

'Hey, what was that for?'

'To thank you for calming me down. Seriously, you were a lifesaver.'

'I'm going to hold you to that beer, you know,' he called after her as she walked towards the studio doors.

Britt turned back with a huge grin. 'No worries, mate!'

On her way back to the dressing room people stopped to congratulate Britt and welcome her to the team. Fran stuck her head out of the make-up room as she passed and gave her a thumbs-up. Even Charlie, the surly runner who she had met at the screen test, gave her a high five as she passed.

Britt couldn't stop smiling. It had been such an adrenaline rush. She felt like she had just thrown herself off the top of a tall building and miraculously survived – and now she couldn't wait to do it all over again.

She was walking down the corridor to her dressing room when a voice stopped her in her tracks.

'Hey, kid, you did great.'

Britt turned to see Josh Bailey walking towards her. It was the first time she had seen him since the party and he looked even more gorgeous than ever. He was wearing a pale blue shirt and slim black trousers, which made the most of his perfect body. The top couple of buttons of his shirt were undone to show off a V of perfectly smooth, tanned skin. Britt idly wondered whether you would find a hairy chest a few buttons lower, then forced all lustful thoughts to the back of her mind. This time she was determined not to make a fool of herself.

'Hi, Josh,' she said, in what she hoped was a brisk, business-like tone. 'I never had a chance to properly introduce myself the other day. I'm Britt Baxter.'

Josh took the hand that she was holding out to him. 'Well, Britt, I guess you and I are going to be seeing quite a lot of each other now that we'll be working together.'

He pulled her ever so gently towards him and she caught a whiff of expensive-smelling, citrusy aftershave. 'That could be fun,' he added softly.

Then Josh smiled at her and his emerald eyes seemed to light up with the suggestion of something that was quite frankly filthy and possibly illegal in most countries. The guy just exuded sex. It took a moment for Britt to realise that she had been holding her breath, and she let it go in a noisy exhale that ended up a sort of wheezy, choked-up cough. *Smooth, Baxter, very smooth.*

'Well, I'd better get going – busy day and all,' he said eventually, letting her hand fall. 'See you around, Britt Baxter.'

She watched him walk away, noting his broad back and tight, high bum. You could see from the way he walked that he was a professional dancer – he moved confidently, like he was in total control of his body.

Please look back, Britt willed as he reached the end of the corridor. *Maybe if he looks back it means he's interested in me.*

Josh disappeared around the corner without another glance in her direction. *Get a grip.* Britt told herself.

The following morning, just a week after she had thrown that cocktail over Ken Chudleigh, Britt presented *Rise & Shine*'s first fashion feature, Style Spot. During the six-minute feature, she introduced models wearing the pick of the high street's jumpsuits (so much easier to do with real girls rather than a spotty runner), and she interviewed a footballer's wife about her new lingerie range. And apart from a rather risqué joke to the WAG about playing with her husband's balls – which had been met by the director's sharp intake of breath in her ear – Britt was told her performance had been pretty flawless.

Toby came to her dressing room straight afterwards. 'That was fantastic, Britt! You're a natural. Didn't I tell you there was nothing to worry about?'

'I guess I just had to find it out for myself.' Britt grinned. She was thrilled with Toby's reaction; he'd taken such a gamble massive on hiring her.

'Well, keep this up and we'll definitely have to talk about making you a permanent member of the team.'

Britt was floating on air. For the first time in her life, it felt like she was finding something she was actually good at. Okay, she'd always been a decent model, but standing in front of a camera in a pretty frock didn't exactly require enormous amounts of skill. Presenting, on the other hand, was something of an art and a hell of a lot more challenging. This could really be the start of something big for her.

On the way home from the studio Britt's phone beeped more or less constantly with messages of congratulations, not just from her mum and Jessie, but from friends she hadn't heard from for donkey's years. There was a voicemail from Scott, too, which was a lovely surprise. They'd kept in touch over email, but she hadn't spoken to her old agent since he'd told her she'd never get a modelling job again – and although she knew Scott loved her, it had hurt when he had acted as if she was a lost cause.

'You totally killed it, babe!' he screeched on the message. 'Seriously, you were divine – like breakfast telly's answer to Katie Adie, but *way* hotter. Oh, and when you see Josh Bailey give him my number. No guy that hot and with those kinds of moves can *possibly* be straight . . . Anyway, call me, precious. Love you. Mwah.'

In fact, the only person who she hadn't heard from by the time she made it back to the flat was Alex.

Standing on the street outside their house, Britt was aware that something wasn't quite right, but to start with she couldn't quite put her finger on it. After a few seconds, she realised what it was: all the curtains in their flat were closed. Britt checked her watch. Nearly lunchtime. Alex couldn't still be asleep; besides, they never closed the living-room curtains, even at night.

She opened the communal front door, climbed the stairs and stood on the landing outside their door, listening. Inside, she could hear soft music playing. What the hell . . . ?

The thought hit her like a bullet. *Alex is having an affair.* Suddenly, it all fell into place. He'd gone off sex, he was avoiding her, he was being secretive and evasive. How could she have been so stupid? He was shagging some floozy right now in their bed! *How could he do this to her?*

Britt stood frozen outside the door, too shocked to cry. Her initial reaction was to turn and leave, but she knew she couldn't run from this.

Dreading what she would find inside, Britt put her key in the lock and pushed open the door.

22

The living room was lit by a dozen fat cream candles that had been dotted along the mantelpiece and on the table, which had been beautifully laid for two. There were fancy folded napkins and matching plates. A bottle of champagne sat in an ice bucket next to a vase with a single white rose – Britt's favourite. And in the middle of the room, grinning a bit sheepishly, was Alex. He was wearing a tuxedo and looked like he'd had a shave and a haircut.

'What . . . what's going on?' Britt was gobsmacked.

'Well, I wanted to take you out for a romantic meal to celebrate your fantastic TV debut, but as you're going to bed at 8 p.m. these days, I thought we could have a candlelit lunch instead.'

'So there's no-one else here?'

Alex looked confused. 'No – why would there be?'

Britt flew straight into his arms, all doubts vanished. It was such a lovely, thoughtful gesture – just the sort of thing Alex used to do for her before things started to go so badly wrong. She kissed him hard on the lips and had begun to feel the stirrings of emotions she hadn't felt for a very long time when suddenly Alex pulled away.

'Britt, I know things have been hard between us, but—'

'Shh, not now.' She pressed her finger on his lips. 'Let's not spoil it.'

The bedroom was lit by yet more candles, and there were what Britt thought were little bits of damp tissue scattered over the bed.

'Rose petals.' Alex shrugged. 'Must have wilted.'

Giggling, Britt pushed him back onto the bed, quickly wriggled out of her clothes and then straddled him. Alex reached up to her, running his hands all over her body.

'God, I've missed you, beautiful. Come here.'

They had been together so long that they knew exactly what to do to turn each other on so the sex, while a little predictable, was fantastic. Afterwards they lay together, a sweaty tangle of limbs, basking in the after-glow.

'I love you, Britt.' Alex picked off a rose petal that had stuck to her damp skin. 'I'll always love you.'

'I love you too,' she smiled, nuzzling into his chest, trying to ignore the fact that, at the point of orgasm, it had been Josh Bailey's face that had flashed through her mind.

The following week was London Fashion Week, so Britt was given an extended time slot on the show and a chance to get out of the studio for some reports on location. Rashida and her team of researchers had secured tickets for most of the big shows, and thanks to her time work-ing in fashion (and Scott pulling some strings on her behalf), Britt managed to get some fantastic backstage interviews and insider gossip.

The week's hottest ticket was Todd Lazarus, the young Londoner *Vogue* had crowned the most talented designer of his generation. Only a handful of journalists had been invited to attend his show – and certainly no TV crews. Luckily, Britt had done a bit of modelling for Todd when he was a struggling fashion design student at St Martin's and the pair had stayed in touch, so as well as making it into the exclusive show, she secured the interview with Todd all her rivals would die for. He told her he was designing a wedding dress for the next big celebrity wedding and Britt's report was followed up in all of the next day's newspapers. Thrilled with the publicity that she was getting for the show, Toby assigned Britt her own desk in the production office next to Rashida so Britt could help come up with ideas for Style Spot.

When Britt arrived at the office after the next day's broadcast, there was a pile of packages waiting on her desk.

'Rashida, what are all these?'

Rashida looked up from her computer. 'Bribes, mainly,' she shrugged. 'From PR companies.'

Britt looked puzzled.

'As far as they're concerned, you hold the key to getting their product on telly, so they send you a sample and then hopefully you'll include whatever it is they're trying to flog on Style Spot,' explained Rashida. 'You get some goodies, they get national exposure and more sales. Get used to it, hon – there'll be a lot more from where those came from.'

While a runner trotted off to Starbucks to get her a cappuccino, Britt sat and opened the boxes. Amongst the haul was a butter-soft leather satchel, a dozen mascaras, some foot cream, a crate of vanilla-flavoured energy milkshakes and a pair of flip-flops with her name picked out in crystals along the side. Keeping the flip-flops and one of the mascaras for herself (plus the handbag for her mum), she shared the rest of the goodies around the girls in the office. Could the job possibly get any better?

Two weeks after starting work at *Rise & Shine*, Britt decided to spend an afternoon tackling all the annoying little jobs that she'd been putting off for weeks, including going for her long overdue smear test.

While she was sitting in the waiting room, she flicked through a copy of *Cosmopolitan* magazine. It was their annual 'Hot Hunks' issue featuring fit, famous blokes in poses, and the centerfold was none other than Joshua J. Bailey. He was naked but for a pair of tap shoes, a big grin, and a sparkly top hat held coyly over his tackle. The shot was far too cheesy to be sexy perhaps, but Britt couldn't take her eyes off his incredible body – perfectly defined without being overly pumped up. *Looks like he wasn't hiding a hairy chest under that shirt after all*, she thought with a smile.

'Britt Baxter? Is Britt Baxter here?' She realised that the receptionist had been calling her name and she'd been lost in a daydream.

She jumped up. 'Sorry, that's me!'

The receptionist nodded curtly. 'Room 3 along the corridor, please.'

A friendly nurse greeted her at the door and told her to go behind the curtain and remove her skirt and knickers, then to lie on the couch. Britt did as she was asked.

'Right, are we all set?' The nurse swished back the curtain along the rail. 'Now this won't hurt at all. Just try and relax.'

It wasn't the most dignified position to be in, so Britt

tried to zone out until it was over. But it seemed the nurse had other ideas.

'Having a good day, are you, love?' she said, angling a light between her legs.

'Oh, um, fine, thanks,' said Britt. 'You know, busy!' She wasn't sure about the etiquette involved in making small talk with someone while they were poking at your cervix. It wasn't like chatting to a hairdresser about your holidays.

'All done.' The nurse snapped off her surgical gloves. 'Look, I really hope you don't mind me asking, but are you that girl off *Rise & Shine?*'

Britt was speechless. She was still lying half-dressed on the couch with just a skimpy sheet of NHS blue tissue covering her bits, for God's sake! But she couldn't very well lie. 'Well, yes, I am.'

'I thought it was you! I love you on that fashion report. Ooh, you're my first celebrity smear!'

Walking back from the surgery, Britt remembered what the nurse had said: '*My first celebrity smear.*' Britt smiled. *Is that what I am now*, she thought with a shiver of excitement, *a celebrity?* She had a quick look round the busy pavement to see if anyone else had recognised her. Then she reached in her handbag for her sunglasses, before suddenly stopping herself short: *Oh, get over yourself, love, you're not Angelina flippin' Jolie!* Britt put the shades back into her bag and continued the walk home. The thought kept creeping back into her mind, though.

Blimey, she was going to be famous.

23

Toby had originally said that he would make a decision about Britt's future after three months, but it was more like three weeks when he asked her up into his office to offer her a permanent job on the show. Overjoyed, Britt immediately accepted.

She couldn't wait to phone her mum and tell her the news. They had fallen into a routine of chatting every morning after the show so she could get Molly's feedback on her performance and check that her mum was okay after her recent health scare, and she knew how excited she would be now Britt was to be a permanent fixture on the show.

At the next morning's conference meeting, when all the presenters and key production staff got together to discuss the show, Toby announced the good news.

'I think we can all agree Britt will be a fantastic addition to the team,' he said to general applause. 'In fact, she reminds me very much of Cherry when she started with us!'

Ken gave a hearty shout of laughter. Cherry smiled thinly.

At the end of the meeting, Ken cornered Britt and gave her a sloppy congratulatory kiss, quietly reminding her that his offer of dinner and a private tutorial still stood. She looked around for Josh, hoping to see how he'd reacted to the news – and she struggled not to feel disappointed when he didn't appear to be in the meeting.

Rashida linked arms with her as they walked out. 'I'm really thrilled we're going to be working together on a permanent basis,' she said. 'You're a real asset to the show.'

'Thanks, Rashida, I couldn't do it without you,' Britt smiled, adding in what she hoped was a casual tone, 'Um, is Josh in today?'

'No, he's at a press junket in LA,' said Rashida dismissively, with a look that suggested she was happy Josh wasn't around. Britt was confused. From the way she'd been speaking to him on the phone the other day, she would have guessed Josh was Rashida's favourite person.

Later that morning, Britt bumped into Cherry outside the green room.

'Such wonderful news, darling,' Cherry said breezily. 'Just . . . super.'

'Thanks, Cherry.' Britt remembered her thin smile. 'I'm obviously still totally new to all this, so do let me know if you have any advice.'

'Well, there is one little thing,' said Cherry. 'Perhaps you've heard the saying that the camera puts on ten pounds . . . ?' She smoothed down her size six Armani trouser suit and shot a meaningful look at Britt's own clingy dress. 'Ciao, darling!'

Britt watched her totter off down the corridor. She couldn't work Cherry out at all. On the one hand she could be charming and helpful, but then she'd go and throw out bitchy comments like that. Most of the people who worked on the show seemed to be terrified of her – apart from Ken, that was. They were famed for their relaxed, easy banter on air, but she had sensed they were less than friends off-screen. In fact, after Cherry's dog Anthea pooped in the corridor later that week, you could hear Ken shouting about '. . . that fucking woman's fucking rat . . .' all the way up in the production office.

Britt decided to quiz Fran about it the following morning while she was having her make-up done. She'd become really fond of the head make-up artist, who she'd come to think of as the show's unofficial mum: always there with an encouraging word, a square of Green & Black's chocolate or a sneaky sip from the cans of Red Bull she kept hidden in the make-up room fridge if you need a pick-me-up.

'So what's Cherry really like?' she asked Fran the next day. 'She can seem a bit . . . frosty.'

'Ah, well, I guess I'm biased.' Fran smiled as she brushed blusher onto Britt's cheeks. 'Cherry and I started here together on the same day and we've been friends ever since. She is the ultimate professional – hard-working, talented and incredibly good at her job. I suppose if you don't know her as well as I do, she can seem a little . . . *cool*, perhaps, but her heart is absolutely in the right place. I really can't say enough good things about her.'

'And how about she and Ken – do they get on?'

Fran looked away. 'They're a great team and have genuine respect for each other.' She promptly put down her brush and undid the bib from around Britt's neck. 'Right, love, you're good to go.'

* * *

148

'They can't stand each other,' grinned Stewie wickedly. He and Britt were sitting in the canteen having their usual post-show drink: a black coffee for Stewie, a fruit smoothie for Britt. Over the past few weeks Stewie had become her closest friend on the show. Loyal, helpful and always ready with a joke to boost her spirits at 5.30 a.m., he was like a ray of Sydney sunshine on a drizzly London morning. With Stewie, what you saw was pretty much what you got. The board shorts and sun-bleached hair weren't an affectation: his true love was surfing, and whenever he could afford it he would pack a rucksack and head off to Hawaii or Costa Rica to catch a wave. Stewie was very much of the 'work to live rather than live to work' school of thought, which was why he had zero ambition to rise up the ranks of the production team. But he was a fount of all knowledge on all things *Rise & Shine* – or *Lies & Whine* as Stewie and the rest of the floor crew called it.

'So why do Ken and Cherry stick it out if they hate each other so much?' asked Britt.

'Because they've got TV's holy grail – a permanent contract. They're not stupid enough to let a little detail like loathing bugger that up.'

Britt drained the last drops of her smoothie. 'I don't think Cherry likes me that much,' she said.

'Oh, don't worry about old Chezza. She's just not that keen on beautiful and talented girls – especially not ones who are young enough to be her daughter. But her bark's worse than her bite, that's for sure. It's Ken who's the real diva on this show.'

'He seems laidback.'

'Christ, no!' Stewie glanced around the canteen to

check they couldn't be overheard and then leaned in closer to Britt. 'You want to know why Ken really lost all that weight? He went around telling everyone it was golf, but the truth is he got a gastric band fitted six months ago.'

'You're kidding!'

'Why do you think we can't have croissants laid out for guests in the green room any more? Ken might have lost the weight, but he sure as hell still has an eye for calories, and so all the food in the studio has to be hidden in case he goes on a binge. Him and Cherry used to present the weekly cookery slot together, but then one day ol' Kenny tried to cram an entire banoffee pie into his mouth on live TV, and since then Cherry has to do it on her own.'

'Bloody hell!' Britt giggled.

'You don't know the half of it.' Stewie rolled his eyes. 'Give it a few months and you'll be as bonkers as the rest of them.'

They sat in companionable silence for a few moments.

'So, what about you, Britt?' Stewie glanced shyly at her. 'Got a boyfriend?'

'Yes, I do. His name's Alex. We've been together for a few years.'

'He's a lucky guy.'

Britt just smiled. She wasn't sure if Alex would necessarily agree. Ever since he had surprised her with the candlelit lunch, he had reverted to being quiet and moody.

'Are you seeing anyone, Stewie?'

'Nah, not at the moment,' he said. 'I had a girlfriend – in fact, she's the reason I came to London in the first place. She's from Kentish Town and she came to Oz on a gap year. She wanted to learn to surf and I was the one giving the lessons. We fell in love and I followed her back here. I was going to propose – got the ring and everything – and then she told me that she'd met someone else. Right punch in the nuts, that was.'

'God, I'm sorry.'

'Yeah, well, better off without her, mate . . .' Britt noticed him shrug and couldn't help but feel touched that he'd opened up to her; he usually seemed to keep so much close to his chest.

After coffee they walked back down the three flights of stairs to the studio floor, where Britt was due to pre-record an item on control pants for next week's show.

Walking down the stairs they could hear raised voices. Britt glanced over the banisters and saw Josh and Rashida standing on the landing below them. Rashida looked hysterical, her face screwed up in anger and her hands waving wildly, while Josh was leaning up against the wall with his arms tightly folded and his face blank. Britt's curiosity was instantly piqued.

'What's going on with those two?' Britt asked once they were back in the studio.

'Trouble in paradise, I'm guessing.' Stewie shook his head. 'Jeez, poor Rashida. She deserves a hell of a lot better than Twinkletoes.'

Britt had been desperate to find out more about their relationship since that time she'd overheard Rashida flirting with Josh on the phone, so she grabbed the opportunity to grill Stewie: he seemed to be the oracle on all things *Rise & Shine*. 'Are they dating?' she asked casually.

'Well, I think they are – or rather were,' he said. 'I reckon Rashida wanted to keep it quiet as they worked together. Looks like it's all gone pear-shaped now, though. Forget the quickstep or the tango, Bailey's speciality is the hump 'em and dump 'em.'

'That's terrible!' Britt was horrified to hear that Josh would behave that way.

Stewie shrugged. 'Yeah, well that's Joshua J. Bailey, I'm afraid – the Prince of Pricks. You'd do well to be careful of him, Britt. He's trouble.'

24

Britt slid open the glass door and walked onto the balcony overlooking the river. The afternoon sun was twinkling on the Thames and she could hear the laughter of people enjoying a drink on the terrace of the uber-trendy bar a dozen floors below. She heard the letting agent come out behind her.

'Stunning view, isn't it?' he said smoothly. 'An amazing location, plus seventeen hundred square feet of beautifully appointed penthouse living space. What more could you want?'

The flat *was* pretty incredible. It had a huge open-plan living area decorated in tasteful tones of beige and cream, a tiny kitchen ('The people who can afford to live in these apartments tend to eat out most nights,' the agent had said) and two generously sized bedrooms (with walk-in wardrobes), the largest of which, Britt was amused to see, had an entirely mirrored ceiling. The bathroom was decked out in Italian black marble and had a shower cubicle that was virtually the same size as Britt's entire flat.

When she had first walked in Britt had felt like an imposter. With its sleek lines and suede furnishings, the place deserved someone who collected modern art and ancient Chinese pottery. Britt's art collection consisted of a *Breakfast at Tiffany's* movie poster and a couple of small watercolours painted by her Nanna Eileen. She didn't fancy waking up every morning to her sleep-rumpled reflection in the bedroom ceiling. She didn't have any use for a shower in which you could fit a whole football team plus the referee and linesmen too. And as much as she enjoyed going out to restaurants, she quite liked cooking at home. But she had fallen head over heels for the amazing view, and the location was pretty much perfect: a five-minute drive along the river from the *Rise & Shine* studio.

'So, what do you think?' The agent leaned on the balcony next to Britt. 'I've had a lot of interest in this apartment, as you can imagine . . .'

Britt loved her flat in Clapham, but she had been there for nearly eight years and it felt like it was time for a change. Besides, since joining the *Rise & Shine* team a month ago she had already seen her salary double. She glanced to her left and saw Tower Bridge slowly opening up to let a boat through. Imagine waking up to that every morning . . .

Taking a deep breath, she turned to the agent. 'I love it, but I'd really want the mirrors taking off the bedroom ceiling and a bigger oven in the kitchen . . .'

'Not a problem,' he replied instantly.

'Okay, then, I'll take it,' she said with a smile, butterflies fluttering in her stomach as she thought about her and Alex's new life together starting there.

Alex, however, was not at all happy about the idea of moving.

'What's wrong with this place?' They were sitting at

the kitchen table having an early dinner of takeaway fish and chips so that Britt could get to bed by 9 p.m.

'Nothing, but wouldn't it be great to have a bit more space? There's a spare bedroom, so we could have friends or your parents or my mum to stay. And as the apartment is so central I could have thirty minutes extra in bed every morning!'

Alex stabbed moodily at a chip. 'I don't want to live in some soulless block in the middle of London.'

'It's a gorgeous penthouse on the river! Come on Al, for the first time in for ever we actually don't have to worry about money, so let's enjoy it.' Britt reached over and squeezed his hand. 'Besides, we won't be able to move in for a month or so as they need to get rid of the mirrors on the bedroom ceiling. Honest to God, Al,' she giggled, 'it looked like something out of a porn film!'

But he was staring back at her, stony-faced. 'I'm sorry, Britt, but I don't want to move.'

'Well, I'm the one paying the bills,' she snapped, before she could stop herself.

Alex pushed back his chair, picked up his keys and calmly walked towards the front door.

'Look, Al, I didn't mean . . .'

The door slammed. Kate Moss shot off the sofa and under the table.

Britt felt terrible. And yet didn't she have a point? Alex was still making no effort to find a job. He moped around at home all day. They made love once in a blue moon. It seemed like the only thing that was keeping them together were the memories of how amazing things had once been – and even those were fading.

* * *

The next day, after the show, Britt arranged to meet Jessie for a girly day of shopping and pampering. She hadn't had a chance to see her friend since starting work on *Rise & Shine* and was dying to catch up. As a special treat, Britt had arranged for a car to collect Jessie from her house and drive her to The Wolseley, where they were meeting for brunch. It was a place she'd read about in umpteen magazines and always thought out of her league.

'You should have seen how excited the girls were when this big black limo pulled up outside the house!' laughed Jessie, giving Britt a huge hug and then joining her at the table. 'Wow, check you out, Miss Baxter! You look all . . . shiny!'

Britt laughed. 'Well, now that I've got to be ready for a close-up at a time when most people are just crawling out of bed, I decided to throw some serious money at the problem.'

It was true. In the last few weeks she'd had a Brazilian blow-dry treatment to de-frizz her hair (saving a good hour's blow-drying time each morning), a permanent manicure in neutral pale pink, a spray tan and an oxygen facial that had left her with the dewy, luminous skin of a Hollywood starlet.

'Well, fame obviously suits you.' Jessie reached over and gave her another hug. 'Oh, it's so good to see you, lovey. I've been dying to hear about how the new job's going. The girls are telling everyone about their famous Auntie Britt and even Tom leaves a bit later for work these days so he can catch you in the morning! We're all so proud.'

'Aw, bless you. I've been missing you all horribly. I must come round and see the girls soon. By the way, how bling is this place? Can you believe we're actually here?' Suddenly, Britt caught sight of a glamorous blonde strutting into the restaurant. 'Oh my God . . .' she gasped. 'Is that . . . ? It can't be! It's only bloody Kate Moss – the real one!'

Jessie squealed. 'Blimey, babe, get us!' They clinked glasses giddily.

Just then the waiter appeared and they ordered caramelised pink grapefruit, salt beef hash with fried eggs and two more glasses of Bucks Fizz. Britt felt herself relax for the first time in ages.

'Mmm, I could get used to this,' sighed Jessie as a basket of flaky croissants arrived unbidden at the table. 'So, anyway, I turned on the TV this morning to see you sitting on the sofa presenting an item with Josh Bailey! Do you two come as a team these days?'

'No, they just rope me in to talk about red carpet fashion when he's been reporting on a big award ceremony or party.'

It was a development that Britt had had mixed feelings about. Since Stewie's warning she had become far more wary of Josh but, nevertheless, she couldn't help but be attracted to him. He was so charming – not to mention knee-tremblingly sexy. And, as it turned out, there was a sizzling on-screen chemistry between the pair of them that the viewers seemed to love.

'So, tell me, what's he like?' sighed Jessie. 'Is he as gorgeous as he looks?'

'Yup, a total fox. I can't even look him in the eye without turning into a dribbling wreck.' Britt picked at the basket of croissants in front of her. 'I'm not sure about him though, Jess. Word on the street is that he's a bit of a player.'

'Well, the good-looking ones usually are.' Jessie topped up their drinks from the bottle of champagne until it was practically all Fizz and no Bucks. 'Talking about fit blokes, how's Alex?'

At the mention of his name, Britt's high vanished. The last thing she wanted to do was spend their day moaning about her boyfriend. But she knew that she'd been sticking her head in the sand about their problems – perhaps it would be good to talk over them with Jessie? So she told her about the row they'd had the previous night over the new apartment.

'I understand why you're upset, but try and see it from Alex's point of view,' said Jessie. 'His girlfriend has become a celebrity overnight and is suddenly earning more money in a month than he probably made in a whole year, while he can't even get a job. You can't blame the bloke for struggling with it a bit. He probably feels like you're the one wearing the trousers now.'

'Well, I'm going to move to this new apartment and Alex can either come with me or stay in the flat. I really don't care any more,' Britt tried to say it like she meant it.

Jessie nodded, but Britt could tell from her expression that she thought Britt was being unreasonable. Britt was relieved when the waiter came over and asked if they wanted coffee so they had an excuse to change the subject.

They were trying out lip-glosses in Selfridges beauty hall after brunch when a woman and her young daughter came rushing up to Britt and asked for her autograph. Jessie was thrilled – and Britt, though taken aback, did get a bit of a kick out of it. Since the smear test humiliation she had been recognised a couple more times and it was still a novelty for her. She signed her name and added two kisses, and then posed for a photo with the young girl, all the while thinking *Is this really happening to me, Britt Baxter from Larkbridge?*

It had been ages since Jessie had been shopping for anything other than nappies and nipple cream, so Britt insisted she had a makeover at the Bobbi Brown counter and then, in a rush of generosity, bought her all the products the girl had used on her. Next, they went up to the contemporary designer floor, where Britt fell in love with the softest grey cashmere Zadig & Voltaire sweater with a skull design picked out in tiny silver studs on the back. She insisted on getting one for Jessie in black, too.

'You can't, Britt, it's too expensive!'

'Please, Jess, it's my treat. I can't remember when I could last afford to splurge on my best mate. I want to.'

The assistant behind the cash desk smiled in recognition as Britt approached.

'I'm sure if you speak to our press office they would be happy to arrange to have these sent to you,' said the woman.

Britt was confused. 'It's okay, I'll just take them now, thanks.'

The woman handed her a card. 'You might find it easier to liaise with the press office directly . . .'

Jessie beckoned Britt to one side. 'I think they're trying to give you them for free,' she whispered.

'Oh! Oh, right.' It seemed sort of wrong that now she was in a position to pay for things, people wanted to just give them to her. Britt went back to the cash desk. 'Thanks so much, but I really am happy to pay.' The woman looked disappointed. 'But I'll be sure to contact the press office next time,' Britt added quickly.

Jessie chuckled as they walked away. 'You're a wonderful friend, Britt, but you really are a crap celebrity . . .'

The following morning, Britt was sitting at her desk in the production office returning emails after the show had finished when she got a call to say there was a visitor waiting for her in Reception. She trotted downstairs and was shocked to find Alex standing by the front desk. They hadn't spoken since their row and she wasn't quite sure whether she had forgiven him yet.

'What are you doing here, Al?' He was wearing an old tracksuit and flip-flops and looked like he had just got out of bed.

'I've come to take my girlfriend out to lunch if that's okay. Don't I get a kiss?'

Britt gave him a perfunctory peck on his cheek, which was sporting several days' worth of reddish-brown stubble. He smelt like he'd just got out of bed, too.

'Look, I'd love to come out with you but I'm afraid I'm just in the middle of something,' she said.

'Don't worry, I'm happy to wait,' said Alex. 'Which way to your dressing room?'

He obviously wasn't going to take no for an answer. Britt sighed and led him to the lifts and then up to the fourth floor. She walked briskly along the corridors with Alex flip-flopping behind her. Not so long ago she would have been proud to be seen with him, but now, she realised guiltily, she was desperate to get him out of the way before anyone saw them together.

But she was too late. As they neared the dressing rooms Toby came round the corner.

'Oh, Britt, don't forget you've got a pre-record in ten

minutes on celebrity fashion disasters.' He turned to Alex. 'Hi, I don't think we've met . . . ?'

'I'm Alex.'

Toby looked blank.

'My boyfriend,' Britt said quickly. 'Toby – Alex.'

'Oh, right, great to meet you,' said Toby. 'Britt, see you downstairs shortly.'

After he'd walked off, Alex instantly rounded on Britt. 'Your boss didn't even know you have a boyfriend! Why the hell have you been keeping me a secret?'

'Come on Al, I've only been here a month,' said Britt, trying to hurry him along. The last thing she wanted was a scene. 'I'm hardly going to share my private life with everyone I work with, am I? Right, this is my dressing room . . .'

She hustled him inside and shut the door.

'Britt, we need to talk,' said Alex. He looked furious.

'I agree with you, but not here. Not where I work. I promise we'll talk later.'

'No, Britt, we need to talk now!' She was shocked by how angry he seemed. 'You're always too tired when you get home. We can't go on like this.'

'Alex, I'm sorry but I have work to do. I can't just drop everything . . .'

'No, it's quite clear that the only thing that you're prepared to drop is our relationship.' He was virtually shouting now. 'That is if we even have a goddamn relationship any more!'

Just then there was a soft knocking and Stewie stuck his head round the door.

'Sorry to interrupt. I was just checking everything's okay in here?'

'Thanks Stewie, it's fine . . .'

'I'm her boyfriend,' Alex snapped.

'Oh, hi there, Alex,' said Stewie. 'Good to finally meet you. I've heard a lot about you.'

This took some of the wind out of Alex's sails. There was an awkward silence.

'I've come to take Britt out to lunch.' Alex sounded like a moody teenager.

'Al, I've told you, I can't come out now,' said Britt. 'I've got to do a pre-record.'

'With that American twat?'

'Yes. I mean, no! It's with Josh, yes, but he's not a twat.' Britt dropped her head into her hands with frustration. 'Al, please, can't we do this later?'

'Why, so you can have a good laugh about me now with all your new friends?'

Stewie stepped in, the voice of calm and reason in the face of Alex's barmy ranting. 'Come on, mate, it's probably best if you go.'

'And what's it got to do with you, *mate*?'

Britt cringed, feeling utterly ashamed of Alex's behaviour and wishing he would just leave. Stewie must think he was a total idiot.

'Like she said, this isn't the place.' Stewie put his hand on Alex's arm. 'I think you need to cool down . . .'

'Like fuck I do!' Alex turned to Stewie and shoved him hard against the wall. Britt yelped and jumped between them, but Alex instantly seemed to realise that he had gone too far. 'Oh Christ, I'm so sorry . . .'

'It's okay, no harm done,' said Stewie. 'But you should leave.'

Alex just nodded. He looked defeated.

'I'll show you out,' said Britt.

Neither of them spoke on the way down to Reception, but when they reached the exit Alex took both of Britt's hands in his.

'I'm so sorry, Britt. It's no excuse, but I was watching you on TV this morning with Josh Bailey and you looked so bloody happy, and I realised I never make you smile that way any more.' His shoulders slumped. 'I'm just a jealous idiot. I'm sorry, Britt. For everything.'

And with that he pushed through the revolving doors and walked out onto the street. Britt thought about running after him, but she let him go.

Still shaken, she decided to walk back upstairs so she had time to compose herself. How dare Alex just burst in and start screaming at her? She hardly knew who he was any more. Perhaps it would be better if they just called it a day . . . But then she thought back to what Jessie had said yesterday, about how he might be struggling with her newfound fame. What if Jess was right? She hadn't even considered that this might be hard for Alex, too. She had a fleeting memory of them standing in the flat they had hoped to buy together all those months ago, back when they both had a job and a future, and remembered the surge of overwhelming love and happiness she'd felt when Alex had talked about starting a family. It was true that so much had happened between them since then that it was like a lifetime ago, but surely it was nothing that couldn't be fixed? She thought of Alex's face when he left, broken and crushed. Britt knew they had something worth fighting for.

She was so preoccupied with her thoughts that it took her a moment to notice the bouquet of flowers stuffed unceremoniously in the bin outside the green room. Britt looked more closely; it was a stunning bunch of lilies, still in their cellophane with the raffia ties intact. Why on earth would someone chuck them away? She was just wondering if it would be a bit skanky to take them out of the bin and put them in a vase in her dressing room, when she noticed a gift card on the floor. It was a little crumpled, as if it had been scrunched up. Looking around to check she wasn't being watched, she picked it up: '*To precious Rashida,*' it said. '*I hate seeing you so sad. What can I do to make you smile? JJB x* '

JJB. Joshua J. Bailey. Britt read the note again. The first thing that occurred to her was that she was now feeling more jealous of Rashida than ever. The second was that Alex never, ever bought her flowers any more. And the third was that this very sweet note certainly didn't sound like the work of a player.

Britt tucked the note in the bin with the flowers and hurried off to the studio as something else struck her: perhaps Stewie had been wrong about Josh after all . . .

25

'Britt, your interview's out!'

Jill, the show's press officer, burst into Britt's dressing room waving that morning's copy of *The Daily Splash*. Britt looked up warily, but Jill was smiling. That must be good. If the interview had been a total balls-up, then surely Jill wouldn't look quite so chirpy. Right . . . ?

It wasn't the first time that Britt had appeared in the press since joining *Rise & Shine*. A couple of weeks before, she had been flicking through a feature on 'Scarily Skinny Celebs' in *Closer* magazine. Her eye had been drawn to a bikini-clad girl running towards the camera, the unfortunate angle giving her the impression of a lollipop head and teeny-tiny frame. *God, she needs to put on a bit of weight*, thought Britt. She had looked a bit closer. *Hang on a minute* . . . The girl in the photo was her! It was an old modelling shot from years ago. How the hell had they managed to get hold of that? Then just a week later she had opened *Heat* to find a photo of herself that had obviously been snapped by one of the paparazzi who hung around the studio gates every morning. She was wearing denim shorts and there was a big arrow pointing to a slight dimpling on her thighs with the caption: 'Time to cut down on the croissants, Britt?' After she'd got over the shock of seeing her cellulite splashed across a magazine, Britt found the whole thing hilarious. Too thin one week, too fat the next.

But the interview with *The Daily Splash*, the newly launched tabloid newspaper that focused heavily on sport, TV and celebs, was the first time she had ever sat down and spoken to a journalist.

Britt had met the newspaper's TV editor for lunch earlier in the week at a discreet brasserie in a boutique hotel in Soho. The editor, a pale woman with dyed burgundy hair and lots of black eyeliner, had seemed friendly, but that did little to ease Britt's nerves. She was wary her every word and gesture was under scrutiny – and the three pre-interview espressos she'd downed in an attempt to stay focused did little to calm her raging jitters. Ordering food had been a particular nightmare. Fear had just about ruined Britt's appetite, so the only thing she felt like was a rocket and parmesan side salad. But then it suddenly occurred to her that the journalist would assume she was on some crazy fad diet if that was all she ate, so she ordered a chocolate fondant with ice-cream to follow, then felt mildly ridiculous for attempting to justify she had a normal healthy appetite and not an eating disorder. *Blimey it's no wonder celebrities got paranoid*, she thought, longing for the interview to be over.

So it was with shaking hands that Britt took the newspaper from Jill, who was still smiling broadly.

'Is it okay?' Britt asked nervously. Apart from anything else, she knew her mum had pre-ordered a dozen copies of the paper and she so wanted her to be proud.

'It's great, you did a terrific job.'

Britt breathed a sigh of relief.

'Apart from the bit at the end,' added Jill.

Oh, shit.

The interview took up a full double-page spread and was accompanied by one of her new *Rise & Shine* publicity shots, in which the stylist had put her in a purple wrap dress and her hair had been blow-dried into glossy waves. Britt hadn't been sure about the photo – her grin was so big and unnaturally white (courtesy of an over-zealous airbrush) that it almost felt like there should be a little star glinting on her front teeth – but Toby and the rest of the team had loved it. Perhaps cheesy was the look they had been aiming for. The article's banner headline read, 'THE GREAT BRITT-ISH BREAKFAST' with a smaller subhead beneath it: 'Why millions of viewers want to wake up with *Rise & Shine*'s new golden girl!'

Hmmm, that wasn't so bad. Britt began to read . . .

Britt Baxter is one of TV's fairytale success stories. The Carlisle-born babe, 26, was waitressing at a party when she offered a canapé to the boss of breakfast show Rise & Shine, *who offered her a job in return. And now, just two months on, the stunner with the megawatt smile has got women switching on for her daily fashion Style Spot – and men turned on by those oh-so-sexy curves!*

Britt cringed, although she supposed she should be grateful the journalist hadn't somehow found out the real story of how Toby discovered her. She skimmed through the next bit, which was all about her personal style and beauty tips, until she reached the part she'd been dreading. The standard love-life question . . .

Sorry to disappoint you fellas, but Britt – who lives in a luxurious London penthouse – currently has a boyfriend. So are marriage and babies on the cards? 'No, I'm still young and having fun right now,' she tells us.

One subject the former model remains tight-lipped on, however, is her relationship with Hollywood heart-throb Josh Bailey. For the past few weeks, the uber-cute couple has been steaming up our breakfast tables with their oh-so-hot chemistry. But when asked if romance is on the cards, Britt says with a suggestively naughty smile: 'Josh and I are just very good friends.'

A suggestively naughty smile? She wouldn't know how to do one of those if she even wanted to! Britt read on.

Britt reveals that she gets on brilliantly with all her new colleagues, including veteran TV presenter Cherry Smith. 'She's been around for years,' she says of Cherry, who Britt laughingly admits is old enough to be her mother . . .

Oh God. This was bad – very, very bad. Britt remembered gushing to the journalist about how she had the utmost respect for Cherry for her years of experience, but she certainly didn't say anything about her age. That would be sheer bloody madness. But it was the last paragraph that really twisted the knife.

Until recently Cherry was the undisputed queen of the Rise & Shine sofa, but with her cover-girl curves, youthful beauty and oodles of down-to-earth charm, it looks like Britt Baxter could be the future of breakfast TV.

Britt stared at the paper in open-mouthed horror. Cherry would be furious! And the same thought had obviously gone through Jill's mind as well.

'Don't worry, hon, I'll smooth things over with Cherry,' she said quickly. 'She knows how the press works.'

But Britt wasn't sure that Cherry would see it that way – and soon, far sooner than she would have liked – she had the chance to find out.

After Jill had left her dressing room, Britt headed over to Make-up and found Cherry sitting at the mirror, a copy of Britt's interview in *The Daily Splash* spread open on her lap.

'Well, if it isn't the future of breakfast TV,' she said as Britt came in. Anthea gave a tiny little mouse-like growl at her feet. Although Fran gave her a little smile when Cherry wasn't looking, Britt felt about as welcome as a vegan at an Angus Steakhouse. Clearly, some serious grovelling was called for.

'I am so sorry, Cherry, but that journalist just made that stuff up. Honestly, I would never have said that about your age, even if I thought it – which obviously I don't! Please, you have to believe me. I would never even dream of thinking I could replace you.'

For a moment it seemed as if Cherry hadn't heard her. She was staring at herself in the mirror, examining her face from different angles, smoothing down the fine lines around her eyes. Then she dabbed some gloss onto her lips, and turned to Britt with a smile.

'Don't worry, darling,' she said. 'I know what journalists are like. Never known to let the facts get in the way of a good story!'

'So you're not angry?'

'Of course not! Why would I get angry about something printed in here?' She – rather viciously – poked the newspaper on her knee. 'The only thing that *The Daily Splash* is good for is wrapping up dog poo. Isn't that right, Anthea sweetheart?' She tickled the dog at her feet.

But Britt still felt uneasy: the look on Cherry's face suggested she was far from happy.

26

Britt knew that Alex had been right about one thing: they needed to talk. So that afternoon they met up at a pub called The Queen's Head near their flat – *Better to meet on neutral territory*, thought Britt – for a long chat about their relationship. And by the end of an emotionally exhausting, often tearful two hours, Britt finally understood what was going on in Alex's head. Despite the problems of the last few months, they agreed that they still loved each other. Alex admitted that being made redundant and then fired had shattered his self-confidence to the extent that it seemed easier to just sit at home rather than risk further humiliation in the workplace. He confessed, just as Jessie had suspected, that he was finding it difficult to come to terms with Britt's sudden success and feared he was going to lose her to the likes of Brad Pitt now that she was famous. He told Britt he would do anything to make their relationship work and, to that end, he promised to find a job within a month, even if it was working in a bar; start exercising again (and shaving and washing); and move to the riverside penthouse without complaint, on the condition that he could have his rugby trophies on display. And finally, they agreed to have a 'date night' at least once a fortnight when they would go for cocktails or a fabulous dinner and spend some precious one on one time together, with optional hot sex to follow.

The inaugural date night was to be the following night.

Britt wanted everything to be perfect so decided to book a table at the hottest restaurant in town, the London branch of Los Angeles' top Japanese restaurant, Kobe. It was causing a riot for its £50 sea urchin sashimi and panoramic views of London from forty floors up. But when she phoned the restaurant the next day, the woman on the other end of the line virtually laughed in her face.

'There is a three-month wait for tables, I'm afraid, madam, but I can put you on the waiting list for tomorrow night,' she said. 'I should warn you though, there are already a number of people ahead of you.'

'Oh, right, thanks.' Britt was ready to hang up and think of Plan B but then something occurred to her. *Would she dare . . . ? Oh, what the hell.* 'Actually, I'm calling on behalf of Britt Baxter,' she said in what she hoped was an airily efficient tone. 'From *Rise & Shine*? It's for a special occasion and I know she would be very grateful if you could fit her in.'

There was silence at the end of the line. Britt felt like a prize plonker. Jessie was right, she *was* rubbish at this celebrity lark . . . But then something totally amazing happened.

'Just let me see what I can do,' said the woman, and she put Britt on hold. After a moment she was back. 'Right, I can offer Miss Baxter and her guest a table at 9 p.m. if that would be convenient?'

Britt was stunned. 'Thank you, yes, that would be

extremely convenient!' she said. 'I – sorry, *Miss Baxter* will look forward to seeing you later.' Bingo!

Now for her outfit. Britt had recently splashed out (or rather *invested*, as she liked to think of it) in a black Donna Karan jersey dress. On the hanger it looked conservative, even boring, with a slash neck, cap sleeves and hemline that reached just below the knee. But when she put it on it was transformed into quite possibly the sexiest dress of all time. By some magical fashion alchemy, it boosted her curves, nipped in her waist, gave her a bottom to rival J Lo's and a wiggle in her walk like Marilyn Monroe. Britt had been saving its debut for a special occasion – and what better time than that night?

Britt tied her hair back in a ponytail and kept her make-up minimal, focusing on strong brows and matte fuchsia lips in her favourite Nars shade, Schiap. She checked her reflection in the bedroom mirror and couldn't help smiling. For the first time, she actually looked like the sort of person who belonged in a riverside penthouse apartment.

Alex's face lit up when she walked into the living room. 'Wow, you look breathtaking,' he said.

He looked pretty bloody gorgeous himself in a black shirt and trousers, and she couldn't help kissing him, leaving a perfect pink lip-print on his cheek. As she rubbed off the smudge with a giggle, it occurred to her they hadn't got dressed up and had a big night out together for ages. Perhaps that was part of the problem – had they been taking each other for granted? Tonight was going to be just what the love doctor ordered.

A double toot of a car horn from outside signalled that their taxi had arrived.

'Your carriage awaits, Miss Baxter,' grinned Alex and offered her his arm.

Kobe occupied the entire top floor of a striking glass skyscraper in the City. Alex gave a low whistle of appreciation as they walked into the room. With its glossy red walls and enormous black lampshades that hovered like low-flying UFOs over the tables, it felt more like a billionaire's private nightclub than a restaurant. In the middle of the room was a circular sushi counter where a team of black-clad chefs waved long knives at ninja speed. And the clientele looked like they'd just stepped out of the pages of *Vanity Fair* magazine. Even in her killer frock, Britt felt like a country bumpkin next to the glossy glamazons at the bar in their tiny dresses, big heels and even bigger hair.

Alex obviously sensed her unease. 'You're the most beautiful woman in this room,' he whispered, slipping his arm round her waist. 'And I am so proud to be with you.'

They were shown to a table right next to the window and before they'd even had a chance to look through the menu, a waiter brought over a couple of lychee martinis with rose petals floating on the top. 'Compliments of the manager, Miss Baxter.'

'Wow,' grinned Alex, 'I'm sticking with you, kid.' He raised his glass to Britt. 'Here's to you, beautiful.'

Britt returned his smile. 'No, here's to *us*.'

After two more martinis they ordered a bottle of champagne. Very soon the delicious buzz of the drinks combined with the magical views of London spread out below them, twinkling with a million lights, made Britt feel like she was floating on a cloud in the night sky. And then the food started to arrive: an endless succession of tiny jewel-like morsels served on huge black plates.

'Here, try this.' Alex picked up a deep red sliver of tuna sashimi in his chopsticks, dipped it in soy sauce and offered it to Britt. Their eyes locked and she felt a shiver of happiness. It was a perfect night.

They had finished the champagne and were trying to decide whether to share the flourless chocolate cake with green tea ice-cream or the baked sesame pineapple when a man strolled up to their table. He had loosened his tie and his cheeks were flushed. Britt had actually noticed him already; he had been sitting at a nearby table with a group of similarly suited men who had been getting progressively louder and rowdier as the night had gone on.

'Hi, Britt,' he said, in a voice that sounded like it was the product of a very expensive public school. 'I just wanted to tell you that I'm a bloody massive fan. I think you're, you know, totally fit.'

'Um, that's really kind of you, thank you.' Britt was still working out how best to react in these situations, but figured being friendly was probably the best bet.

'You really are bloody gorgeous, you know,' said the man, grinning woozily. Then he turned to Alex. 'You're a lucky bloke.'

'Thanks,' said Alex shortly. He looked decidedly unimpressed. 'Now if you don't mind . . . ?'

But the man didn't move. 'Can I get a quick photo with you, Britt?'

She looked at Alex, who shrugged dismissively.

'Okay, but then I really must get back to my dinner.' Britt stood up and the man threw one arm round her shoulder, pulling her up close to him, and in the other held his phone out in front of them and snapped a picture. Then he kissed her sloppily on the cheek and Britt giggled out of sheer embarrassment and discomfort. A few tables away, his equally posh friends whooped their approval. She stole a glance at Alex again; his jaw was rigid with tension. She tried to pull away, but the man kept a tight hold. Desperately uncomfortable but not wanting to be rude, Britt just carried on smiling, trying to steer clear of the man's breath, which was rank with stale champagne fumes.

'All done?' she said pointedly.

'Yeah, thanks, baby.' He reluctantly let her go. 'You really are smoking hot, you know . . .'

'That's very sweet of you, thanks. Bye.'

Finally the man sauntered off and Britt sat down, rolling her eyes at Alex as if to say, *What can you do?*

But Alex looked furious. 'What was all that about for Christ's sake?' he hissed.

'I'm sorry?'

'You were flirting with that bloke.'

It seemed so ludicrous that Britt actually laughed.

But Alex wasn't joking. 'I saw you, going all girly and giggly when he kissed you. It was pathetic.'

'Well, what was I supposed to do, slap him round the face?'

'Yes.'

'Come on, Al, please, let's not spoil our night. I was just being friendly.'

'No, you weren't. You were all over him, pushing your tits in his face.'

Britt was stunned. 'What the hell has got into you?'

'Screw this,' said Alex, his face distorted with anger. 'I'm not going to sit here and let you make a fool out of me any more. Enjoy the rest of your night. I'm sure your new friends over there would be happy to entertain you.'

And with that he threw down his napkin and stalked towards the exit.

Britt watched him go, convinced he would turn and come back to the table, but he went straight to the lift and disappeared without a second glance. Frozen with shock and disbelief, Britt felt tears pricking her eyes. *What just happened there?* For a moment she wondered if she actually *had* been flirting with the man, but the idea was ridiculous. She glanced around the restaurant; she might have imagined it, but it felt like all the other diners had been watching what happened and were now whispering and pointing in her direction. Her cheeks flushed with shame. How could Alex do this to her?

'Can I get you anything else?' The waiter had materialised at her side.

'No, just the bill, thanks,' said Britt, hoping that he hadn't noticed the tear fall down her cheek.

An hour later, Britt was lying in bed, staring at the bedroom ceiling. Alex hadn't come home. There had been no reply to her increasingly desperate messages and when she'd tried phoning him, her calls had gone straight through to voicemail. Britt replayed the night's events over in her mind, trying to work out what had gone so badly wrong. She looked at the clock: 2 a.m. She would have to get up in a few hours' time. Feeling horribly lonely and wondering where on earth Alex could be, Britt rolled onto her side and began to cry again.

27

When Britt's alarm went off at 4.30 a.m. she was still alone in bed. Now she was seriously worried; what if something had happened to Alex? His phone was still turned off. She imagined him lying in a gutter somewhere, beaten or stabbed; he could be hurt.

By the time she got to the studio she was in such a state that when Stewie stuck his head round her dressing-room door at 6 a.m. to see if she wanted a coffee she burst into tears again.

'Hey, what's the matter, doll?' He came straight over and put his arms round her. 'Can I help?'

Between choked-up sobs, Britt told him about their row and Alex's subsequent disappearance.

'What if he's been attacked,' she wailed, 'or even murdered!'

But Stewie didn't seem at all concerned. 'Blimey, us blokes can be proper wankers, can't we? Don't worry, Britt, he's a big boy. I bet you fifty quid he'll turn up later today with his tail between his legs and a stonking hangover.'

With a rush of relief, Britt realised that Stewie was probably right. Alex was six foot three inches of former rugby player. He was unlikely to have been mugged.

'He's probably on his way home right now,' continued Stewie, 'if he hasn't got back already, that is. Nah, the only thing I'd be worrying about, if I were you, is how hard you're going to kick him for putting you through this.'

Despite herself, Britt giggled and wiped away her tears. 'Thank you, Stewie. You're a star. Right, shall we go and get that coffee?'

But just then her phone rang. It was Alex's name that flashed up on the screen. She showed the phone to Stewie, who just shrugged. Britt let it go to voicemail. A split-second later it started ringing again, and then a third time. Clearly, he wasn't going to give up.

'I'd better get this,' she said apologetically.

'No worries. Give him hell.'

As soon as Stewie had gone, Britt answered the call.

'What?' she snapped. She was no longer worried or upset; she was livid.

'Britt, please, don't hang up,' said Alex.

'Where the bloody hell have you been?'

'Around. I don't know. In a few bars.' He sounded terrible.

'Alex, you're drunk.'

'Yeah, and who the hell are you – the fun police?'

'How . . . *dare* you?' spluttered Britt. Suddenly, something snapped inside her and the weeks of worry and resentment came flooding out. 'I don't know if you've noticed, but for the last few months I've been working my backside off to keep a roof over our heads, trying to be sympathetic about your total inability to find a job, while all you've done is mope around the house watching daytime TV! Right now you have a more meaningful relationship with *Loose Women* than you do with me. We never have sex and when we do, you can't even finish what you've started half the time because you're drunk. In fact, it's been so long since you got anywhere near satisfying me that I'm seriously considering buying a vibrator. So don't you *dare* talk to me about fun.' There was a stunned silence at the other end of the phone. She'd gone too far but she couldn't stop herself. 'And another thing,' Britt went on, 'any idiot would be able to see that I wasn't flirting with that dickhead in the restaurant last night, apart from my boyfriend who apparently seems to think I'll jump into bed with just about anyone!' She was so angry that her voice disappeared in an outraged squeak.

Eventually, Alex managed to speak. 'I'm sorry about last night, it was unforgivable. I just got so jealous, I . . . I lost it. It was a really shitty thing to do, I know that.'

'And what possible reason have I ever given you to be jealous?'

'Josh Bailey,' he said immediately – he didn't even have to think about it. 'You don't know what it's like, sitting at home watching the two of you together on TV. It's so bloody obvious that the pair of you fancy the pants off each other.'

Britt didn't say anything; at this point she wasn't sure what she could say.

'Just tell me I'm not going completely insane here, Britt.' Alex's voice was pleading. 'Admit it, you fancy him.'

'Okay, I find him attractive,' she said. She never could lie to Alex. 'But that doesn't mean I'm shagging him, because I'm not.'

'I bloody well knew it!'

Britt felt utterly exhausted; all the fight had gone out of her. She was tired of fighting and sick of trying to fix something that was clearly broken.

'What's happened to us?' she said, trembling. 'We used to have the most amazing relationship. Do you remember what you used to say? 'I've always thought you were The One, and now I know we're The Two.' I used to think that was so lovely, and you were absolutely right – we completed each other. All I wanted was to marry you and have your babies.' Oh God, she was going to cry again. Britt took a deep breath, desperate to hold it together. 'But we can't go on hurting each other like this. I . . . I'm sorry Al, I don't think I can do this any more.'

And with that she punched the 'End call' button. The phone started ringing again almost immediately but she turned it off and threw it in her bag.

Britt felt horribly empty. For all his faults, she still loved Alex, but she knew that she was right: there was no way they could go on like this. She glanced at the clock over the mirror and then at her reflection: she would be live to the nation at 8.30 a.m., just a couple of hours' time, and right now her face was so red and puffy from all the crying she looked like she was suffering an allergic reaction. *Right, sort yourself out, Baxter.* First she would get a coffee from the green room and then she would go to Make-up and let Fran deal with the disaster zone that was her face.

But when she opened her dressing-room door she bumped straight into the one person she really would have liked to avoid: Josh Bailey. Even in an old grey sweatshirt and black track-pants with a frayed Chicago Bulls baseball cap he still looked gorgeous. In fact, if anything, just-got-out-of-bed Josh was even sexier than the camera-ready version.

'Hey, are you okay?' he asked. He looked touchingly concerned at the sight of her.

'Oh, hi, yes, all fine,' she managed. 'Just off to Make-up.'

'I think Fran will be able to wait. Come on, let's grab some breakfast from the canteen and have a chat.'

The last thing Britt wanted was to sit opposite Josh, she was still reeling from the trauma of the past twelve hours.

'So, do you want to talk about it?' asked Josh, once they'd got coffee and toast and sat down at a quiet corner table.

'I'd rather not, if that's okay.' She grimaced. 'Boyfriend troubles.'

'Ah, yes, Britt Baxter's mysterious unnamed boyfriend.' He took a sip of coffee and leaned back in his chair. 'Well, if it's any consolation, I've been having those as well.'

'Boyfriend troubles?' she spluttered. Christ, perhaps she had totally misread the signs and Scott had been right about him after all . . .

'Oh, yeah,' said Josh, staring ruefully at his cup, seemingly lost in his thoughts. 'Jeez, relationships can be hard work . . .'

Still none the wiser as to whether he was gay or not (and if he was, what the hell was going on with Rashida?) Britt decided she would need to tread carefully. 'So, what sort of, um, boyfriend troubles are we talking about here?'

Josh suddenly looked up at her, surprise etched across his face. 'Boyfriend troubles? Oh, man, we've got our wires crossed here.' He started to chuckle. 'Britt, I'm not . . . I mean, I can assure you I don't have a boyfriend. I was talking about *girlfriend* troubles. Well, not even those actually. It's Rashida.'

'Oh, yes,' said Britt, startled by the surge of relief at the discovery that he was straight after all. 'I heard that the two of you were dating.'

'But we're not, that's the whole point!' Josh took off his cap and ran his hand through his hair. 'Rashida's a very sweet girl, but she's rather fragile. Look, can I talk to you about something? It's a bit . . . *delicate*. I'd really appreciate your advice.'

Britt nodded. Despite herself, she was desperate to know what was going on between the two of them.

'Okay, so a few months ago, Rashida got it into her head that there was something going on between us. We'd always got on well and, yes, I know I can be a bit flirty, but it had all been completely innocent – at least it was on my part. But suddenly Rashida seemed to think we were dating. She'd phone me day and night, demanding to know what I was doing. She started sending me long, rambling love letters which she'd sign off 'The Future Mrs Bailey'.'

Britt was stunned – Rashida really didn't seem the bunny-boiler type. But then she thought back to the time she'd overheard Rashida on the phone to Josh and just how clingy and desperate to please she had sounded. And when Britt had spotted them arguing in the stairwell the other day, Rashida had certainly looked like a woman possessed.

'But I'd never even kissed her!' said Josh. 'So in the end, I just stopped answering her calls. It just seemed like the kindest thing to do, because by this point Rashida was living in a dream world and she could spin anything I said into some crazy fantasy. The calls eventually stopped, but since then she's been so mad at me that it has started to become a problem at work, so the other day I sent her some flowers. You know, just to tell her that I care and that I'm there if she needs to talk. I didn't know what else to do. The atmosphere has been terrible.'

Britt *had* noticed a change in Rashida over the past few weeks. She had been strangely moody and snappy, even making one of the new runners cry when they got her breakfast order wrong, which was totally out of character. Suddenly, everything started to fall into place. It looked like Stewie *was* wrong about Josh, after all.

'Didn't you speak to Toby about all this?' asked Britt.

'I didn't want to get Rashida in trouble. She means well. There's no malice in the girl – she's just lonely.'

Then Josh smiled a sad, lovely smile and Britt had to stop herself reaching over and wrapping her arms around him.

When Britt got home later that morning, Alex was sitting at the kitchen table. His hair was wet from the shower, but the dark shadows under his eyes and shaking hands betrayed the state he was in. He leapt up when she came in, as if he had been waiting for her.

'Please, before you say anything, just hear me out,' he said. He pulled out the chair next to him, but Britt shook her head.

'I'll stay standing if you don't mind,' she said.

Alex slowly sat back down and put his head in his hands. 'I'm so, so sorry. I'm a drunk, stupid, jealous arsehole and I wouldn't blame you for dumping me. But please, you can't doubt for a moment how much I love you.' He looked up at her imploringly. 'You're my life, Britt. All I want is to make you happy.'

'You've had a pretty funny way of showing that recently.'

'I know, I know. I've been a total loser. All I can say is that I'll change, I promise. I'll sort myself out, just give me one last chance.'

She looked at his face, his eyes wide with desperation. She wanted to believe him. Every relationship had its hard times. That's why they put all that, 'For better, for worse' stuff in the marriage vows, right? Trouble was, they weren't even married yet, and right now the worse already far outweighed the better.

She sat down next to him. 'One last chance,' she said finally. 'But this time we have to make it work and if we don't, we call it quits. Okay?'

Alex looked like he'd just been told he'd won the lottery. He leaned over and swept her up into an enormous hug. 'Thank you, thank you, so much,' he murmured into her hair. 'I won't let you down, I promise.'

Then he pulled away and rummaged in his pocket, bringing out a flat, black box about the size of his palm.

'This is for you. To show how much you mean to me.'

Britt opened it up and was stunned at what she found inside. It was a pendant of rose quartz surrounded by tiny diamonds, the exact one she'd fallen in love with in a magazine. She'd pointed it out to Alex, but hadn't dreamt for a moment he would buy it. It was absolutely breathtaking – and breathtakingly expensive.

She felt the smooth, cold stone between her fingers. 'Alex, it's beautiful, but . . .'

'Don't you like it?'

She looked up at him. 'How on earth did you afford it?'

'You don't need to worry. You deserve it.'

'Really, I want to know,' said Britt gently. 'It's such a lot of money. Where did you get it from?'

Alex looked agitated. 'I thought it was rude to ask that sort of thing?' he muttered.

'It's important to me. Please.'

Alex sighed. 'I . . . I borrowed the money from my parents,' he said eventually, but he wouldn't meet her gaze.

Britt nodded, but didn't say anything. She had known Alex for long enough to be able to tell when he was lying.

28

The following Saturday Britt woke up at 6 a.m. She had the prospect of a much-needed lie-in, but she was still up at the crack of dawn. *Pesky bloody body clock . . .* Alex was still fast asleep, so she slipped on some Uggs and a cardigan over her pyjamas and then trotted down to the newsagents at the end of the road for some milk and the morning papers.

'Morning, Ahmed,' she said cheerily to the shop's owner, who was busy unbundling stacks of newspapers. It usually took Britt a good five minutes to get out of the shop – only once Ahmed had finished chatting – but today he just gave her a brief, embarrassed smile and then seemed to remember he had something very important to attend to at the back of the shop.

I suppose I do look a bit of a sight, thought Britt, looking down at her pink flannel PJs. Thank goodness the paparazzi didn't venture as far south as Clapham. She would have to buy herself a glamorous full-length coat for the weekend newspaper run once they moved into the new place, which the agent had assured her was going to be ready to move into in a couple of weeks. She'd seen a gorgeous camel MaxMara one she might splurge on on Net-A-Porter that would do the job perfectly. Britt smiled to herself. It was still a huge novelty that she could afford to treat herself to such lovely things.

She had picked up a carton of semi-skimmed milk and was just browsing through the papers on the shelf when she noticed it: a photo of herself on the top right of the front page of *The Daily Splash*. She grabbed the paper and looked more closely. It was only a tiny picture, but it was the words that accompanied it that made Britt's stomach lurch: 'BREAKFAST BRITT'S SEX SHOCKER: See page 5'.

A feeling of panic churning her insides, she frantically scrambled through the pages to find the story – and what she saw made her gasp in shock. Most of the page was taken up by a photo of her wearing skimpy black underwear, kneeling on a bed while sucking seductively on a lollipop. The photo had been taken years ago, as part of a modelling shoot for a tacky high street lingerie chain. Britt remembered it as one of the less enjoyable jobs of her career: the photographer had been a bit of a perv and the scratchy g-string knickers and bra that pushed her boobs up to her chin were definitely not the sort of thing she'd ever wear. Not that anyone looking at the picture over breakfast this morning would realise any of that. They'd just assume she was a bit of a slapper with crap taste in pants.

Britt tore her eyes away from the photo and scanned the bold black type of the headline: 'SEX-MAD TV BREAKFAST BABE: I'm desperate to bed Josh Bailey!'

For a moment she felt like she was about to be sick. She swallowed noisily. She began to read the article with shaking hands:

She might be giving Britain's fellas a good morning every day of the working week, but Rise & Shine *babe Britt Baxter has confessed that she hasn't had sex for* MONTHS!

In a sensational heart-to-heart with pals, the foxy TV star, 26, claimed that she was so desperate to be satisfied that she was going to buy a SEX TOY.

'I'm seriously considering buying a vibrator,' she cheekily admitted.

But the top-rated breakfast show's millions of viewers will be stunned to learn that what the curvy star really wants is a little snap, crackle and pop with fellow presenter Josh Bailey.

Although Britt has insisted that they are just good friends, The Daily Splash *can exclusively reveal that in private she has made no secret of her insatiable LUST for the Hollywood hotty.*

'Yes, I find Josh attractive,' Carlisle-born Britt gushed, hinting to pals that she plans to SEDUCE the former movie star.

Ex-model Britt also admitted that her three-year relationship with her hunky boyfriend, former rugby star, Alex, is on the rocks.

'All I wanted was to marry him and have his babies,' she said. 'But I don't think I can do it any more.'

According to our source, the couple's relationship started to crumble after Britt shot to stardom earlier this year, and pals blame her jealous behaviour for their troubles.

The Daily Splash *has learnt that in a shocking rant last week the paranoid presenter ACCUSED her boyfriend of bedding the stars of ITV show* Loose Women, *outrageously claiming that Alex was having a 'meaning-ful relationship' with at least one or more of the popular female presenters.*

'Britt is behaving like a woman possessed,' said a friend. 'We're all worried about her.'

A spokesman for the Loose Women *stars declined to comment.*

Britt barely noticed the newspaper sliding from her hands and fluttering into a heap on the floor. She stood frozen in shock for what felt like a lifetime. She noticed Ahmed looking at her from behind a stack of tinned peas. Still standing there, she was unable to move until the whirl-wind churning through her mind gradually began to form itself into discernable thoughts. *Where had they got this from? Who were these 'pals' that had made up such a pack of lies? Could she sue? Would she ever be able to face Josh again? And what the hell was Alex going to think?*

And then, with a rush of horror that hit her with the force of a jumbo jet, everything fell into place. Alex! She thought back to the argument they'd had the other morn-ing and the awful things she'd said in the heat of the moment: *'Right now you have a more meaningful rela-tionship with* Loose Women *than you do with me . . . It's been so long since you got anywhere near satisfying me that I'm seriously considering buying a vibrator . . . All I wanted was to marry you and have your babies.'* And the killer blow, the one that really put the cherry on the whole awful cake: *'Okay, I find Josh Bailey attractive.'*

Jesus Christ . . . it could only have come from Alex! The journalist might have added their own grubby spin on things, but the quotes at least were lifted word for word from the phone conversation they'd had last week. Alex'd sold her out to *The Daily Splash* – and for what? A few hundred lousy quid? It was the lowest sort of betrayal. How could he do this to her? And then something else occurred to her. *The pendant.* So that was where he had got the money to pay for it!

'Are you alright, dear?' An old lady was standing next to her, looking at her with an expression of concern.

'Yes . . . yes, I'm fine,' Britt managed. 'Thanks very much.' She noticed that the woman was holding a copy of *The Daily Splash*. What if her mum got hold of a copy? The thought made her feel like she was going to throw up. Molly usually only read the *Daily Telegraph*, but if she saw her daughter's name on the cover she was bound to take a look. Britt glanced over at the huge stack of newspapers and briefly considered buying up every copy, then realised she only had two quid in her pocket. Besides, she couldn't very well get to every shop in the country, could she? Britt gathered up the pages from the pile at her feet, slammed her money on the counter and ran out of the door.

Alex was still asleep when she got back to the bedroom. She flicked on the light and he groaned and stirred.

'Ouch, turn that off would you, babe?' he grumbled. 'Bit much first thing . . .'

But Britt kept the light on. She stood at the end of the bed, her fists clenched by her side to stop herself lashing out in fury.

'How could you do this to me?' she asked, her voice low and trembling.

Alex pushed himself up on his elbows and fumbled his hair out of his eyes, squinting under the bright light.

'Do what? What are you talking about?'

'This,' she spat, throwing the newspaper on the bed. Alex picked it up and started reading. His expression gradually changed from confusion to shock and finally to horror. Britt had no idea he was such a talented actor.

'How did you think you'd get away with it, Alex?' She was literally shaking with rage. 'Does our relationship really mean so little to you? I had no idea you could stoop so low. This is the worst thing anyone has ever done to me.'

But Alex was ashen-faced. 'Britt, I had nothing to do with this! You have to believe me.'

'You've got a nerve! How can you deny it when it's there in black and white? Those quotes couldn't have come from anyone but you. I will never forgive you for this. *Never.*'

'But it wasn't me, Britt! How could you think it was? I would never do this to you – I wouldn't do it to my worst enemy! You must know, deep down, that I wouldn't do something like this. Someone must have heard.'

He jumped out of bed and reached out for her, but Britt furiously shook him off. She had never hated anyone more.

'I know it was you, Alex. Those quotes came from a private conversation between the two of us. And the pendant – how else could you have paid for it?'

'I told you, I borrowed the money from my parents! I know I've been useless recently and I wanted to get you something to apologise. Please, Britt, you have to believe me!'

Britt shook her head. 'Get out,' she said quietly,

backing towards the bedroom door. 'Pack up your things, and get out of my flat.'

'You can't be serious . . . ?'

'Just get the hell out,' she screamed, breaking into hysterical sobs, 'or I'm calling the police!'

29

Britt wasn't sure how long she'd been lying on the sofa, crying into the cushions, when the phone rang, but it must have been at least an hour after Alex had left. He had stood at the front door, tears rolling down his face, his rucksack crammed with his possessions at his feet, and begged her to believe him, but she had told him to get out and never to contact her again. She knew it was the only thing to do after the way he'd treated her, but right now it felt like her heart was breaking from the pain.

When her phone rang the first time she ignored it; the second time she looked at the screen. It was Jessie.

'Britt, I've seen the paper. Are you okay?'

Britt collapsed into a fresh round of wails.

'Shh, don't worry, love, this will have blown over by tomorrow,' said Jessie. 'No-one believes the stuff they read in those papers, anyway. Come on, pet, don't cry.'

'It's not that . . . I'm just . . . Oh, Jess, it was Alex,' Britt sobbed. 'He sold the story to *The Daily Splash*.'

'You're joking!' spluttered Jessie. 'Are you sure that he's behind it?'

'He has to be. There's no other way the papers could have got all that detail. There was stuff in the article lifted virtually word for word from this big row we had the other day. He's had no money, but now he's buying me flash presents – it all makes sense! Oh, Jess, can you believe it?'

There was a silence at the end of the line.

'No, I'm sorry, I can't,' said Jessie finally. 'Whatever his faults, there is no way that Alex would do that to you. He's a good guy – and he adores you. There must be another explanation for how this crap got in the paper. Couldn't you have been overheard?'

Britt sniffed and wiped her eyes. 'Jess! Will you please listen to me? There is no way it could have been anyone else. No-one else could have known the things that were printed in the article! Don't you understand, it was a private conversation!'

'What does Alex say about it?'

'Well, of course he says he didn't do it. But he wouldn't admit it, would he?'

There was another pause as Jessie obviously tried to make sense of what had happened. 'Right, I'm coming straight over,' she said eventually. 'But I think you should believe Alex, I really do.'

What the hell was wrong with Jessie? Britt saw red. 'What about taking my side for a change?' she asked furiously. 'All you've done over the past few months is stick up for Alex over and over again. What about supporting me? I'm the one whose life has been totally ruined here! I'm beginning to think you prefer him to me! I mean, do you fancy him or something?'

'That was low, Britt,' said Jessie quietly.

'Yeah, well, I meant it. Don't bother coming over – or calling back,' she stammered. She just didn't know what to think or who to trust any more.

Britt spent the rest of the afternoon holed up in the flat, torturing herself over and over with the thought of people around the country reading the story and laughing at her for being a sex-crazed psycho who thought her boyfriend was shagging the cast of a TV talk show. Christ, what would Molly think? If her mum didn't see a copy of the paper, someone was bound to mention it to her. Larkbridge was a tiny place – you couldn't go for a wee without old Mrs Reynolds in the village shop telling everyone about it. Britt hated the thought of her mum getting upset, especially after she'd been ill. As for what Josh would think of the whole thing – well, she hadn't even let herself explore that area of potential humiliation yet. It was too painful to even think about.

Looking at her mobile, Britt realised she'd had a couple of missed calls from Stewie, but he hadn't left a message and she couldn't face speaking to anyone from work right now. She would save that ordeal for Monday.

At 6 p.m. Britt ordered an Indian takeaway as she couldn't face leaving the flat. But she was convinced the motorbike delivery boy gave her a weird look that suggested he'd seen the article, and it killed any appetite she'd had. In the end, Kate Moss had most of a chicken dhansak and a poppadum for her tea.

Britt had had no idea that cats liked mango chutney quite so much.

That night, she watched *Sex and the City* DVDs back to back and drank a whole bottle of white wine that she hadn't even bothered chilling. By 10 p.m. she had fallen into an uneasy sleep.

Britt woke early the next morning and stretched out in bed, enjoying the sensation of the soft pillows and cool sheets. *Mmm, Sunday,* she thought happily, *a whole day of doing nothing.* But then she realised that Alex wasn't there and that actually, her head was aching quite a lot.

It was bad enough that she was hungover, but suddenly the horrible events of the previous day came crashing down on her. If anything, Britt felt worse than she had yesterday now that she was beginning to consider the implications of that horrible, scummy newspaper article. Her relationship with Alex was over – and in the worst possible way. And what if she got fired from *Rise & Shine*? She longed to call Jessie, but she was still angry about what she'd said yesterday. So she reached for her phone on the bedside table and called her mum. If anyone could make her feel better, it was Molly.

'Britt, darling, how lovely to hear from you! How are you?'

She wasn't surprised that her mum hadn't seen the story; after all, she didn't read this paper, but she was quite surprised no 'concerned neighbour' had dropped by with the story. Without going into the gory details (she doubted her mum would even know what a vibrator was – she certainly hoped not) Britt told her about the newspaper story and Alex's betrayal. But Britt didn't get the supportive shoulder she had hoped for. Her mum was worried about her, sure, but Molly was adamant that Alex couldn't be to blame.

'Oh, no, he wouldn't do something like that,' she said instantly.

Britt immediately lost her rag. *God, it was Jessie mark two!* 'Why does everyone seem to think Saint Alex couldn't possibly be responsible?' asked Britt furiously.

'Because he's a decent man and he loves you more than anything in the world,' said Molly.

'Well, that just goes to show how sheltered you are up there in the sodding sticks,' stormed Britt.

'Britt, there is no need for language like that.'

'Yes, there is!' Britt snapped. 'Mum, you can just be so flipping naïve! You have absolutely no idea what all this is like for me.'

'Come on, love, I was just—'

'Oh, forget it.' And she slammed the phone down, feeling more desolate than ever.

Britt hardly ever argued with her mum and instantly felt terrible about the way she'd spoken to her, but it seemed like everyone had forgotten that *she* was the one whose life was spiralling out of control! She reached out to give Kate Moss a cuddle but she dashed off the bed and out of the room. Great, even the cat was giving her the cold shoulder.

Britt pulled the duvet over her head, feeling like she had no-one left to turn to. One thought kept coming back to her: would she be fired on the spot?

30

Britt had thought about phoning in sick on Monday morning, but she was going to have to face everyone at some point and there was no point in putting it off.

Things did not start off well. She pulled up outside the studio just as Ken was getting out of his car. She considered asking Reg, her driver, to go around the block a few times until the coast was clear, but Ken had already seen her and was waiting for her on the pavement.

'Hi, Ken,' she said sheepishly, walking over.

'Well, well, well, I always suspected you were a bit of a minx,' he sniggered as he tried to kiss her on the lips. By now experience had taught Britt to dodge at the last minute, so he got her cheek instead. But he didn't let her brush-off stop him. 'Shall we?' He offered her his arm and she had no choice but to let him accompany her into the studio. 'May I just say, you looked just ravishing in that photo in the newspaper. Quite spectacular. Brightened up my morning no end . . .'

So much for making a low-key entrance, cringed Britt. Thankfully, Ken was eventually stopped by a runner and she was able to head into the studio alone, but not before he was able to take one parting shot: 'Now, you know where I am if you need me, ducky,' he said with a lascivious wink and a nudge that was straight out of a *Carry On* film. 'No need to waste your money on a vibrator, is there now? Eh, love? Eh?'

Britt watched him walk away, chuckling to himself. 'In your dreams, Chudleigh,' she muttered crossly, under her breath.

It was a horrible feeling walking along the corridors and knowing everyone who greeted her had seen the article. The worst part was that they now all knew she had the hots for Josh Bailey. It reminded her of when she was a gawky fourteen-year-old with a crush on the school hunk, a sixth former called Sam who had never looked twice at her. One of her so-called friends had scrawled, 'BRITT WANTS TO SHAG SAM' in foot-high letters across the common-room window. When Sam saw it he had laughed and said, so everyone could hear, 'What, that skinny kid with the frizzy hair and goofy teeth? Ugh, no thanks!' Britt hadn't lived down the humiliation for weeks. The thought of her workmates having a good old laugh over the fact that she fancied Josh but didn't have a hope in hell with him made her want to dash out of the studio, never to return again.

She was about to reach the safety of her dressing room when she spotted Toby standing outside the green room. Fighting the urge to flee in the opposite direction, she took a deep breath and walked over. *Might as well face the music now . . .*

'Ah, Britt, hi.' Was it her imagination, or did he look pissed off with her? 'Bit of a rough weekend in the papers, I noticed.'

'Yes, I'm so sorry about all that, Toby,' said Britt. 'It was total nonsense, but it turns out my boyfriend – or rather ex-boyfriend – had sold the paper a few quotes.'

'Right, I see. Well, I'll speak to Jill in the press office, get her to call the news editor at *The Splash* and kick up a bit of a fuss. Everyone gets it at some point, though. Goes with the territory, I'm afraid.'

His phone bleeped and he glanced at the screen. 'Sorry, Britt, I've got a meeting. Just be aware that now you're in the public eye you're considered fair game by the papers, so if there are any skeletons in your cupboard then I recommend you have a thorough clear-out. Okay?'

She nodded miserably and watched as he strode away down the corridor. Perhaps she'd imagined it, but it seemed like Toby couldn't get away from her fast enough. She couldn't really blame him: she'd single-handedly turned *Rise & Shine* into a laughing stock.

Britt got to her dressing room and shut the door behind her, relieved not to have to face anyone else for the time being. Then she noticed a small, folded-up piece of paper on the floor that had obviously been pushed under the door. It had her name written on it. Intrigued, she picked up the note and read it: '*Don't worry, I know* The Daily Splash *is 100% bullshit. They once wrote that I was marrying Graham Norton in Britain's first gay Catholic wedding. JJB* x ' And there was a P.S. at the bottom: '*If it's any consolation, I find you attractive, too.*'

Britt couldn't help but smile. Incredibly, Josh didn't seem to think of her as 'that skinny kid with the frizzy hair and goofy teeth' after all. She knew he was probably only saying the stuff about finding her attractive so she didn't feel such an idiot, but despite the heavy cloud that had been hanging over her since she'd split from Alex, her stomach gave a little flip of excitement.

'Hey, anybody home?' Stewie's sunny blond head appeared around the door. Britt beckoned him in.

'I tried phoning you at the weekend,' he said.

'I know, sorry not to call back.' Britt shoved Josh's note in her pocket. 'I wasn't really in a state to talk. Turns out that Alex sold those quotes to the paper.'

'Jeez, really?' Stewie's eyebrows shot up. 'What a complete tosser! You okay, mate?'

'Yeah, well, I've finished with him now. It's for the best.' Britt said it with more conviction than she felt. The anger had begun to fade, but there was still a horrible ache of sadness in her chest every time she thought of Alex.

'It gets easier, I promise.' Stewie put his arms round her and drew her to him in a friendly hug. It felt so nice to have some physical contact after her horrible weekend that she rested her head on his shoulder and relaxed into the embrace. He had this knack of making her feel safe and protected, like the big brother she never had.

'I've got an idea,' Stewie said suddenly. 'How about I take you out after the show has finished today and get you blinding drunk? We'll go on an old-school pub-crawl. By the end of it, you'll be too sick to worry about all that bull in the papers.'

'Deal,' she said with a smile.

Thankfully, most of the people she worked with seemed happy to ignore the fact that Britt had been outed as a sex-mad hussy in the weekend's papers, and Josh was out on location with Rashida, so the morning's show passed off largely uneventfully.

Britt was rounding off her Style Spot with an item on home pedicures: '. . . and so, if you want pretty feet all summer, it looks like exfoliation is the way to go. I'll certainly be getting out my trusty peppermint foot scrub tonight! Now it's back to Ken . . .'

'Thank you, Britt,' smiled Ken, shuffling his papers. 'And may I say you're looking very pretty this morning in that lovely flowery dress.'

'Why, thank you, Ken.' She did a little bob and a twirl. 'It's called a tea-dress.'

'Ah, well, now I know,' he chuckled. 'Doesn't Britt look lovely today, Cherry? Really young and summery.'

'She does indeed,' said Cherry with a rictus grin. 'And Britt will be back on the sofa with Josh tomorrow, which I'm sure she's *very* excited about.'

Meow.

Britt did her best to style it out. 'I certainly am, as Josh will have all the gossip about next weekend's Golden Globe Awards, and I'll be giving you my predictions on the red carpet style winners and losers. It's going to be a great show!'

As they cut to the ads, Britt heard Toby giving Cherry a hard time over talkback and worried at what the repercussions might be.

Britt and Stewie kicked off their pub-crawl at The Bay Tree, a favourite with the floor crew because it was situated just across the road from the studio. It was a proper old man's pub with fruit machines, a jar of pickled eggs on the bar and only two beers on tap: Heineken or Guinness. Britt was wearing a grey marl T-shirt with a little floral skirt and a baseball cap pulled low over her face.

'It's my incognito look,' she laughed as they carried their pints to a table in the beer garden round the back.

Stewie snorted. 'You should put away those legs if you don't want anyone to look at you, mate.'

They sat in the bright May sunshine, sipping their pints and eating dry roasted peanuts out of little foil packets. There were only a couple of other people in the garden – tourists from the look of their bulging rucksacks and guidebooks – and Britt began to relax. It was so good to feel the sun on her face. The beer was icy cold and the nuts were deliciously salty and savoury. The first pint slipped down easily.

Inevitably, the conversation eventually got round to the article.

'What Alex did really sucked,' said Stewie, 'but everyone will have forgotten about it by tomorrow – if they haven't already.'

'I won't have forgotten, though, will I? And what about my career?' said Britt. 'No-one's going to take me seriously after that article.'

'You're kidding, aren't you? If anything, this will give your career a boost. A bit of scandal is the magic that can turn a celebrity into a superstar. Look at Paris Hilton. Just another poor little rich kid until that sex tape surfaced.'

'Yeah, well I hope Toby sees it that way,' said Britt. 'Oh, and by the way, there is *definitely* no sex tape.'

'Let's make one then,' Stewie grinned. 'Really give people something to talk about.'

Britt giggled. She needed cheering up and Stewie was doing a fantastic job. He was such a good mate – and he could make her laugh like no-one else. She couldn't put her finger on it, but something about him seemed different today. Perhaps he'd had a haircut . . . ? He was certainly dressed differently, in a spotless white T-shirt that set off his tan, with a pair of Levi's rather than his usual crumpled shorts. It had never occurred to Britt before, but he really was quite handsome. True, he was some way off sex-god territory but there was something so attractive about that crinkly-eyed grin and air of rugged manliness that Britt suddenly wished she'd put on a bit of make-up. God, only one pint in and the beer goggles were already on!

Stewie drained the last of his pint. 'Want another beer?'

'Yeah,' she smiled. 'Why not?'

By mid-afternoon they had visited three pubs, and while Britt had downed a few pints of water in between the beers she was feeling decidedly drunk – and her tummy was rumbling loudly.

'There's this really lovely pub near my flat in Shepherds Bush,' said Stewie. 'Sort of a posh gastropub; does a killer steak and chips if you can be bothered to trek west?'

'Let's do it,' said Britt. She realised she had barely eaten since Friday evening and was suddenly ravenous.

A thirty-minute taxi drive later and they arrived at The Haverhill, which sat at the end of a row of pretty terraced cottages on the edge of a green: it felt like they were in a country village, even though they were only metres from a tube station. With its mismatched vintage wooden furniture and hanging baskets of pansies, Britt loved it. It had an air of cosy boho chic that had probably taken thousands of pounds to achieve, but looked like it had just been effortlessly thrown together.

They ordered a bottle of rosé and the food and found a table outside. She quickly devoured the huge portion of ribeye steak with a bowl of golden thick-cut chips, followed by salted caramel ice-cream for pudding. The warmth of the late-afternoon sun combined with a full stomach and yet more alcohol left Britt feeling deliciously relaxed. She looked over at Stewie, who was smiling back at her.

'Thanks so much, Stewie,' she said happily. 'You're always there for me. You're a true friend.'

She leaned over and gave him a kiss on the cheek. As she pulled away, he reached out and gently touched her face. He was so close that she could feel the warmth of his breath on her cheek. She noticed a pale sprinkling of freckles on his nose. Stevie leaned in closer and kissed her. His lips felt different from Alex's, firmer and cooler, but the kiss sent a spark of electricity shooting through her. After a few moments, she felt Stewie's arms wrapping round her waist, pulling her closer to him. She felt dizzy with lust.

Britt had a brief moment of doubt when they got to the front door of his flat. She was drunk. She had just split up from her boyfriend. Stewie was her friend. Oh lord. This probably wasn't the best idea. Or maybe it was just what the doctor ordered to help mend a broken heart?

While Stewie fixed them a drink in the kitchen, Britt looked at the pictures on his living-room walls, telling herself she would just have one drink, make her excuses and then get a taxi home. Her eye caught photos of him in a wetsuit riding the most enormous rolling waves like a total pro. She hadn't realised quite how sexy surfing could be. He walked back in the room, came straight over to her, put the drinks on the table and before she could protest he started kissing her again and suddenly they were falling into bed.

They were both tipsy, so the sex wasn't exactly like it

was in the movies, but it was certainly a lot of fun: Stewie fell over when he was trying to wriggle out of his jeans, which left them both in fits of laughter. He kissed her from her chin in a straight line down to her stomach and kept telling her over and over again how beautiful she was and how much he wanted her, but that made her giggle too. Yet although it was strange being with someone new after so long, Stewie obviously knew what he was doing and as he touched her she started to relax and lose herself in the moment. Gradually, the excitement built inside her until there was no turning back and afterwards they collapsed into yet more giggles.

It was only later, after the sun had gone down and they were lying together in Stewie's bed, as the heady buzz from the alcohol had started to fade to be replaced by the creeping queasiness of a hangover, that Britt realised she had just made a monumental mistake. She had to work with this guy every day. She glanced at Stewie snoring gently beside her, his arm thrown across her naked stomach, and a tsunami of panic crashed over her. Oh. My. God. What about Alex? Her Alex. For as long as she would remember it had been Britt and Alex, Alex and Britt. They were a team. *What the hell have I done?*

31

Britt's eyes flew open. Christ, she felt awful. Her head was throbbing and her insides lurched as if she had just got off Detonator at Thorpe Park.

She became aware of someone lying next to her in the pre-dawn gloom: Stewie was stirring and stretching. It was then that Britt remembered where she was and what she had done. Suddenly, throwing up seemed the very least of her worries.

Stewie groaned. Britt lay next to him, rigid with discomfort, the duvet pulled up tight under her chin as if 2.5 togs would be enough to block out reality. For a moment all was deathly quiet but then she felt the mattress shift and dip as he pushed himself up onto his elbow, leant over and kissed her gently on the cheek. She hoped he didn't sense her flinching at his touch.

'Hey there, sleepyhead.'

'Hi,' said Britt. She felt horribly self-conscious, as if she was naked in bed with a stranger – which actually wasn't that far from the truth.

'Sleep okay?'

'Yes, fine thanks.'

'I'll just jump in the shower and get out of your way, then I'll fix us a coffee.'

'Sounds great,' she said, with as much enthusiasm as anyone with a stinking hangover, a hefty dose of guilt and a side order of mortification could manage.

After showering as best she could (Stewie only seemed to possess a small tablet of soap, whereas Britt would usually use at least five products to get herself top-to-toe clean) she dressed in the day before's clothes and went reluctantly into the kitchen, where he was sitting at the table. His face lit up when he saw her.

'I don't know how you manage it, but you still look bloody gorgeous at 4.30 a.m.' He pushed a mug of coffee towards her. 'I've put in a couple of sugars. Thought you might need them.'

Britt forced a smile and sat down opposite him. 'Stewie, about last night . . .'

'It's okay,' he grinned. 'I know you were drunk. Things happened faster than they should have.' To her enormous relief, he seemed to feel the same way as she did.

'Oh, thank God you understand!'

'Yeah, we probably did jump into bed a bit too quickly . . .'

'We certainly did,' said Britt enthusiastically. 'It was a big mistake. Huge!'

'Well, I'm glad we're both agreed that we've done things in completely the wrong order,' smiled Stewie. 'So the question is, when are you going to let me take you for a proper date?'

Shit. That wasn't what she had meant at all. This would have to be handled carefully.

'Um, Stewie, I think you're a fantastic guy and if I was in a better place now I'd definitely want to be spending more time with you. But after what happened with Alex, I'm just not ready for another relationship right now.'

Oh God, she sounded like she was channelling a women's magazine advice column. Next thing she'd be telling him, 'It's not you, it's me', and prescribing an evening with a tub of Ben & Jerry's and a box-set of *Friends*. But at least it seemed to reassure Stewie.

'Of course I understand,' he said, reaching for her hand and giving it a squeeze. 'And don't worry, I'll give you as much time as you need. I'm happy to wait.'

'Ah, thanks,' she smiled. She thought it best not to mention that giving her all the time in the world might not be enough. Stewie was sweet, kind and undeniably attractive (and, from what she could remember, pretty good in bed, even after consuming a week's worth of alcohol units in one day) but right now she couldn't imagine ever thinking of him as anything other than a very good friend.

Britt drained what was left in her mug. 'Right, I'd better get going. Any idea where I can get a taxi?'

'You might as well get a ride in with me on the scooter,' said Stewie. 'Don't worry,' he laughed, seeing the expression on her face, 'I'll drop you at the top of the road and you can walk the last bit. I don't fancy being studio gossip fodder, either.'

Thankfully, their plan worked and an hour later, Britt made it to her dressing room without the horror of being spotted by anyone in the day before's clothes. She couldn't ever remember feeling so horrifically hungover, but that would be nothing compared to the ordeal of all her colleagues knowing that she'd spent the night with Stewie – especially after the article portraying her as a needy nymphomaniac.

With a few hours to kill before the show, Britt had another shower, turning it cold at the end as a combination of medication and self-punishment, and then headed off in search of one of the runners who might take pity on her and fetch her a bacon sandwich from the canteen.

She found two of them – Charlie the moody runner and a new girl called Lulu – in the green room, hunched over a pile of newspapers on the coffee table. They were pointing and giggling at something, but when they noticed Britt they suddenly pretended to be busy tidying up. Charlie even started whistling.

'Alright Britt?' he said, jumping to his feet with uncharacteristic agility. 'I've just . . . got to go to the studio with Lulu.' The girl, who with her pudding-bowl bob and heavy-framed glasses looked exactly like Velma from *Scooby Doo*, nodded energetically. 'Right, then see you later, yeah?' And with that they both dashed out.

Britt went straight over and rifled through the papers until she found *The Daily Splash* and then flicked through the pages until she came across what she desperately hoped she wouldn't find.

Above a photo of her and Stewie sitting drinking in the beer garden of The Bay Tree was the headline: 'A BRITT ON THE SIDE!' The snaps were blurry and poor-quality, obviously taken from a distance, but despite the baseball cap you could clearly see it was her. She was laughing and touching Stewie's arm flirtatiously. The only good thing was that he had his back to the camera, so even people from work wouldn't be able to identify him. She really didn't want to drag him into her ten-car pile-up of a life, or face the questions that would inevitably be asked.

Britt quickly scanned the article. The gist of it was that she had a new man, that she'd moved on already.

Sexy TV presenter dumps rugby player boyfriend ... Breakfast star canoodles in the sunshine with mystery hunk just TWO DAYS after split ... Britt's lust for co-host Josh Bailey put on ice ... Pals fear besotted babe is heading for heartbreak.

On and on it went in lurid, invented detail, repeating everything from the weekend's article to pad out the new story. Not that there was any story – just some fairly innocuous photos and a truckload of insinuation – but anyone flicking casually through the newspaper would instantly think she had been cheating on her boyfriend to be this cosy with another man already. *And Alex would assume that too*, she realised with a stab of horror.

Britt was so wrapped up in this fresh new torment that she didn't hear the door to the green room open and someone walk over to where she sat.

'They're like sharks, aren't they? Once they smell blood they won't stop until they've torn you to pieces.'

She looked up to see Cherry standing over her.

'Sorry, what was that?' said Britt tetchily. The last thing she needed right now was Cherry rubbing salt in the wound; Britt didn't get why she was always there at just the wrong moment, armed with a dig. But to her surprise, Cherry looked sympathetic – almost concerned. She sat down next to Britt and took a deep breath.

'Britt, I wanted to tell you that I . . . *regret* what I said yesterday about you and Josh. I know what it's like to be on the receiving end of this kind of thing' – she waved a hand dismissively over the newspaper on Britt's lap – 'and it's not nice at all. We're in this together after all. But you can console yourself with the fact that at least *you* weren't caught snorting coke off a Premiership footballer's freshly waxed chest.'

Despite herself, Britt managed a smile.

'And if you need any help or advice,' Cherry went on, 'please, just ask.'

Britt was stunned. 'Thank you, Cherry,' she said. 'That's really kind of you.'

Cherry gave a gracious little nod, patted Britt's knee and then got up to leave.

'Oh, and by the way, I've asked Fran to take special care of you – you need to make a bit of an effort with your appearance when you're in the middle of a newspaper scandal.' She brushed a bit of non-existent fluff off her spotless white sheath dress. 'Don't want to disappoint the viewers, darling . . .'

Britt had desperately hoped that would be the last of it, but the following morning she popped up in *The Daily Splash* once again. She was beginning to be as regular a feature as the weather – and it looked like another shitstorm had been forecast today. This time a reporter had somehow found a bloke who she had dated a couple of times in her late teens to corroborate Britt's scarlet woman credentials – although from the way he was portrayed in the paper, you would think they'd been practically married.

'She's insatiable,' the guy was quoted as saying. 'Britt is the sexiest woman I've ever been with. She left me panting with lust!' It seemed a funny way to describe a quick snog outside Pizza Express, but there you go . . . If stories about her sex life continued to pop up relentlessly in the press, wasn't it inevitable that Toby was going to sack her? She would surely be fired and the only surprise was that the axe hadn't fallen sooner. *Rise & Shine* was a family show after all. Britt imagined he wouldn't be thrilled at one of his presenters being described as '. . . boy-crazy with a taste for naughty lingerie'.

Britt had been doing her best to avoid Toby since their awkward conversation at the start of the week, ducking into doorways and behind desks, but after the show that morning there was a knock on her dressing-room door and Toby walked in. This time there was nowhere to hide.

'Britt, we need to have a chat,' he said. ' This is getting out of hand.'

32

Toby was sitting at his desk when she came to his office. After he had left her dressing room, Britt had buttoned a long, charcoal-grey cardigan over her stripy T-shirt dress and wiped her face clean of make-up, in a last-ditch attempt to convince Toby that she wasn't a slut.

'I'll be with you in a moment, Britt. Just take a seat over there, will you?'

She sat down on the yellow sofa closest to the window and waited nervously while Toby tapped away at his laptop. Talk about prolonging the agony. She'd rather he'd just tell her to get out and be done with it. Britt glanced over to where *Rise & Shine*'s haul of awards sat proudly on a shelf. Best Daytime Programme, Most Popular Presenter, The Bruce Forsyth Award for Broadcasting Excellence . . . Last time Britt had been sitting in this spot was when Toby offered her a permanent job on the show and she remembered looking at all the trophies and imagining herself winning one and making a gushing acceptance speech. *'I'd just like to thank my mum, my best friend Jessie and my darling boyfriend Alex . . .'* At the time, it hadn't seemed like such an impossible dream. Now, however, it looked as likely a prospect as her marrying Prince Harry.

Toby came over and sat opposite her. 'Right, I wanted to talk to you about this.' He threw a copy of Saturday's *Daily Splash* on the table. 'And this' – yesterday's paper – 'and this' – that day's copy joined the pile. He looked pissed off.

'Toby, before you say anything, I want to assure you that this is all rubbish. The bloke in the picture was actually Stewie; he just took me out for a drink yesterday to cheer me up. And as for this other bloke they've dug up . . . well, I hardly knew him!'

'Yes, but the newspaper doesn't think that, and unfortunately that's all that matters.'

Britt nodded miserably. He was right.

'Now, I've been trying to think how to deal with this, as it'll probably just get worse,' said Toby. 'You're on their radar now and will probably be tailed round until they find something juicier to distract them. We're going to have to take action.'

'Of course,' nodded Britt sadly. 'I completely understand.'

'Which is why I've made a decision.' Britt held her breath, preparing herself for the blow. 'I've decided to send you to Los Angeles this weekend to report on the Golden Globes with Josh.'

Britt was confused. 'So I won't be leaving the show until I get back from the States?'

'Who said anything about you leaving the show? No, that would be a terrible shame. You're doing an excellent job.' Toby smiled at her. 'Now Cherry usually accompanies Josh to the Globes to do the red carpet fashion, but I think it makes more sense for you to go this year. Not only does it get you out of the way until this fuss in *The*

Splash blows over, but you are our style correspondent after all, and I've been really impressed with your location reports to date. Kills two birds with one well-aimed stone and all that. How does that sound?'

Britt was struggling to take it all in. Instead of getting the boot, it looked like she was being offered an all-expenses-paid trip to Los Angeles with Josh Bailey as her own personal tour guide. Screw marrying the second in line to the throne, this really was the stuff of fairytales!

'I think that all sounds fine,' she said eventually, struggling not to do a Tom Cruise and jump on the sofa and punch the air with a delighted whoop.

'Great,' said Toby, 'I'll get the production team to book flights and sort out the necessary press accreditations for the two of you, plus a small crew. You and Josh will fly out after the show on Friday.'

When Britt got home later that day, she immediately noticed that there was a blank space by the front door where a framed photo of her and Alex used to hang. It was a lovely black-and-white close-up of their laughing faces, taken on a weekend break to Rome where Alex had first told her that he loved her. They had been sunburned and tipsy on prosecco at the time; Britt never failed to smile whenever she looked at it. And now all that was left of that wonderful moment was a forlorn-looking hook.

Staring unhappily at the spot, Britt became aware of Kate Moss rubbing herself around her legs. The poor thing hadn't got any dinner last night; she must be starving. Britt went straight to the kitchen and piled her bowl high with cat food and then reluctantly explored the rest of the flat. Some time in the last thirty-six hours Alex must have been back for his stuff. Everything that had belonged to him had gone: his clothes, toiletries, pictures, books, CDs – even the bottle of hot chilli sauce he used to splash over all his food. There was no note. The only evidence that he had ever been there were his door keys on the kitchen table.

Over the last few days, Britt had been careful not to dwell on the fact that their relationship was over, but now she let herself tumble into the chasm of pain and loneliness where her heart had once been.

It was dark by the time she managed to haul herself out again. She dragged herself off the sofa and went to the bathroom to splash cold water on her face. Catching sight of herself in the mirror, her face all red and blotchy, Britt realised it was time to give herself a stern talking-to: *Come on, Baxter, pull yourself together. That chapter of your life is now closed*. She patted her face dry and tried out a smile in the mirror. *It's time to move on*. Perhaps if she said it enough times, she'd be able to convince herself.

Britt went and poured herself a large glass of red wine, pulled a tub of Ben & Jerry's Phish Food out of the freezer, and hung one of Nanna Eileen's watercolours on the empty hook by the front door. With the empty space filled, she rifled through her collection of DVDs until she found the one she was looking for and put it in the player.

'Come on, Mossy, you're going to enjoy this,' she said to the cat, who had been sitting on the kitchen table, tail curled neatly around her, watching what Britt was doing.

They settled on the sofa together as the intro music to *Dance Delirium* blared out, a cheesy eighties rock anthem that had stayed at the top of the charts for weeks. Britt sung along at the top of her voice.

The opening, moody-looking shot was of Josh – his character, Mitch Rider, was walking along the side of a dusty road, a cigarette dangling from his lip. The camera panned lovingly over his clingy white T-shirt, jeans and battered brown cowboy boots. There was a black leather biker jacket tossed over his shoulder, movie shorthand for Bad Boy.

A battered red pick-up truck appeared on the road behind him in a cloud of dust. There was a group of young guys in the cab, one of whom leaned out the window as they pulled up alongside him.

'Hey, Mitch, you need a ride?'

'Nah, I feel like walking.'

'You're gonna be late for class again. Gregson's gonna be spittin' mad at you, man . . .'

Josh shrugged, then ground his cigarette out in the dirt. 'He'll get over it.' Under the bright sunlight, his taut, tanned skin shimmered with sweat. 'Catch ya later, Tommy.'

Britt giggled, scooping up a spoon of ice-cream. She hadn't watched the movie for years, but she must have seen it dozens of times and, like most women her age, virtually knew it off by heart: the scene where Mitch practises his dance moves while working at the local store, leaping over piles of food cans, jumping off shelves and vaulting over the counter. The bit where his dream girl leaves a party with his arch-enemy and Mitch storms out into the rainy night to do an impromptu angry dance to a soaring power ballad while his T-shirt gets fetchingly wet and see-through. And the movie's climax, where he wins the girl and they do their final spectacular dance in the school hall, a routine that countless newlyweds across the world had since tried to recreate for their first dance with varying degrees of success.

As Mitch took his co-star in his arms and then slowly leaned in for their first, magical kiss, whispering the now-famous line: 'I have wanted to do that since the moment I first laid eyes on you – and now I never want to stop', Britt felt a shiver of anticipation. She was single for the first time in years, and in just a few days' time she was going to be jetting off to California with Mitch Rider. Boy, it was the stuff her teenage dreams were made of.

33

Britt gawped out of the tinted windows of the black SUV that was ferrying the *Rise & Shine* team from Los Angeles International airport to their hotel. It was Friday afternoon: less than a week since the shit-storm had first struck, yet right now it felt like a lifetime ago. She had never been to LA before, but was thrilled to see that it was exactly the same as it was in the movies: monster cars, six-lane highways, bright blue skies and palm trees everywhere she looked. It wouldn't really have surprised her if Arnold Schwarzenegger had driven past in a Hummer, puffing on a fat cigar.

But while LA was fulfilling every expectation, Britt's fantasy of spending the weekend getting to know Josh better wasn't quite working out the way she'd hoped. For a start, he'd barely spoken to her since they met at Heathrow. He had gone straight to sleep on the flight and since getting off the plane had been constantly on the phone to people with names like Brad and Zane making exciting-sounding plans, none of which appeared to involve her. Then there was the fact that there was a crew tagging along with them – and not just the location producer, Jasper, and the two cameramen, Phil and Dan, as she had expected. Toby had also sent along a new researcher, a Sloaney graduate trainee called Caggie who was apparently the daughter of someone very important at the production company that made *Rise & Shine*. Britt had been put next to her on the plane and Caggie had wittered on about her recent holiday to '. . . Daddy's finca in Ibiza with *darling* Assisi Jagger' and getting 'the best table in the house with Pixie and Alexa at El Divino' for most of the ten-hour flight, pausing only to order a half-bottle of champagne that she polished off without offering Britt a drop. And not only was she deeply annoying, Caggie also just happened to be the spit of Sienna Miller. Britt groaned inwardly when she clocked her endless legs and radiant smile at airport check-in. Of all the researchers, why did Toby have to send *her*? Why not one of the boys? With Josh's reputed eye for the ladies, his attention was sure to be focused on the hair-tossing, eyelash-fluttering Caggie. And finally there was the thorny issue of work. In short, there seemed to be a hell of a lot more of it than Britt had been expecting. She had assumed they would do their report from the Globes' red carpet on Sunday and then have the rest of the time off for sunbathing and shopping, before heading home on Monday. But Jasper, the officious Oxford graduate producer, was keen to prove himself to Toby and had other ideas.

'When we get to the hotel you'll have a couple of hours to unpack and read through this research' – he handed a thick sheaf of papers around the car – 'and then let's meet at 6 p.m. tonight for an early dinner when we can discuss this further. I think we should all try and get a reasonably early night so we're in good shape for tomorrow. We've got lots to sort out before Sunday, guys.'

Suddenly, Britt's fantasy of zipping around Hollywood in a sporty red convertible with Josh at the wheel seemed, well, just that. Complete fantasy.

They were staying at The London, a boutique hotel moments away from the bright lights of Sunset Strip. Britt's room was cool and quiet, boasting a bed the size of a bus piled high with crisp white pillows. Inviting though it was – it was 4 p.m. LA-time which made it way past bedtime back home – after being stuck on a plane for so long Britt was keen to get out in the sunshine, so after she had showered and unpacked she slipped into a black Melissa Odabash bikini with a white mini-kaftan (teamed with a pair of high-heeled Miu Miu sandals – *heck*, she thought, *I am in LA, after all*) and found her way up to the hotel's roof terrace.

The first thing Britt noticed – apart from the dazzling turquoise pool – was that the only natural boobs on show belonged to her and a fat bloke eating a club sandwich. The women were without exception toned, tanned and ruthlessly groomed from the top of their (blonde) heads to the tip of their perfectly pedicured toes. Feeling glad she'd at least had a spray tan and a wax before jetting out, Britt settled onto one of the cushiony sun loungers and stretched out, luxuriating in the feeling of the sunshine and soft breeze caressing her skin. Wow, if only Molly could see her now!

'Hi, my name is Jet and I'll be your waiter today.' She opened her eyes to see what looked like an Abercrombie & Fitch model standing over her. He was wearing a dazzling white fitted T-shirt that matched his teeth and trousers. 'May I get you something from the bar, ma'am?'

he smiled. 'Vanilla soy and mango smoothie? Mineral water? Champagne?'

Britt was beginning to like LA.

'Yes, I'll take the smoothie and a bottle of mineral water, thank you.' *Oh, what the hell.* 'And the champagne, too.'

Jet flashed her another blinding smile. 'Sure thing. I'll be right back.'

Britt lay back, listening to the gentle lapping of the pool and admiring the panoramic views of the shimmering city. She gave a contented little sigh and closed her eyes. Jasper's research could wait.

At 6.30 that evening, they dined at Cecconi's, the legendary Italian restaurant that was just a short stroll from their hotel. Britt wore a ruffled silk Lanvin mini-dress (a total steal on The Outnet website), and when Josh caught sight of her before dinner he raised his eyebrow, Roger Moore style.

'That's a very nice dress you're almost wearing, Miss Baxter.'

He said it flippantly, but his eyes locked on hers, holding greedily on to her gaze until she had to look away. They were standing in a busy hotel foyer, but he had the power to make her feel like they were the only two people in the room. Yet any hopes Britt had of continuing the flirtation vanished once they started to walk to the restaurant. Phil, one of the cameramen, immediately fell into step with her and started chatting away about the last time he was in Hollywood for the Academy Awards. Jasper and the other cameraman, Dan, walked out in front, engrossed in a technical conversation about key lights, surveying pans and buffer shots, leaving Josh and Caggie – who was looking effortlessly gorgeous, damn her, in a simple top and skinny jeans – to bring up the rear.

While Phil was rattling on about bumping into Nicholas Cage in the gents' toilet at the Oscars, Britt could not help but hear what Caggie was saying – it was hard not to. Caggie evidently spent most of her time shrieking across the VIP rooms of Boujis or Mahiki and was stuck at that volume.

'Woah, check that out!' she screamed as they walked past an enormous billboard poster of Cameron Diaz advertising her latest rom com. 'Ooh, Josh, I guess you must have had your picture on a billboard like that when you were in *Dance Delirium*. That must have been, like, *OMFG*!'

'Yeah, it was pretty surreal,' he chuckled. 'Nothing like seeing your face blown up ten feet high to give you a few insecurities about your nose . . . Have you ever been to LA before, Caggie?'

'Well, my friend Sahara who's like this *amazing* stylist asked me to come out here with her last year as she was invited to this major fash thing by one of the Olsen twins, but the dates clashed with my internship at *Vogue* so I couldn't go which was like *super* annoying . . . Perhaps you could show me round?' Britt imagined Caggie looking up at Josh, her blue eyes sparkling, and angrily clenched her teeth.

'Well, I lived here for years back in the day,' he said, 'so I'd be happy to point you in the right direction. Just give me a shout.'

'I'll *totally* hold you to that,' gushed Caggie, a flirty smile in her voice.

I'm sure you bloomin' will, fumed Britt to herself. *And I'm betting that's not the only thing you'd totally like to hold him to* . . .

Even though it was still early, the restaurant was buzzing with activity when they arrived. Britt was starving and ordered wood-oven roasted scallops with pancetta and rosemary, followed by melt-in-the-mouth pumpkin tortellini. They drank a delicious bottle or two of Californian pinot noir and gawped at the array of celebrity diners, which included a couple of starlets from the *High School Musical* films, and Jennifer Lopez with a mystery man. Britt couldn't work out why J Lo was always referred to as curvy; the woman was absolutely tiny. Apart from that famous derrière, she almost disappeared when she turned sideways.

But then Jasper turned the evening into a board meeting. Britt's heart sank as he ran through the jam-packed schedule for the rest of their trip: a recce of the location the following morning (thankfully, for the camera guys only), another meeting after lunch, interviews with a celebrity stylist and dress designer on Sunday morning and then the awards themselves on Sunday afternoon. He'd even got some post-production voiceovers lined up for Monday. She knew she was there to work, but surely they could have squeezed in a bit of fun, too?

Britt was polishing off her passion-fruit sorbet when Josh's phone started to ring, interrupting Jasper's flow.

'Sorry, man, I gotta take this . . .' Shrugging apologetically, Josh pushed back his chair and went a discreet distance from the table to take the call.

Britt clocked Caggie watch him walk away and then rummage in her bag and pull out her Dior lip-gloss, which she hurriedly reapplied. *Really*, she thought crossly, *could that girl make it any more obvious that she fancies him?*

Just then Josh appeared back at the table. 'Guys, if you don't need me any more I'm gonna go hook up with some friends. Catch you later.'

'Don't forget, production meeting at 2 p.m. sharp tomorrow,' called Jasper as he walked away.

'Got it. Adios amigos.' Josh waved to the table without looking back. Britt's only comfort was the look of disappointment that flashed across Caggie's face.

Later that night, unable to sleep, Britt sat propped up on the heap of pillows in her enormous bed and watched TV. Almost every channel featured pre-ceremony coverage of the Golden Globes, with feverish speculation over who would win and what they'd be wearing. This really was a big deal, second only to the Oscars – and she was going to be on the red carpet with the stars! Turning off the light and snuggling under the feather-light duvet, Britt vowed to leave the silly schoolgirl crushes to Caggie and focus on her career.

But the next day she went up to the roof terrace for breakfast to find Josh already sitting at a table in the early morning sunshine, looking tanned and sexily sleep-rumpled in a linen shirt, cargo shorts and Ray-Ban aviators. All of her good intentions immediately dived off the roof. He was flicking through *Variety*, but when he caught sight of her he put down the magazine and broke into a delighted grin.

'Hey, babe, pull up a seat. Did I miss much last night at dinner?' He was just finishing off a plate of scrambled eggs and grilled mushrooms.

'Only Jasper micro-managing his way through coffee and the bill.'

'Jeez, that guy needs to lighten up . . .'

Just then a waiter – possibly even *more* gorgeous than Jet – appeared (did they have a factory that cloned them somewhere?). Britt ordered a double cappuccino and pancakes with bacon and maple syrup.

'You could get put in jail for eating like that round here,' smirked Josh. 'This is the land of the egg-white omelette and no-fat, dairy-free decaf latte.'

'Sunshine always makes me hungry.' Britt reclined in her seat and put her face up to the startlingly blue sky, sighing with pleasure as the sunshine touched her skin. 'You know, I really could get used to this place . . .'

'Yeah, it's quite a town. Gaad, I miss it – the weather, the beach, the people . . .' Josh took a sip of juice. 'Y'know, I'm hoping to come back here to live one day, perhaps once I've found the future Mrs Bailey.' He turned to face her as he said it, fixing her with his piercing green eyes.

She glanced at him, her stomach doing a back-flip at his smile. *Am I reading too much into that comment?* she thought. *Is he flirting with me . . . ?* As a whirlwind of emotions churned inside her, she busied herself with pouring a glass of orange juice from the jug on the table. 'So,' she said, swiftly changing the subject, 'what are you up to this morning?'

'I thought I'd go shopping,' he said. 'Hey, you want to come too? I could show you round.'

'Sounds good,' she smiled. 'You can help me find a new dress for tomorrow. Now I'm here, the one I've brought with me just doesn't feel LA enough. I think I need one with a bit more wow . . .'

'It will be my pleasure.' Josh got up to leave. 'Let's meet in the foyer in an hour.'

Britt bolted down the rest of her breakfast and then dashed back to her room to get ready. Making-up her face to look naturally sun-kissed, she applied tinted moisturiser, a YSL peach cream blush and her favourite Daly Face Glow highlighter under the brow to widen her eyes, and then she carefully styled her hair into loose waves. (Thankfully the permanent blow-dry was still keeping the frizz at bay – in this humidity, she'd usually be rocking a decidedly non-funky afro by now.) She wanted to look her best for the date – well, semi-date – with Josh.

Catching sight of her reflection in the elevator mirror as she went downstairs, Britt smiled despite her butterflies. *Not too bad*, she thought. In her loose, pale pink Isabel Marant T-shirt and Zara cut-off denim shorts, she looked glossy but not over-groomed – ironic, considering the look had taken the best part of an hour and a bagful of make-up products to achieve.

Britt got down to the foyer and spotted Caggie standing by the front entrance in a simple white sundress with her hair tied in two loose plaits. *Damn*. She really didn't want her hanging around looking like a sexy Swedish milkmaid when Josh turned up.

'Hey, Britt!'

'Hi, Caggie, where are you off to? I suppose Jasper's got you running around all over the place this morning . . .'

'Not really,' she said. 'He's gone off on a recce of the location with the camera chaps, so I've got the morning off. Yay!' She gave a little thumbs-up. 'So what are you up to?'

Britt supposed she should come clean. 'I'm going shopping with Josh.'

'No way – me too! He asked me last night.'

'Last night?' Britt was trying to work out when he would have had the chance.

'Yah, I met up with him and some of his buds at the bar of the Chateau Marmont after we'd had dinner,' gushed Caggie. 'We got squiffy on cocktails and I got my photo taken with Katy Perry, who was like *totes* divine and had the best boobies I've ever seen.' Her hands flew to her face. 'Seriously, I was like, *screeeeam!*'

Britt's heart plummeted. Josh had invited Caggie out partying with him after dinner. He obviously hadn't even thought of including her. How many more times did she need to be humiliated before she got the message?

34

Josh turned up moments later, smiled breezily at Britt, and asked the doorman to get them a cab to The Grove.

'You're gonna love this place, girls,' he grinned as they climbed into the backseat together. He rapped on the Perspex partition between them and the driver. 'Hey man, take us the scenic route, will ya?'

Britt stared out of the window as they sped past sights so familiar from countless photos and movies: Hollywood Boulevard, where Grauman's Chinese Theater stood on the Walk of Fame with its mile of brass celebrity stars embedded in the sidewalk; billionaire's shopping mecca Rodeo Drive; the iconic Hollywood sign nestled high up in the hills. She was torn between childlike excitement – *You're in Hollywood, baby!* – and annoyance at Josh's rejection. It didn't help that his shorts-clad thigh was pressed firmly against her bare leg. It occurred to Britt that there was actually plenty of room in the back of the cab and he didn't really need to sit quite so close, but she refused to start thinking it was a sign that he was interested. She was over making a fool of herself.

If there was one thing guaranteed to take Britt's mind off Josh it was shopping – and The Grove turned out to be the perfect distraction. They joined the stream of shoppers browsing the designer boutiques and big-name stores, arranged around a tree-filled park with a magnificent musical fountain. If there was a heaven, and if it had a shopping mall (and without one it wouldn't really be heaven, would it?), Britt decided it would look a lot like The Grove.

Josh turned out to be the perfect man to go shopping with: just feminine enough to be interested, but with a straight man's eye for a sexy frock or killer pair of shoes. Meanwhile, Caggie bounced around like a small child after too much pick 'n' mix – she nearly started hyperventilating when she spotted Paris Hilton coming out of Barneys. She was no less subtle in her pursuit of Josh, dragging him into Victoria's Secret (Britt trailing behind), then holding up a succession of increasingly skimpy bits of lingerie and coyly asking his opinion.

In the event, though, Britt was actually quite glad that Caggie had come along. The three of them were leaving J Crew when they walked straight into a pack of British paps, who told Britt that they had been given a Victoria Beckham tip-off and were waiting for her outside. No doubt they would have gone into a frenzy if Britt had been there on her own with Josh, but as Caggie was clinging to him like a pretty limpet it looked like they were a couple and Britt was simply playing gooseberry. For once she was relieved that Caggie had dug her claws into Josh.

By 1 p.m. Britt had bought several Abercrombie T-shirts, dolls from American Girl Place for each of Jessie's daughters, and a silk scarf for her mum, but she still hadn't found anything suitable for the Globes.

'Let's try Michael Kors,' suggested Josh. 'I'd like to take a look at the menswear, anyway.'

Caggie wrinkled her pretty nose. 'The clothes are a bit too *old* for me, I think. Josh, why don't we go to Guess and meet Britt later?'

She was already dragging Josh away by the arm, but he pulled back and told Caggie to go on by herself and they'd meet her there. For a moment Caggie pouted like a sulky teenager, but she still managed a wink to Josh as she left them to it.

A helpful shop assistant, who with her gym-sculpted limbs and glossy chestnut hair looked like she should actually be modelling the clothes rather than selling them, took Britt under her wing and in moments she was on her way to the dressing room with an armful of gorgeous frocks. There was a black full-length draped number, a short white skater-style dress, a rose-pink Grecian gown and an unpromising-looking green number that the shop assistant had insisted she try on. 'Trust me, honey, with legs like yours this will look fierce,' the woman told her, flashing a Tipp-Ex-white smile. Britt glanced round for Josh, but he had wandered off to look at man bags and was nowhere to be seen.

Despite her high hopes, Britt's heart sank as each dress she tried on failed to meet its promise. She was left with only the green one to try. She wriggled it reluctantly over her head, unsure of what to expect when she looked in the mirror. *Wow*. It fitted perfectly, clinging to her curves, while the colour looked stunning against her skin and wavy hair.

When it came to getting dressed, Britt's mantra was legs or cleavage, never both, and although the hemline was thigh-high her boobs were kept under wrap, with just a single bronzed shoulder exposed by the toga-style top. But it looked all the sexier for it. Britt admired herself in the mirror, for a moment feeling like a movie star. Wanting to see what it looked like with heels, she came out of the dressing room to ask the assistant if she could borrow a pair. As she walked out she came face to face with Josh. His jaw literally dropped when he saw her.

'Oh, wow, that looks . . .' He tailed off, shaking his head in admiration. 'Seriously, Britt, you gotta buy that dress. You look incredible.'

'You don't think the colour's a bit dull?'

He laughed, raising an eyebrow. 'Dull would be the last word I'd use for how you look right now.'

Britt checked the price tag – $1,175. *Ouch*. No way. She could not afford to spend that much on a frock. But she knew she just had to have it, even if it meant eating beans for months on her return to London. And it was in dollars, so it would probably be, like, half the price in pounds or something. Plus it would look just sensational with the brown and gold Kurt Geiger platform sandals and gold Lara Bohinc cuff she just happened to have in her suitcase. And the expression on Josh's face when he'd seen her was worth the price tag alone . . .

'Okay, I'll get it,' she smiled, with a frisson of guilty excitement.

Britt went back in the fitting room, thinking about Josh's reaction. She just couldn't work the guy out. He was charming and flirty with her, but then he was charming and flirty with Caggie, too. And with the girls who had stopped him for an autograph in Barneys. And the woman who had served them iced coffees and muffins when they stopped for a snack. And with the man who had rung up his purchases in Gap. It seemed that Josh's default setting was charming and flirty. *All the more reason to stop mooning over him and move on*, Britt scolded herself as she headed for the cash desk with her trophy.

After grabbing some enchiladas for lunch from a Mexican stall at nearby Farmers Market, they made it back to The London a few minutes after 2 p.m. Jasper was already waiting in the hotel's conference room when they got there, tapping a pencil on the desk in annoyance. Dan and Phil wandered in a few moments later.

'Right people, let's get started. We've got a lot to get through.'

That evening, Josh persuaded Jasper that they should all go to the very trendy Sushi Roku for dinner, rather than staying in and discussing work over a room service sandwich as Jasper had initially suggested.

Several cocktails and a feast of truffled lotus root, miso-glazed sea bass and spicy octopus hand roll later and even Jasper had chilled out. By 10 p.m. though, he was ready to throw in the towel and head back for an early night. Phil and Dan went with him, leaving Britt alone with Josh and Caggie.

'Right, now we can really get the party started,' grinned Josh, rubbing his hands. 'Drink, ladies?'

'Definitely,' smiled Britt.

'Hell, yeah!' whooped Caggie, who had already had at least two Mojitos too many. 'Let's paaaarty!'

'Let's go to Soho House,' said Josh. 'An old producer buddy is a member, so we should be able to get in.'

* * *

A lift whisked them up to the penthouse floor of a building on Sunset Boulevard where the club was situated. As the lift doors opened, Britt felt like she'd walked into some A-lister's private house party. The first thing she saw was a magnificent marble staircase, enormous chandeliers, and floor-to-ceiling windows with panoramic views of the ocean and the San Gabriel mountains. There was a friendly, almost homely feel to the place, but then she'd glance over to the bar and see Mila Kunis chatting to Justin Timberlake.

Britt was standing in the toilets washing her hands when she noticed a gorgeous brunette standing next to her, touching up her lipstick in the mirror. The woman looked sort of familiar – perhaps they'd worked together on a modelling job? – so she said a cheery 'Hiya.' Encouraged by the woman's warm smile (God, she really was beautiful) Britt ploughed on.

'You know, I think we might have met before,' she said as she pumped out a dollop of hand cream from the dispenser on the sink and rubbed it in. 'Are you a model?'

'No, I'm an actress,' the woman said in a husky Spanish accent.

Then suddenly Britt remembered where she'd seen her before. It was back in Clapham, at the local cinema. Her jaw dropped. The woman was Penelope Cruz.

'Oh, right, okay,' she managed. 'Well, lovely chatting to you!'

Cringing with embarrassment, Britt scuttled back to where Josh and Caggie were sitting on comfy sofas next to an open fire, and decided not to mention the fact she'd just mistaken an Oscar-winning actress for a Primark model.

'A-listers love it here,' Josh was saying, 'because there's

an underground car park so they can leave at the end of the night without any photographers catching them looking drunk or high.'

'Or leaving with someone they shouldn't,' muttered Britt, nudging Josh as an extremely famous married movie star walked past with his arm round a young starlet at least four decades his junior.

A few rounds of Grey Goose and tonic later, Britt noticed that Caggie was getting progressively more drunk and giggly. She was stroking Josh's arm flirtatiously, whispering to him, leaning over to show off her cleavage and ruffling his hair. Britt found the whole display highly embarrassing, though, she noticed with a flash of annoyance, Josh didn't seem to mind.

After a while, she couldn't stand it any longer. 'I think I'll just go for a look round,' she said, getting up quickly before either of them could come with her. 'See you later.'

Dashing out of the loos she walked slap bang into none other than the rapper, P Diddy, almost slamming her jewelled clutch into his nether regions in the process.

'Gosh, *really* sorry! My fault, I'm *so* clumsy,' she babbled.

'Hey no worries pretty lady. I'm digging that accent.' Britt smiled her thanks and started to sidle away. 'Hey! Not so fast English, I'm having a party tomorrow at my place. A pool party. Why don't y'all stop by?'

'Y'all?' Britt asked, this all felt slightly surreal – as if she were watching it happen to someone else.

'Sure,' he drawled. 'Bring a girlfriend. My man here will check your number.' He gestured to the sharp-suited security guard standing a respectful few feet away. Britt glanced over and he nodded in acknowledgement.

'Er, I have to *work* tomorrow, but thanks all the same. It's awfully nice of you,' Britt stammered, unsure of why she had suddenly developed a prim and proper accent that Julie Andrews would've been proud of. She quickly made her excuses and left. *Crikey, they're not backwards in coming forwards in La La Land.*

Britt wandered around, trying not to gawp at all the famous faces, until she found herself out on the terrace. They might be in the middle of a city, but it was quiet out there, with just the murmur of traffic many storeys below and the soft buzz of conversation from inside. Despite the late hour, the air was so warm that it felt like she was wrapped up in a cashmere shawl.

Britt leant on the balcony rail and looked out over the city and beyond. By the light of the full moon the view was breathtaking, and she had reached for her BlackBerry to try and capture it on camera when she noticed the message light flashing. It was a text: 'Hope ur having a great time, mate. Looking forward to catching up when u get back. Stewie x'

Britt read the message and smiled. She was surprised by just how much she missed him. And then she thought about Alex and was hit by a wave of loneliness so intense that it left her welling up. What was the point of being somewhere this magical without anyone to share it with? It might just as well be a dream . . .

Lost in her thoughts, it took her a moment to realise that there was someone standing next to her. She turned – and there was Josh.

'Quite a place,' he said, looking out at the mountains. In the moonlight, his profile seemed to be carved out of marble, like a statue of a Greek god.

'Just breathtaking,' agreed Britt, not sure if she was even talking about the view any more. 'Where's Caggie?'

Josh turned to her and smiled. 'Last seen chasing after P Diddy at high speed. Man, that girl is going to have one heck of a hangover tomorrow.'

They stood together in silence for a while, breathing in the velvet-soft night air and listening to the chatter of the cicadas. They were just inches apart, and Britt wondered if Josh could feel the electricity fizzing in the air between them. Just as she was thinking about making her excuses and calling it a night, Josh suddenly reached out and put his hand on top of hers as it rested on the rail. Her skin burned at his touch. She turned to him in surprise, but for once he wasn't smiling. He looked thoughtful – almost solemn.

'Britt,' he said, his voice low and urgent, 'there's something I wanted to say to you . . .'

'Heeeey, guys, so that's where you're hiding!' Caggie tottered out onto the terrace, stumbling in her heels. 'You'll never believe it, I just met Ashton Kutcher! Omigod, he is like sooo fit!' Then she tumbled over in a giggly heap. 'Oops, I might be a teensy-weensy bit drunk.'

'No shit, Sherlock,' muttered Britt, going over to help her up. 'I think we should get her back to the hotel,' she said to Josh. 'Don't want to get her fired.'

He gave a resigned shrug and together they hauled Caggie to her feet and then half-dragged, half-carried her in fits of giggles to the lift. But Britt couldn't stop thinking about the way that Josh had looked at her in the moonlight. She was desperate to know what he'd been about to say to her.

35

Over the years, Britt had watched TV coverage of superstars arriving on the red carpet at the Golden Globes, the awards night that was second only to the Oscars for prestige and glitz. The frocks! The jewels! The plastic surgery! It always looked like a glamour bomb had exploded in the middle of Hollywood, showering everywhere with diamonds, glitter and lip-gloss.

Shame they didn't show what it was really *like*, thought Britt furiously, as an Italian reporter with false eyelashes and fake boobs like two half-grapefruits clamped on her. No wonder they called the enclosure they were standing in a press 'pen': reporters and crews from around the world were crammed in like livestock. Britt wasn't sure why she had bothered spending all that money in Michael Kors – a flak jacket and steel-toe boots would have been far more appropriate.

Josh had been his usual upbeat self at breakfast that morning but had made no further mention of needing to speak to her, so Britt had plucked up the courage to find out.

'By the way,' she had said as casually as she could, 'was it anything important you wanted to talk to me about last night?'

'Oh, just a few details about the shoot,' he had replied, his usual grin unwaveringly in place. 'Nothing important.'

Britt had put it firmly to the back of her mind. She had probably been reading too much into the situation, as usual.

They had arrived to set up their equipment at 1.30 p.m., two hours before the first guests were due to turn up. Unlike the celebrities whose limos would deposit them at the foot of the red carpet, they'd had to stack-park their satellite van nearly a mile away, as all the streets surrounding the venue had been closed off except for VIP access, and then hike the rest of the way on foot. By the time they got there, Britt was wilting in the heat and had a blister the size of a five-pence-piece on her toe. Thank God for her cameraman, Phil, who had been through all this before with the Oscars, and who did a brilliant job in bagging them a plum spot right by the side of the carpet. And at least she wasn't struggling with a killer hangover like Caggie, currently running around after Jasper, her face a similar shade of green to Britt's dress. Josh looked bloody gorgeous in his tux. Britt glanced over to where he was standing on the red carpet, looking like James Bond's foxier younger brother.

Britt quickly got caught up in the magic of the occasion. Every time a famous face appeared, the fans sitting on the bleachers running alongside the red carpet roared and whooped with delight. Josh managed to grab a succession of superstars for a chat, many of whom he appeared to know personally, while Britt was so starstruck that she just stood there gawping as the likes of Brad Pitt and Angelina Jolie paraded past. It took a swift nudge from Phil to remind her that she was actually there to work and she remembered that perhaps she should be trying to find out about what they were wearing.

Just then Johnny Depp appeared through the crowds.

'Johnny! Johnny!' screeched Britt, waving furiously until, to her astonishment, he sauntered over to the barrier where she was standing. Excellent, her first red carpet interview and it was with possibly the sexiest man alive!

'Hi Johnny, I'm Britt from *Rise & Shine*, it's so great to meet you,' she babbled, trying her best not to squeal *'You're Johnny Depp! JOHNNY DEPP!'* into his beautiful face. 'Can you tell the viewers what you're wearing today?'

'Clothes,' he deadpanned.

'Um, right. Ahahaha! Thanks, Johnny!'

He walked off, leaving Britt cringing with embarrassment. Humiliated by Willy Wonka. The shame. *God, I'm an idiot*, she thought. *Come on, girl, pull yourself together . . .*

Phil poked his head out from around the back of his camera and gave her an encouraging smile. 'Don't worry, you're doing great,' he said kindly.

Next, Britt grabbed a chat with a very lovely elderly English actress who had been nominated for a Globe for her supporting role in a small art-house movie, only for Jasper (who was dashing back and forth between her and Josh) to hiss furiously into her ear – was she aware Nicole Kidman *and* Jennifer Aniston had just walked past while she was talking to bloody Miss Marple?

Britt had more success as the afternoon went on. She managed to collar Julia Roberts to talk about her vintage Dior dress and how her body had changed since becoming a mom.

'Oh, sure, my body's changed since having my babies but I really don't care,' the actress told Britt. 'I've got more important things to worry about these days. Plus, I just love pizza too much!'

This left Jasper punching the air. 'Brilliant quote, all the newspapers will pick that up!' he said happily. 'Way to go, Britt!'

Then Colin Farrell wandered over, without Britt even needing to scream for his attention like she had with all the other celebrities, and after a brief chat about his Armani tux he whispered to her how gorgeous she was and asked for her number.

Britt gawped at him. 'Are you serious?'

'Deathly,' he said softly, in his knee-tremblingly gorgeous Irish accent.

Britt flushed and giggled, not caring that Phil was still filming, and before she knew it, she had reeled off her mobile number, trying to imagine what it would be like going on a date with Colin Farrell. Was he even single? She seemed to remember reading in one of the gossip mags that he'd got married. Oh, Jeez, she wasn't going there, but still, she had just been chatted up by Colin bloody Farrell!

As he entered her number into his phone and kissed her on the hand, she was pleased to see her pushy Italian neighbour shooting daggers in her direction. Okay, so he'd probably never call, but Britt's immediate thought was that she must text Jessie to tell her that she was standing on the red carpet at the Golden Globes, and oh, by the way, her number was in Colin Farrell's iPhone! And then Britt remembered what had happened the last time they spoke and the terrible things she'd said. With a pang of guilt, she vowed to call Jessie as soon as she could to apologise.

By the time the last guest had been whisked off the red carpet and into the auditorium, Britt felt like she'd just been to a particularly brilliant party. She had bagged some great interviews for the show, and had her dented self-esteem pumped up by the delectable Colin Farrell. Jasper was thrilled with the footage and eager to get back to the satellite van to knock their report into shape for Monday morning's show – due to start back in Britain in just five hours' time.

Britt kicked off her heels, not caring that the red carpet was by now absolutely filthy. She was helping Phil to pack up his equipment when Josh appeared at her side. It seemed unfair that he still looked cool and unruffled when she was such a sweaty mess.

'Nice work, Baxter,' he said. 'You wouldn't know it was your first time. You enjoy it?'

'Loved it!' she grinned. 'I just wish I could go to the ceremony.'

'Believe me, this is the fun bit. After you've been sitting in your seat for four hours and they're announcing the winner of 'Best Original Song in a Foreign Animation', the novelty has worn off.'

Britt giggled. He was right – and she *was* looking forward to relaxing now that her work was officially over.

'Right, that's us ready to go,' Phil called over. 'You guys coming?'

'Sure,' said Britt, but as she turned to follow him she felt Josh gently grab her arm.

'Listen, Britt, do you want to go get some dinner?'

'Great,' she said. 'Let's go and round up the rest of the team . . .'

'No, you don't understand.' He was now gazing at her with the same, strangely intent expression that he'd had on the balcony the night before. 'I meant just you and me,' he said softly. 'On our own.'

36

Britt eyed him warily, wondering if she was misreading the signs yet again.

'But what about Caggie?'

'Caggie?' Josh looked puzzled.

'Yes. You asked her out with your friends on Friday night, so I assumed . . .'

'You're kidding, right?' snorted Josh, as if she'd just accused him of fancying Ken Barlow. 'Caggie kept badgering me until I said she could come along. She's a nice girl, but she's like my kid sister: cute, but annoying. There's definitely *nothing* happening there.'

As Britt nodded slowly, it sank in.

'So what do you say about dinner? My favourite restaurant in the world is just down the road, and I can't think of anyone I'd rather go there with.'

Britt finally broke into a beaming smile. 'That sounds perfect.'

Somehow, Josh had a black limo waiting for them around the back of the venue and moments later, they were speeding out of the urban sprawl of Hollywood and then out onto the Pacific Coast Highway to Malibu with its breathtaking views of the ocean.

Neither of them spoke much during the drive. Britt felt

dizzy with apprehension and excitement. Josh stared out of the window seemingly lost in his thoughts. Then, just as the sun was setting, they turned off the highway and bounced down a dusty, unmade track towards the beach. They came to a halt in a makeshift car park amongst the sand dunes, just in front of a shabby wooden building with a hand-painted sign reading 'The Spotted Crab', lit up by a string of white light bulbs.

'We're here,' smiled Josh. 'Believe me, you're in for a treat.'

But inside, it seemed to be more trick than treat. There were a few rickety tables with mismatched chairs and a bar running the width of the room, behind which a huge man with a bushy Captain Birdseye beard stood polishing glasses with a tea towel.

'Hey, Marvin,' said Josh, reaching over the bar to shake the man's meaty paw.

'Josh! Great to see you again, man. How ya been?'

While the two of them caught up, Britt looked round the restaurant. There were two guys in baseball caps and plaid shirts sitting at the bar sipping bottles of beer, and a couple playing pool at a table in the corner. A neon 'Coors' sign flickered at the window. The place was stuffy and smelt of fried food.

Britt had been worried that she was looking a bit dishevelled for their date after the scrum of the press pen, but in here she felt spectacularly over-dressed. She wasn't sure what she'd been expecting, but it sure as hell wasn't this.

'You guys take a seat and I'll bring you some beers,' said Marvin.

'Thanks, man,' said Josh, then turned to Britt and reached for her hand. 'Come with me.'

247

He led her through the restaurant and then out of the back door onto a wooden deck – and the sight that greeted Britt made her gasp with delight. They were standing in a garden surrounded by olive trees and dotted with plant pots containing large, exotic shrubs with flowers of vivid pinks and reds, through which she could see the glittering expanse of the Pacific just a hundred or so metres away. The branches of the trees were festooned with strings of tiny white fairy lights and hung with jam jars, each containing a softly glowing candle. There were more candles in storm lanterns on each of the dozen or so tables, all of which were occupied by loved-up couples or laughing parties of diners, apart from one in the far corner beneath a rose-covered arbor, which was where Josh headed now. Above the murmur of happy chatter, Britt could hear the waves crashing on the beach just beyond the trees.

'So, what do you think?' he asked as they sat down. She noticed a handwritten sign reading '*Reserved for JJ Bailey*' propped against the salt cellar.

'It's perfect,' she breathed.

He smiled, pleased at her obvious happiness.

Marvin brought them out two bottles of ice-cold beer and a pitcher of iced water and then deposited a large platter of what looked like deep-fried calamari at a neighbouring table. As the delicious smell wafted over, Britt realised just how hungry she was.

'Are we going to order food?' she asked.

'No need. They just cook up whatever's been pulled out of the ocean that day. I promise you won't be disappointed . . .'

Sure enough, Marvin soon reappeared with two

enormous plates of grilled lobster topped with garlic butter, salad and a mountain of crispy matchstick-thin fries. Moments later he was back with a bottle of rosé wine in a cooler.

'From your vineyard?' asked Josh, as he filled their glasses.

'Sure is,' said Marvin. 'I'll get you a case if you like it. It's the 2009 – a particularly good year, I think. Bon appétit, guys.'

Britt watched him lumbering off, vowing never again to judge a book by its cover. 'Marvin used to work at one of the big movie studios,' said Josh. 'In fact, I think he pretty much used to own it, until he gave it all up for this place and the simple life. He's single-handedly turned a fishing shack into LA's best kept foodie secret.'

Britt had never tasted lobster like it – or fries, for that matter. And the wine was so drinkable they had finished the whole bottle before they'd even started on dessert, a sinful brownie topped with vanilla ice-cream and a buttery lake of hot fudge sauce.

After their plates had been cleared Britt leant back in her chair, staring up at the star-filled sky, and rubbed her tummy contentedly. 'That is without doubt the best meal I've ever eaten.'

Josh chuckled. 'We aim to please, ma'am.'

Just then Britt became aware of soft music. She looked round to see a guitarist sitting beneath one of the trees. To her horror, Josh, seeing that she'd noticed, stood up and held out his hand. 'Will you dance with me, Miss Baxter?'

'Oh God, no way!' giggled Britt. 'I'm a terrible dancer.'

In fact, looking round, she couldn't even see a dance floor, just a patch of scrubby grass. After the beers and the wine she was more than a little bit drunk, but even so, the thought of standing up in front of the other diners and busting some inexpert moves with a man who had starred in probably the best dance movie of all time was beyond mortifying. And while she could just about jiggle to Abba at weddings, the guitarist was playing some sort of complicated jazz number. Britt had no idea what it was, but it sure as hell wasn't 'Dancing Queen'. 'Come on, Britt,' insisted Josh. 'Just follow my lead. I promise to look after you.'

He looked so gorgeous, still in his tux, his eyes sparkling in the candlelight, that Britt reluctantly stood up and let him lead her between the tables to where the guitarist was playing. Then he put his arms around her – just like she'd seen ballroom dancers do on TV – and started moving her, gently but insistently, in a fluid pattern around the moonlit garden.

'Just relax, baby,' he whispered, his breath warm and velvety against her ear.

And so Britt stopped worrying that she'd trip or trample on his feet and let Josh take the lead. He really was an incredible dancer, strong and graceful, and she thrilled at the feeling of being pressed up against his chest. She was dancing with Mitch Rider!

'See, you *can* dance,' smiled Josh as they whirled together. Then suddenly he lifted Britt up and effortlessly spun her around. 'Is this a waltz?' she gasped, as Josh gently lowered her back down, then looped her round and around in a series of dizzying turns.

'It's called the American Smooth.'

'Is that you or the dance?' Their eyes locked and Britt instantly knew that the night would end in a kiss. It was such a ludicrously romantic moment, with the sound of the ocean merging with the soft music and the lights twinkling like a galaxy of stars in the trees, that Britt almost laughed out loud.

The guitarist came to the end of the number and, gripping her tightly in one arm, Josh swooped her down until it felt like she was floating in mid-air, dipping her so low that her hair brushed the ground. She smiled up at him, delighted, as the other diners broke into spontaneous applause. Then, still holding her there, Josh slowly leant down and gently pressed his lips against hers, sending sparks shooting wildly through her body.

'I have wanted to do that since the moment I first laid eyes on you,' he breathed, staring into her eyes. 'And now I never want to stop.'

Oh my God, it was The Line from her favourite scene of the movie, the one that she had re-enacted countless times in her bedroom mirror as a teenager. *Was this actually happening to her?*

He pulled her to her feet and kissed her again, harder and more hungrily this time, as the guitarist started on another number. Before she knew where she was, they were somehow back in the limo, oblivious to their surroundings, pulling at each other's clothes, touching and kissing with an urgency that bordered on desperation. Britt had never wanted anyone so much. When Josh moved his hand over her breast and gently brushed her nipple with his fingertips, she thought she would explode with lust.

Britt lost all sense of time and, what felt like just

moments later, they were back in Josh's room. The door was barely closed before he pulled off her dress and then slid down her knickers, leaving her standing naked in just her jewellery and heels.

'You are perfect,' he gasped, kissing her neck and then moving down over her body, his hands knowing exactly what to do. She moaned softly as he caressed every inch of her skin. 'Lie back on the bed, baby,' he said softly.

Josh was still fully dressed, but Britt didn't feel remotely self-conscious as she stretched out on top of the cool, smooth sheets. Under the smouldering gaze of his cat-like eyes, she felt like a goddess.

There was a bottle of champagne in an ice bucket next to the bed and Josh poured them both a glass. He handed Britt hers, then positioned himself between her legs, took a mouthful of champagne and bent down to kiss her. She moaned as the ice-cold, bubbly liquid ran down the inside of her thighs while the warmth of his tongue made her shudder in ecstasy.

'Please, don't stop,' she gasped, as he took another sip, his mouth moving harder against her this time, leaving her writhing on the bed in a frenzy of delicious anticipation.

'You don't know what you're doing to me, Britt,' muttered Josh as he pulled away from her to look greedily over her body. 'I've wanted you for so long . . .'

And suddenly he was ripping off his clothes and then grabbing her and pushing himself deep inside her. They both exploded in shouts of pleasure.

They barely slept that night, dozing in each other's arms before waking again and again to make love. They just couldn't get enough of each other. As Britt relaxed back onto the pillows after yet another mind-blowing orgasm, she vaguely wondered if Josh was so incredible in bed because he could dance, or whether he could dance because he was so incredible in bed. *Either way, I'm a very lucky girl*, she thought as she closed her eyes and fell asleep, a cat-that-got-the-cream grin on her lips.

The next morning, they ordered a room service breakfast, made love again and stayed in bed until, with just forty minutes to go before the taxi was due to leave for the airport, Britt reluctantly wrenched herself away from Josh's hot body to shower and pack.

As she left, he pushed himself up on one elbow, his skin golden against the rumpled white sheets. 'Missing you already, sweetheart,' he said with a lazy smile.

'So what happened to you guys last night?' asked Jasper once they were in the SUV on the way to the airport. 'You were missed at dinner. We tried calling, but neither of you were answering your phones.'

'We had an early night,' smirked Josh.

Sitting next to him on the backseat, Britt sniggered like a naughty schoolgirl. They could hardly have made it more obvious if they had been wearing a placard around their necks reading, 'BEEN SHAGGING'.

Jasper rolled his eyes, while Caggie stared out of the window, chewing her nails. But Britt didn't care; in her blissed-out haze, nothing much seemed to matter apart from when she could start kissing Josh again.

They had seats next to each other on the flight and Britt had been hoping to continue where they had left off that morning under a blanket – or perhaps even in the bathroom. The idea of joining the mile-high club suddenly seemed very attractive . . . *Blimey what's got into you Baxter? Bucket of ice for one please.* But as soon as the 'Fasten seatbelt' sign had gone off, Josh had leaned over to give her a quick peck, put on his eye mask and fallen asleep.

Britt flicked through a magazine. She glanced over at him, taking in the soft lips that just a few hours ago had kissed every inch of her. *Obviously he's tired after last night*, Britt reassured herself with a shiver of pleasure at the memories . . . But then *she* was managing to stay awake, wasn't she? Perhaps he wasn't tired after all. Perhaps, it occurred to her with a sudden surge of dread, he was trying to avoid her now he had got what he wanted? And he hadn't made any mention of meeting up again once they were back in Britain. What was it that Stewie had said of Josh's behaviour? *Hump 'em and dump 'em.* Wouldn't that just serve her right for behaving like a raging nympho without a conscience rather than someone who'd just split from their long term boyfriend and love of their life? Britt's heart started racing in panic. Oh God, what if she meant nothing more to him than a quick shag?

37

When it was time for Josh and Britt to go their separate ways at Heathrow, Josh had kissed Britt on the lips and murmured, 'Thanks for an amazing time, baby.' There was no suggestion of meeting up. No offer of dinner. Definitely no 'I can't wait to see you again.' Not even an annoyingly vague, 'I'll call you.' He just sauntered off towards his taxi, bag slung casually over his shoulder, leaving Britt fighting back tears.

The next day she rushed to her BlackBerry every time it beeped with a message, but it was never Josh – or Colin Farrell, for that matter. She thought about calling Josh, but dismissed the idea as borderline stalker. No, if he wanted to see her again he would get in touch. And if he didn't . . . well, really, that was her fault for bedding two men in the space of a week. *Oh my God*, she thought, *what have I done?* It was so out of character. Before this she had only ever slept with her first boyfriend and Alex, who she had believed was the love of her life. The thought of him left her close to tears. *Oh, Alex, why did it have to go so terribly wrong?* Feeling utterly wretched, Britt busied herself with her unpacking, washing and ironing, then spent some quality time playing with a wildly purring Kate Moss. She at least was overjoyed to see Britt.

After polishing off an M&S lasagne and garlic bread for dinner (jet lag made her crave carbs), Britt was trawling through the dozens of emails that had arrived during her weekend – and comfort-shopping on topshop.com – when her home phone started to ring.

Resisting the urge to jump on it, she let it ring a few times and then purred 'Hello', in what she hoped was a seductive yet off-hand fashion.

'Britt, it's me, Jessie.'

She instantly felt a surge of disappointment that it wasn't Josh, but that was quickly replaced by guilt at being such a terrible friend.

'Jess! It's so good to hear from you. I've been meaning to call . . .'

'That's okay. From the look of things you've been busy. I saw your report from the Golden Globes yesterday morning. You were fantastic – and you looked gorgeous. When you were talking to Julia Roberts it looked like you were the movie star and she was the bint from breakfast TV . . .'

Despite what had happened when they last spoke, they quickly fell into easy conversation. Britt lounged happily on the sofa, picking at a bag of Revels while she caught up on all Jessie's news: Poppy had made the swimming team and Rose had squirted a whole bottle of waterproof sun-cream all over the carpet that now wouldn't come out. In turn, Britt told Jess all about LA, about Johnny Depp's put-down and being chatted up by Colin Farrell. This sent her friend into fits of excitement.

'Calm down, love, he hasn't called and I very much doubt he's going to,' giggled Britt. Speaking to Jessie again had made her realise how horribly she'd missed her. It suddenly felt vitally important that she should clear the air.

'Look, Jess, I'm so sorry about what happened when we spoke. I know you don't fancy Alex, I just . . . It was such a horrible shock when I saw that story and I just wasn't feeling supported. I overreacted.'

'It's okay,' soothed Jessie, 'I'm sorry too, I didn't handle it at all well. I just couldn't believe Alex would do such a thing. I still don't, to be honest, but your friendship is very important to me and I promise that whatever happens in your life I'll be there for you. I love you.'

Britt smiled into the phone. 'I love you, too.' Now would seem the perfect time to talk to Jessie about Josh. She desperately wanted to tell her what had happened, to get a bit of perspective on things. 'Jess, when I was in LA . . .'

'Yes?'

But Britt couldn't bring herself to say the words. Jessie was her best friend, but it was only a week since her split from Alex. What would she think of her if she told her she'd slept with not one, but two of her work colleagues? Besides, she didn't actually know what *was* happening with Josh. Right now it looked like a big fat nothing.

'I was just going to say that when I was in LA I bought some presents for you and the girls,' said Britt eventually. 'We'll have to arrange a time to meet up soon so I can give them to you.'

As she arrived at the studio the following morning, Britt hoped to be able to put her feelings about Josh to one side, but thanks to bloody Caggie it looked like what had happened between them in LA was already common knowledge. To make matters even worse, it turned out that Josh was off for the rest of the week (a fact he hadn't bothered to mention to her, she noted angrily), so she was left to face the nudges and whispers on her own. Also, she wasn't sure how many people were aware of what had happened between her and Stewie last week. At this rate she was going to get a reputation as the office bike. From the way Charlie perved at her when he brought her a coffee, maybe she already had?

Britt hurried into the morning's pre-show production meeting studiously avoiding eye contact with anyone and took a seat at the back, where hopefully she could keep a low profile. But when Toby arrived he immediately sent all heads swivelling in her direction.

'Britt! Great to have you back,' he boomed across the table. 'You did a fantastic job in LA, well done. The papers went mad for your Julia Roberts quotes.'

She grinned sheepishly, stealing a glance round the room. To Toby's right was Rashida, whose pretty heart-shaped face expressed a mixture of pity and disappointment, while across the other side of the table Cherry just looked livid.

At the end of the meeting, Britt was scuttling out of the room when she heard someone call her name. It was Rashida.

'Can I have a quick word?' Her dark eyes were wide and anxious.

'Sure,' said Britt reluctantly, following her out into the corridor.

'I know it's none of my business but do be careful of Josh,' said Rashida. 'The guy only cares about one thing, and that's himself.'

'It's okay, you can save your breath,' said Britt, a little

more harshly than she had intended. 'There's nothing going on between us.' But as she said the words, each one felt like a dagger in her heart. It had actually been the most romantic night of her life, but to Josh she was evidently just another notch on his bedpost.

Rashida looked relieved. 'Oh, that's good to hear. You deserve so much better.' She checked her watch. 'I should get going. See you later.'

You're just jealous that you couldn't have him, thought Britt crossly as she watched her disappear off down the corridor.

The other person who she had been dreading seeing was Stewie. Clearly he didn't want to see her either, as he didn't come and visit her before the show as he usually would. But they couldn't avoid each other when he came to mic her up just before she went on air.

'Britt.' He couldn't look her in the eyes.

'Stewie, I just wanted to say . . .'

'Really, no need.' She noticed that he was wiring her up with lightning speed. 'It's none of my business. As long as you're happy, that's the main thing.'

He gave her a sad little smile, leaving Britt in no doubt as to how deeply she'd hurt him. She would almost have preferred him to scream at her and call her a slut.

'Canteen after the show as usual?' she said brightly, as he turned to leave.

'Nah, think I'll take a rain-check.'

'Another time then, perhaps . . . ?'

But Stewie had already gone.

On the way back to Clapham from the studio later that morning, Britt stared out of the car window feeling wretched. She had lost her best friend on the show and been turned into a laughing stock by Josh. *That's it*, she thought, *I'm swearing off men for at least a year. I shall be one of those career women who wears expensive Armani suits and has a personal trainer. By this time next year I'll be presenting* Newsnight *and have adopted an orphan from Iraq*. But behind the bravado, a little voice piped up, *All I really want is Josh to call . . .*

Britt let herself in through the front door and was just thinking about phoning Jessie and spending the rest of the afternoon with her and the girls when she spotted a parcel wrapped in brown paper just inside the communal doorway. It had her name on it. And she instantly recognised the loopy, sloping handwriting. *Josh*.

38

Her hands shaking with anticipation, Britt dashed upstairs to her flat and tore off the paper. Inside, there was a package wrapped in cream tissue tied with black ribbon and an envelope. She opened it up and read the note inside: '*I haven't stopped thinking about you. Dinner at Hix, 8 p.m. on Friday night? Please say yes . . . JJB x PS: I look forward to seeing the enclosed lying on your bedroom floor.*'

Ripping open the tissue paper she found the most beautiful set of La Perla lingerie in dove-grey silk and nude lace. It was super sexy without being tarty, the sort of thing a girl would choose herself as opposed to the scratchy black lace stuff that blokes usually went for. Whooping with delight, she dashed to the bedroom to try it on. It fitted perfectly, and she felt a shiver of excitement as she imagined Josh peeling it off her.

As she looked at herself in the mirror, it occurred to her that she should get another spray tan if she *really* wanted to look her best. And a wax. And a mani/pedi, an oxygen facial and what about those eyelash extensions that everyone seemed to be talking about? And possibly one of those inch-loss seaweed wraps as well.

Britt spent the rest of the afternoon booking

appointments and then trying to put together a killer date outfit. It took almost until dinnertime as most of her clothes had been packed away in boxes ready for her move to the new apartment at the weekend, so she had to empty them all out and then fold everything away again. In the end she decided on a pair of black J Brand 'Agnes' trousers with the sexy zips up the side of the legs and a leather Vince vest top.

As Britt laid out the outfit and started to think about accessories (okay, so the date was two days away but better to know now if she needed to buy a new necklace or shoes), it fleetingly occurred to her that she was supposed to be arranging a visit to see Jessie, but she instantly shoved it to the back of her mind. That could wait. Jess would understand.

Just after 8 p.m. on Friday Britt climbed out of her taxi and into the bustle of Soho's Brewer Street, pushing through the stream of tourists and after-work drinkers sauntering along the pavement, and into the restaurant with its anonymous black front door.

The girl sitting at Reception smiled at her arrival. 'Good evening, Miss Baxter, are you dining with us tonight?'

Britt shrugged off her coat and handed it to the girl. 'Yes, I—'

'She's with me.' Britt turned and looked straight into Josh's emerald eyes. He looked like an old-school Hollywood matinee idol, with his dark hair smoothed to the side and a crisp white shirt and chinos. 'I've missed you so much, baby,' he whispered, wrapping his arms around her and pulling her in for a long, lingering kiss.

He didn't seem to care that they were standing right at the front of the restaurant in full view of all the diners. Britt felt like she was in a dream.

'I'm so sorry about not getting in touch when we got back,' he said as they sat down. 'I got home to a message from my sister that our mom had been taken ill back home in Chicago. It was too short notice to go out there, but Toby gave me the rest of the week off to sort things out from here.'

'Oh God, I'm sorry, is she okay?' Britt felt terrible. There she was, obsessing hysterically over whether he was going to call while the poor guy had been in the middle of a family crisis.

'I hope she will be,' he said, although his expression seemed to suggest it was unlikely. 'I've made sure she's getting the best care. Only time will tell if she'll make a full recovery.' He reached out and took her hand. 'But let's not talk about that now. I want to spend the next few hours focusing on you.' He leant towards her and said in a whisper: 'You look so goddamn gorgeous you're making all the other women in here jealous . . .'

Britt barely ate anything. She was too hungry for Josh to have much of an appetite for dinner. The atmosphere was thick with lust and longing and Britt was relieved when Josh asked for the bill straight after they had finished their main courses – well, finished pushing the food around their plates a bit.

As they left the restaurant, they were greeted by an explosion of flashes from a pack of paparazzi that had been lurking outside. Of course, she had been papped before, but that had been like posing for a friendly family snap compared to this . . . *ambush*. There must have been at least a dozen photographers and they were all shoving and shouting her name – it was terrifying. Britt froze in shock, but instead of covering his face or hanging back to avoid them being photographed together, Josh was totally prepared. He put his arm around Britt's shoulders and plastered on his most dazzling smile, as if he wanted the world to know they were together.

He elbowed them a path through the pack and they jumped into a waiting taxi as the paps pressed their lenses up against the windows.

'Where d'you live, babe?' asked Josh, seemingly totally unruffled by the scrum.

A shell-shocked Britt reeled off her address, then instantly regretted it. She should have suggested going to his place instead. What was Josh going to think about her poky little flat?

But then it occurred to her that as she was moving to the penthouse in the morning, she really had to go back to Clapham anyway to let in the removal men, and then Josh started to kiss her and the only thing she could focus on was her desperate urge for him.

They were tearing each other's clothes off before they were even through Britt's front door. If anything, the sex was better than it had been in LA. She had never been with anyone who seemed to know so instinctively where to touch her and what to do. She stopped counting at five orgasms. And it wasn't flashy sex, where a new partner seems intent on dazzling you with their repertoire – 'And now, for my next trick . . . !' – rather than fully surrendering themselves to the moment. It might have been premature to admit it, but Britt felt like they were really making love rather than just, well, sex.

Afterwards, she lay with her head in the nook of his arm, lulled into a dreamless sleep by the rhythmic rise and fall of his chest.

The next morning, Josh was still lounging around in his Calvin Klein briefs when the removal men arrived. Although Britt had shelled out an extra three hundred quid for the 'premium' removals option – which meant the blokes would pack up all her belongings in boxes for her – there still seemed to be an awful lot to do, and Britt was quite relieved when Josh suggested he get a taxi back to his place in Chelsea and then drive back later to take her to the penthouse. In the end, he didn't arrive back in his zippy black Porsche 911 until after 3 p.m., but Britt couldn't really blame him. Despite the fact that the removal men were doing most of the hard work, moving house wasn't exactly a sexy way to spend a Saturday.

It had been well over a month since Britt had seen the apartment and she was nervous it wouldn't live up to her initial excitement, but as she wandered around the huge, airy space, taking in the sexy L-shaped suede sofa, the balcony that made you feel like you were flying above the Thames and the hi-tech coffee machine in the kitchen, she knew she'd made the right choice. And Josh, with his golden tan, designer T-shirt and Rolex looked far more at home there than Alex ever had.

'Quite a pad you got here, babe.' He emerged from the bathroom with a glint in his eye. 'I'm just going out to buy a celebratory bottle of champagne, then you and I are gonna christen that shower . . .'

That night, after Britt had unpacked the most useful of the boxes while Josh made some work calls, they stretched out on the sofa with a Thai takeaway and watched old movies on the huge flat-screen TV built into the wall. They didn't even discuss whether Josh would stay the night; it just felt the natural thing. And as the next day was Sunday, they could have a proper lie-in.

When Britt woke the next morning in an unfamiliar bed it took her a moment to remember where she was, but then she felt Josh's warm body asleep beside her and saw the morning sunlight creeping in through the slats of the blinds and she smiled to herself. *The luckiest girl in the world.* She was just getting out of bed when Josh started to stir.

'Not so fast,' he murmured sleepily, grabbing her hand and pulling it under the sheets to rest on his crotch. It was obvious he wanted her.

Britt dropped a kiss on his chest then wriggled out of his clutches. 'You'll just have to wait. I need to get some milk, so we can try out the coffee machine.'

As she walked naked over to the fitted wardrobes, which stretched the entire length of the room, Josh sat up in bed and watched her.

'You going out like that?'

Britt pulled out her new MaxMara coat with a flourish. 'Almost,' she said, wrapping the coat over her naked body with a naughty smile.

'Christ, you're so goddamn sexy. Hurry back.'

Britt's apartment was housed in a building that used to be part of old Victorian docks, and millions of pounds had been spent restoring the area to its former glory, with pretty cobbled streets and black-painted ironwork – although without the rats and open sewers, obviously. She found a newsagents a few doors down and picked up some provisions and the papers.

It wasn't until Britt was back in the lift, humming happily to herself as she flicked through *The Daily Splash* that she noticed that her and Josh's dinner date on Friday night had made it onto page 5. There they were, with soppy grins and their arms round each other, looking nauseatingly loved-up. There was another snap of them snogging in the back of the taxi.

'BED AND BREAKFAST! *RISE & SHINE* DUO'S STEAMY SECRET DATES' read the headline. It was hardly a surprise that the photos had ended up in the press, but that didn't make Britt feel any less uncomfortable. She didn't think she'd ever get used to seeing her private moments made public. Reluctantly, she read on.

Breakfast TV pin-ups Britt Baxter and Josh Bailey have embarked on a secret romance after their sizzling on-screen chemistry spilled over into real life.

Dance Delirium hunk Josh, 33, has been linked to a string of famous beauties, but friends say that he's serious about Carlisle-born babe Britt, 26. The tasty twosome were reportedly inseparable during a recent work trip to LA, sharing a room and sneaking out for romantic dinners.

A pal told us: 'They can't keep their hands off each other. Josh is crazy about her . . .'

Josh was sitting up in bed with a glass of juice when she came in.

'Look at this.' She climbed into bed next to him and showed him the story. 'I'm so sorry.'

She expected him to be pissed off, but as he read through the article he just laughed.

'Great picture of you, babe.' He held the paper up for closer examination. 'Not so hot of me, though. Assholes got my bad side.'

'But aren't you angry about the story?'

'Why should I be? We *are* dating, we clearly can't keep our hands off each other and I *am* crazy about you.'

'You are?'

'Yes!' Josh threw the paper on the floor and pulled her closer to him. 'I don't do this sort of thing with my friends, believe me . . .' He began to unbutton her coat, tantalisingly slowly. 'I adore you, Britt, haven't you realised?'

As he slipped off her coat, she lay back on the pillows and surrendered as he started to kiss her.

'But what about Toby?' she murmured, as Josh stroked the inside of her thighs, making her shudder with anticipation. 'And what are the viewers going to think?'

'Shhh, just play the game, baby. The public are gonna go crazy for this, you'll see . . .'

39

Josh was right. The following Tuesday, when the new issues of the celebrity weeklies hit the shelves, every magazine featured the pictures from their Hix date together with stories breathlessly claiming to have the inside story on their whirlwind romance. *The Daily Splash* followed up its original scoop with a story on how 'BROODY BRITT WANTS BAILEY BABIES' and then a few days later reported on a bookmaker that was offering odds of 6–1 that the couple would wed within the year. Even the broadsheets picked up on the story, with *The Times* quoting television industry experts who predicted that Britt and Josh could become the next Richard and Judy.

Suddenly Britt couldn't leave her flat without someone stopping her for an autograph or a photo. Van drivers would lean out of their windows and shout, 'Oi, Baxter, where's the Yank?' as she walked down the street. She started doing her supermarket shopping online after someone snapped a picture of her buying tampons in Sainsburys and sold it to the tabloids. But this was nothing compared to the blizzard of attention when Britt and Josh went out together. Wherever they were, a pack of paparazzi would magically appear and start snapping away.

Over the next two weeks they were invited to every premiere, launch party, charity ball and awards ceremony in the showbiz calendar. They were inundated with requests for press interviews and photo shoots. In short, the public couldn't get enough of what *The Daily Splash* was calling 'The TV love story of the year'.

But although they were out virtually every night at some glitzy showbiz bash, they hardly ever got any time alone together. Josh would stay at her place a couple of nights a week – and the sex was always amazing – but he would never invite her back to his. They hadn't been out on a proper date, one where they could have a really good chat, since that dinner at Hix. And although Britt would watch Josh work a party, charming the pants off everyone, and feel a shiver of pride, she couldn't help wishing it could be just the two of them at home, snuggling on the sofa with only a DVD and a takeaway curry for company. But then he would look across the room and smile at her, and Britt's silly worries would vanish in a puff of lust.

News of their romance was greeted less effusively at the *Rise & Shine* studios. Soon after the story broke Rashida requested a transfer from Style Spot to work on Sport. Britt could only assume she believed Britt had lied about her relationship with Josh. And although still always polite, Stewie now seemed desperate to get out of her company whenever work pushed them together.

Toby, however, was thrilled with all the extra publicity that their relationship was generating for the show, and when fans started inundating the show's website message boards with requests for Josh and Britt to appear together on the sofa more often, he decided to try them out as the main anchors for one day a week, replacing Ken and

Cherry on the sofa every Friday. Although Britt wasn't surprised that Ken was happy with the new arrangement as he had been angling for a four-day week for some time – 'Need to work on my golf handicap,' he had chuckled to her – she was amazed that Cherry seemed to accept it too, even coming to Britt's dressing room to wish her luck. The rumours in the green room were that she was keen to have more lie-ins as there was a hot new toy-boy on the scene, but when Britt tried to quiz Fran about it one morning as she was having her concealer applied, Fran swiftly changed the subject.

In amongst all the fuss, Britt had completely forgotten about meeting up with Jessie. Her friend left a phone message for her, teasing her for not mentioning Josh to her when they spoke and asking for all the juicy details, but Britt somehow never found the time to call back and besides, when she wasn't with Josh she seemed to have countless interviews and appointments to fulfil. *She'll understand*, thought Britt guiltily, when she noticed yet another missed call from Jessie. She sent her a text promising to get in touch soon and got one of the production secretaries at the studio to courier round the presents she'd bought in LA to Jessie's house.

Two weeks after *The Daily Splash* broke news of their romance, the *Rise & Shine* press office arranged for Britt to do an exclusive 'at home' chat with *Wow!*, the top-selling weekly celebrity magazine. On the morning of the interview Britt rushed home after the show and was just straightening up when there was a knock at her door. It was Josh.

'Hey, baby,' he smiled, taking her in his arms. She

thought she'd mentioned she was going to be busy with the interview. 'I hope you don't mind me stopping by,' he said, 'but you looked so gorgeous at work today that I couldn't wait to get my hands on you.'

'I'm sorry, Josh,' she said. 'I've got a team from *Wow!* magazine arriving any minute to do an interview.'

'Oh.' He pulled away from her, sounding disappointed.

'I just thought you wouldn't want to be around when the journalist arrived. They're bound to make our relationship the focus of the feature if we're here together . . .'

'Are you ashamed of me?'

'What? No! God, no. Absolutely not!'

'Then let's do the interview together,' he said with a grin, going to sit on the couch. '*Really* give people something to talk about!'

Suddenly Britt felt like she'd had enough of people talking about them. She was sick of seeing 'body language experts' analysing their photos in the women's weeklies and then commenting on the state of their relationship. She didn't want everyone to know about what they had for dinner on a date last week. It felt like they never had a private moment to themselves.

'Josh, I'm not sure I'm ready to do something like this just yet,' she said carefully: the last thing she wanted to do was give the impression that she was somehow rejecting him. 'I want to try and keep some things just for us. Do you know what I mean?'

To her relief, Josh got it immediately.

'Oh, baby, I'm so sorry.' He patted the seat next to him and she came and sat down. 'I just get carried away. I know we've only been together for a few weeks, but I've fallen for you in a big way. For the first time in my life I've met a woman who I want to spend every minute with, and I guess I just want to shout that from the rooftops. But you're absolutely right. We should take things slowly. And if you want to do the interview alone, I totally understand.'

But as she looked into his dark-lashed eyes, nothing seemed important apart from making him happy. And besides, wasn't it better that they told their side of the story, rather than let the endless fictitious 'sources' in the press do it for them?

'No, it's okay, I'm just being silly,' she said with a smile. 'Let's do this.'

When the journalist arrived, a hard-faced blonde called Chrissy, wearing too much make-up and a pair of teetering cork wedges, she was overjoyed to discover that she had somehow landed a world exclusive: Britt and Josh's first ever joint interview. Also, she obviously had a raging crush on Josh that she did little to hide.

'It's *so* good to see you again,' Chrissy gushed, fluttering her false lashes so furiously it looked like she was trying to swat flies. 'Our readers just can't get enough of Josh Bailey!'

The pair of them settled down together on the sofa, while Chrissy sat opposite on a leather armchair and put her Dictaphone on the coffee table between them. Britt eyed it nervously. She still got terrified she'd say something stupid and it would end up as front-page news.

'So, Josh, you've got a reputation as something of a stud,' said Chrissy, shooting him such a knowing look that Britt immediately wondered if they'd slept with each other, but the journalist wasn't exactly gorgeous so she dismissed the idea. 'Are things serious with Britt?'

'Oh yes,' said Josh. 'The way I feel about Britt . . . It's like nothing I've had before.'

'So you might say that she's tamed JJ Bailey?'

Josh laughed. 'Britt has got me wrapped around her beautiful little finger if that's what you mean.' He leant forwards, an earnest expression on his face. 'I'm in my thirties now, Chrissy, and for the first time in my life the idea of settling down with someone and having babies seems really quite attractive.'

'So could Britt possibly be that someone?'

He turned to look at Britt with a look of tenderness in his eyes. 'I very much hope so.' The way he said it, it almost seemed like he was asking her a question. Britt caught her breath as the implication of what Josh had said sunk in. *Oh my God, he wants to marry me!* Then he turned back to the journalist. 'All I can say, Chrissy, is watch this space. And if, or rather *when*, anything does happen, then *Wow!* will be the first – well, second – to know!'

It was the following Friday, Britt's day to co-host the show with Josh. The pair of them had been out the night before at the star-studded launch of a new boutique hotel in Notting Hill so had only managed to get a few hours' sleep.

While Josh was his usual sparkling self, Britt was running solely on caffeine and adrenaline. With only fifteen minutes of the show left to go, she was just about managing to hold it together and couldn't wait to go home and crawl back into bed.

But as the floor manager cued them for the next item, an interview with a young solider who had just received the Victoria Cross for saving seven of his colleagues in Afghanistan, Britt began to feel very strange indeed. She had broken out in a cold sweat and her stomach was churning ominously. It couldn't be a hangover, as she'd only had a couple of glasses of champagne the night before.

'Hi, and welcome back to *Rise & Shine*,' said Josh beside her. 'Now the word 'hero' is used a lot these days, but few people have been quite so deserving of the name as our next guest. Corporal Robert Tyler was on a tour of duty in Afghanistan earlier this year when his unit came under attack from enemy fire . . .'

As Josh was talking Britt kept a smile plastered on her face, but inside she was beginning to panic at the increasingly urgent griping in her guts. Suddenly her stomach let out such a loud gurgle that Josh glanced at her in alarm, before quickly recovering his composure.

In her ear, the director told Britt to ask about the soldier's family life.

'So, Rob, you've got a wife and small daughter back in Bristol,' she said, shifting uncomfortably on the sofa as another terrifying groan rose from somewhere deep in her intestines. She spoke a bit louder in an attempt to cover the noise. 'Were you thinking about them when you ran towards the machine-gun fire to save your colleagues?'

He started to answer, but Britt was no longer listening. Her sole focus was the urgent cramping in her bowels and the terrible realisation that she had to get to the toilet *right that second* or else suffer the mother of all humiliations on live TV.

40

'. . . so to answer your question, in the heat of the moment I wasn't really thinking of anything but helping my mates,' concluded Corporal Tyler, with a modest shrug.

Suddenly, Britt stood up. Josh stared at her, surprised. In her ear, the director was screeching at her to *Sit the fuck down!* She noticed Stewie standing behind the cameras, a worried expression on his face, mouthing 'Are you okay?'

'Well, I think your story is an absolute inspiration,' gabbled Britt, crossing her legs, 'and it's a pleasure to meet you, but I'm afraid I'm going to have to excuse myself and leave you in the capable hands of Josh.'

And with that she ran out of the studio as fast as her Givenchy heels would allow, leaving the entire floor crew staring after her, and nearly crashing straight into Rashida who was hurrying along the corridor outside.

'Hey, watch out,' cried the assistant producer, the first words she'd actually said to Britt since Britt had started dating Josh.

'I'm so sorry!' cried Britt, shoving past her to the toilets – although, even in her dire state, she couldn't miss the look of contempt that flashed across Rashida's pretty face.

The show was long finished by the time Britt finally emerged from the toilet feeling so shaky and drained she had to steady herself on the wall as she tottered along the corridor. Thank God she'd somehow remembered to turn her mic off on the way in . . . What the hell could have made her so ill? It couldn't have been the two glasses of champagne. And she very much doubted it was the trendy vegan canapés they'd served at the hotel launch. She'd never heard of anyone getting food poisoning from a carrot. God, what if she was pregnant? Her jeans *had* been feeling a little tight lately . . . But no, it was called morning sickness, not morning squits. And she and Josh had (mostly) been very careful on that front . . .

'Hey, you okay, Britt?' Fran appeared out of the make-up room, her face etched with concern. 'Everyone's worried about you.' She put her arm around Britt's shoulders and looked into her face. 'Gosh, you're very pale, love. I really think you should come and sit down for a bit.'

The idea of curling up on the make-up-room sofa and letting Fran look after her was desperately tempting, but Britt knew she had some urgent explaining to do after dashing off in the middle of a live broadcast.

'It's really lovely of you, but I think I should go and find Toby.'

Fran considered her for a moment, then nodded. 'Okay, if you insist, but just hold on a minute.' She disappeared and then came back with a can of Coke, which she handed over. 'Here you go – first aid. And you must promise me you'll come back here for a lie-down once you've spoken to the boss.'

Britt smiled weakly. 'Thanks. And if you see Josh, tell him I'm really sorry and I'll explain later.'

Toby looked up from his computer when she came into his office.

'There're a lot of concerned viewers on the message boards asking what happened to you earlier when you ran out on the interview with Corporal Tyler,' he said, gesturing for her to sit opposite him. 'I'm quite interested to know the same thing.'

'I'm so sorry, Toby. I got a violent attack of the runs and had to get to the toilet. The last thing I wanted was to interrupt the broadcast, but I didn't really have any choice.'

'Are you feeling better now?'

'Yes, a bit shaky, but I think the worst is over.'

'That's good to hear.' Toby propped his elbows on the desk and steepled his fingers. 'Look Britt, I appreciate that it's hardly your fault that you're ill, but I've noticed in the papers that you and Josh have been going out an awful lot lately. Obviously I want my presenters to have a social life, but when it starts affecting their work then it becomes a concern.'

'I'm not hungover, if that's what you mean,' protested Britt, realising she sounded a bit like a defensive teenager. 'I barely drank anything last night . . .'

'That's as maybe, but I think you might want to cut down the partying a bit for the time being and focus on your career. This is a demanding job, Britt, and you need to take good care of yourself to stay on top. Image is so important in this game. You've got a chance to really make a success of this and I'd hate to see you screw that up for the sake of a few wild nights. I've seen too many promising talents crash and burn to risk letting it happen to you. Do you understand where I'm coming from?'

Britt nodded miserably. Toby had a point – she had pretty much been living on canapés and late-night restaurant dinners recently, and couldn't remember the last time she'd felt like she'd had enough sleep.

'I do understand, Toby, and I really am sorry,' she said.

'That's good to hear.' He gave her a fatherly smile. 'And I hope it goes without saying that I'm immensely pleased with your work on *Rise & Shine*. Now you get home and have a quiet weekend and I'll see you on Monday.'

Britt walked out of his office feeling like a total screw-up. She hated disappointing Toby as she knew he'd taken such a huge gamble in giving her a job. But she couldn't help feeling a little bit victimised. She bet he wouldn't be having this chat with Josh.

Britt was just walking past the studio on her way back to the dressing room when she spotted a small pill bottle lying on the floor near the bin. She picked it up and shook it: empty. Britt went to throw it away, but as she did so she glanced at the name of the drug on the label. *U-Go-Fast*. And in small letters underneath were the words, 'Stimulant laxative'. Britt stared at the bottle as the awful realisation dawned on her.

'Look at this.' After a quick glance round to check if they were being watched, Britt placed the laxative bottle on the table in front of Josh. He had insisted that she come up to the canteen for a restorative cup of tea before he escorted her back home.

Josh picked it up and looked at it. 'And?' he shrugged.

'Read the label,' she urged. '*U-Go-Fast*. Bit of a coincidence, don't you think?'

Josh pulled a face. 'You really think someone slipped these in your drink?'

'Well, it seems a bit odd that one moment I'm pretty much fine, and the next I'm having to sprint off to the toilet like Usain Bolt.'

'Oh, get real, babe, they probably belong to Ken. That guy's like an anorexic teenager . . .'

'Come on, Josh, you really don't find it suspicious that I get the runs and then find an empty laxative bottle?'

'We're working in a TV studio. If they don't belong to Ken, there are plenty of other people here vain enough to pop laxatives to shit away the excess pounds. Come on, baby, you're just being silly.'

'I guess you're right,' she said eventually.

'I am. Now let's get you home so I can do my Doctor Bailey bit. If you're feeling up to it, I think a full body examination might be in order . . .'

Britt smiled, but inside she couldn't shake off a feeling of uneasiness. If her suspicions were right, who the hell would want to do something like that to her?

41

It was Saturday morning, and Britt and Josh were lying in bed together with the sun pouring in through the floor-to-ceiling windows. She was stroking his freshly waxed chest, marvelling yet again at how perfect his body was. Honest to God, he had a six-pack like that bloke from the Dolce & Gabbana perfume advert.

They were at her flat, as usual. Britt had given up asking Josh if he wanted them to sleep over at his place for a change. 'It's just so small compared to your apartment, baby,' he would say, 'and girls have so much more shit than boys.' And then he would start to kiss her and she would forget all about why it seemed remotely important. But Britt couldn't help wondering what the famous Bailey bachelor pad in Chelsea was really like. She bet it had a cinema room and those special windows that go opaque when you press a button, instead of curtains. Probably a hot tub, too. No doubt she'd see it soon enough.

'D'you know, it will be our two-month anniversary next weekend?' Josh was propped up on one elbow, tracing circles on her naked tummy.

'Mmm,' murmured Britt, relishing his touch. Right now, she felt like she never wanted to move.

'So how about we go away somewhere for a couple of

nights, maybe one of those English country-house hotels with four-poster beds and butlers, and we can spend the whole weekend doing this.' Josh dropped a kiss on her lips. 'And this.' He kissed her neck. 'And then maybe something like this . . .' His lips moved downwards, brushing over her body, making her sigh with ecstasy.

'I'd say that sounds like an excellent idea,' she purred, stretching like a contented cat. But then suddenly her eyes flew open. 'Oh no! My mum's coming to stay next weekend.'

'What?' Josh frowned. 'You didn't mention that.'

Britt sat upright. 'I know, I'm so sorry, hon, but it's been in the diary for ages and I really can't cancel. I haven't seen her for so long.'

In fact, she realised guiltily, she hadn't seen Molly since that week in Larkbridge all those months ago, and they'd barely spoken since the awkward phone call in the wake of her split from Alex.

'Hey, perhaps the three of us could go for dinner on the Saturday night?' she said. 'I'd love you to meet her, and we can raise a glass for our anniversary, too. I know it's not ideal, but we could do the hotel another weekend. What do you think?'

Josh shrugged back the covers and climbed out of bed. 'Yeah, okay babe, whatever works for you,' he muttered over his shoulder, heading for the bathroom.

Damn. Why did Molly's visit have to be this weekend, out of all the ones that it could have been? As a rule, Britt didn't get to see much of Josh at the weekend. He had just landed a regular gossip spot on a top American radio show and between researching and recording the interviews he was usually too busy to see her. Not only that, but this was the first time he'd ever suggested they go away together and she so didn't want to turn him down. Perhaps she could ask her mum to swap dates . . . Oh God, no, she really couldn't. Although her mum understood how busy she was these days, Britt felt guilty that she'd been ignoring her – especially as she'd been ill. Besides, she was looking forward to showing her the new apartment. It was just a shame that Molly's visit screwed up her precious weekend away with Josh.

'Goodness, love, do you really need all this space?' Molly was standing in the doorway of Britt's new flat, gawping like a tourist. 'And is that a *suede* sofa? Dear me, must be the devil to get marks out of . . .'

Britt rolled her eyes. Why couldn't her mum just be pleased for her? But she immediately swallowed her irritation. Her life had totally changed since they'd last met and while it had been a gradual process for her, for Molly it must be as if her daughter had morphed overnight into a shiny-haired celebrity with a chauffeur-driven car (Britt had asked Reg to pick her mum up from the station) and a luxury penthouse apartment. They had stopped for lunch on the terrace at Pont de la Tour on the way back, and when a man had come up to their table to ask for Britt's autograph she had caught Molly looking at her as if she was a total stranger. She mustn't forget how weird this must all be for her mum.

'Here, Mum, come and check out the view,' she said, leading her over to her balcony. 'Look, you can see Tower Bridge!'

At last Molly's face broke into a delighted smile. 'Well, I never! Britt, this is . . . well, I've never seen anything like it, love. I can't believe my little girl lives in a place like this!'

'Make yourself at home and I'll put the kettle on,' said Britt, buzzing off her mum's excitement, as they wandered back into the living room. 'I thought we could go for a bit of a stroll by the river this afternoon, then tomorrow I'm going to take you shopping and maybe have a wander round a few art galleries. The Tate Modern is just along the river.'

'Sounds lovely,' said Molly, perching gingerly on the sofa.

'And then tomorrow night we're seeing Josh for dinner.' Britt came and sat next to her. 'I can't wait for you to meet him, Mum.'

Molly squeezed her hand. 'Me too, love,' she smiled. Britt knew how much her mum had loved Alex, but she felt sure that she would fall for the famous Bailey charm. 'How does he get on with Jessie?'

'Um, he hasn't met Jess yet.' She noted Molly's look of surprise. 'You know what it's like, Mum, we've all been really busy . . .'

Molly nodded, but of course they both knew it was a feeble excuse. The truth was that Jessie had repeatedly asked them round to join her and Tom for dinner at home in Streatham, but it was impossible to persuade Josh to leave central London. 'I get a nosebleed if I go that far south,' he had joked. She knew she should really try and arrange a meal at a restaurant in town, but she just never seemed to get round to it.

'Right, I think I'll freshen up,' said Molly. 'Which way to the bathroom?'

'Second door over there on the left.' Britt watched her

mum close the door and then waited with a smile. *One, two, three . . .*

'By 'eck!' came Molly's shriek. 'Will you look at the size of this shower!'

The next day a taxi picked them up at 9 a.m. and whisked them off to Harrods, where Britt treated her mum to a Burberry trench coat and a pair of Giuseppe Zanotti grey suede ankle boots. After all the sacrifices her mum had made over the years it was wonderful to now be in a position to spoil her. They had lunch at the brasserie in the Mandarin Oriental Hotel and then it was more shopping, including a stop at the lingerie specialists, Rigby & Peller.

'Isn't this where the Queen buys her smalls?' Molly asked the sales assistant.

Britt cringed. She knew that mothers were meant to be embarrassing, but it was different now that she was famous and an ill-judged comment could lead to a tabloid headline. She decided to tackle the subject over an afternoon tea of vanilla macaroons and a pot of Earl Grey at the Ladurée café back in Harrods.

'Mum, I know you mean well, but can you try and be a bit less . . . *chatty* with everyone? We're not in Larkbridge now.'

'What do you mean, love?' Just then a waitress appeared and asked if they wanted anything else. 'I think we're alright, love, thank you,' smiled Molly. 'Ooh, unless you have a nice slice of fruitcake?'

'Mum, this is a *patisserie*,' snapped Britt. 'They don't serve Dundee cake.'

'Just the bill then, thanks,' said Molly, looking a little hurt.

Britt instantly regretted snapping at her. 'I'm so sorry, it's just that people recognise me from *Rise & Shine* and you wouldn't *believe* the sort of stupid stuff that ends up in the press. I have to be really careful these days . . .'

'No, *I'm* sorry love, I just can't get used to the fact that my little girl is famous. I promise I'll be on my best behaviour at dinner tonight . . .'

At 8 p.m. their taxi pulled up outside the iconic stained-glass windows of The Ivy in Covent Garden. Britt wanted to take her mum to a restaurant that she read about in the celebrity magazines, and Molly was excited about the fact that she might be dining next to Ant and Dec or Simon Cowell.

'Do I look okay, Britt?' she asked, patting nervously at her hair as they stood outside the famous double doors. 'It's just I don't get dressed up very often these days . . .'

'You look absolutely gorgeous, Mum.' And she did. Molly had spent ages getting ready and looked twenty years younger in a floral dress teamed with the new boots, her glossy auburn hair loose about her shoulders. 'Don't worry, you'll fit right in.'

They were shown to one of the best tables with a view of the whole restaurant, a few seats over from where Big Brother's Brian Dowling was giggling with a friend and behind them were Chris Moyles and David Walliams laughing over their Dover Sole.

As they were sitting down, Britt's phone bleeped with a text. It was from Josh: 'Sorry babe, just finishing up a drink with a friend. Be with you in 20 minutes x'

With a flash of annoyance, Britt deleted it without replying. He knew how important tonight was to her.

Why couldn't he have finished his flipping drink a bit earlier?

'Everything okay, love?' asked Molly.

'Yes, fine,' said Britt quickly. 'Josh is just running a few minutes late. He'll be here shortly. Now, let's order some champagne . . .'

In the end, he didn't turn up until over half an hour later, but when Britt spotted him making his way across the restaurant to their table, his gorgeous face a picture of apology, her anger instantly evaporated.

'I'm so sorry, babe,' he whispered, as he leaned in for a kiss, 'I got caught with an old work colleague. I'll make it up to you, I promise.'

Then he turned to Molly with his most dazzling grin. 'And I don't believe I've met your sister . . . ?'

It was the corniest of lines, but there were few who could resist Josh Bailey when he turned up the charm to full volume and, sure enough, Molly dissolved into girlish giggles as he bent over and kissed her hand.

'It's lovely to meet you, Josh,' she said. 'I've heard a lot about you.'

'And you too, Mrs Baxter. I know how much you mean to Britt, so it's great to finally meet you.'

'Please, you must call me Molly.'

Britt watched the exchange with a smile. She was desperate that Josh and Molly – the two most important people in her life – should get on. After all, they might soon be family . . .

'Have you been enjoying your stay so far, Molly?' asked Josh.

'Ooh, yes, it's been lovely. Britt took me to Harrods today and bought me these fancy boots.' Molly stuck a foot out from under the table. 'Spoilt me rotten she did. Nearly two hundred pounds, weren't they, love?'

Britt nodded enthusiastically. They had actually cost three times that much, but there's no way her mum would have allowed Britt to treat her if she'd known.

Just then a waiter appeared and stood by their table, his pen hovering expectantly over a pad.

'Mum, are you ready to order?' prompted Britt.

'Oh, yes, let me just see . . .' Molly fumbled in her bag for her reading glasses. The pair of them had polished off a few glasses of champagne while waiting for Josh, and she seemed a bit merry. 'Right now, please could you tell me what 'Char' is?' She pointed to the menu.

'Arctic Char is a type of fish, similar to salmon,' said the waiter.

'Oh, right. Very nice, I love a bit of salmon . . . And what's this – 'scallions'?'

'Spring onions.'

Britt felt a twinge of embarrassment. 'I could have told you that, Mum,' she muttered under her breath.

'It's okay, he doesn't mind,' said Molly, beaming up at the waiter. 'It's your job, isn't it, love?'

'It is indeed, madam,' he smiled, with a gracious nod of his head.

Britt glanced over at Josh. Was it her imagination, or did he just roll his eyes? No, she was just being over-sensitive.

Once they had ordered the food, they had begun to chat away about Josh's movie career when Molly suddenly yelped and started furiously nudging Britt. 'Look over there!' she gasped. 'It's Donald Sutherland!'

Britt looked over to where Molly was pointing and,

sure enough, the white-haired Canadian movie star was sitting at a corner table, dining with a female companion.

'Ooh, I absolutely loved him in *Don't Look Now*,' said Molly. 'Such a handsome young man he was!' And then suddenly she pushed back her chair, put her napkin on the table and started off in his direction.

'Mum, what are you doing? Sit down!'

'Sorry, love, but I'd never forgive myself if I was in the same restaurant as Donald Sutherland and I didn't go and say a quick hello. Wish me luck!'

'Mum, please, come back!' But it was too late. Britt watched in horror as her mum bustled over to his table. She put her head in her hands. 'Oh God . . .'

Beside her, Josh drained his glass. 'Perhaps we should have taken her to Pizza Express.'

'I'm sorry, hon, she just gets a bit . . . over-excited.'

'Yeah, well, you might have told her that the reason stars come to The Ivy is to avoid exactly *that* sort of thing,' said Josh, jerking his head over to where Molly was now crouched next to Donald Sutherland's table.

Moments later she was back. 'What a lovely man,' she said, her eyes shining. 'I told him I was his biggest fan and we had the nicest little chat. Do you know he actually visited Carlisle once, back in the seventies? And look!' She waved something at them. 'Donald Sutherland signed my new Nectar card!'

From then on, the evening went downhill. Josh was as polite and charming as ever, but Britt recognised it as the sort of patronising politeness he used with difficult guests on the show. Thankfully, Molly was too tipsy to notice. By the time they had finished pudding, Britt was desperate to get home and end the disaster that the evening had become.

'I'd better just nip to the Ladies,' trilled Molly after Britt had asked for the bill. 'Few too many shandies, I think!'

As soon as she had left the table, Josh turned to Britt and rested his hand on her arm. 'Listen, baby, I've been thinking,' he said. 'You know what it's like here – there'll be the usual gang of paps waiting outside, and we don't want to put your mom through that. If you're not used to the attention it can be quite frightening. Much better if she leaves the restaurant first and waits in the car while we make our exit, don't you reckon?'

Britt frowned. She didn't want her mum to think she was embarrassed by her. But Josh had a point. There were bound to be photographers waiting outside – there always were – and no doubt there would be a bit of a scrum when they left. She imagined Molly tottering out, clinging on to her arm, probably waving at all the paps and asking if they could get a picture of her with Donald Sutherland . . .

She said, 'I'll talk to Mum.'

'Talk to Mum about what?' Molly was standing at the table, smiling expectantly.

'Well, the thing is,' said Britt, 'there will be a load of paparazzi waiting outside the restaurant and it can all be a bit crazy when they start snapping away, so I think it's probably better if you leave before us. Just to avoid the worst of it,' she finished lamely. It had sounded far more convincing the way Josh had put it a minute ago.

'Oh. Right.' Molly's smile had faded slightly. 'Well, yes, that does sound a bit much.'

'Honestly, Mum, these guys push and shove you to try

and get a photo, and it's no fun. You can go and get in the car without any hassle and then we'll come straight out after you.'

'Of course, whatever you think is best,' Molly said, picking up her bag and glancing around her for the exit. 'Just this way is it, love? See you shortly then.'

But as Molly left, stumbling slightly as she walked around the tables, Britt caught a glimpse of her mum's expression. She looked ashamed, like she knew she was an embarrassment, and Britt immediately felt terrible. How could she have done that to her mum?

But then she felt Josh put his arm round her shoulders. 'Hey, you did the right thing, babe,' he said softly, kissing her on the cheek, reassuring her. 'She knows you're just looking out for her.' Then he stood up and smoothed back his hair. 'Right, what do you reckon – jacket on or jacket off?'

Molly was meant to stay until Wednesday, but when Britt got home from work on Monday there was no sign of her. When she looked in the guest room her mum's things had gone and the sheets had been stripped off the bed. Britt was stunned and more than a little bit upset – she couldn't believe her mum would leave without saying goodbye. She wandered into the kitchen to make a coffee, trying to figure out what had happened, and propped up on the counter she found a note:

Dearest Britt,

First things first. I've left a casserole for you in the fridge. I saw you didn't have much food in the house and I had a bit of time to kill before my train so I put something together for you. Stick it in the oven at gas mark 5 for about 45 mins. It might be nice with some dumplings/mash if you can be bothered. And maybe some green beans or those ones with the French name. Monge something or other?

Anyway, I'm sorry to leave without saying goodbye but I can see how busy your life is here in London and I didn't want to get in the way, what with your job etc. Thank you SO much for my coat and boots, and for dinner at The Ivy. It was lovely to finally meet Josh. I really hope I didn't embarrass you both too much with my 'country ways'!

Hopefully speak to you soon. I hope you know how proud I am of you, love.

Mum x

42

Britt stared at the note. She felt wretched. Her mum was far too lovely to ever say anything, but Britt knew that she'd hurt her. She dialled Molly's mobile to apologise but it went straight to voicemail, so she left a message wishing her a safe trip home and promising her she would come and visit her in Larkbridge very soon. And then she phoned Josh and told him what had happened.

'Hey, don't beat yourself up, baby,' he soothed. 'You did the best you could. You and your mom live in such different worlds these days, it was never going to be easy. This is why so many celebrities end up dating each other – it's hard for civilians to understand the stresses of being famous. I'm sure she had a great time.'

'I guess you're right . . .'

'I *am* right. Hell, Donald Sutherland signed her fricking Nectar card! She'll be dining out on that for months.'

Britt giggled. Josh was good at making her feel better.

'Now,' he said, 'how about you go out and buy a sexy new dress and I'll take you to this new members' club launch in Shoreditch tonight? Sounds like it's going to be a pretty A-list affair.'

'Okay,' said Britt. 'You're amazing, you know that?'

'I just want the girl I love to be happy, that's all.'

Britt almost dropped the phone in shock. 'You . . . love me?'

Josh laughed. 'Isn't it obvious, babe? I'm head over fucking heels! Now go do some serious shopping. I'll pick you up at seven.'

She put down the phone, any concern about her mum's hurt feelings momentarily forgotten. *Josh was in love with her!*

Later that week, Britt was sitting at her desk after the show, doing some research for next week's Style Spot, when she glanced up and saw Toby walking through the production office accompanied by a tiny brunette in a tight pink dress. From this distance, he looked like he was giving her a guided tour. Britt squinted across the office – was that . . . could it be . . . Cheryl Cole? But as they got nearer she saw that she was mistaken, although this girl shared the singer's killer figure and elfin features.

'Britt, I'd like to introduce you to Mandii Parsons,' said Toby, as they approached her desk. 'Mandii is going to be joining us as our new weather girl.'

'It's great to meet you,' said Britt, getting a proper look at the new girl. She had the sort of girl-next-door prettiness that made lads' mags fly off the shelves: wide-apart eyes, a tiny nose, a heavily lip-glossed smile and a mane of glossy dark brown hair – plus, of course, a pair of outrageously pumped-up boobs. She also looked vaguely familiar. 'Have you done much on TV before?' asked Britt.

'I was Miss England last year,' said Mandii in breathy Scouse. Of course, that was it! Britt remembered there had been a bit of a scandal when she'd posed topless for a magazine soon after winning the crown. And then she noticed the chickpea-sized rock glittering on Mandii's French-manicured finger and remembered reading something else about her getting engaged to a Premiership footballer. It seemed Toby was hoping to cause a bit of a stir with his latest signing.

Even before her debut forecast, Mandii certainly caused a stir amongst the *Rise & Shine* team. She couldn't walk down the corridor without attracting a drooling male escort, usually either Ken or Charlie. And Mandii played up to the attention shamelessly, dressing in tiny vests and short shorts despite the fact that they were now into autumn. Unsurprisingly, her arrival didn't go down particularly well with Cherry, who was overheard screaming expletives in Toby's office after Mandii had told Cherry that her granddad fancied her.

But at least Cherry's truce with Britt still held. In fact, to Britt's surprise, Cherry had recently started to drop by her dressing room every now and then for a coffee and a chat. If she didn't know better, Britt would think she was actually being friendly.

Her big worry, however, was how Josh would react to the sexy new arrival. It wasn't that Britt was insecure, but judging from the rest of the crew's reactions, Mandii Parsons was to men what the new Bottega Veneta ostrich tote bag was to her. An object of instant and unequivocal lust.

Britt broached the subject when she cooked Josh dinner that Friday.

'So, what do you think of the new girl?' she asked casually as she stacked up their plates.

Josh looked up from a copy of *Reveal* magazine in which there was a new interview with him, complete with the customary shirt-off photos.

'Mandii something, isn't it?' He frowned. 'Nice enough, but looks a bit of a tramp. No class. Seems like an odd choice for a *Rise & Shine* weather girl, but I'm sure Toby knows what he's doing.'

And with that he went back to reading the magazine.

It was Monday, and Britt was rounding up that morning's Style Spot by announcing a new competition, reading the details from the autocue: 'We're offering one lucky viewer and a friend an all-inclusive week at the exclusive 'Los Relaxos Spa' in Tenerife for the ultimate in pampering indulgence.' She paused for effect, her eyes wide with excitement. 'Ooh, sounds fabulous, doesn't it? I could certainly do with a week of massages and manicures in the Spanish sunshine! All you need to do to be in with a chance of winning this amazing prize is to answer the following question. What is—'

Suddenly the screen of the autocue went blank. The words just vanished, as if the power had failed. Britt tried not to panic. She hadn't got a clue what the question was – and she couldn't very well make one up. Okay, stay calm. There was obviously some sort of technical glitch and no doubt it would be sorted soon.

'Well, I'll bring you that all-important question in a moment, but in the meantime, I'll just tell you a bit more about this fabulous prize.'

Britt waffled on about a spa that she knew nothing about until, after what felt like hours but was probably just a few seconds, the autocue suddenly flickered into life once more and she gratefully finished reading the competition details.

Once she was done, Britt walked back to her dressing

room, feeling pleased with herself at how well she'd handled the situation, when she was stopped outside the green room by a furious Toby.

'Britt, what the hell happened in there? You just went off on a tangent for twenty seconds!'

'I was just filling as best I could while the autocue was fixed,' she said, bewildered by his reaction. What on earth had he expected her to do – stand there in silence?

But Toby was staring at her blankly. 'What are you talking about? The autocue was fine. No-one reported any problems from the gallery.'

'But I . . .' Britt didn't know what to say. Was she going mad? 'Toby, I swear, the words suddenly just disappeared from the screen. Why would I make something like this up?'

But it was obvious he didn't believe her. 'I don't know what's going on, but I really don't want to have to talk to you about your performance again. Please, Britt, for your sake as much as that of the show, cut down on the late nights and the partying and start focusing on your job.'

And with that he stalked off back to the gallery, leaving Britt close to tears. Surely *someone* must have noticed that the autocue wasn't working? She thought about going to talk to Stewie, to try and get a technical explanation for what had happened, but he was still doing his best to avoid her. So instead she went to Josh's dressing room. A kiss was bound to make her feel better.

Britt tapped on the door and went straight in. 'Hi, gorgeous, you'll never believe what . . .'

But the sight that greeted her inside left her frozen in shock.

43

Josh was perched on the edge of his dressing table and, sitting in the chair next to him, so close that it looked like he might at any moment tumble into her eye-popping cleavage, was Mandii Parsons. They were laughing about something and she had her hand resting on his leg, white-tipped talons gripping his thigh. When Josh spotted Britt his face lit up in a grin of greeting, but Mandii looked altogether less relaxed. Guilty, was the word that sprang to Britt's mind.

'Oh, hey, baby,' said Josh. 'I was just giving Mandii the low-down on Ken's gastric band. Crazy shit, huh?'

Britt nodded slowly, her mind whirling as she desperately tried to work out what – if anything – she had just walked in on.

Mandii stood up and gave a little shimmy to wriggle down her barely there skirt. 'Well, I guess I should get going, the weather's not going to read itself. See ya, Britt. Bye, Josh.' She gave him a sexy little wave and wiggled out on her red-soled stilettos. *Surely there should be a law preventing slappers like that from buying Louboutins*, thought Britt furiously as Mandii sashayed out.

'So, what was it you wanted to say to me, baby?' Josh reached for her, but Britt took a step back.

'What the hell was going on there?'

Josh frowned. 'What do you mean?'

'You and Mandii,' she spat. 'You were all over her.' Britt knew that she sounded jealous, but she didn't give a damn. The image of Josh and the weather girl sitting together, all cosy and giggly, was burning into her mind.

'You seriously think there's something going on between us?' Josh sat back in the chair and pulled a protesting Britt onto his lap. 'Come here, silly. Right, listen to me. First off, Mandii's engaged. Secondly, she's *definitely* not my type. Thirdly – and most importantly – when are you going to get it into your head that I'm crazy in love with you?' He put his finger under her chin, moving it so she was looking into his eyes, and then kissed her gently on the lips. 'Okay, I'm a bit of a flirt, but honestly, babe, you gotta believe me – you're the only girl for me.'

Britt suddenly remembered a magazine article she'd read about the signs to look for when a person is lying. Something about touching their nose or ears and hunching their shoulders . . . ? But Josh wasn't doing anything like that – and he certainly wasn't avoiding eye contact, which as far as she could remember had been the clincher. Quite the opposite: his eyes were firmly locked onto hers. At once the panic that had gripped her moments ago started to fade.

'I love you, baby,' he said. 'I'd never do anything to hurt you.'

'I love you, too,' she said, snuggling into his shoulder and smiling to herself, making a mental note to pull herself together. She wasn't even the jealous type, for goodness' sake . . .

* * *

There was great excitement in the production office. Johnny Depp was in the UK for two weeks to film scenes for his new movie, and he had granted his one and only interview to *Rise & Shine*. It was a major scoop, as all the other big TV shows had been trying to get the actor as well. Seeing as how they had already met (albeit briefly), it was decided that Britt should do the chat. Determined to get the best out of the ten-minute interview slot, she had stayed up late the night before researching his life and career, and by the morning of the interview would have easily passed a Johnny Depp GCSE with an A grade – possibly even an A*.

The morning's show had just finished and Britt was sitting at her desk in the production office running through her research one last time when her computer pinged with an email. It was from Jasper, the location producer for the interview, and was headed 'CHANGE OF PLAN!!' with a little red flag denoting that it was urgent.

'Sorry, Britt,' it read, 'the interview with Johnny Depp will be at the Dorchester, NOT in his trailer on the movie set in Islington as per the call sheet. See you in the hotel reception at 11 a.m. Jasper.'

That's lucky, thought Britt smugly. It would have been a real schlep to get up to north London from the studio, whereas the Dorchester was just a fifteen-minute taxi ride away. Plus with an hour and a half to kill before the interview, she could go via Selfridges and pick up that new Phillip Lim brown leather jacket she had on hold. Excellent.

At a few minutes before eleven, Britt arrived at the Dorchester and strode up to the reception desk. She knew she was looking good (in the gorgeous new leather jacket over a white and blue bird-print Tibi chiffon dress), and that helped reinforce her confidence and calm her nerves.

'Hi, I'm Britt Baxter from *Rise & Shine*. I'm here to do an interview with Johnny Depp,' she said. 'Please can you tell me which room he's staying in?'

'Johnny Depp? The real Johnny Depp?' The reception-ist questioned as she checked a computer screen in front of her. 'I'm sorry, madam, we don't have Johnny Depp staying here.'

Oh, that was right, Hollywood stars never used their real names in hotels so they weren't pestered by fans.

'It's okay, I'll just wait for my producer,' she smiled. 'He has all the details.'

But after ten minutes and with no sign of the crew, Britt was beginning to worry. Reaching for her phone, she was horrified to see that she had twelve missed calls from Jasper. Damn, she had forgotten that she'd switched it to Silent so that it didn't ring in the middle of the interview.

Jasper answered his phone on the first ring, as if he'd already had it in his hand.

'Where the fuck are you?' he screeched.

'At the Dorchester Hotel, like you told me.'

'*What . . . ?* It clearly says on the call sheet that the interview is in his trailer on set!'

'I know,' she said patiently, 'but then you sent me that email telling me it had changed to the Dorchester.'

There was a moment's silence at the other end of the line. 'Britt, I have no idea what you're talking about, but the interview is and always has been on the movie set. I am standing outside Johnny Depp's trailer and for the last ten minutes he has been waiting for you to come and interview him.'

Shit. 'Okay, I'll jump in a taxi, I'll be right there . . .'

'It's too late, he's about to be called back onto set. We've missed our chance.' Jasper sighed in frustration. 'You'd better meet me back at the studio. Toby is going to be furious that we didn't get this interview, and you are going to have to explain why.'

An hour later, Britt found herself sitting next to Jasper on the sofa in Toby's office, while their boss paced up and down in front of them running his hands through his hair. She had rarely seen the executive producer looking so angry.

'So let me get this straight,' he said. 'Britt, you say you got an email from Jasper this morning changing the location of the interview to the Dorchester. Is that right?'

Okay, stay calm, thought Britt. *You know you're in the right here*. 'Yes, that's right.'

Toby looked at Jasper. 'Well?'

'I'm sorry, Britt, but I didn't send any such email.'

'For God's sake, this is ridiculous . . .' huffed Britt. Why was Jasper lying? There was only one way to sort this out. 'Come on,' she said, 'if you don't believe me, I'll show you.'

The three of them trooped down to the production office and huddled around Britt's computer as she switched it on and scrolled down the messages. But to her horror, the email wasn't there.

'It must be in the deleted items,' she said, as panic started to grip her insides.

But there was no trace of it anywhere.

'I . . . I don't know what happened,' she stammered.

'I *swear* I got an email from Jasper. Why would I make something like that up?'

'Britt, you're an excellent presenter,' said Toby quietly, 'but any more silly mistakes and we're going to have to have a serious chat about your future at *Rise & Shine*.'

Lying in bed that night, Britt went over and over the events of the last few weeks. First the laxatives, then the jammed autocue and now the mysterious email from Jasper that had somehow vanished from her computer. Okay, so they might just be a series of accidents. But what if they weren't? Perhaps someone had deliberately planned them to try and make her look bad? *Jasper?* No, the idea was ludicrous. Why would he? And this was real life, not bloody *EastEnders* . . . But how else could an email just have disappeared, unless someone had hacked into her computer and deleted it? And who the hell sent it in the first place if it really wasn't Jasper? The questions swirled endlessly, dizzily, around Britt's head, but by the time she fell into a restless sleep way past midnight, she had made up her mind.

Someone at *Rise & Shine* was trying their best to ruin her.

44

Britt was going to mention her suspicions to Josh, but after the way he'd dismissed her suggestion about the laxatives she decided to wait until she had further evidence. If there did turn out to be a perfectly innocent explanation for what had gone on, she didn't want him thinking she was paranoid. So instead, she just put herself on high alert whenever she was at work. She printed out all her emails. If she was given instructions she double-, triple-checked them. She refused to drink or eat anything she hadn't prepared herself. It got her some funny glances, but that was better than getting the sack. If someone *was* trying to ruin her career, Britt was determined that they sure as hell weren't going to get another chance.

But as the weeks rolled by without further incident, Britt gradually started to relax again: there were far too many exciting things going on for her to stay focused on conspiracy theories for long. Josh had been treating her like a princess, showering her with presents and constantly telling her how much he loved her. He even hinted in a newspaper interview that he was planning to whisk Britt off to Chicago at Christmas and propose. Not that he'd said anything about it to her, but he must be pretty certain of his plans to mention it to a journalist, mustn't he? It was just a shame he had to travel so much for work: they still only saw each other a couple of days a week at most and rarely at weekends. And, okay, so he *still* hadn't invited her back to his flat, but was that really so important?

And it wasn't just her personal life that was going so swimmingly. To her delight, Britt was nominated for Best Entertainment Presenter *and* Best Newcomer in the prestigious British Television Awards, which would be taking place in a few months' time. Toby was so thrilled that he started to talk about getting Britt and Josh to co-host the show on Wednesdays as well as Fridays, which would mean another pay rise. With her star on the rise again, Britt was relieved that she hadn't mentioned her sabotage theory to Josh. It was time to put all that behind her. Even the dull ache in her stomach that she'd been feeling everytime she thought about Alex had begun to subside.

Britt was sitting in her dressing room trying her best to calm her nerves. Cherry had given her some calming chamomile tea, which had no effect at all other than making her need to wee a lot, and now she was mainlining Bach's Rescue Remedy. On the bottle it had recommended putting a few drops on the tongue, but Britt had unscrewed the lid and was now taking long swigs straight from the bottle.

In just twenty minutes' time, she was due live on air to interview the world's biggest movie star. Powers Buckman was an all-American action hero who still looked as good now in his fifties as he had when he shot to stardom as a teenage sensation. Famously private, he rarely gave interviews – so when it was announced that he was going to be visiting the UK to promote his latest blockbuster and that during the visit he would be gracing the *Rise & Shine* sofa, the press went mad. It felt like the world would be watching.

Draining the last of the Rescue Remedy, Britt glanced up at the clock to check the time and caught sight of the enormous bunch of white roses that were sitting in a vase on her dressing table. Josh was in Los Angeles for two weeks, but he'd sent her the bouquet to wish her luck for the interview with Powers. She caught a whiff of their delicate scent and smiled at the memory of the card that had accompanied them. '*To my superstar girlfriend*,' it had read in that familiar looping handwriting. '*All my love, always, JJB* x'

A tap on her dressing-room door broke her concentration.

'Come in!' she shouted.

The door opened and there, looking desperately uncomfortable, stood Stewie. Britt was stunned. It was the first time he had come to her dressing room since she'd been dating Josh. He hadn't even spoken to her in weeks.

'Stewie, it's so good to see you!' And she meant it – seeing him in the doorway made her realise how much she'd missed him.

'Do you have a moment?' he asked. 'I need to talk to you about something.'

'I'd love to catch up, but I'm about to go on air to do this big interview. Can it wait? Perhaps we could go for a coffee after the show . . .'

'No, I'm sorry, Britt, this is important.'

He certainly looked like he had something weighty on his mind, so she gestured for him to sit down.

'It's okay, I'll stay standing, thanks,' he said. 'I don't quite know where to begin, so I'll just come right out with it.' But he didn't come out with anything; he just stood there, shuffling from foot to foot, unable to even look her in the eye.

'Stewie, I'm sorry but I'm really pressed for time . . .' Britt said gently.

'Right, okay. God, this is really awkward.' He took a deep breath. 'I'm sorry to tell you this, but Josh is cheating on you with Mandii Parsons.'

Britt froze. Her stomach lurched horribly. 'That's bullshit, Stewie.'

'I wish it was, but it's been going on pretty much since she started. They've been screwing in the disabled toilets on the third floor after the eight a.m. weather bulletin every day. I wanted to tell you because—'

'Because what?' Britt said, suddenly furious. 'Because you hoped I'd fall into your arms and screw you instead? Admit it, you've been jealous of my relationship with Josh from the word go.'

Stewie shrugged miserably. 'Yeah, I have. Guilty as charged. It kills me to see the two of you together. But this has nothing to do with that. He's a total bastard, Britt, and I hate to see him making a fool of you like this.'

Britt was shaking her head in disbelief. 'How can you do this to me – just as I'm about to do the most important interview of my career? You're incredible, you know that? Lying about Josh to try and break us up.' But inside she was in turmoil. She replayed the moment she'd walked in on Josh and Mandii in his dressing room. It couldn't possibly be true – *could it . . . ?*

'Please, Britt, just listen to me,' urged Stewie. 'I

overhear things in this job. Private things. When you're putting microphones on people all day you can't help but eavesdrop on people's personal conversations.'

The words swirled through Britt's mind: '*I overhear things . . . private things . . . you can't help but eavesdrop on personal conversations . . .*' And then suddenly, in a flash, it was as if a mist had been lifted and finally she saw the truth laid out in front of her in crystal-clear detail. *Oh god, did she have her mic on when she had that row with Alex?*

'It was YOU!' she gasped, as the pieces slotted into place. 'You were listening in on me! You sold the story about me and Alex to *The Daily Splash* after I told you about our problems! You tipped off the papers about my new 'mystery man' and God knows what else. How the hell could you do this to me? I thought you were my friend!'

Stewie looked like he'd been slapped in the face. 'What . . . What are you talking about?' he stammered. 'That was ages ago, why are you bringing that up now?'

But there was no other explanation. *How could she have been so stupid?*

'The worst part is that you let me believe it was Alex that had betrayed me!' Britt was choking back the tears. 'I dumped him – and all because of your lies. Get out of my room!'

'Britt, please, just listen to me, there's something else. I need to warn you about—'

'I don't want to hear anything else you've got to say,' she shrieked, hands flying to her ears. 'Just get out!'

When Stewie had gone, Britt struggled to regain her composure. There was so much she had to deal with, so many consequences from her shocking discovery that it was Stewie who was to blame for selling her out, but she had ten minutes before the interview with Powers Buckman and right then that had to take precedence over her personal dramas.

After wiping away the teary smudges of mascara and blotting her face with loose powder, she tried to focus on the final page of the Powers research notes. It was all familiar territory: the hit movies . . . the marriages . . . the beautiful twin girls . . . the foster son . . . But then, in the final paragraph, the bombshell. All thoughts of Stewie and Alex were instantly banished from her mind as she read that Powers Buckman, the granite-jawed action hero who had only just celebrated his third marriage to a twenty-something *Sports Illustrated* model called Janey, had late last night held a press conference at which he had declared he was gay.

Britt stared open-mouthed at the page. There had been persistent rumours in the media, of course, but Powers' famously ferocious lawyers had always slapped down any queries over his sexuality. In celebrity terms, this was one of the biggest stories of the decade. And she was going to get the first interview! But Britt had read all the morning's papers and there was nothing about Powers Buckman coming out. Surely if it were true, it would be all over the front pages? She had just three minutes before she was due on the sofa.

Gathering up her notes, she dashed along the corridor to the make-up room, where Fran was tidying up her kit.

'Sorry to interrupt, hon,' panted Britt, 'but did you hear anything about Powers Buckman admitting he was gay last night?'

'God, yes, unbelievable, isn't it? Apparently he gave an impromptu press conference at the Ritz in the early hours of this morning, so none of the newspapers were in time to run it in their first editions.' Then Fran looked at her in wide-eyed astonishment as the realisation sank in. 'Blimey, Britt, you'll get the first interview!'

'I know,' she grinned. 'This is seriously big news.'

'Well, best of luck, love.' Fran came over and gave her a hug. 'You'll be brilliant. I'll be watching!'

Britt blew her a thank-you kiss and ran out of the room.

Seconds before they were due to go on air, Powers strode manfully through the studio accompanied by a retinue of hangers-on including a woman who was powdering his nose and another who was tweaking his famous blond mane while he walked. He was every bit as handsome as he was on screen, but surprisingly short in real life – even in the pair of stacked Cuban heels he was wearing. Powers greeted Britt with a huge smile and a firm handshake.

'Britt, isn't it?' he said in his famous honey-dipped voice, settling down opposite her on the sofa. 'Great to meet you.'

'Thank you so much for coming on the show, Powers,' she smiled. 'I'm a huge fan.'

The floor manager indicated that they had twenty seconds before going live. Britt had just enough time to brief the actor on their chat: 'So we'll talk a bit about the new movie and then, if it's okay with you, I'll move on to the more . . . *personal* side of things.'

Powers grinned. 'Guess I really can't avoid it, huh? Just promise you'll go gentle on me, sweetheart.'

And with that the floor manager pointed in Britt's direction and they were live.

'Welcome back to *Rise & Shine*. Now our next guest is a man – a legend – who needs absolutely no introduction. With one Oscar, two Golden Globes and countless hit movies under his belt, he is the most successful movie star of his generation and a bona fide box-office legend. I am delighted to welcome the one and only Powers Buckman to the sofa.' She turned to him with a beaming grin. 'Powers, thanks so much for stopping by.'

He bowed his head graciously. 'Well, that was quite an introduction you gave me, Britt,' he chuckled. 'I just hope I can live up to it!'

It was one of those fantastic interviews that seems like a casual chat rather than a stilted Q&A. The pair of them fell into relaxed and easy banter and, after they had chatted a bit about his new movie – an action rom com in which Powers played a secret agent who went undercover as a 'manny' – Britt felt ready to tackle the subject that the millions watching at home would no doubt be waiting for.

'Now, if we can just leave your movie career to one side for a moment and move on to your recent big announcement,' she said gently – this would have to be handled with the *utmost* sensitivity – 'can you tell us why you chose this particular time to come out?'

'Well, obviously it's something I've been passionate about for some time,' said Powers with a happy grin. Britt had been terrified about broaching the subject, so was desperately relieved – and more than a little impressed – at how relaxed he seemed. 'You know, if it had been up to me I would have been shouting about it from the rooftops some time ago, but unfortunately that hasn't been possible until now.'

'What, because of your wife's reaction to the news?'

For a moment, Powers looked blank. 'Janey? No, she was fully supportive about the decision. She had to be! She loves Jake – that's his name, I'm now happy to reveal – just as much as I do.'

Christ, thought Britt, *perhaps they were having some strange* ménage a trois? *Perhaps best not to go down that route on breakfast telly* . . . 'Well, that must make things so much easier to have Janey on board,' she said to Powers with an encouraging smile. 'So, why didn't you feel ready to come out before now?'

'Well, it's more to do with the fact that at first I wasn't exactly sure about the nature of my relationship with Jake,' said Powers. 'Was it going to be long term? There have been so many boys I met, so many who I felt a connection with, but it wasn't until I met Jake that I really felt I could make the commitment.' *Shit, this really is sensational stuff*, thought Britt, imagining the newspaper headlines. 'POWERS BUCKMAN: I went cruising the streets to pick up young boys!' She might even get some sort of journalism award . . .

'It's been real hard,' Powers continued, 'but Jake really is the best thing that's ever happened to me.'

'I'm sure,' said Britt. 'And, of course, such a brave thing for a man in your position to admit that he is gay.'

But the words were barely out of her mouth before Britt realised something was wrong. Powers sat, his eyes wide open, making a sound like a cat trying to cough up a particularly troublesome hairball. Over talkback there was a sharp intake of breath and then a high-pitched wail from the director that made Britt's hand fly to her ear.

'What the FUCK are you doing?' he shrieked. 'Powers Buckman has never admitted he's gay!' And then with a rush of horror, Britt remembered something in the research notes about Powers and his wife Janey announcing that they had fostered a child. A two-year-old boy. Who was called Jake.

Oh God. Oh God, no. Britt tore her eyes away from Powers, who now appeared to be struggling for breath, and glanced out at the studio floor. A sea of appalled faces stared back at her, no doubt mirroring the viewers' expressions at home. For Britt, it was as if the world was standing still as the terrible realisation sank in. She had been set up. There had been no late-night press conference. Britt had effectively just outed the most powerful star in Hollywood live on *Rise & Shine*.

45

Suddenly Powers seemed to recover his faculties. He jumped up from the sofa, his face screwed up with anger, and tried to rip his microphone off. 'I have never in all my years . . .' he spluttered, twisting and tugging furiously at the wires. 'I can't believe . . .' But as he gave the battery pack a particularly vicious tug, his shirt ripped open to reveal that Powers Buckman, renowned super stud and ripped movie god, was in fact wearing a flesh-coloured support girdle.

With a howl, he strode off set (was it Britt's imagination or was he actually mincing?). She came to and realised she was sitting stunned in front of the cameras.

She had just humiliated the world's most famous movie star on live television. *Rise & Shine* would probably get sued for millions. She would *definitely* get fired. And alongside all the fear and panic and embarrassment, a seed of anger was growing by the second. There was no doubt in her mind now about her suspicions of sabotage. But why the hell would Fran do this to her?

She reluctantly turned to face the camera. 'Um, I think we might have had a bit of a misunderstanding here, folks. I don't think Powers quite got our famous British irony.' She gave a weak laugh, trying to concentrate as the director shrieked that they were '. . . going to the fucking ads right this fucking second' in her ear. 'Right, so we'll be back in a few moments,' said Britt, 'but for now – Powers Buckman, thanks for coming into *Rise & Shine*, it was a pleasure to have you on the sofa.'

Sure enough, as soon as they were off air all hell broke loose. Powers was screaming for someone to get his '. . . fucking lawyer right fucking now', while his entourage swarmed protectively around him with faces set like thunder – well, as thunderous as all the Botox would allow. A red-faced, bald man (Powers' agent, perhaps?) was now laying furiously into Toby, who had dashed down from the gallery after Britt had uttered the 'G' word.

Toby was grovelling profusely. Britt knew that she had no choice: she would have to face the music. As she walked slowly across the studio floor to where Toby was prostrating himself in front of the red-faced man, the crew stared after her with a mixture of horror and pity. They knew as well as she did that she was a doomed woman.

'Um, hi there, excuse me!' Britt began nervously.

Toby and Powers' rep turned to face her. Their expressions were murderous. Britt took a deep breath and ploughed on.

'I am so, so sorry about what I said during the interview. Obviously I was given the wrong information. I would never dream of suggesting—'

But Toby cut her off. 'Shut up, go to your dressing room and do not move until I get there,' he hissed. 'I will deal with you later.'

As she slunk out of the studio, her eyes pooling with tears, it suddenly occurred to her. The research notes with the information about the press conference! If she could show those to Toby then surely he would believe that she'd been set up. But then she remembered. She had left them in the make-up room with Fran; God only knew where they would be now.

Toby turned up to her dressing room half an hour later. If anything, he looked even angrier than he had in the studio. Britt tried to explain what had happened but he wouldn't listen.

'You're fired, Britt. I want you out of this studio in half an hour. If Powers Buckman's people have their way, you might just have managed to single-handedly destroy *Rise & Shine*.' He glared at her angrily, shaking his head. 'I had high hopes for you, Britt. I can't believe how wrong I was.'

After he left, Britt let the tears freely flow down her cheeks. Stewie had sold her out. Fran had killed her career. There was no way she would get another job after this. Whoever said 'All's fair in love and war' had obviously never worked in breakfast television.

Without any holdalls or suitcases in which to pack her belongings – how she had managed to accumulate quite so much crap in four months she had no idea – Britt was emptying her dressing table drawers into Tesco carrier bags when she heard the door open. She looked up to see Cherry standing in the doorway, arms folded.

'Leaving us, are you, darling?' she said lightly. 'Such a shame.'

'Cherry, it was Fran,' sobbed Britt. 'She set me up!'

'Are you quite sure about that?' asked Cherry, her mouth set in a smirk of triumph.

'What . . . what are you saying?'

316

'Let me spell it out for you, darling.' Cherry smoothed a stray hair away from her face. 'Fran might have been the puppet, but it was me who was pulling the strings.'

Britt stared at her in horror. 'How . . . how could you do this to me?'

'Oh, it was very easy, really,' shrugged Cherry. 'I persuaded Fran to crush up some laxatives in your lip-gloss – bit of a master-stroke that one, I thought! – and then the rest of it was easy when you've been working in TV as long as I have. To be honest, I didn't think you'd fall for the Powers Buckman story. You must be as dumb as you look.'

'What have I ever done to you?'

'You stole my job, darling, it's as simple as that.' Cherry said it as if her behaviour was entirely reasonable. 'I couldn't risk being elbowed off *Rise & Shine* by a jumped-up waitress. It's nothing personal, honest.'

'Why Fran?' asked Britt weakly. She had always thought the make-up artist had been a friend.

'Once I'd explained to her about how you'd been bitching about her behind her back, she was happy to help.'

'But I didn't! I would never . . .'

'Well, I'm afraid that Fran thinks you did. And after all, no-one likes being called fat and frumpy, do they? Anyway, Fran will be totally loyal to me. I am her idol, you see.'

'I'm going to tell Toby everything,' said Britt, her voice shaking with emotion. 'You're not going to get away with this, you evil cow.'

Cherry gave one of her brittle, tinkling laughs. 'Be my guest, darling. He won't believe you. He already thinks you're delusional.' Cherry turned to go, but then paused in the doorway. 'Oh, and by the way, in case you hadn't realised, that fame-hungry pretty boy is only with you to raise his profile. So don't expect too much sympathy from JJ Bailey now that you're the TV equivalent of swine flu.' And with that she gave her a smug little 'Ciao!' and waltzed out.

Britt looked around for something to throw at her, but Cherry's bony size six backside had already disappeared. How could anyone be so cruel? And then trying to twist the knife by claiming Josh was only interested in her for the publicity? What utter bollocks. Britt was sure it wasn't true, but there was only one way to find out. She glanced at the clock: 9.26 a.m. It would be the early hours of the morning in LA, so she couldn't possibly phone Josh now. Perhaps she should leave a message to call urgently when he woke up . . . ?

But Britt didn't get the chance, as just at that moment one of the security guards appeared at her door – a nice old bloke named Clive.

'Sorry, Britt, I don't want to do this but the boss has asked me to see you out.'

'That's okay. I know you're just doing your job.'

He insisted on carrying her belongings and she followed him along the corridors, feeling like a common criminal. They passed several familiar faces, but although some of her colleagues – now ex-colleagues – offered her a sad smile, no-one spoke to her.

'Right, well, best of luck then, Britt,' said Clive, handing over her bags at the exit to the car park. 'We'll miss you round here.'

'See you, Clive.' She gave him a hug and then watched

as he headed back inside, leaving her standing alone in the street.

So, what now? A taxi was waiting outside the studio with its light on and Britt started towards it, but then she realised she wasn't going to get her travel expenses paid any more. Or a clothing allowance. Or, in fact, any sort of salary at all.

With a heavy heart, she took a firmer grip on the handles of her plastic bags and set off towards the tube station.

As she was weaving her way between the rows of vehicles in the car park, she noticed a bright red – *cherry* red – BMW convertible. In the back window hung a cutesy pink sign reading 'PUPPY ON BOARD'. Britt put down her bags and stared at the car. It was Cherry's car. A wave of anger ripped through her. Before she knew what she was doing, she'd dragged the keys she'd been clutching in her hand along the paintwork leaving a white gouge in the glossy paintwork. She felt dizzy when she recalled Cherry's smug expression as she gloated about how her little plan to ruin Britt had worked. She wasn't sure what she'd imagined she would feel when she scratched Cherry's precious car – it was hardly as if she had carved 'I AM A CONNIVING COW' across the bonnet, no matter how justified she might have been to do so – but as she composed herself and gathered up her plastic bags again, even the thought of the look on Cherry's face when she saw her car wasn't enough to make Britt feel better. If anything, it made her feel worse – that she'd stooped to Cherry's level.

She was making her way to the station when suddenly one of the bulging bags split and its contents

– make-up, hair clips and tampons – skittered across the pavement. Britt wearily bent down to pick it all up. *Well, at least this day can't get any worse*, she thought, scrabbling in the gutter. But then she heard someone shouting her name and turned to see Stewie running down the street towards her and realised that her day could get worse – and just had.

'Britt!' He was waving his arms. 'Britt, I need to talk to you!'

He had a bloody nerve. She abandoned the rest of her stuff and started jogging towards the station.

'Please,' he shouted. 'Just hear me out!'

Well, that was the last straw. Britt swung round to face him.

'Get the HELL away from me,' she screamed. It was a struggle to stop herself from taking a swing at him. 'You have ruined my life!'

'You're wrong, Britt, I would never do anything to hurt you. It wasn't me that sold those stories, honest. And I tried to warn you about Cherry . . .'

'I don't believe you. Just leave me alone.'

She stumbled away, tears springing hotly to her eyes.

'Please, Britt, you didn't let me finish – there's something you need to know!'

But Britt kept on running towards the station, pausing only to scream at Stewie over her shoulder: 'I don't ever want to speak to you again!'

46

It was dark when Britt woke suddenly from a bizarre dream in which she had been thrown out of S Club 7 for forgetting the words to 'Reach For the Stars'. She lay still in bed for a moment, listening. There were no cars on the road or birds singing. It must be horribly early. She reached over for her BlackBerry: 3.57 a.m. With a groan, Britt flopped back on the pillows: she'd never get back to sleep again now. Although she'd been in this bed – the one in Jessie's spare room – for most of the past few days, she had probably only slept for a few hours in total. Even the bomber sleeping pills that Jess had managed to get hold of for her had hardly helped.

Britt lay on her back and stared up at the skylight over the bed. Her body ached as if she'd run a marathon. It had been four – or was it five? – days since her spectacular exit from *Rise & Shine*. After getting back to her flat on the morning she was fired, Britt had locked herself away and sobbed into the sofa cushions at the unfairness of it all, while a traumatised Kate Moss rested her fat furry paws on her back and kneaded at her like a ball of wool. *That poor cat is going to need therapy after all this trauma*, thought Britt miserably. Then at about 5 p.m. it had occurred to her that without a job there was absolutely no way that she would be able to afford the rent on the riverside apartment – not to mention the cleaning bill for a tear-stained suede sofa – so she had phoned the management company and reluctantly given her notice. On day two she had crept out to get the news-papers and was relieved to see that there was nothing in them about her outing Powers Buckman or being fired, apart from a few lines in *The Daily Splash* ridiculing her ill-judged 'joke' about the infamous movie stud being gay. She then had plucked up the courage to call Jessie.

Britt really wouldn't have blamed her friend for refus-ing to even speak to her after the way she had ignored her over the past few months, but when she had explained what had happened Jessie drove straight over to the flat, scooped up Britt, Kate Moss and a bagful of clothes, then drove them all back to Streatham. That afternoon when Poppy, Willow and Rose had got home, they had jumped all over Britt, showering her with kisses and showing her pictures and cards they'd painted for her over the last few months, and she had felt even more awful at having been such a neglectful godmother. She had put fame and all the fickleness that went along with it before the people who really loved her – who really *mattered* to her – and the thought made her sick with guilt. Yet Jessie had been an absolute angel and insisted she stay with them until she sorted out what she was going to do. Right at this moment, however, Britt had absolutely no idea what that would be.

And then there was Josh. Or rather, there wasn't Josh. Anywhere. The one person she needed more than any other had simply disappeared, and the agony of not being able to get hold of him, of not knowing whether he was cheating on her, was almost worse than the pain of her public humiliation and losing her job. She had left him a rambling phone message explaining that she had been sacked, but she didn't hear from him until the following day when he had sent her a short text: 'Sorry to hear about what's been going on, babe. Cherry's such a f–ing bitch!! Things are crazy busy at this end. I'll call you as soon as I can. JJB x' But, since then, despite her repeatedly phoning, texting and emailing him, Josh had gone silent on her. She was desperate to feel his arms around her, to have him tell her that everything was going to be okay. Jessie kept reassuring her that there must be a perfectly reasonable explanation for why he hadn't got in touch, but at the back of Britt's mind, and growing by the second, was the awful fear that Stewie had been right about him.

Stewie. The thought of him opened up a whole other world of pain. Someone who she had trusted as a friend, who she'd even gone to bed with, had betrayed her in the worst possible way. On top of all this, Britt was struggling to come to terms with the horrible way she had treated Alex now that she knew he hadn't sold the story after all. Perhaps she'd still be with him if she'd believed his denials? How could she not have believed him in the first place? She couldn't believe she'd let all the hype cloud the fact that the man she knew, the man she loved, could never have done something like that. She knew she should phone and apologise to him now she knew the truth, but it had been hard enough admitting to Jessie that – just as her friend had suspected – Alex hadn't sold the story after all. Britt was too ashamed to even write him a letter. She resolved to revisit the matter when the dust had settled. Besides, she was struggling to focus on anything apart from what the hell had happened to Josh . . .

She must have fallen into a fitful doze because she was woken again a while later by a knocking at the door. It was light now, but it still felt early.

'Britt, are you awake?' Jessie's head appeared around the door, a worried look on her face. 'Sorry, love, but you've got to get up.'

'What time is it?' She rubbed her eyes.

'About eight. There's someone here to see you.'

Britt's heart leapt. *Josh!*

'Okay, let me just throw on some clothes.' She scrambled out of bed, catching sight of herself in the mirrored wardrobe door. Christ, she looked a proper sight. Her unwashed hair appeared to be forming into dreadlocks and there was a shadow of flaked and smudged mascara stretching halfway down her bed-creased cheeks.

'Give me five minutes,' she said, rifling through the pile of clothes she hadn't yet got round to hanging up. 'Who is it, by the way?' she asked, as she tried to hide the hopeful tone in her voice.

Jessie looked uncomfortable. She came over and put her hand on Britt's arm. 'Hurry up, love, please,' she said urgently. 'It's the police. They've said they need to talk to you about something.'

Britt's heart sank like a rock at the news that it wasn't Josh, and she had to fight an overwhelming urge to crawl back into bed. But then something truly horrible occurred to her. Maybe the police were there to tell her that something had happened to Josh. Perhaps there had been an accident? That would explain why Josh had simply disappeared. But then she remembered. *Cherry's car.* They must have got the footage of her keying it on CCTV. Would Cherry be so vindictive as to press charges after everything she had done to Britt? *Of course she bloody would*, thought Britt miserably, *this was Cherry*.

As she walked down the stairs she remembered seeing mugshots of Hollywood stars like Paris Hilton and Lindsay Lohan splashed over the press. That was going to be her. 'DISGRACED EX-TV PRESENTER ARRESTED FOR VANDALISM'. Perhaps she should put on a bit of make-up and brush her matted hair, try to look a bit more like a respectable and responsible citizen? No. At the very least she would get an Asbo – her life was ruined – so she might as well look the part.

Sitting at the kitchen table were a man and a woman, both in plain clothes, with mugs of tea in front of them. Rose was standing by the table staring intently at the visitors, thumb in mouth, but as Britt came in Jessie ushered the toddler out of the room. 'I'll call you later, love,' she whispered as she passed. 'I've got to take the kids to school.'

The man stood up when he saw her. He must have been in his fifties; he wore a brown suit and tie, and looked like he was fairly senior: that belly didn't look like it belonged to a beat-pounding bobby.

'Britt Baxter?'

'That's me.'

'My name is Detective Inspector Perkins from Scotland Yard. This is Detective Phillips.'

'Hello,' said Britt, trying her hardest not to look guilty.

The man sat back down and signalled for her to do the same. She was wondering when they'd get to the bit about having the right to remain silent and thinking that that would actually be the best course of action, when DI Perkins said, 'Miss Baxter, we wondered if you knew someone called Gaz Dobbs?'

Britt was confused. 'Um, I think I might have heard of him,' she said. 'Who is he?'

'He's a journalist on *The Daily Splash*,' said Detective Phillips, who was a couple of decades younger than her colleague.

'He edits the newspaper's showbiz pages,' DI Perkins added helpfully.

Of course, that was how she knew the name Gaz Dobbs. Britt had seen his by-line on several stories he had written about her, including the original one about her and Alex that had started all this mess. 'Miss Baxter, your name and mobile number has been found in the files of a private detective who we believe is an associate of Mr Dobbs,' said DI Perkins. 'He also had a list of people you'd phoned, places you frequent and transcripts of personal phone calls. We have reason to believe this man has been listening to private conversations and intercepting the voicemail messages of a number of high-profile people, yourself included.'

'To put it bluntly, Miss Baxter,' added Detective Phillips, noting Britt's dazed expression, 'Gaz Dobbs is under investigation for suspected phone hacking and we're pretty sure that you are one of his victims.'

Britt was struggling to take it all in. *Phone tapping?* Well, that would certainly explain why *The Daily Splash* seemed to have access to her private conversations. She shuddered. It felt as much of a violation as if someone had been rifling through her knicker drawer.

'We don't have enough information to press charges as yet,' continued Detective Phillips, 'but it would certainly help our case if we could ask you a few questions to try and establish how Mr Dobbs might have got hold of your details.'

Britt told them she would help in any way she could, but her head was spinning with questions. So did that mean Stewie hadn't sold her out after all? Oh God, she'd been so awful to him . . . And how had this Gaz Dobbs got hold of her number and personal information in the first place?

47

Once the police had left after nearly an hour and a half of questioning, Britt was more desperate than ever to talk to Josh. He *must* be back from his trip to LA by now, but every time she called she just got those smooth American tones asking her to leave a message and promising he would call back '. . . just as soon as I can'. It was Friday today, which meant she would definitely be able to find him at the *Rise & Shine* studios on Monday, but she couldn't wait until then to speak to him – especially after the phone-tapping bombshell; after all, it was highly likely that Josh was being bugged, too.

It struck Britt that she didn't have a clue where her boyfriend lived. Why hadn't she realised before how weird that was? Short of wandering the streets of Chelsea, her only option was to get his address from the one place that was sure to have it: *Rise & Shine*.

In the end, getting hold of it proved far easier than Britt had hoped. After dismissing her original plan to send Jessie round to the studio disguised as a policewoman, Britt moved on to Plan B, which was to call up the production office and simply ask for it, using some feeble excuse about wanting to send him some gifts from a new fashion label. Luckily, a temp getting some work experience answered and was only too pleased to prove herself efficient as she happily repeated the address on the phone without question.

After putting down the phone, Britt stared at the address she had scrawled on her pad: *Flat C, 15 Morpeth Terrace, Chelsea SW3*. One way or another, everything would become clear when she got there.

She shampooed the matted mess of her hair three times, applied a deep conditioner and then blow-dried it straight. Make-up wise, she kept it simple: tinted moisturiser with mascara, blush and the trusty Clinique lip-gloss. Then she put on a pair of Nudie skinny jeans, ankle boots, vest top and biker jacket (the look was a bit Olivia Newton-John at the end of *Grease* but she knew Josh liked that sort of thing) and set off for the station, a mixture of nerves and excitement bubbling up inside her.

Less than an hour later, Britt was standing outside the iron railings of a grand old redbrick building on Morpeth Terrace in Chelsea, amid the squillion-pound residences of oligarchs, aristocrats and Arabs. She had imagined Josh's flat to be a hi-tech bachelor pad, but this five-storey mansion block, with its porticoed entrance and net curtains at most of the windows, looked like the sort of place where someone's rich old maiden aunt might live. There was no doubting it was the right address, however, as she spotted Josh's black Porsche outside.

Britt stood there for a moment, staring up at the lead-paned windows, wondering why Josh had tried so hard to keep her away from there – and what she would find inside. She was about to press the bell for Flat C when she had a moment's uncertainty. Would Josh be angry if she just turned up on his doorstep? But she was his *girlfriend*, for God's sake! And anyway, it was his fault she'd been forced to snoop around like a bloody stalker.

Giving her hair a shake and adjusting her top to show off just the right amount of cleavage, Britt took a deep breath and pressed the buzzer. But it was a bit of a shock when, a few seconds later, Josh's voice came over the intercom. Up until that point, she had still been half-convinced that he might have been lost at sea or kidnapped by Colombian drug runners.

'Hello?' he said, sounding his usual laidback self.

'Josh!' Her voice was trembling despite her best efforts to stay calm. 'It's me. Britt.'

There was a momentary pause, but if he was surprised to hear from her then he certainly didn't show it.

'Hey, babe,' he said casually. 'Come on up. Third floor.'

As she climbed the richly carpeted staircase, the walls of which were hung with enormous gilt-framed oil paintings of horses and hunting scenes, Britt fought to stay calm amid a whirlwind of emotions. Despite everything, she was still crazy for Josh, but that was tempered by anger at the way he had treated her. Whatever happened, Britt assured herself, she would remain cool and calm. She would handle this like the mature, sophisticated woman that she was.

When she got to his front door it swung open to reveal a smiling Josh. She had to fight the urge to throw herself at him, cling to his gorgeous body and shower it with kisses. It must have been sunny during his trip to LA as he was looking more tanned than ever, setting off the dazzling green of his eyes and whiteness of his teeth, while the hairs on his forearms had bleached blond in the sun.

'Hey, great to see you, babe,' he said. Yet despite the broad grin, there was a strange hardness in his eyes. He made no move to kiss or touch her. He just stood there, his hands wedged in his pockets, looking at her as if she was a Jehovah's Witness. He stood in the doorway.

'Are you going to let me in? Aren't you surprised to see me?' she finally managed.

'I guess.' He shrugged, looking as if he didn't give a shit. 'What's up?'

'What's up? *What's up?*' Britt was gawping in disbelief. 'If you had bothered to listen to any of my dozens of messages, you would have a pretty good idea what's bloody up!'

'Woah, babe, chill out . . .'

'No, Josh, I will not chill out,' said Britt, her voice quivering with the effort it was taking not to grab his shoulders and shake some sense into him. 'I have been having the worst week of my whole life and my boyfriend hasn't even bothered to get in touch to check how I am. Unsurprisingly, that has made me quite upset.'

'Like I said in my text, I've been busy.' He folded his arms and leant against the doorframe. His body was filling the doorway and he still made no move to invite her in. 'No need to get hysterical, I told you I'd get in touch when I was free. But then I guess you have more time on your hands to worry about these things now that you don't have a job.'

Britt was stunned. She was struggling to get her head around what was going on. What had happened to her kind, adoring boyfriend – the boyfriend that just a few weeks ago was telling the world that he was going to propose to her?

Josh glanced down at his Rolex. 'Was there anything else, babe? It's just I've got a friend stopping by for a beer any minute.'

Well, that was it. *Screw staying calm.* Britt needed some answers.

'There is something else, yes. On top of the fact that you've been completely ignoring me for the past week, Stewie informs me that you've been shagging Mandii Parsons behind my back. I told him it was bullshit, but the way you are behaving I'm starting to think he was right.'

Josh sighed and shook his head. 'Gaaad, that Stewie is such a fucking idiot . . .'

Despite everything, Britt felt a glimmer of hope. 'So it's not true about you and Mandii?'

'Well, yes, but then we never said that we wouldn't see other people, did we?'

His words hit her like blows. 'But you said you loved me . . .' She had to put her hand on the wall to steady herself. 'You told that journalist that I was 'the one'. You said you wanted to have babies with me, for God's sake!'

'Ah, but that was before you went and got your ass fired, babe,' said Josh with a sardonic smile. 'You'll understand that kinda changes things between us.'

'What are you talking about?' asked Britt weakly.

'You're washed up, babe, and I don't date losers.' He said it in a matter-of-fact sort of way, like, *The earth is round and why the hell would you think otherwise?* 'No hard feelings, eh?'

'How can you . . . ? I can't believe . . .' But she couldn't get the words out. She sank to the floor and let the tears flow. How had her Prince Charming turned into this evil monster?

Josh was just standing in the doorway, looking at her with a vaguely unsettled expression, as if embarrassed that she was making a scene. And then amid the pain and humiliation came a memory of sitting in the studio canteen with him all those months ago, talking about Rashida. What was it that he'd said to her? *'In the end, I just stopped answering her calls. It just seemed like the kindest thing to do, because by this point Rashida was living in a dream world . . .'*

So Rashida hadn't been stalking Josh after all. She'd probably been in a relationship with him, just like Britt had – until Josh decided that he'd had enough and just blanked her. Just like he had with Britt. How could he be so cruel?

Suddenly the buzzer inside Josh's apartment sounded.

'Hang on a sec,' he said, ducking back in to answer it. Britt sensed he couldn't get away from her quickly enough. 'Hello?' Britt couldn't tell who it was over the crackle. 'Oh, yeah, hi,' said Josh, 'come on up.'

Then he turned to Britt with an apologetic smile. 'Sorry, babe, it's been great catching up but you're gonna have to leave. Three's company an' all.'

It took all her strength just to haul herself off the floor. It was going to be humiliating enough coming face to face with Mandii Parsons without the weather girl finding her collapsed on the floor in a sobbing heap. But as she got shakily to her feet, she heard someone bounding up the stairs and then – to her surprise – a man's voice. 'Mate, how are you?' said the visitor in a rough London accent. 'I've been gagging to know what this big news is that you've got for me!'

Britt turned and looked at Josh's visitor. The men were

probably about the same age, but if Josh was at the peak of physical perfection, this bloke was way down at the other end of the scale. With greasy black hair that hung down to his shirt collar and a thin black moustache, he had the sickly complexion of someone who spent their life indoors.

The man's milky blue eyes narrowed in recognition when he saw her and he broke into a weasly grin. Britt wasn't sure where, but she knew she had seen him somewhere before.

'Well, if it isn't the lovely Britt Baxter!' Up close, he smelt like an old pub carpet. 'I've been hearing some very interesting rumours about you, darlin'.'

'Hey, buddy, you're late,' grinned Josh, giving his visitor a warm hug. 'Good to see you, man.'

Then he turned to Britt and in a few short words turned her world completely upside down. 'Sorry, babe, I'm forgetting my manners. You know Gaz Dobbs from *The Daily Splash*, don't you?'

48

Britt stood there in a daze, her head flicking back and forth between the men's grinning faces. Josh looked uglier than she had ever thought possible. That Californian tan now seemed to have a weird orange tinge, like it was out of a bottle, and his suspiciously line-free complexion suggested Botox rather than youthfulness. And then there was the other one. *Gaz Dobbs.* The man who just a few hours ago the police had revealed had been tapping her phone and who now appeared to be on man-hug terms with Josh. She was struggling to take it all in. Not only did Josh not love her any more – never had by the sound of things – it now looked entirely likely he had been selling stories about her and their relationship to *The Daily Splash.*

Of course, it all made sense when she gave it a bit of thought: the paparazzi who always seemed to know exactly where she and Josh would be; the way he always grabbed her for a perfectly choreographed snog whenever there were cameras around; the endless gushing interviews about how much he loved her and was planning to propose. What she had thought was proof of his undying love was actually just a way to boost his profile and bank balance. It turned out Cherry was spot on: Josh had only been with her for the publicity.

A wave of hatred surged up inside her. Without thinking, Britt stamped as hard as she could on the foot of Gaz Dobbs, glad she had decided to wear her new wooden-soled Mulberry ankle boots.

The journalist howled in pain and hopped around the hallway clutching his foot.

'Woah, easy, tiger!' chuckled Josh, looking at her with amused surprise.

'You bitch!' squealed Gaz Dobbs. 'You've broken my toe!'

'It would have been your nose but I didn't want to waste a manicure on you,' said Britt. 'And as for you,' she said, turning to Josh, who infuriatingly appeared to be finding the whole thing funny, 'I might be a loser, but at least I'm not a failed movie actor who cocked up his career so spectacularly that the only time he gets near a red carpet nowadays is when he's interviewing the *genuine* stars.'

Britt was gratified to see a cloud pass across Josh's face. She knew how sensitive he was about his movie career, and that would have hurt him far worse than she had Gaz Dobbs' foot.

'Oh, and by the way, Josh,' she said loudly (hoping the neighbours would hear), 'waxing your balls doesn't make your dick look any bigger. Without the hair it just makes it obvious how tiny it really is.'

And with that she picked up her handbag and strode down the stairs with her head held high. No doubt there would be a particular vicious story about her being sacked from *Rise & Shine* in tomorrow's paper, but she didn't care. It had been worth it just to see the look on Josh's face.

336

Unfortunately, Britt's 'I Will Survive' mood abruptly vanished as soon as she got out onto the street and started looking around for a taxi to take her home and the realisation hit her like Josh's speeding black Porsche: she didn't *have* a home. Or a job. Or, it would now seem, a boyfriend. Fighting back more tears, she quickly started walking – not caring where she was going, just needing to get as far away from Josh as possible.

Britt eventually found herself in a park just off the King's Road and sat on a bench amidst crowds lured out by the unseasonably warm late October weather. She wasn't crying any more; she just felt numb. Right now the worst thing to deal with was the number of people she had hurt. Alex, her mum, Stewie, Rashida . . . How could she have been so stupid? *Because you were in love with the idea of being loved by a movie star*, a little voice inside her piped up. It was true. The thought that JJ Bailey – the legendary Mitch Rider – had wanted her, a girl with big feet and frizzy hair from Carlisle, had left her deaf to Stewie and Rashida's warnings and to her own suspicions that it was all too good to be true.

'Excuse me?' Britt looked up to see a woman standing in front of her, laden down with carrier bags from Oasis and Warehouse. She must have been in her early twenties and was dressed in one of the floral jumpsuits that had been so popular that summer.

'Ooh, I thought it was you!' she smiled. 'Please could you sign this? My boyfriend loves you.'

Britt felt like telling her not to waste her time, that she was now an ex-celebrity, but she scribbled her name anyway.

'Thanks!' said the girl. 'And say hello to that sexy American of yours.'

'Oh, we're not together any more,' said Britt. 'I came home to find him dressed in my underwear with a full face of make-up on.'

The woman gawped at her, gave an embarrassed half-laugh and then scuttled off. Despite herself, Britt managed a small smile.

She sat watching the people in the park come and go. They all seemed so happy and carefree; right now she could never imagine feeling that way again. She noticed a young mum playing hide and seek with her toddler, chasing her around the fountain as the little girl gurgled with delight, the woman switching direction at the last moment to scoop her daughter up and cover her with kisses. Seeing the joy on both their faces, Britt was overwhelmed by sadness. It felt like her chance of a family of her own was further away than ever. Then she thought about her mum and the terrible way that she'd treated her during her visit, scolding her just for being *chatty*, for God's sake, and letting Josh talk her into making Molly leave the restaurant alone before them. Not out of concern, she realised now, but so she didn't spoil his precious photo opportunity! Cringing at the memory, Britt immediately pulled out her phone. She couldn't change the past, but she could do her best to make things right now.

'Mum? It's Britt.'

'Hello, darling!' Her mum was so warm, so lovely – not a trace of reproach in her voice. 'So good to hear from you. I was going to call you earlier this week, but I thought you must be on holiday somewhere nice with Josh as the two of you haven't been on telly all week.'

'Yeah, well, something like that.' At the moment, Britt

was too upset to explain. 'Anyway, I want to know how *you* are. I'm so sorry I haven't been in touch for ages.'

'Oh, don't worry, love, I know how busy you are. And I seem to have had an awful lot on my plate since we last spoke . . .'

Her mum happily chatted away, filling her in on the latest goings-on in Larkbridge, how Biscuit the border collie was going to need a hip replacement and about the hoo-hah over the local farmer's plans to breed ostriches. Her familiar voice soothed Britt as effectively as if someone was stroking her hair. And speaking to Molly made her realise how much she had missed her. She really must go and visit her, spend some time with her mum and clear her head, perhaps even stay up there for a while . . .

'. . . and then Alex helped me put up those shelves in my bedroom,' Molly was saying, 'which look really fantastic with all of Nanna Eileen's china bits and bobs on them.'

Suddenly, Britt snapped back to attention.

'Sorry, what was that, Mum? Did you say Alex? *My* Alex?'

'Yes,' said Molly. 'He's been helping me with a bit of DIY. Oh goodness, you don't mind do you? I know you said you were worried about him selling stories to the newspapers or some such, but he's such a nice lad.'

'No, of course I don't mind, but . . . I mean, why was he in Larkbridge?' Britt had assumed he'd headed back up north, but had no idea where he was.

'I bumped into him in the village shop when he came to visit his uncle, and I invited him over for coffee,' said Molly. 'Since then he's been stopping by every now and then, helping me out with any odd bits that need doing

339

around the house. He did a lovely job on the hallway skirting board.'

'What's he up to these days, then?' Britt asked as casually as possible.

'Well, he's actually doing rather well. He's set himself up as something called a 'personal trainer' in Carlisle. People pay him an astonishing amount of money to make them run round the park and do star jumps and the like. Quite the market for it, apparently! It's so successful that he's even got a couple of people working for him now. Like I said to him the other day, he's become a proper Alan Sugar.'

Well, good for Alex, thought Britt. Maybe splitting up with her had been just the motivation he had needed to sort his life out. He was better off without her.

'Such a shame that the two of you couldn't work things out,' Molly was saying. 'He always asks after you. He knows you're happy with Josh, though.'

After she had said goodbye to her mum, promising to call again in a few days, Britt headed to the shops on the King's Road. She didn't want to go back to Streatham just yet. She knew that Jessie would be sympathetic, but she couldn't face seeing that 'Told you so' look flash across her friend's face – however fleeting and deserved.

There was also something else she needed to do, something long overdue, and she had to psyche herself up with a bit of retail therapy first.

A pair of black patent boots and two pairs of Calvin Klein knickers later, Britt headed back to her bench in the park, got out her phone again and dialled Alex's number. Hopefully he would forgive her. Perhaps, further down the line, they might even be friends? She imagined meeting him in a cosy country pub for a couple of beers (or maybe he only drank wheatgrass now he was a personal trainer?) and the thought made her smile.

When the call connected it rang and rang, but just as she thought it would go to voicemail, someone answered. It wasn't Alex, though; it was a girl.

Britt was thrown. 'Oh, hi, um, is Alex there?'

'No, he's away on a business trip, I'm afraid. He'll be home next week,' she said, 'but you can reach him on his work mobile or I can take a message. Who shall I say called?' The voice sounded sweet and kind; just the sort of girl Alex should be with.

49

'It's okay,' Britt finally managed. 'I'll call back sometime.'

She quickly ended the call, afraid she might burst into tears again if she stayed on the line a moment longer. It wasn't that she begrudged Alex happiness – he deserved every good thing that had come his way – but it put into sharp focus what a God-awful mess she had made of her own life. And it also made her realise how terribly she missed him. She had a sudden vision of him in their flat, a memory from back when things were still amazing between them, of him coming into the bedroom after a shower, filling the doorway with his broad shoulders, a little towel wrapped round his waist and his shaggy hair slicked damply off his smiling face. She had been lying in bed and as he had walked over to her, she remembered thinking how lucky she was to have such a gorgeous boyfriend, and then . . . well, the memory of what had happened next was too painful to dwell on. Instead, she ran over the dying months of her and Alex's relationship: the rows, the jealousy and frustration. Could she have been more patient with him, more understanding? *Perhaps.* Every relationship had its rocky patches and if it was worth fighting for, then you did just that. But it was too late for regrets, no matter how much she wished things could be different. That chapter in her life was now closed.

The thought made her more miserable than ever.

The next day, just as Britt had feared, Gaz Dobbs took revenge for his sore foot in *The Daily Splash*.

'Well?' asked Jessie nervously, when Britt got back from the newsagents, clutching the paper. 'How bad is it?'

'Short of claiming I was Osama bin Laden's mistress and responsible for the death of Princess Diana, it couldn't be much worse.'

Jessie winced. 'Let's have a look then.'

Britt spread the newspaper out over the kitchen table. Under the headline: 'YOU'RE FIRED!' was the subhead: 'TV bosses ditch breakfast Britt after diva strops and boozy benders' with a photo of her looking squiffy at some showbiz bash a few months ago (she had actually been stone-cold sober, but was squinting at the camera flash) and an article that went as close as it legally could to hinting that she was an unstable, coke-snorting, gin-guzzling egomaniac who enjoyed the seedier side of S&M without actually coming right out and saying it:

Until her recent dramatic breakdown, pals reveal that the failed presenter used to go to a different showbiz party every night to load up on free booze and designer goody bags.

'Britt would go to the opening of an envelope,' admitted a source close to the star. 'It was quite tragic, really.'

And although Britt, 33, insisted in interviews that she led a healthy lifestyle, pals have been left wondering

343

exactly how she had the energy to party all night and then get up for work the next morning.

'Drugs are freely available at those showbiz parties,' said a source. 'We were all really worried about her.'

'Wow,' gasped Jessie, as she scanned the story. 'Ooh, and that's nice, they seem to have aged you by seven years too.'

'Yeah. And I particularly like the next bit,' said Britt gloomily.

Rise & Shine hunk Josh Bailey, who was dating the troubled star until her crazed antics left him with no choice but to end their relationship, told our reporter: 'Britt would call me at all hours of the day and night and turn up at my flat screaming and demanding to know where I'd been. But I pity her more than anything. I just hope she gets the professional help she so desperately needs'.

Jessie shook her head. 'What a wanker.'

'Yeah,' agreed Britt. 'Gaz Dobbs has really outdone himself this time. In fact, if I wasn't so pissed off about the fact that this article has killed off any remaining hope I had of getting another job in TV, I would actually be quite impressed.'

It was the following Monday morning and Britt was sitting at Jessie's kitchen table in her pyjamas drinking her fourth cup of tea of the day. She had the house to herself. Tom had left for work, while Jessie had taken the older girls to school and Rose to toddler swimming class. Britt, however, had nowhere to go and nothing to do. Just a week ago, the prospect of a weekday with no work or commitments would have filled her with joy, but now she was desperate for something to fill the void that was now her life.

'Don't you dare switch on the TV until *Rise & Shine* has finished,' Jessie had warned her as she flew out of the door with the girls at 8.30. 'You'll just torture yourself.'

Jess was absolutely right, of course: it would be a really stupid thing to do. And for a few minutes, Britt managed to stay away from the remote control by making her fifth cup of tea and eating another bowl of Coco Pops. But at 8.36 she could stand it no more and turned it on to catch Cherry simpering her way through an interview with some Irish stand-up comedian about his new tour. Next up it was Mandii. *Talk about a warm front*, fumed Britt as Mandii jiggled her ridiculous boobs at the camera as if she was posing for a *Nuts* magazine lingerie shoot. Ken was seated, as usual, on the sofa, doing a link to showbiz gossip with Josh (assholebastardwanker). The sight of him brought all the horrible memories crashing back, but like a rubber-necker staring at a motorway collision Britt couldn't tear her eyes away. She sat through the whole of his report wondering for the umpteenth time how she had let herself be so taken in by him. Why hadn't she noticed before how stupidly white his teeth were? They were like oversized Tic-tacs. As for that hair! Honest to God, if she didn't know better she'd have thought it was a wig. And had he always made that idiotic *hur-hur-hur* sound when he laughed?

It suddenly occurred to Britt that she had never really loved him. What she had thought was love was actually just a mix of lust and insecurity. *Josh played me from the start*, she thought bitterly, keeping her on her toes by never fully committing, then showering her with compliments and presents. God, she was *so* much better off without that loser.

Now if only someone would relay that message to her poor aching heart.

The show had finished and Britt was flicking half-heartedly through one of Jessie's recipe books, thinking she might smother her unhappiness with some freshly baked brownies, when her phone rang. She glanced at the screen: unknown number. She let it go to voicemail and whoever it was didn't leave a response. But a few moments later her phone rang again and this time there was the beep that indicated she had a new message. When she listened to it, to her surprise it was Toby.

'Hello, Britt, I was hoping to speak to you today about something quite urgent. It's a rather, um, *sensitive* matter so I'd really prefer to discuss this face to face. Sorry about the short notice but perhaps we could meet for coffee later this morning, say elevenish at the Bridge Café near the studio? I'm just heading into a meeting now, but if you can make it, please give the office a call and let my PA know. Thanks. Oh, and if you don't mind, I'd rather you didn't mention this to anyone – I'll explain all later. Anyway, apologies for the subterfuge and hope to see you soon. Bye.'

Britt's immediate reaction was that Toby could, quite frankly, eff off. *He's got a bloody cheek*, she thought furiously, *expecting her to come running after the way he had handled things*. But then it occurred to her that it was possible that he was calling to offer her her old job back. The idea sent her hopes soaring. Toby's tone of voice didn't give anything away, but really, *what else could it be?* Perhaps she should go and hear what he had to say. It wasn't like she had anything else to do.

At just after 11 a.m. Britt arrived for their rendezvous at the little greasy-spoon café, which was tucked away down a side street out of sight from the pack of paps who always hung about the studio gates. The formica tables were all empty apart from the one in the far corner away from the window, which was occupied by Toby. He had obviously been looking out for her and jumped up as soon as she came in, offering an awkward smile and raking his hand through his hair. He looked almost sheepish, an expression she'd never before seen on the hard-nosed executive producer's face. It gave her confidence a much-needed boost.

'Britt, thanks so much for meeting me. I would have understood if you hadn't wanted to come.'

'Yes, well, I'm here, aren't I?' she said, taking a seat opposite him and signalling to the waitress for a black coffee. 'What's this about?'

'Right, okay,' he said, as if psyching himself up. 'Well, the thing is, Britt, I've discovered I owe you an apology. A very big apology. Since we last spoke—'

'You mean since you had me thrown out of the studio.'

'Um, yes, God. I've handled this so badly.' Toby grimaced. 'Well, to cut a long story short, I've found out that Cherry set you up. I know about the doctored research for the Powers Buckman interview, the laxatives, the jammed autocue and the fake email from Jasper. I am truly sorry, Britt, I should have listened to you.'

She nodded for him to go on, trying to take in what he was telling her.

'And the worst part of this whole mess,' he said sadly, 'is that I can't make you a public apology or offer you your old job back as the only reason Powers Buckman isn't suing the show and the channel is that we blamed it all on you, and if you're reinstated, all hell would break loose. Believe me, Britt, I wish we *could* have you back on board. You were the best thing that had happened to *Rise & Shine* in years.'

'Thanks,' said Britt, but inside she felt crushed. As sweet as it was of him to say all this, it didn't change the fact that she would still have to be Cherry's fall guy. And an apology wasn't going to pay the bills, was it?

But Toby hadn't finished. 'So I have a suggestion for you,' he said. 'I might not be able to have you back on the sofa, but I will do everything in my power to help you find another job in television. It's a small world, and I know a lot of production companies who would kill for a presenter like you. You've got the full package, Britt – beauty, brains and charm – and it would be a tragedy if all that talent went to waste.'

'I appreciate the offer, Toby, but I don't think anyone will employ me after that story in *The Daily Splash* at the weekend.'

He waved his hand dismissively. 'Bollocks. That isn't even an issue. Everyone in the industry knows that paper's full of bullshit. If you want, I'll ring round all my contacts and put in a good word for you. I'm not promising anything, but I'll do my very best. What do you say?'

Britt thought about it. She had loved TV presenting and it had finally felt like she'd found something she was good at. The thought that she might get another job made her heart do a little pirouette of happiness.

She smiled at him. 'Thanks, Toby. That would be fantastic.'

He looked relieved. 'Oh, that's great, I'm so pleased. And if it's any compensation, Cherry's contract won't be renewed when it expires in a couple of months. If I had my way I'd have the scheming witch out today, but the channel doesn't want another scandal.'

'And Josh?' asked Britt. 'You know he's been selling stories to *The Splash*?'

'I had a pretty good idea, yes, but I can't get rid of him for that, I'm afraid, much as I'd like to after the way he treated Rashida – and now, I understand, you,' said Toby, pulling an apologetic face: he had never been very good at the touchy-feely stuff. 'He's a huge favourite with the viewers. Sorry, Britt.'

'Not your fault,' she shrugged. 'Thanks.'

They both got up to leave.

'Oh, just one thing,' said Britt. 'How did you find out about Cherry setting me up?'

'It was Stewie. He really went into bat for you, collected together all this evidence to show me and after that there was no question. He's one of the good guys, Britt – and he obviously worships you.'

50

After saying goodbye and promising to stay in touch, Britt got the train back to Jessie's thinking over everything Toby had said. It really was very nice of him to offer to put in a good word for her with his producer buddies, but now she'd had some space to think, she refused to let herself get too excited about the chance that anything might come from it. For a start, whatever Toby might think, she now – thanks to the charming Gaz Dobbs – had a reputation for being a hard-partying pisshead. No doubt the storm would blow over in a few years and she might be able to get a gig flogging mops on QVC, but right now what employer would want to take the gamble? But at least her name had been cleared (even if it was only within the confines of the *Rise & Shine* studio) and it was all thanks to Stewie. Sweet, wonderful Stewie, who was still looking out for her despite the fact that she'd been a total cow to him. *I should call him*, thought Britt, as she walked up the hill to Jessie's house. *I'll get back, have a bit of lunch and then I'll phone him.*

But she never got the chance: as she walked up to the house she saw there was someone standing outside holding a large bunch of flowers and, as she got nearer, she saw who that visitor was.

'Well, I guess that's why you weren't answering the door,' said Stewie as she walked up the path towards him.

He was wearing his usual knee-length shorts, his only concession to the autumn weather being a yellow hoodie and a pair of trainers in place of the usual flip-flops.

'Stewie!' She ran up the path and gave him a big hug. He smelt of fresh air and surfboard wax, even though the closest he'd probably been to the sea that day was Bob's Fish Bar next to the station. It felt so good to be back in his arms, like nothing bad could happen to her there.

'This is so weird,' she said, 'I was just about to call you.'

'Beat you to it.' When he pulled back from her embrace, he was grinning from ear to ear. 'I hope you don't mind me stopping by. I wasn't sure if you were speaking to me so I thought I'd just come knocking. I got the address from your file at the studio – Jessie was listed as your emergency contact.'

'Of course I don't mind, come in, come in!' She opened the front door and led him through to the kitchen. It looked like Jessie wasn't yet home. 'To be honest, I'm surprised you're speaking to me after the way I've behaved.'

He gave a dismissive shrug. 'Water under the bridge, mate. Here, these are for you.' He shyly held out the bouquet.

'They're beautiful, thank you.' They sat opposite each other at the kitchen table, Stewie looking just as awkward as she felt. But certain things needed to be said, so Britt took a deep breath. 'Stewie, I can't begin to tell you how sorry I am for everything. I've just been to see Toby and he told me what you did for me, how you convinced him that Cherry set me up. And after all those horrible things I accused you of! I can't thank you enough.'

'It's okay. Though I can't pretend I wasn't gutted when you hooked up with that Bailey a-hole.'

'Yeah, and you were absolutely right.'

'Well, you can't help who you fall in love with, as I know all too well,' he said, staring at his hands on the table. Then he looked up at her, his eyes full of hope. 'I do love you. I have done almost since the first moment I saw you.'

'Stewie, I—'

'Please, just hear me out.' He walked round the table and crouched by her chair. 'I'm not asking for you to fall into my arms. God knows you probably need a bit of time to sort your head out after everything that's gone on. But I'm crazy about you, Britt, and you know we have a good time together, don't we?'

She smiled and nodded. He was right, they did.

'So what do you say we let the dust settle, then maybe try going on a date? A proper one this time, not a pub-crawl. I know I could make you happy, Britt. Just give me a chance.'

He put his hand on her leg and then slowly started to lean towards her. It would be so easy to kiss him right now – and from what she could remember through the haze of drunkenness, last time it had been really rather good . . . *But you're still in love with Alex*, a little voice inside her said. *You always have been.*

It was true, thought Britt miserably, but Alex has got a girlfriend and there's no point wishing things could be different. Maybe she *could* be happy with Stewie? She hesitated . . . But no, she couldn't do this now. Her head was all over the place. She needed time to think.

'I'm sorry,' she said, pulling away. 'You truly are an

amazing guy, one in a million, but right now I just need a bit of space.'

'I was afraid you'd say that.'

'Just give me some time and we'll see how things go, okay?'

'Okay. But if you change your mind, then—'

'Then I know where to find you.' She kissed him on the cheek. 'You've been a real friend to me, Stewie, and I can never thank you enough for that.'

They stood up and Britt gave him a warm hug.

'Keep in touch, mate,' he smiled a little forlornly. 'I'll see myself out.'

After he had gone, Britt sadly busied herself arranging the flowers in a vase. She was a million miles away when her mobile rang.

'Hello?'

'Is this Britt Baxter?' It was a man's voice she didn't recognise.

'It is.'

'Hello, Britt, sorry to call out of the blue but I've been given your details by Toby Livingstone of *Rise & Shine*. My name's Justin Dornan, and I'm the producer of a new talent show. Would you have a moment for a quick chat?'

Would she ever! 'Yes, that would be fine,' said Britt, trying to sound as calm as was possible while doing a little jig of excitement around the kitchen.

The show, Justin told her, was to be the Saturday-night star of next season's TV schedule. Over three months, a group of celebrities would learn to dance, with each specialising in a different style: tap, ballet, hip-hop, ball-room and even Irish dancing. They would compete each week in front of a panel of expert judges. Britt didn't know whether to laugh or cry when Justin told her that one of them would be Josh Bailey.

'The reason I'm calling is that we're looking for a female anchor to host the show alongside Tommy Forbes,' he said, mentioning a young comedian who'd had hit shows on every channel and was currently the hottest property on television. 'I've been very impressed by your performance on *Rise & Shine* and Toby can't say enough good things about you, so I was wondering if you would like to come in to meet me – say, on Thursday?'

'Let me just grab my diary, Justin,' said Britt smoothly, although of course she knew very well it was totally empty.

As she listened to Justin talk, the doorbell rang. She ignored it, but a moment later there was another long ring. It was probably Stewie, back to try and convince her to reconsider. She should answer it, as by the sounds of things, he wasn't going to give up ringing the bell, and after all that had gone on she owed him another hearing.

'Sorry, Justin, would you mind holding on a second? There's someone at the door.'

Britt wedged the mobile between her ear and shoulder and trotted to the door. But when she opened it, it wasn't Stewie. It was the last person Britt had expected to see standing on Jessie's doorstep.

51

It was Alex.

Britt couldn't believe he was stood there in front of her. She was totally thrown. He looked great. In fact no, he looked amazing – the best Britt had ever seen him look. He'd had his shaggy hair cut short, the better to show off his Brad Pitt jawline and the cheekbones that were looking more chiselled than ever now that he'd shed the extra pounds he had put on during those last boozy months in London. As for his body – well, those daily workouts had clearly paid off. Britt felt a sickening surge of jealousy at the thought of him wrapping his new girl-friend in those strong arms and whisking her off to bed. But the changes weren't just physical; Alex seemed to glow with a newfound confidence.

'Hey,' he said with a smile.

'Hey.' It was all she could manage.

The seconds ticked past as they just stood there, staring at each other.

'Er, Britt, are you on the phone?' said Alex eventually.

'Oh, right, oh god, yes.' She fumbled with the handset, almost dropping it. 'Justin? Hi, sorry about that – Thursday would be great, thanks. Okay, looking forward to it. Bye.'

She ended the call and looked back at Alex again.

'That was Justin,' she said, still in a daze. 'We're having a meeting. On Thursday.'

Alex smiled. 'It's good to see you, Britt.'

'What . . . what are you doing here?'

'Well, I was just in the area and wondered if you wanted a personal trainer.'

'Not really. I can't afford one.'

'Oh, right. Cup of tea and a chat then?'

'Deal.'

She showed him into the kitchen, wishing she'd made a bit more of an effort that morning instead of tying her hair in a messy topknot that she'd secured with a biro, and then just throwing on a pair of jeans and her sweatshirt with a weird stain down one arm. It was definitely not the sort of outfit you wanted to be wearing when you met up with your ex – especially when he was looking so bloody hot. She bet his new girlfriend wouldn't be seen dead looking such a state. For the umpteenth time, Britt wondered what she looked like. Blonde, probably – Alex had always been a sucker for the Pamela Anderson look. Fighting another wave of jealousy, she busied herself making tea, stealing the occasional glance over to where Alex was leaning against the kitchen countertop.

'So, what are you doing in London? How did you know I was here?' she asked, pouring milk into their mugs.

'Jessie told me,' he said. Britt swung round in surprise. 'Don't be mad at her, but she's been in touch every now and then, letting me know how you are. I'd read stuff in the paper and I was worried about you. And I missed you, too. I suppose speaking to Jessie was a way of keeping you in my life.'

Britt handed him the tea, hoping he wouldn't notice that her hands were shaking.

'Thanks,' he smiled. 'So, I guess you're wondering why I've really come round?'

'I was, rather.'

'Well, three things, really. The first is to see how Kate Moss is.'

Britt laughed. 'She's fine. Missing you, obviously. She's probably asleep on the spare-room bed; go up and see her if you like.'

'Great, I'll pop up in a bit. The second is to apologise.'

'Apologise?' Britt gawped at him. 'What on earth for?'

'Because of the way I behaved in those last months we were together,' he said. 'I'm sorry, Britt, I was a total idiot. I can't blame anything but my own stupid ego, but when I lost my job I literally went into freefall. My life seemed to be going to pieces, whereas you were this incredible overnight success. I didn't know how to cope with it all, so I ended up destroying the one good thing in my life, which was us. Then after that story appeared in the papers . . .'

Britt cringed. 'God, I feel terrible about that . . .'

'Well, you mustn't,' he said passionately. 'I don't blame you in the least – it must have seemed that I was the only possible culprit. And in the end, it was the best thing you could have done for me. When I saw you were with Josh, it gave me just the kick up the arse I needed to finally sort my life out. I guess I had to hit rock bottom before I could start to climb back up again. And now I have, and things are going good – well, great, really.'

Britt nodded slowly, feeling more awful than ever. Not only had her disastrous fling with Josh helped screw up her career, it had propelled Alex into the arms of his lovely new Pamela-Anderson-clone girlfriend. *Nice work, Baxter . . .*

'Yes, Mum told me what a success your business is,' she said. 'I'm really thrilled for you, Al. And I'm glad you're happy in your personal life, too.'

'Sorry?'

'Your girlfriend.' Alex looked at her blankly. 'I tried to call you to apologise on Friday,' said Britt, 'and she answered the phone.'

'Oh, you mean Liz!' Alex shook his head as the penny dropped. 'She works for me, Britt. Does book-keeping, that sort of thing.'

'So . . . you're not dating?'

'No, we're not,' he said with a wry smile. 'Apart from anything else, I don't think Liz's husband would be very happy about that.' Then he put down his mug and took a step towards her. They were close enough to touch, but he didn't reach out for her. 'I'm single, Britt,' he said softly. 'I have been since we split up.'

Britt barely dared to breathe. 'You said you were here for three things,' she said, her voice just a whisper. 'But you haven't told me what the last one is.'

Alex took another step closer and took her hand in his. 'The third and most important thing,' he said, 'is to tell you that I love you. That I have never stopped loving you. That I think about you every minute of every day and what I want most in the world is to spend the rest of my life with you.' He grasped her other hand and gazed deeply into her eyes. 'So I suppose all that's left is for you to decide if that's what you want, too.'

Britt felt like electricity was shooting through her body,

lighting her up from the inside. At that moment, she knew for certain that the way she felt for Alex knocked anything else out of the park. Britt couldn't believe she'd lost sight of how much Alex and her friends and family meant to her. There might have been a few bumps along the road, but she had never been so sure about anything in her life: Alex was The One.

'It is *exactly* what I want,' she said, breaking into a smile of pure joy that was reflected by Alex's own. 'But,' she said, putting a hand on his chest, 'you need to agree to a few conditions first.'

'Okaaaaay . . .'

'The first is that you never, ever make me run round a park or do star jumps.'

'Agreed,' he said, wrapping his arms round her and pulling him towards her.

'The second is that we listen to the radio in the morning instead of watching breakfast TV.'

'Fine.' Alex started to slowly lower his face to hers until he was so close that she could feel his breath on her cheek.

'And the third,' she whispered, her voice thick with desire, 'is that you kiss me right this second.'

And without a word, Alex swept her to him and pressed his lips against hers, until Britt felt dizzy with love and longing and a happiness that she han't dreamt possible just minutes ago. She'd suddenly gone from being jobless and single to being reunited with the love of her life with a possible job on a primetime television show. This time she wasn't about to let it slip away.

Suddenly, Alex pulled back and looked at her. 'Well, in that case, I have a condition of my own, too.'

'Anything,' she murmured, her body tingling with bliss, every bit of her wanting him.

'Britt Baxter,' he said slowly, smiling down at her, 'will you marry me?'